Praise for *Tweet Cute*

"From meme wars to social media marketing, Lord accurately depicts various sides of today's online culture. Amid all the digital hoopla is an engaging story about family loyalty and pursuing one's own passions. . . . A just-right combination of sweet and cheesy." —*Kirkus Reviews*

"A precursor to the way teen love stories will be told for years to come." —*Booklist*

"Lord's snappy debut features a strong contemporary beat and a host of sympathetic characters." —*Publishers Weekly*

"Filled with humor, heart, and a dose of social media reality . . . debut author Lord packs a punch in this adorably fun novel."
—*School Library Journal*

"*Gossip Girl* meets *Mean Girls* mixed with *To All the Boys I've Loved Before* with a touch of *You've Got Mail.* It's basically impossible not to like." —*Hypable*

"Sweet and fun! An adorable debut that updates a classic romantic trope with a buzzy twist." —Jenn Bennett,
author of *Alex, Approximately* and *Serious Moonlight*

"A witty rom-com reinvention for the Twitter age, *Tweet Cute* pairs delicious online rivalry with deeply relatable insights on family pressure and growing up. This fresh, funny read had us hitting 'favorite' from page one."
—Emily Wibberley and Austin Siegemund-Broka,
authors of *Always Never Yours* and *If I'm Being Honest*

"*Tweet Cute* delivers in every possible way: a perfect enemies-to-lovers romance, a whip-smart plotline, and endearingly real characters. I devoured it." —Francesca Zappia, author of *Eliza and Her Monsters*

"A hilarious and adorable rom-com with a spot-on teen voice and characters whose vulnerability and open hearts will make them feel like lifelong friends. Readers will be cheering for Pepper and Jack from beginning to end . . . and waiting with anticipation for them to fall in love."

—Kacen Callender, author of *This Is Kind of an Epic Love Story* and Stonewall Award–winning novel *Hurricane Child*

"Take it from a rom-com fanatic: *Tweet Cute* will make your heart feel warm. It is, in a word, delicious. Emma Lord is an exciting new voice in YA and romance, and this book has me on the edge of my seat waiting for the chance to read whatever she cooks up next." —Alanna Bennett, culture writer and writer for *Roswell, New Mexico*

Emma Lord

TWEET CUTE

WEDNESDAY BOOKS
NEW YORK

For my favorite writers, Mom and Dad

This is a work of fiction. All of the characters, organizations, and events portrayed in this novel are either products of the author's imagination or are used fictitiously.

Published in the United States by Wednesday Books, an imprint of St. Martin's Publishing Group

Printed in the United States of America. For information, address St. Martin's Publishing Group, 120 Broadway, New York, NY 10271.

www.wednesdaybooks.com

Designed by Anna Gorovoy

The Library of Congress has cataloged the hardcover edition as follows:

Names: Lord, Emma, author.
Title: Tweet cute / Emma Lord.
Description: First edition. | New York : Wednesday Books, 2020
Identifiers: LCCN 2019036362 | ISBN 9781250237323 (hardcover) | ISBN 9781250759627 (international, sold outside the U.S., subject to rights availability) | ISBN 9781250237330 (ebook)
Subjects: CYAC: Love stories. | Twitter—Fiction. | Social media—Fiction.
Classification: LCC PS3612.O744 T84 2020 | DDC 813/.6—dc23
LC record available at https://lccn.loc.gov/2019036362

ISBN 978-1-250-75043-3 (trade paperback)

Our books may be purchased in bulk for promotional, educational, or business use. Please contact your local bookseller or the Macmillan Corporate and Premium Sales Department at 1-800-221-7945, extension 5442, or by email at MacmillanSpecialMarkets@macmillan.com.

First Wednesday Books Paperback Edition: 2020

10 9 8 7 6 5 4 3 2 1

PART ONE

Pepper

To be fair, when the alarm goes off, there's barely even any smoke rising out of the oven.

"Um, is the apartment on fire?"

I lower the screen of my laptop down, where my older sister Paige's now scowling face is taking up half the screen on a Skype call from UPenn. The other half of the screen is currently occupied by the *Great Expectations* essay I have written and rewritten enough times that Charles Dickens is probably rolling in his grave.

"Nope," I mutter, crossing the kitchen to shut the oven off, "just my life."

I pull the oven open, and another *whoosh* of smoke comes out, revealing some seriously blackened Monster Cake.

"Crap."

I grab the stepladder from the pantry to shut off the fire alarm, then open all the windows to our twenty-sixth-floor apartment, where the Upper East Side sprawls out beneath my feet—all the scores of towering buildings with their bright lights burning even long after anyone in their right mind should be asleep. I stare at it for a moment, somehow still not quite used to the staggering view even though we've been here nearly four years.

"Pepper?"

Right. Paige. I pull up the laptop screen.

"Under control," I say, giving her a thumbs-up.

She raises a disbelieving eyebrow, then mimes sweeping at her bangs. I raise my hand to touch my own, and end up streaking the Monster Cake batter all the way down them as Paige winces.

"Well, if you do end up calling the fire department, prop me up on the taller counter so I can see the hot firefighters bust in." Her eyes shift on her screen away from me, no doubt to look at the unfinished post on the baking blog we run together. "I take it we're not getting any pictures for the entry tonight?"

"I have three other pans of it from earlier I can snap once they're frosted. I'll send them later."

"Yeesh. How much Monster Cake did you make? Is Mom even back from her trip yet?"

I avoid her eyes by looking at the stove top, where my pans are all lined up in a neat row. Paige barely ever asks about Mom these days, so I feel like I have to be extra careful with whatever I say next—more careful than, say, the state of academic distraction that led me to nearly burn the kitchen to the ground.

"She should be back in two days." And then, because I apparently can't help myself, I add, "You could come up, if you wanted. We don't have much going on this weekend."

Paige wrinkles her nose. "Pass."

I bite the inside of my cheek. Paige is so stubborn that anything I say to try to bridge the gap between her and Mom will usually just make things worse.

"But you could come down to Penn and visit me," she offers brightly.

The idea would be tempting if I didn't have this *Great Expectations* essay and a whole slew of other great expectations to deal with. An AP Stats test, an AP Bio project, debate club prep, and my first official day of being captain of the girls' swim team, to name a few—and that's only the tip of my figurative, ridiculously stressful iceberg.

Whatever face I'm making must say it all for me, because Paige holds her hands up in surrender.

"Sorry," I say reflexively.

"First off, stop saying sorry," says Paige, who is now waist-deep in a feminist theory class and embracing it with aggressive enthusiasm. "And second off, what is going on with you, anyway?"

I fan the last of the smoke toward the window. "Going on with me?"

"This whole . . . weird . . . Valedictorian Barbie thing you've got going on," she says, gesturing at the screen.

"I care about my grades."

Paige snorts. "Not back home, you didn't."

By "home," she means Nashville, where we grew up.

"It's different here." It's not like she'd know, considering she never actually had to go to Stone Hall Academy, a private school so elite and competitive that even Blair Waldorf would probably burn within two minutes of crossing its threshold. The year Mom moved us here, Paige was a senior and insisted on going to the local public school, and she already had grades from her old school to buoy her applications. "The grading scale is harder. College admissions are more competitive."

"But you aren't."

Ha. Maybe I wasn't before she ditched me for Philadelphia.

Now my peers know me as the Terminator. Or Two-Shoes, or Preppy Pepper, or whatever moniker Jack Campbell, notorious class clown and the metaphorical thorn in my very irritated side, has decided to grace me with that week.

"Besides, didn't you apply to Columbia early decision? You think they're gonna care about a lousy B plus?"

I don't think they will, I know they will. I overheard some girls in homeroom saying a kid at another school down the block from ours had their Columbia acceptance pulled after a bout of senioritis. But before I can justify hinging my paranoia on this extremely unsubstantiated rumor, the front door opens, followed by the *click click click* of my mom's heels on the apartment's hardwood floors.

"Peace," says Paige.

She ends the call before I even turn back to the screen.

I sigh, shutting the laptop just before my mom walks into the kitchen, decked out in her usual airport fare: a pair of tight black jeans, a cashmere sweater, and a pair of oversize black sunglasses that, frankly, look ridiculous on her given the late hour. She pulls them off and perches them up on her perfectly coiffed blonde hair to inspect me, and the hurricane that used to be her spotless kitchen.

"You're back early."

"And you're supposed to be in bed."

She steps forward and pulls me into a hug, and I squeeze her a little tighter than someone covered in cake batter probably should. It's only been a few days, but it's lonely when she's gone. I'm still not used to it being so quiet, without Paige and Dad around.

She holds me there and takes a demonstrative whiff, no doubt inhaling a lungful of burnt baked good, but when she pulls away, she raises the same eyebrow Paige did and doesn't say anything.

"I have an essay due."

She glances over at the pans of cake. "It looks like a riveting read," she says wryly. "Is this the *Great Expectations* one?"

"The very same."

"Didn't you finish that a week ago?"

She has a point. I guess if push really comes to shove, I can pull up one of the old drafts and submit it. But the problem is, the figurative pushing and shoving at Stone Hall Academy is more like maiming and destroying. I'm competing for Ivy League admissions with legacies who probably descended down from the original Yale bulldog. It's not enough to be *good*, or even *great*—you have to crush your peers, or get crushed.

Well, metaphorically, at least. And speaking of metaphors, for some reason, despite having read this book twice and annotating it into oblivion, I'm having some trouble interpreting any of them in a way that wouldn't put our AP Lit teacher to sleep. Every time I try to write a coherent sentence, all I can think about is tomorrow's swim practice. It's my first day as acting captain and I know Pooja went to a conditioning camp over the summer, which means she might be faster than I am now, which means she has every opportunity to undermine my authority and make me look like an idiot in front of everyone and—

"Do you want to stay home from school tomorrow?"

I blink at my mom like she grew an extra head. That's the last thing I need. Even missing an hour would give everyone around me an edge.

"No. No, I'm good." I sit up on the counter. "Did you finish up your meetings?"

She's been so dead set on launching Big League Burger internationally that it's practically all she ever talks about these days—meetings with investors in Paris, in London, even in Rome, trying to figure out which European city she'll take it to first.

"Not quite. I'll have to fly back out. But corporate's been having a cow over the new menu launches tomorrow, and it just didn't look good for me to be away in the middle of it." She smiles. "Also, I missed my mini-me."

I snort, but only because between her designer digs and my wrinkled pajamas, right now I look like anything but.

"Speaking of the menu launches," she says, "Taffy says you haven't been answering her texts."

I try to keep the twinge of annoyance from my face. "Yeah, well. I gave her some ideas for tweets to queue up, like, weeks ago. And I've had a lot of homework."

"I know you're busy. But you're just so good at what you do." She sets her finger on my nose the way she's done since I was little, when she and my dad used to laugh at the way I'd go a little cross-eyed staring at it. "And you know how important this is to the family."

To the family. I know she doesn't mean for it to, but it rubs the wrong way, considering where we started and where we are now.

"Ah, yeah. I'm sure Dad's losing all kinds of sleep over our tweets."

My mom rolls her eyes in that affectionate, exasperated way she reserves solely for Dad. While plenty of things have changed since they divorced a few years back, they still love each other, even if they're not so much "in" love, as Mom puts it.

The rest of it, though, has been whiplash. She and my dad started Big League Burger as a mom-and-pop shop in Nashville ten years ago, when it was just milkshakes and burgers and we were barely making rent every month to support it. Nobody ever expected it to franchise so successfully that Big League

Burger would become the fourth largest fast-food franchise in the country.

I guess I also didn't expect my parents to get amicably and almost cheerfully divorced, Paige to totally freeze Mom out for being the one to initiate it, or for Mom to one-eighty from a barefoot cowgirl to a fast-food mogul and move us to the Upper East Side of Manhattan either.

Now with Paige in college in Pennsylvania, my dad still living in the Nashville apartment, and my mom's fingers near surgically attached to her iPhone, the word *family* is a bit of a stretch for her teenage daughter guilt-trip campaign.

"Explain to me this concept of yours again?" my mom asks.

I hold in a sigh. "Since we're launching the grilled cheeses first, we're 'grilling' people on Twitter. Anyone who wants to get 'grilled' can take a selfie and tweet it at us, and we'll tweet something sassy at them about it."

I could go into detail—pull up the mockups we made of potential responses to tweets, remind her of the #GrilledByBLB hashtag we're going to push, of the puns we've come up with based on the ingredients of the three new grilled cheeses—but I'm exhausted.

My mom whistles lowly. "I love it, but Taffy is *definitely* going to need your help with that."

I wince. "Yeah."

Poor Taffy. She's the mousy, cardigan-wearing twentysomething who runs the Twitter, Facebook, and Instagram pages for Big League Burger. Mom hired her right out of school when we were first starting to franchise, but after we expanded nationwide, the marketing team decided that Big League Burger's Twitter presence was going to go the way of KFC or Wendy's—sarcastic, irreverent, fresh. All the things that Taffy, bless her overworked, Powerpuff Girl heart, has no experience with.

Enter me. Apparently in the vast arsenal of useless talents that aren't going to help me get into college, I am really good at being snarky on Twitter. Even if these days "good at being snarky" generally means photoshopping an image of Big League Burger on the Krusty Krab and Burger King on the Chum Bucket—which happened to be the first one I made, when Taffy took that trip to Disney World with her boyfriend last year and Mom asked me to pitch in. It ended up getting more retweets than anything we'd ever posted. Mom has been pushing me to help Taffy ever since.

I'm about to remind her that Taffy is long overdue for a raise and actual subordinates so she can get some sleep sometime this year, when my mom turns her back to me and squints at the cake in the pan.

"Monster Cake?"

"The one and only."

"Ugh," she says, picking at the pan I already sliced from. "You should hide these from me, you know. I can't stop myself."

It's still strange to me, hearing my mom say stuff like that. If she hadn't been such a proud foodie, she and my dad wouldn't have opened Big League Burger in the first place. It sometimes doesn't seem like that long ago I was standing on the porch of the old Nashville apartment with Paige, while our dad crunched numbers and emailed suppliers and my mom made exhaustive lists of bonkers milkshake combinations, reading them all off for our approval.

I don't think I've seen her have more than a few sips of milkshake in half a decade—now she's way more into the business side of things. And while I've leaned into that by helping with the tweets and trying to make New York work, the shift only seemed to make Paige even angrier with her. Half the time I feel like she's only so committed to our baking blog as some kind of sticking point.

But no matter what else happens, this one thing my mom has always had a weakness for—Monster Cake. A perilous invention from childhood, the day Paige and Mom and I decided to test the limits of our rinky-dink oven with a combination of Funfetti cake mixed with brownie batter, cookie dough, Oreos, Reese's Cups, and Rolos. The result was so simultaneously hideous and delicious that my mom fashioned googly eyes on it out of frosting, and thus, Monster Cake was born.

She takes a bite of it now and groans. "Okay, okay, get this away from me."

My phone pings in my pocket. I pull it out and see a notification from the Weazel app.

Wolf

Hey. If you're reading this, go to bed.

"Is that Paige?"

I bite down the smile on my face. "No, it's—a friend of mine." Well, kind of. I don't actually know his real name. But Mom doesn't need to know that.

She nods, pulling up some cake residue from the bottom of the pan with her thumbnail. I brace myself—it's about now that she usually asks what Paige is up to, and yet again I have to play the middleman—but instead, she asks, "Do you know a boy named Landon who goes to your school?"

If I were the kind of girl who was stupid enough to leave diaries laying out in my bedroom, this would be reason enough to tailspin into full-blown panic. But I'm not the kind of girl who is stupid enough to do that, even if Mom were the kind of parent who snoops.

"Yeah. We're both on the swim team, I guess." Which is to say—*Yeah, I had a massive, irrational crush on him freshman year, when you essentially dropped me off in a lion's den of rich kids who've known each other since birth.*

That first day was about as painfully awkward as a day could be. I'd never worn a school uniform before, and everything seemed to itch and not quite tuck in properly. My hair was still the frizzy, unruly mess it had been in middle school. Everyone was already secure in their own little cliques, and none of those cliques seemed to include anyone who had six pairs of cowboy boots and a Kacey Musgraves poster hung up in their closet.

I nearly burst into tears on the spot when I finally got to my English class and realized, to my horror, there had been summer reading—and there was a pop quiz on the first day. I was too terrified to actually say something to the teacher, but Landon had leaned over from his desk, all tanned from the summer with this broad, easy smile, and said, "Hey, don't worry about it. My older brother says she just does these quizzes to scare us—they don't actually count."

I managed a nod. Sometime in the split second it took for him to lean back over to his own desk and look down at his quiz, my stupid fourteen-year-old brain decided I was in love.

Granted, it only lasted a few months, and I've spoken to him approximately six times since. But I've been way too busy for crushes in the time between then and now, so it's pretty much the only blueprint I've got.

"Good, good. You should get to know him. Invite him over sometime."

My jaw drops. I know she went to high school in the nineties, but that does *not* excuse this fundamental misunderstanding of how teenage social interaction works.

"Um, what?"

"His father is considering a massive investment in taking BLB international," she says. "Anything we can do to make them feel more at ease . . ."

I try not to squirm. For all the bad poetry and light angsting to Taylor Swift songs that Landon inspired a few years back, I don't actually know all that much about him, especially since he's so busy now with some app development internship off campus that I barely even see him in the hallways. Landon's been too busy being Landon—exceedingly handsome, universally beloved, and probably out of my mortal league.

"Yeah, I mean. We're not really friends or anything, but . . ."

"You're great with people. Always have been." She reaches forward and tweaks me on the cheek.

Maybe I was, back at my old school. I had so many friends in Nashville, they basically made up half of the original Big League Burger's revenue, hanging out there after school. But I never had to do anything to make those friends. They were all just there, the same way Paige was. We grew up together, knew everything about each other, and friendship wasn't some sort of conscious choice so much as it was something we were just born with.

Of course, I didn't know that until we moved here into this whole new ecosystem of other kids. That first day of school, everyone stared at me as if I were an alien, and compared to my Manhattan-bred peers who were raised on Starbucks and YouTube makeup tutorials, I basically was. That day I came home, took one look at my mom, and started to bawl.

It spurred her into action faster than if I'd come home literally on fire—within the week, I had more makeup products than my bathroom counter could hold, lessons with a stylist about blow-drying, one-on-one private tutoring so I could catch up to the elite curriculum. My mom had put us into this strange new world, and she was determined to make us both fit.

It's weird, that I kind of look back on that misery with a fondness. These days my mom and I are too busy for much more than this—weird post-midnight encounters in the kitchen, both of us already poised with one foot out the door.

This time I beat her to it. "I'm gonna go to bed."

My mom nods. "Don't forget to leave your phone on tomorrow, so Taffy can reach you."

"Right."

I should probably be annoyed that she thinks Twitter takes priority over my actual education—especially considering she put me in one of the most competitive schools in the country—but it's nice, in a way. To have her need me for something.

Back in my room, I lean on the mass of pillows on my bed, pointedly avoiding my laptop and the mountain of work still waiting for me by opening the Weazel app instead and typing a reply.

Bluebird

Well look who it is. Can't sleep?

I think for a moment Wolf won't respond, but sure enough, the chat bubble opens again. There's a certain kind of thrill and an even more certain kind of dread—a hazard of using the Weazel app. The whole thing is anonymous, and supposedly there are only kids from our school on it. You're assigned a username when you log on for the first time, always some kind of animal, and stay anonymous as long as you're in the main Hallway Chat that's open to everyone.

But if you talk with anyone one-on-one on the app, at some

point—you never know when—the app reveals your identities to each other. Boom. Secrecy out the window.

So basically, the more I talk to Wolf, the likelier the odds are that the app will out us to each other. In fact, considering some people are randomly revealed to each other within a week or even within a day, it's kind of a miracle we've gone two months like this.

Wolf

Nah. Too busy worrying about you butchering Pip's narrative.

Maybe that's why, lately, we've started getting a little more personal than usual. Saying things that won't quite give us away, but aren't all that subtle either.

Bluebird

You'd think I'd have an advantage. Pip's whole rags-to-riches thing isn't so far off my mark

Wolf

Yeah. I'm starting to think we're the only ones who weren't born with silver spoons in multiple orifices

I hold my breath, then, as if the app will out us both right there. I want it and I don't. It's kind of pathetic, but everyone is so closed off and competitive that Wolf is the closest thing I've had to a friend since we moved here. I don't want anything to change that.

It's not really that I'm afraid he'd disappoint me. I'm afraid I'd disappoint him.

Wolf

Anyway, milk it for all it's worth. Especially cuz those assholes probably paid a much smarter person to write their essays for them.

Bluebird

I hate that you're probably right.

Wolf

Hey. Only 8 more months 'til graduation.

I lie back on my bed, closing my eyes. Sometimes it feels like those eight months can't go by fast enough.

Jack

People should be banned from sending emails before 9 a.m. on Mondays. Particularly if said email is going to wreck my day.

To the parents and eager learning beavers of Stone Hall Academy, it begins. A clear sign it's from Rucker, full-time vice principal and part-time thief of joy.

> It has come to the faculty's attention that members of the student body are engaging in anonymous chats on an app called "Weasel." Not only is it not sanctioned by the school, but it is a growing cause for concern. The risk of cyberbullying, the potential spread of test answers, and the unknown origins of this app are all reason enough for us to enact a schoolwide ban, effective immediately.
>
> Parents, we urge you to have a frank discussion with students about the dangers of this app. From this day forward, any student caught engaging in "Weasel" on campus will be subject to a disciplinary hearing. Anyone

with information about this app is encouraged to come forward.

Have an enriching day,
Vice Principal Rucker

I shut my screen off, throwing myself back onto my pillow and closing my eyes.

Weasel? Of all the hills I'm willing to die on, this should probably be the last one, but I'm irked by the misnomer anyway. It's "Weazel," my slightly cheeky homage to early-era apps that abused *z* and disavowed vowels (I figured leaning into that second one and calling it "Weazl" was a little too much, even for me).

But more importantly, nobody's using it to cheat or cyberbully or whatever the hell Rucker thinks teenagers do when they finally find a space to interact without adults breathing down their necks. First of all, if anyone at Stone Hall wants to cut any academic corners, odds are a big fat check will do a hell of a lot more than a list of Scantron answers will. And second of all, I'm so vigilant about monitoring the Hallway Chat and erasing any messages that come close to cyberbullying or cheating that now most people know better than to even try.

My door swings open.

"Did you *see* this?"

Ethan is fully in my bedroom before I'm even awake enough to properly scowl at him. Naturally, he's already in his school uniform, his hair gelled, his backpack slung over his shoulder. He always gets to school early to make out with his boyfriend on the front steps, and I guess do whatever it is you do when you're too damn popular for your own good. Read: being student council president, captain of the dive team, and a star pupil so beloved by our teachers that I heard two of them arguing once in the staff lounge over whether he should win the departmental award for English or math at the end of our junior year, since he wasn't allowed to win both.

All of which would be annoying if Ethan were just my brother, but are made at least ten times worse by the fact that he is my identical twin. There's nothing quite as awkward as living in a shadow that is quite literally the same shape as yours.

Not that I'm a loser. I have plenty of friends. But I'm definitely more the class-clown variety of high school clichés than my brother, who is basically the Troy Bolton of our school, minus the jazz hands.

(Okay, maybe I'm a little bit of a loser.)

"Yeah, I saw the email," I mutter, a pit sinking in my stomach.

The thing is, nobody knows I made Weazel. I didn't ever mean for it to become such a—well, for lack of a better word, such a *thing*. Ethan asked my parents for a book on app development one Christmas so he could join some club his friends had started, and when he abandoned the idea by New Year's, I picked it up and found out I actually had a knack for it. I made a few rinky-dink chat platforms and location-based apps, but was way too busy helping my parents out in the deli to do much more than that. Then the idea for Weazel popped into my head and wouldn't let go.

So I made it. Polished it up. And then one day in August, after I'd had a beer at some party with Ethan and yet another classmate approached, chatted me up for thirty seconds, and abruptly abandoned me when she realized I was *not* my brother, I'd decided I had had enough of dealing with our peers face-to-face for the night. Only this time, instead of spending the next few hours feeling sorry for myself the way I usually do when this kind of stuff happens, I ended up making a throwaway account and posted a link to download the app on the school's Tumblr page.

There were fifty students on it by the next morning. I had to immediately put safeties on it so you could only make an account with a Stone Hall student email address. Now there are three hundred, which means there are only about twenty-six people in the entire school who *don't* have it—which is maybe for the best, because honestly I'm so low on random animal identities to assign them that the most recent user was just dubbed "Blobfish."

"What email?" Ethan asks. "I'm talking about the tweets."

"Huh?"

Ethan grabs my phone off my mattress and does that incredibly irritating twin thing where he unlocks it using his own face. He pulls something up and then promptly shoves it under my nose.

"Wait, what is this?"

I squint down at the tweet from what appears to be the Big League Burger corporate account. It's introducing a new menu item, one of three new "handcrafted grilled cheeses"—the one in this tweet is called "Grandma's Special." I read the ingredients and my confusion hardens into anger so instantly that Ethan can practically feel it like a ripple of air in the room, immediately saying, "*Right?*"

I look at him, and then back down at the screen. "What the *hell*?"

We don't exactly have license on the words "Grandma's Special" or on specific combinations of ingredients that go on grilled cheese. But there's no way it's a coincidence. "Grandma's Special" has been a mainstay at our family deli since Grandma Belly introduced it to the menu, based on a sandwich *her* grandma had made. And now dozens of years of Campbell family grilled cheese innovation was just straight up stolen by one of the biggest burger chains in the country, down to the name and five of its very specific ingredients.

We may not be some massive corporate name, but Girl Cheesing has been an installation in the East Village for decades. Every New Yorker worth their salt knows about our legendary sandwiches—particularly "Grandma's Special," our top-selling grilled cheese, and its prolific secret ingredient. There's literally an entire wall of pictures of people posing with it and Grandma Belly, including a photo of some pop star from the eighties that I'm fairly certain my mom prizes more than the photos of me and Ethan taken moments after our birth.

"Dad says to just ignore it," says Ethan, his nostrils already flared in that way I know mine are too. I can see the gears turning in his head, his fingers curling into fists. I'm right behind him, the rage jolting me awake faster than any stupid email from Rucker ever could.

The world can mess with me however it wants, but I draw the line at it messing with Grandma Belly.

"Yeah, well. He didn't tell *me* to ignore it."

Ethan's lips quirk upward. "That's what I was hoping you'd say."

For all of our differences, at least in this regard, we're always agreed. Ethan may have begged off most of his shifts at the deli over the last few years—the summer before high school he opted into some volunteer trip to build houses with a group of the more popular kids in our class, and basically came back their new king—but no matter how in demand he is outside of the deli, the loyalty is always there. It's so bone-deep in both of us that it feels more shared than anything else, even more than being each other's spitting images.

I pull up the Girl Cheesing Twitter account from my phone. We're both logged into it, mostly because our parents can't be bothered keeping up with any of the deli's pages. If my dad had his way, we wouldn't have any social media presence at all.

"We're a word-of-mouth establishment," he's constantly saying, with that same stubborn pride he's always had. Which is all well and good, except that "word of mouth" has not exactly been helping us stay afloat lately. He and Mom haven't talked about it much, but I'm in the deli practically every day after school—and by virtue of the insane private school education they've insisted on, I'm no idiot. Our loyal customer base is aging or leaving the city. The lines are shorter. Our sales are dwindling. We need to get people in the door.

It's not like I haven't tried to pull my dad into the twenty-first century. I even pitched a few ideas for social media pushes or apps that we could develop to try to generate more buzz. But before I could tell him that was something I could do myself, he said we needed to put our energy into the store, and not waste it on all the "background noise."

"Apps, websites—that's all useless to me," he'd said at the time. "You're what matters to this store. This whole family. We just need to work a little harder, is all."

It still stings, how fast he dismissed the whole thing—but not nearly as much as the crap Big League Burger is pulling on us right now.

I'm still half delirious from sleep when I draft the tweet. It's honestly not my best work. It's just a picture of our menu board, which proudly declares we sold our millionth "Grandma's Special" in 2015, next to a screenshot of Big League Burger's tweet, which reads, "Nobody grills a cheese like Grandma League can."

I almost write something as pissed off as I actually am—*Who do you asswipes think you are?* is the first unhelpful one that comes to mind—but my parents would murder me if I wrote anything rude on the company social media. In the end I decide my safest option to throw just enough shade but not so much that we inspire our parents' wrath is to write sure, jan on the text above the screenshots, along with a side-eye emoji. I hold the screen up to Ethan for approval, and he nods, mirroring my smirk, and hits "Tweet."

It's not going to make the slightest difference. We have a handful of followers to their behemoth four million. But sometimes even shouting into a void feels better than just staring into it.

Jack

I manage to calm myself down to non-Hulk levels by the time I reach the 6 train platform, leaving a good twenty minutes after Ethan. The only silver lining to all this bullshit is that Grandma Belly, at least, probably won't see it—I'm pretty sure she's never even opened Twitter before. At eighty-five, she's not exactly a huge fan of the internet.

But then again, that might be changing. She's been winding down a bit—going on shorter walks, going to more doctor's appointments. But it's one of those things we seem to sweep under the counter like the deli's finances, or what exactly is going to happen when my parents want to retire—as long as nobody actually says that Grandma Belly's health is waning, we can all act like it isn't happening.

My phone buzzes in my hands, pulling me out of the tangle of my thoughts. I open the Weazel app, trying not to smile too obviously on the platform when I read the message waiting for me.

Bluebird

afkgjafldgjalfkjahlfkajgd

Wolf

I don't speak zombie. Did that mean you finished your essay?

Bluebird

"Essay" is certainly a word for it. Whether it will compete against the ghostwriter Shane Anderson's mom hired is another issue entirely

The 6 train rolls into the station, and I shove my phone into my pocket, Bluebird along with it. She's been doing this lately—this game of elimination. Not that it helps much that she's eliminating a guy in our class who has fewer brain cells than fingers, because even if she *were* massively catfishing me, I'm pretty sure it's not Anderson on the other end. Bluebird's too quick-witted for that. (The ghostwriter Anderson's mom hired, on the other hand . . .)

Maybe I should know who she is even without the hints. I barely ever interact on the Hallway Chat, where all the users can post and stay anonymous, and I never initiate any chats with people who do. But at one point I posted a link to a free SAT test prep book online, which was met with a resounding silence from my peers and their $200-an-hour tutors—that is, until about an hour later, a private chat came from Bluebird. It was a picture of The Rock mid-flex at the gym, and a text that read Me after devouring all that sweet, sweet Protein Punch—a reference to one of the first math prep questions about a fictional protein company whose products came in powdered and liquid form.

Her profile said she was a girl and she was a senior, so that was initially all I knew. That, and she wasn't chugging so much Stone Hall Kool-Aid that she was above using free test resources. Still, even after all we've talked since—first making dumb jokes about the test prep questions, then our teachers, and sometimes things way beyond school—nothing really seems to narrow it down. I can't think of a single girl at our school who she might be.

Which, to be fair, might not be so difficult a feat if I paid attention to something other than the dive team and my phone every once in a while.

The truly weird thing about this is that I could just blow the whole thing wide open right now. I have access to the emails attached to the different usernames, for one thing. But I've never looked, and it feels like cheating somehow to check on Bluebird's. Like it would wreck it a little bit, in some way, because I'd feel like a liar. Like I'd pulled one over on her. I'd rather us just stay on level ground.

But I guess I already have pulled one over on her. Technically, the app should have given away our identities weeks ago. That's the whole point of the name—Weazel, for "Pop! Goes the Weasel" (not the most clever reference, but it was three in the morning when I patented it). But I messed with the code and stopped it from happening between us for reasons I'm still not entirely sure of. Maybe it's just nice to have someone to talk to who *gets* it—the whole fish-out-of-water thing. At least, nice to talk to someone who doesn't have the exact same stupid face as me.

Maybe it's just nice to finally be honest with someone at all. Ethan's all too willing to pretend we're as well-off as our peers, but I can't separate School Jack and Home Jack the way Ethan does—or at least not as easily. It feels like it takes up way too much space in my brain, trying to make myself fit, but when I'm talking to Bluebird, I never have to switch between the two. I just am.

Not that I'm not grateful and all—Ethan and I may have both worked our asses off to get into Stone Hall, but my parents continue working their asses off to pay for it. My mom went there when she was a kid, and even though she has adjusted to the rest of it—the whole comedown from "uptown princess" to "wife of a deli owner" that must have been some hell of a whirlwind romance before Ethan and I existed—she has always been adamant about our education, and my dad has always been adamant on backing her up on it.

Which is why I find myself on a Monday morning, walking up the steps of a school that looks like it fell out of Disney's *The Hunchback of Notre Dame* and nodding at kids whose bank accounts are hefty enough to buy the Starbucks down the street for kicks.

And so commences my least favorite part of every day—the part where people's eyes graze my face, light up hopefully, and then immediately dim when they realize I am not, in fact, their treasured Ethan, but still just regular me. No amount of letting my hair grow out slightly longer and messier than his or switching up my backpack and shoes or generally walking around with my head in my phone screen has done anything to prevent it.

What I really need is a new face. But since I'm actually partial to it, I'll settle for waiting for Ethan to blow the Popsicle stand that is Manhattan and go to some yuppie university far away from here.

"Yo. *Yo.*"

I glance up from my locker to find Paul, who is all of five-foot-five and basically what would happen if the Energizer Bunny and the leprechaun from Lucky Charms had a very ginger, very excitable baby.

"Did you see? Mel and Gina were like, *necking* in the hallway," he informs me, his eyes shining with glee.

I pull out my history textbook and shut the locker. "In 1954? Because I'm pretty sure we call it making out now."

Paul frantically pats my arm. "So here's what happened," he says, with the urgency of an intern reporting something to their boss on the way into work. "They were chatting on the Weazel app, and, y'know, flirting and stuff, and then the app revealed their names to each other and *now they are dating.*"

Paul is grinning one of those manic grins, and for once, I find myself grinning manically back. To be honest, this has been the coolest part of Weazel—people actually connecting on it. Like, the Hallway Chat is sometimes just people shitposting for kicks, but sometimes it gets *real.* People talking about how freaked out they are about college admissions, or their parents putting pressure on them. People cracking jokes about a test we all failed to lighten the mood. All the tiny little cracks in our armor that we never actually show each other in person, because sometimes this place feels more like a watering hole where we all have to establish ourselves as predator and prey than an actual institution of learning.

But this—this is the stuff that makes all those hours monitoring the app worth it. When people connect with each other on the one-on-one chats. Mel and Gina aren't the first people to either start dating or strike up a friendship because of it. In fact, so many people were bitching about our calculus midterm that there's a full-on study group that meets twice a week in the library now.

We round the corner and there, sure enough, are Mel and Gina, going at it so enthusiastically that it is a genuine miracle neither of them has gotten detention yet. It almost makes me worry that something has happened to our dear old friend Vice Principal Rucker, whose sonar for teenage affection usually rivals bomb-sniffing dogs.

"*Hot*, right?"

I put a hand on Paul's shoulder, knowing full well it will do nothing to calm his seismic level of excitement, and also knowing full well that he's only calling it "hot" because he thinks he's supposed to.

"You're going full Hefner," I say, because we've talked about this kind of thing before. "Dial it down."

"Yeah, right, right."

If there is one person in this school I feel more sorry for than myself, it's Paul—who, despite having all the trappings of a filthy-rich Stone Hall legacy, is basically what would happen if a Nick Jr. cartoon became three-dimensional. I think if it weren't for the diving team being so fiercely protective of their own, this place might have eaten him alive.

"Let's get to homeroom."

I'm still kind of high on the buzz of my own inflated sense of ego as I sit, itching to check my phone, to see if there's another message from Bluebird. I'm suddenly bursting to tell someone—*I made this happen. I was a small part of something cool.* And of all the people in my world, weirdly, it's the person whose face I don't even know that I want to tell most.

Well, that's the other weird thing. I *do* know her face, whoever she is. I know everyone in our year. It could be Carter, who's highlighting a set of notes in the front row, or Abby, who's blowing an impressively large bubble gum bubble, or Hailey or Minae, whose heads are ducked down in a heated discussion about what definitely sounds like *Riverdale* fan fiction. In some ways, it's like Bluebird is nobody and everybody at the same time—like every time someone looks up and notices me glancing at them, I could be looking right at her.

Or worse—she could be looking right at me.

Jack

Once the final morning bell rings, I find out pretty fast why Rucker wasn't around to hit lovesick teens with his metaphorical broomstick.

"Good morning, eager beavers of Stone Hall," says the nasally voice that probably haunts at least half the school's dreams over the intercom. "By now you have seen the schoolwide email warning about the 'Weasel' app, and disciplinary action that will be taken for any student caught using it. Students are encouraged to report to any faculty members if they observe any of their peers communicating on the app."

Yikes. The thing Rucker is most notorious for—aside from sporting a collection of patterned pants that even the local Goodwill would burn upon sight—is his loyal little rat pack of students. I don't know any names for certain, but I have suspicions—namely Pooja Singh and Pepper Evans, two fellow seniors who seem to be in some kind of silent authority-figure-pleasing competition at all times, and some of the kids on the golf team, who seem to be otherwise overlooked because . . . well . . . golf. I don't know if he's offering them extra credit or college recs or *what*, but he seems to have at least three narcs in every year who are all too willing to sell the rest of us out. Ethan has taken to calling them Rucker's "little birds" like that dude in *Game of Thrones*, but honestly, "complete assholes" suits them just fine.

Paul leans over. "Okay, that's *1984* as heck."

I try not to look over at him too obviously. Our homeroom teacher, Mrs. Fairchild, is a big fan of silence. I personally suspect it's because she is nursing a hangover most of the time, which, respect. If I had to deal with hormonal teenagers who carry black AmEx cards, I'd probably be buying out the Trader Joe's wine store in Union Square too.

"No kidding."

Then the door swings open, and in comes Pepper Evans herself. The only reason I'm not entirely sure that Pepper isn't a robot is that she's captain of the swim team, and I haven't seen any circuits actively frying when she gets into the pool. All the other evidence decidedly points toward her being SkyNet material. She's top of the class, has a GPA that makes mere mortals weep, and is never, ever late.

Which means that if she's walking in five minutes after the bell, it can only be for one reason.

"So?" I ask, as she slides herself into the seat right next to mine. She either doesn't hear me or pretends not to. "How many?"

Pepper barely turns to acknowledge me, her face flushed under her freckles and her eyes trained on the chalkboard, where Mrs. Fairchild is half-heartedly writing some reminders about volunteer hours being due by the end of the week.

"How many what?" she mutters, tucking her overgrown bangs behind her ear. Within a second, they're fanning back over her face, a blonde curtain that, unlike the rest of her, she can never quite seem to tame.

"How many people did you rat out to Rucker?"

She scowls that uneven scowl of hers, one of her eyebrows creasing just a bit more than the other. It is bizarrely satisfying, getting any kind of reaction out of her—like when the machine at Chuck E. Cheese in Harlem used to malfunction and spit out a few extra tickets. I lean forward in my desk, forgetting for a moment about Mrs. Fairchild's wrath.

"What'd he offer you?" I ask. "A's on all of your midterms?"

Pepper's lips thin into her teeth, but her body stays very still. She has this uncanny ability to sit like a statue. I wouldn't be surprised if pigeons have landed on her in the park.

"Unlike you," she says, the words perfectly clear even though her mouth hardly moves, "I don't *need* any help with my grades."

I put a hand on my heart, wounded. "You think I'm dumb?"

"Last year I watched you put Kool-Aid mix in pool water and drink it. I *know* you're dumb."

"It was for a bet."

She arches one perfectly groomed eyebrow before devoting her full attention back to her notebook. I grin and shake my head, turning back to the front. Truth is, I actually don't mind Pepper. She's one of the few people who knows, sometimes without even glancing up from her textbook, that I'm me and not my brother.

Which, to be fair, is probably a lot easier for a robot.

Still, it's kind of unnerving. Even people who've known us since kindergarten get tripped up, and she came in out of nowhere and seemed to have me sized up the moment she got to Stone Hall. Sometimes freshman year, I'd notice her staring—not just at me, but at everyone. At that point we were all in that bumbling part of puberty where we were pretending not to notice each other, but Pepper was actively and unabashedly observing everyone, like she was trying to figure out the whole of us before trying to make herself fit.

I still can't quite figure out what was so weird about it—Pepper specifically, with the keen blue of her eyes on me, or just the fact of feeling seen at all. But I missed the weirdness of it when it was over, when within the month, she was just like everyone else here, so tunnel-visioned about her grades and her SATs that she couldn't see past her nose, let alone see anyone else.

It's probably why I rib her, in particular, more than the other Goody Two-shoes in our class—the nicknames, the teasing, the occasional foot-tapping on the back of her chair. Because I miss that strange, undivided attention. Because I know she wasn't always like this. Once, she was every bit as out of place here as I feel every day.

Homeroom only lasts for thirty minutes, but as usual, Mrs. Fairchild manages to make them as excruciatingly boring as possible. All around me, I can see students with varying degrees of subtlety pulling out their phones and texting—from my desk alone, I can see at least three people on Weazel. I scan the room, looking to see if I can find any more. Then I notice Pepper bent over slightly, her perfect posture just a degree off.

"Are you *texting*?" I hiss.

She jumps. Literally jumps up in her seat, getting an impressive inch of air.

"None of your business."

"Are you on Weazel?"

Her eyes are hard. "You saw Rucker's email. I wouldn't be caught dead on that app."

Um, ouch.

She settles her fingers back on her phone screen and types without breaking eye contact with the whiteboard, which even I have to admit is impressive.

"This is a place of *learning*, Pepperoni."

She rolls her eyes and shoves her phone into her open

backpack. I wonder if she really thinks I was going to bust her for texting in class. The idea of that is oddly more insulting than the whole "I watched you drink Kool-Aid" bit (which, in all fairness, was among the most disgusting things I have ever done because of peer pressure).

I'm about to say something conciliatory, but just then I see Paul's mouth drop open out of the corner of my eye. Not that I need any peripheral vision to see it—about half the class does, because Paul's emotional states are generally so demonstrative that I'm pretty sure people in Brooklyn can lick their pointer fingers, hold them to the wind, and know exactly what kind of state Paul is in at any given moment. But as soon as he looks up and his eyes meet mine, I know that whatever it is that has him worked up, it does *not* bode well for me.

He sucks in a breath to say something, and then, mercifully, the bell rings before he can blurt whatever it is out into the open. Instead, he scrambles out of his desk so fast his bony knees almost knock it over, and yanks on the sleeve of my uniform.

"Did you *see*?"

I glance to my right—Pepper's already halfway out the door.

"See what?"

Paul's hands are shaking as he shoves his phone into my line of vision—an impressively stupid move, all things considered. Weazel aside, we're not allowed to have our phones out during school hours. But I see the familiar Twitter handle for Girl Cheesing and all of my concerns about future detentions fly out the window.

"Oh my god."

"*Right?* This is amazing."

"Amazing?" I grab his phone from him, holding it up to my face and blinking at it as if I can blink away the literal *three thousand* retweets and the ungodly number of likes on the tweet I sent from the deli's account this morning. "My parents are going to gut me like a fucking *fish*."

"Language," Mrs. Fairchild mutters, evidently not even caring about the contraband in my hands.

My heart is halfway up my throat, beating in my skull. My dad doesn't even like that we're on Twitter, let alone going viral on it. "How the hell did this happen?"

We have 645 followers. The fact that I know the exact amount is a testament to how very rarely that number changes. Up until now, the most engagement we've ever gotten from a tweet on the deli's account was a meme about early dive team practices that Ethan accidentally posted and a bot retweeted before he realized what he'd done.

"Marigold retweeted it," says Paul.

My throat feels like sandpaper. Marigold, as in the eighties pop star my mom is obsessed with, who still comes into the deli every now and then.

Marigold, as in the eighties pop star who just unwittingly got me grounded into next year. It was one thing when I thought I might take some heat for tweeting it in the first place—now I'm going to be working unpaid shifts at the deli and smelling like turkey until Christmas.

Because Marigold, as it turns out, has a whopping 12.5 million followers. I don't need to be coasting in AP Calc to know that translates to roughly a bajillion retweets every time she breathes. And it looks like she only *just* retweeted us—in the time I've stood here staring at Paul's phone with my mouth unhinged, it's gotten another 250 retweets.

I tap on her profile and see there's another tweet she sent herself, right after her retweet. "Shame on Big League Burger!" it reads. "Girl Cheesing perfected Grandma's Special before that punk was even born."

By "that punk," I assume she is referencing the Big League Burger mascot, a cartoon of a chubby-faced, freckled little boy in a baseball cap with a melting ice cream cone in his hands. In commercials he's always hamming it up to the camera, getting into some kind of annoying shenanigans and saying, "Welcome to the big leagues!" The commercial ends before anyone bothers disciplining him for anything. I better figure out what the secret to that is, and fast, because my parents are going to be none too pleased when I get home.

"You're famous," says Paul, elated.

"I'm doomed."

I hand him back his phone, scanning the hallway for Ethan, wondering if he's seen. Not that it matters—nothing is going to get me out of what is sure to be another long lecture in our dad's roster of them. I'm thinking this one will be in the *patience is a virtue* variety, subsection *you need to think before you act.* And admittedly, I do have a slight habit of opening my mouth before my brain fully filters what is and isn't appropriate to say (or, y'know, tweet).

But if I'm bad, our mom is *way* worse. She once scared a guy with a literal knife trying to hold up the deli by throwing a ham and screaming at him. It's not like my hotheadedness is some kind of anomaly.

Still, this is one of those moments I wish I'd taken Dad's advice. It'll be a miracle if I get out of this unscathed—thanks to Marigold, I'm about to be the level of grounded that will make me flinch at every "Best of the '80s" playlist for the rest of my life.

Pepper

Wolf

Haven't heard from you all day, so I'm going to assume you're among the chosen few and Rucker confiscated your phone. Godspeed, soldier.

I press my forehead to the locker of the changing room. The final bell rang ten minutes ago, and by then Taffy had texted me a whopping total of thirty-two times.

What about this one? reads her latest message. I squint at the screenshot of a tweet she's sent me. It's a selfie of a guy holding up a full McDonald's bag, his mouth crammed with fries, captioned grill this, bitch. It's one of a few thousand tweets we've gotten, tagged to the corporate account for the #GrilledByBLB initiative, but we're trying to respond to at least two hundred of them with funny comebacks today.

And by "we" I really mean me, because Taffy does not have a sarcastic bone in her entire body.

I draft a tweet and send it to her so fast that I don't even have to break my stride: it's illegal to burn trash.

Taffy has it up within the minute, which means it's going to be another five minutes before she finds another contender, and another ten minutes after that for her to give up on thinking about a tweet on her own and text me. By then, though, I'll be in the pool—something I'm actually looking forward to for once, since it is the only definitive way to make myself unavailable these days.

It's not that I don't like swimming. Paige and I swam in summer leagues growing up, and even as young as six, I was swimming laps around all the other kids. It was fun back then—less about racing and more about playing Uno in the grass between races and begging my parents to let us get those massive baked potatoes at the food truck down the street after swim meets. Once we moved, though, there was no more swimming for fun. People are only here to collect the varsity letter they get every season and slap a line about it on their college apps. Hundreds and hundreds of hours and sweat and chlorine-bleached hair and occasional tears, all reduced to a few printed words.

"Hey, Pep? You want me to run warm-ups or are you gonna be out in a sec?"

Pep. I hate that nickname. Possibly even more than *Pepperoni*, another Jack Campbell original.

Or maybe it's less about being called *Pep* and more about the person who's saying it.

"I'll be right out," I tell Pooja, shoving my backpack into one of the lockers. It feels like I'm shoving Taffy in there with it. Wolf too.

Pooja pushes a lock of hair into her swim cap, then gives me a thumbs-up. "If you're sure!"

I wait until she's turned the corner to roll my eyes. The

whole exchange was innocuous enough on the surface, sure, but I know Pooja—the two of us have been neck and neck with everything since my first year at Stone Hall. We're constantly within one point of each other on exams, within milliseconds of each other on our racing times, in all of the same teachers' office hours. Competing with her has become such a constant in my life that I'm pretty sure on my deathbed, I'll get a call from her casually bragging about how she bets she's going to get to die first.

Our eventual mortality aside, there's no way in hell I'm letting her lead warm-ups on the first day of the season. I earned my spot as the captain of the girls' team. For once, I had a clear-cut victory over her: I'd gotten the votes. I'd won the numbers game. Coach Martin made her a co-captain in some attempt, maybe, to soften the blow, but if anything, that just made me all the more determined not to let her undermine me in the first hour of the season.

I head out to the pool deck, the smell of chlorine heavy in the air. I probably shouldn't love the smell so much—and maybe I don't. It's the kind of smell that aches, that takes up too much space in your lungs and displaces you in time. It could be last season, or five years ago, or back to a kiddie pool with my floaties on all at once.

I'm knocked out of whatever lingering nostalgia I have, though, when I look down at the pool and see a bunch of people already in it, their arms and legs cutting through the water.

For a second I am frozen, horrified at the idea that Pooja just walked out here and led practice on her own. That I'm going to look like an idiot in front of the whole team because I took an extra minute to write another one of those stupid tweets. But then I see Pooja striding up to me, looking livid.

"We've got a problem."

I follow her scowl to the wall of the pool, realizing I don't actually know the person who is clinging to the edge of it, shaking water out of her goggles. I look farther up the lanes of the pool and see that really, there is only a cluster of fifteen or so swimmers—just enough to take up most of the three lanes the school is allowed to use at this pool, but not enough for it to be our team.

Someone swims toward the wall and does a flip turn so aggressive, it manages to soak me and Pooja both. I can't see his face from underwater, but whoever it is seems to be *smirking*, like I can feel the smirk all over his body. And that's when I realize it's none other than Jack Campbell and the band of misfit toys that is our dive team.

Pooja is still sputtering in shock when I take a step toward the pool and mutter, "I'll handle this."

I run up to the edge of the pool for momentum and get enough air on my dive that I'm only a few feet behind Jack when I hit the water. I catch up to him in another few seconds, tapping his foot. He keeps kicking as if he hasn't felt it. I speed up, rope my fingers around his ankle, and yank. Hard.

After a moment of floundering in surprise, Jack emerges from the water, shaking out his dark hair. For a moment, he looks ridiculous without a swim cap on, like a shaggy dog who jumped overboard from someone's rowboat. Then he runs his fingers through his hair and pushes it back so fast that it's almost striking, seeing his brown eyes wide on mine, close enough that I can see they're already tinged with a bit of red from the chlorine.

"*Yeesh*, Pepperoni," he says, grabbing the lane line. "No need to go all *Sharknado* on me."

"What do you think you're doing?"

"Um. Right now? Wondering if the lifeguard will stop you from drowning me, mostly."

"You can't be here. We booked the pool. Besides, don't you guys have a plank to go jump off?"

Jack grins one of those half grins of his, the kind that means he's about to say something he thinks is super clever. I usually manage to ignore it—but even when it's not aimed at me, it's something I've come to notice after four years of him in the periphery, interrupting peaceful silences in class or the library or when the rest of us are trying to nap on the pool deck in between heats at swim meets. Jack is the kind of person who fills silences. The kind of person who doesn't necessarily command attention, but always seems to sneak it from you anyway.

The kind of person who steals your pool lanes and makes you look like an idiot on your first day as team captain. And even though Jack has seemed determined to knock me down a peg for years, this time there's way too much of my pride on the line to let him.

"You talk a big game for someone who's terrified of that plank."

My eyes narrow. "I don't know what you're talking about."

Jack's eyes gleam from under his goggles. We both know I absolutely do.

The swim team and the dive team sometimes stay late after Friday practices to play informal water polo games with a beat-up soccer ball, and there's always some dumb bet based on who loses. It's why I have some rather off-putting memories of Jack and his brethren gagging on a Kool-Aid–pool water concoction after a loss, and why the swim team was forced to jump off the high dive after we bit it once freshman year.

Except I didn't exactly jump. It turns out whatever evolutionary compulsion not to die that's hardwired into my brain is a lot louder than the rest of the team's, because I stared at that infinite distance between the diving board and the water and immediately climbed back down so fast, I don't even remember making a conscious decision to do it.

Unlike Jack, who seems to remember the incident all too well.

But I'm not taking the bait. "Your season hasn't even officially started yet. Get your team out of our pool."

Jack blows out a breath, the grin's wattage going down a notch. "Ethan's our captain this year," he says, more to the pool than to me. "Take it up with him."

"Everything okay over there?" I hear someone call. "What's going on?"

Despite my not-crush on Landon, my cheeks go red on reflex—as though the sound of his voice triggers something Pavlovian in the blood vessels in my face. I turn toward it and see him standing on the edge of the pool deck, somehow *still* tan from the summer despite it being the middle of October. He's filled out a bit since last season too, and judging from the diameter of the eyes of the sophomore girls hanging out on the bleachers, I'm not the only one who's noticed.

"We're fine," I call back. "The dive team was just leaving."

Jack snorts.

"What's the holdup, Ethan?" Landon asks.

I don't have to be looking at Jack to feel his eye roll. I push myself through the water to get closer to the wall, my mom's voice unhelpful in my ears: *Anything we can do to make them feel more at ease.*

The problem is, Landon's at ease just about everywhere he goes. He doesn't need any help.

I am struggling to think of something clever to say, something that will make some kind of lasting impression, but by the time I hit the wall, I've got nothing. How is it I can fire off a stupid text to a guy I literally call *Wolf* without thinking twice, but when I'm actually confronted with a human being I know, my brain decides to take a hike?

I'm rescued from stammering something dumb when I see Ethan push himself out of the water.

"Hey, sorry—are you guys supposed to have the pool right now?" Ethan asks.

"I mean, it's all yours, man," says Landon. "My internship's got me beat. I'll take a nap if it's all the same to you."

It's probably my cue to laugh—the sophomore girls sure don't miss the opportunity—but I'm too thrown off to do anything but get back out of the pool, hyperaware both of my authority being more undermined by the second, and of the fact that I'm pretty sure I have a slight wedgie. For something we do half naked, swimming really is just about the least sexy sport there is.

"Our coach said we needed to put in more laps this year to strengthen up in the preseason," says Ethan, half to Landon and half to me. He at least has the decency to look apologetic for it. "Cross-training, and all."

"Where *is* your coach?" I ask.

"Well, he said he was visiting his mom for the week, but he definitely just posted an Instagram story from Cáncun," says Ethan with a shrug.

By now Coach Martin has emerged from the lobby of the gym, where she's been talking to the parents of the new members of the team about the weekend swim meet schedule. She takes one look at all of us in various states of half wet on the pool deck and doesn't bother holding in her sigh, or asking where the dive coach is. Sightings of Coach Thompkins are so rare that he's become something of a myth anyway. Considering what a hot mess the dive team is the first few weeks of every season, I guess I can't blame them for trying to get their shit together without him.

She pulls me and Ethan aside. "I have no idea when Thompkins is going to be back, so in the meantime, we need to work out a schedule. Can you guys meet after practice and figure out who's going to use the lanes and when?"

"We've never shared the lanes before," I protest.

Coach Martin offers me another one of her trademark *I don't know what to tell you* faces. "Technically the school budget for the pool rental times is for both teams, so we can't tell them no. Work it out."

Ethan nods, and we make plans to meet up at the coffee shop across the street once practice is over. Already I can feel the seismic shift of trying to adjust my schedule to compensate for it—if I spend twenty minutes with Ethan that means twenty fewer minutes for AP Calc homework, which means it will eat into the time I'll undoubtedly be answering Taffy's texts, which means I probably won't even get to work on my college apps tonight, which, in turn, means I probably won't be texting Wolf back anytime this century.

I shake the last thought out of my head before I hit the water again. Of all the priorities I'm sinking under right now, banter with some guy I don't even know should be the absolute last.

Pepper

Two hours later I feel like my entire body has been whipped. I practice often enough in the off-season that it's not too much of a shock getting into the swing of things, but nobody's self-directed workouts can reach even half the intensity of Coach Martin's. I barely have the energy to drag myself over to the coffee shop, let alone run ridiculous negotiations for a pool we shouldn't be sharing in the first place.

Even if it weren't for that, the city just makes me nervous in general. I've carved myself a little world here in a neat seven-block radius: the apartment, the school, the pool across the street, the bodega where I get my bagels, the drugstore, the good pizza place and the better taco place, and the salon where my mom gets her blowouts. I don't like leaving my orbit. I know, on a rational level, this part of the city is on a grid, and in the age of smartphones it's impossible to get lost. But everything is so cramped here, so *dense*—I hate that I can turn one corner and see an entire world I don't recognize, have to navigate a street with a completely different mood than the one a few steps away.

I hate that I feel like I have to be a different person to match. Some people can weave in and out of these streets like chameleons, but four years have passed, and I still feel like the same kid who rolled up here in a U-Haul wearing cowboy boots—stubborn and unchanged.

In Nashville, there was order. Or at least it felt that way. There was downtown, with its restaurants and honky-tonks and the massive CMA Fest crowds in the summer. There was East Nashville, all earthy and young and hopeful. There was Bellevue, where we lived in the outskirts of the city in an apartment, just beyond Belle Meade, with all of its absurdly decked-out mansions. And then in the city, in the middle of all of it, Centennial Park with its giant Pantheon replica, which to me seemed like the heart of everything, as though all the roads and tangles of freeways led back to it, pumped people in and out each day on their way to and from work.

I miss that. I miss the transition of knowing *this is who I am when I'm downtown* and *this is who I am when I'm home* and *this is who I am when I visit the restaurant*, the original Big League Burger, which was just a stone's throw away from all the recording studios and publishing houses lined up on Music Row. I miss being able to prepare for things, and knowing where I fit. Not even *knowing*, really, because when you grow up somewhere, you don't have to think about fitting into it. You just do.

When Paige is on break from UPenn and deigns to stay with us for a few days at a time, she forces me out of the orbit. We get ramen in the East Village and window shop in Soho and take dorky historical tours that start in different parks. But since she and my mom don't really talk, the rest of the year it's just me, a rat in a seven-block cage, wishing something as stupid as walking into an unfamiliar coffee shop didn't fill me with dread.

Once I actually get inside, I see someone at a table by the

window bent over a cup of coffee, wearing Ethan's baseball hat and holding Ethan's backpack, with Ethan's coat draped over the chair. I walk over to him and put my hands on my hips.

"Are you seriously trying to *Parent Trap* me?"

Jack looks up, brows puckered with disappointment, like he's a little kid and I just stuck a pin in his balloon. "What gave it away?"

I gesture in the direction of his lanky frame. "Your general Jack-ness."

"*Jack*-ness?"

"Well. That, and you're a little bit of an ass."

I smirk—a small peace offering—and he returns it and then some, with another one of those half grins. It's so unabashed that I straighten up a bit, glancing away.

"So where *is* your brother? Is he in on this little prank of yours? Because if it's all the same to you, I want to wrap this up quick."

Jack cocks his head toward the window. "Ethan is currently preoccupied making out with Stephen Chiu on the steps of the Met."

"So he sent *you*?"

Jack shrugs. "My brother's an important dude, in case you haven't noticed."

I have. It's hard not to. Ethan's one of those man-of-the-people types—always has something nice to say, an extra few minutes to give someone, some practical solution to a problem. Which is why I had been counting on this meeting being a quick one.

Enter Jack, who seems to have absolutely no qualms with wasting time.

My phone pings in my backpack, and I realize with a lurch I haven't checked it since I got out of the pool. I drop my bag, tell

Jack to keep an eye on it while I go grab a tea, and look down at my phone.

Nine texts. Holy *crap*.

The most recent ones are from my mom: Where are you?? and Is everything okay? My stomach sinks—I never told her I had practice after school today because I didn't think she'd be home. But then I scroll down and realize that although she is very much worried about my welfare, she was initially more worried about a "Twitter emergency" that needs attending.

I shoot her a quick text to let her know I'm alive and open the ones from Taffy, who—bless her heart—actually remembered I had practice, and broke down the situation with screenshots.

I'm caught up by the time I reach the cashier. Apparently some tiny little deli in the city is claiming Big League Burger copied their grilled cheese recipe, and the accusation now has ten thousand retweets. A Twitter account dedicated to the welfare of small businesses has even co-opted the #GrilledByBLB hashtag, so #KilledByBLB is trending instead.

Jesus. The internet moves fast.

Your mom wants us to fire a sassy tweet back, Taffy has texted. Which is Taffy code for, *I know this is a terrible idea, but your mom is my boss and I'm too scared of her to press the point.*

I guess I'll have to, then. I send my mom what I hope is a pacifying text, telling her we should either just let it go or sit on it for a bit and see if it actually merits some kind of apology. I'm no PR professional, but attacking an itty-bitty deli that can't rub two Twitter followers together can't be a good look for a goliath like BLB no matter how you slice it.

By the time the barista puts my tea on the counter, my mom is calling. She starts talking before I can even say hello.

"What do you think our next move is?"

I walk over to the counter, prying off my lid to add sugar and milk. I peer out of the corner of my eye to make sure Jack hasn't made off with my stuff, but he's just staring out the window, tapping his foot to the beat of whatever he's listening to with one earbud in his ear.

"I don't think we should tweet anything at them. People actually seem kind of mad."

"Well, let them be mad," says my mom dismissively. "We're not going to take this lying down."

"Okay—but maybe you should—I don't know, talk to them? Not send a tweet?"

"There's no point in talking to some sandwich place looking for attention. Give me something to fire back at them. I can't waste time right now."

It feels like a gut punch through the phone. I clutch my tea, letting it burn against my palms, waiting for it to anchor me. I want to push back, but I know how this goes—it sounds like the beginning of half of Paige and Mom's fights. One of them would push, and the other would dig their heels into the cement, and before I knew it Paige would be stalking off into Central Park, and Mom would be on the phone with Dad trying to figure out how to deal with her.

I don't want to be someone she has to deal with. Things are already weird enough between the four of us without me making waves.

"Just, uh . . . send that GIF from *Harry Potter*. The 'excuse me, but who are you' one."

There's a beat. "You're in the right direction, but let's go edgier than that."

I close my eyes. "Fine. I'll text you something else."

I text Taffy and my mom the idea, walking over to the table, where Jack is still so very clearly *Jack* that it's ridiculous he tried to pretend otherwise.

I can't lie—despite his shenanigans, it is kind of fascinating, watching him and his brother. How two people can be so strikingly similar, with the same build and the same open face, the same rhythm in the way they talk, and still present it to the world in such different ways. Where Ethan is almost coolly self-possessed, like some kind of politician, Jack is an open book—his eyes unguarded and unselfconscious, his tall frame always strewn across chairs like he has settled into himself earlier than most people our age, his dark eyebrows so expressive and honest that it's laughable he even tried to pull one over on me in the first place.

While I'm staring without meaning to, Jack takes a very long slurp of his coffee. "So. This pool thing."

I lean forward, leveling with him. We are two people at odds—me rigid and immovable, him just as at ease as ever, meeting my stare with faint amusement.

"What *exactly* did your coach want?"

"Ethan says we're supposed to do a half hour of lap swimming a day."

We only have the pool for two hours at a time. Every single year before this one, they've taken the area by the diving board, and we've taken the lanes. Half of me wonders if this is Coach Thompkins's way of getting under Coach Martin's skin—they are notorious for not getting along, especially when it comes to using the swim and dive budgets—but that doesn't mean we can't deal with it.

"How's this: you get the pool for twenty minutes a day," I propose. "The last twenty minutes we have rented."

"And where will the swim team go?"

"We'll do dry land exercises. Push-ups and lunges."

"And you're going to lead that?"

"I'll ask Landon to do it."

Jack blows out a breath. "Sounds like it's all settled, then."

I blink, surprised. I don't know Jack all that well, but I'm not used to him being so . . . reasonable.

"Wanna go heckle my brother?"

Ah. There it is.

My phone pings from the table—it's a text from Taffy, letting me know she's in a meeting. My mom immediately texts and asks me to pull up the corporate account on my phone and tweet it instead.

I wait for a beat, wondering why I feel a pinch of guilt sending it. This isn't my business, and it's not my Twitter account. It ultimately has nothing to do with me at all. I'm just a set of fingers on a keyboard.

Big League Burger @B1gLeagueBurger
Replying to @GCheesing
extremely ms. norbury voice
do you even go to this school? go home
4:47 PM · 20 Oct 2020

I hit tweet and steel myself. Something feels . . . grimy about the whole thing. Like I've done something wrong.

"They're only, like, three blocks away."

I put my phone on the table, the screen facing down. "I know where the Met is," I say, sounding overly defensive even to my own ears.

But Jack doesn't even seem to notice. "So?" he asks—an invitation.

I feel like I am itching at my seams, compelled to open the phone back up to the corporate account and see what people are saying back to the tweet. It's strange, how I can't seem to untangle myself from the company, even though it looks nothing like it did when it first started. When I was little, the whole of the restaurant felt as if it were *mine.* Paige and I were so defined by it—everyone who worked there knew our names, let us make up ridiculous milkshake combinations, snuck us leftover fries when my parents were in meetings that ran late. The franchise is so corporate that it's way beyond me and my dessert whims now, but no matter how big we get, I can't quite squash the part of me that takes it personally.

There's no way I'm going to be able to focus on anything tonight, not with the stupid notifications piling up. The idea of it is suddenly so suffocating, the last thing I want to do is go home.

"Yeah. Yeah, let's go."

Jack blinks. "Yeah?"

"Why not?"

Pepper

We take our drinks and head out, and it occurs to me as soon as we hit the sidewalk, into the cool October air, that I don't actually have any idea what to say to Jack. I don't usually have to come up with small talk for anyone, really. I walk to school alone, I walk back alone, and everywhere else I go tends to be in a group.

But Jack Campbell is nothing if not good at filling up silence. "Where are you from, anyway?"

I wince. It's not that I lied about it or anything, but after the first few reactions I got name-dropping a city in the South, I decided not to advertise it. "I'm that much of a sore thumb?"

"No, actually. You fit in alarmingly well." I'm not sure if this is meant to be a compliment or not, and from the slight bitterness in his tone, I'm not sure if he is either. He clears his throat, the edge in his words softening. "But you were one of like, two people we didn't already know freshman year, so I'm guessing you moved from somewhere."

I'm never quite sure whether I'm embarrassed or proud of it. Today I settle on some mix of the two.

"Nashville, actually."

"Huh." Jack seems to mull this over, his tongue pressing into the side of his cheek. I can see something shift in the way he considers me, and it makes me uneasy—the not knowing.

I clear my throat. "If you're about to make a cowgirl joke, you can save it."

"Nah, it was gonna be Taylor Swift–themed."

"In that case, you may proceed. But with caution. I was really into her when she was still country."

"Was?"

There's that little half grin again. I wonder if Jack has ever smiled with his whole mouth. Someday when he's an old man, he'll probably just have wrinkles on the one side.

"Am," I concede. Just two days ago Paige and I were blasting "Shake It Off" so loudly on a three-way Skype call with our dad that he threatened to start singing himself if we didn't quit. At that point, considering he has neighbors on both sides of him, it was our civic responsibility to shut it down.

We turn the corner and hit Fifth Avenue, which is emptier now than when I usually see it on the weekends. Today it's mostly tourists and joggers who have gotten home from work. "Where are you from?"

"Born and bred," says Jack, gesturing out in the direction of downtown. "We live in the East Village. Have since my great-grandparents."

I feel an unexpected pang, then. An unwelcome kind of longing. My grandparents are still in Nashville too—on both my mom's and my dad's side. It seemed like Nashville was the root of our family tree, like there would never be any conceivable reason for leaving. Even now, four years on the other side of it, I haven't fully come around to the idea.

I shove my bangs behind my ear, but the wet curl pops out, stubborn as ever. My hair is never more unruly than it is after practice, when I can't style it between school and home.

"So you're like some kind of unicorn."

Jack's lip quirks. "What?"

"When's the last time you met someone in New York whose family is actually *from* New York?"

Jack laughs. "Up here? Not for a while," he says. "But where I'm from . . . well. You meet a lot more New Yorkers downtown than you do up here."

It is a true testament to how enthusiastically Ethan and Stephen are going at it with each other that I notice the two of them on the steps before I notice anything else in the surrounding area—not the intoxicatingly sweet smell of the nut vendor on the curb, or the massive fountains, or the group of little kids squealing and running up and down the iconic steps of the Met. The two of them are utterly oblivious to all of it, kissing like one of them is about to go off to war.

I clap my hand to my chest before I even realize what I'm doing, as if I'm watching one of the ridiculous rom-coms Paige puts on whenever she comes to visit. "Aw. Let's just leave them be."

"What? Where's the fun in that?" Jack crows.

"They look so happy."

"They *look* like they need to get a room," says Jack. But he's the one who starts walking away first, shaking his head with a rueful smile. "I should have known you'd be a terrible pranking partner."

"How exactly were you planning on *pranking* them, anyway?"

"I guess now you'll never know," he says, elbowing me in the shoulder.

I rock to the side and push him back without thinking, the gesture so mindless and natural that only after it happens do I stop breathing for a second, sure I've crossed some kind of line. Sometimes it feels as if I've been interacting with everyone here from behind some kind of veil—as though I'm allowed to be here, but not engage. To look, but not touch. Like the entire social order of this place was decided long before my arrival, and any involvement I have in it is out of mercy from the people who actually belong.

But Jack is just smirking that faint smirk, walking farther down Fifth.

"So, seeing as I'm captain of the dive team now—"

"Is that so?"

"Well, you've seen that Ethan is clearly interested in other varieties of diving at the moment."

"So you've decided to elect yourself?"

Jack shrugs, the smirk taking on a new sharpness. "What's the point of having an identical twin if you can't schlep your workload onto them every now and then?"

I hold his gaze. "That doesn't seem fair."

Jack is uncharacteristically quiet for a moment, watching a group of siblings stand very, very still for a caricature artist as their fanny pack–clad dad flits around them taking video of the whole thing.

"Yeah, well, I've got nothing better to do, so." He licks his upper lip. "So, we should probably start coming up with ideas for fundraising. Before the coaches get on our asses about it."

"Yeah, probably."

"What else do we have to square away?"

I'm not sure how seriously I'm supposed to entertain this. Is

Jack really just going to take over duties for Ethan and let him take the credit? I love Paige more than anyone in the world, but I can't imagine giving up that much of my free time this close to trying to impress college admissions boards.

"Uh . . . well, there's fundraising. And picking out options for people to vote on for the team shirts this year. And Ethan and I were supposed to meet up every week to plan things for meets—like sending out directions to other pools for away meets, and who's bringing snacks. And write up the newsletter for the parents." I'm sure at any second he's going to interrupt me and back out of this massive time suck, but he just stares back, waiting for me to finish. "It's—kind of a lot."

Jack doesn't miss a beat. "Fundraising, shirts, newsletters, snacks. Got it." He shoots a glance back in Ethan's direction, even though he's well out of sight. "How about we grab food after practice?"

I stop walking. "Are you asking me out?"

The mischief in his eyes makes me regret asking before I even finish the sentence. I brace myself, sure he's going to do that thing guys do, that thing Paige warned me about—*Wow, someone thinks highly of themselves*, or some similar belittling comment. Instead, he stretches his back and says, "Well, I wasn't. But now that it's on the table . . ."

I cross my arms over my chest.

"Not a date," says Jack, holding his hands up in surrender, the eternal Jack grin still branded across his face. "Just to work out the season. We can go once a week, like you and Ethan planned."

I consider him for a moment, still waiting for some kind of punchline, some ulterior motive. I don't find any, so I offer my hand for him to shake. He raises his eyebrows at me. I raise mine right back.

Then he claps his hand to mine, shaking it firmly, just once. There is something warm and grounding in it, something that seems to mark a shift between Jack Campbell then and Jack Campbell now. Like maybe I have misjudged the idea of him I had in my head for the last few years.

Jack hikes his backpack up onto his shoulder and looks down Seventy-Eighth Street. "I'm gonna catch the 6 train home. See you tomorrow?"

"Yeah, see you then."

It's only then I realize we left my seven-block bubble a few blocks back. I stand on the sidewalk for a minute, feeling ridiculous for the jolt it sends through my system, staring at the back of Jack as he waits for the light to change as if he's some sort of compass. He pulls his phone out of his pocket, still within earshot when he scrolls for a moment, pauses, and lets out a low "Shiiiiiiiiiit."

I touch my own phone, buried in the pocket of my jacket. It's back to reality for us both.

Jack

Wolf

Do you ever just do something really, really stupid

Bluebird

No, actually. I'm perfect and I've never done a single stupid thing in my life

Bluebird

But actually all the time, always. You good?

Wolf

I mean, my parents are less than pleased with me right now. Well, my dad's not pleased. I think my mom secretly is, but is trying to do that whole solidarity thing

Bluebird

So what did you get busted for?

Wolf

The usual. Selling hard drugs. Joining a cult. Starting an underground fight club for teens, except the one rule is you HAVE to talk about it. Don't know why my parents won't just get off my back

Bluebird

Seriously. Cults are a big commitment. They should have more respect.

Bluebird

But I feel you. Also experiencing some not so great parental pressure

Wolf

College stuff?

Bluebird

Hah. I wish

Wolf

Would joining a fight club help?

Bluebird

Now that you mention it . . .

Bluebird

Ugh, I don't know. Sometimes I think my mom and I have very different ideas of what I should be doing with my time/my life in general

Wolf

Yeah. I get that

Wolf

My parents are kind of like that too

Bluebird

What do you want to do?

Bluebird

Haha that sounds so dumb. Like, "what do you wanna do when you grow up?" But I guess we're sort of getting to that point, huh?

"You'd better put that phone away before your dad spots you."

I flinch. "Jeez, Mom, you're like a freaking ninja."

"Former ballerina, but I'll take it," she says wryly. She plucks my phone from my hand. "I think you've done enough damage on this bad boy for one day."

Fair enough. I could delay my return home with practice and impromptu field trips with Pepper all I wanted, but that did nothing to get me out of a Supreme Dad Lecture of the highest order. The kind where he doesn't even wait for me to get upstairs to the apartment we live in above the deli, but raises a thumb and jerks it to the booth in the back, which my mom dubbed the "Time-Out Booth" when we were kids. These days it's more like the break booth, where we'll scarf sandwiches mid-shift or do our homework during lulls, but every so often it seems to revert back to its original purpose to suit my parents' needs.

The truly demoralizing thing about it reverting to the Time-Out Booth is that I haven't done anything worthy of it in ages. And now that I have, it isn't over anything edgy, like when our upstairs neighbor Benny hotwired a motorcycle, or when Annie, one of our regulars, got caught with a joint in Roosevelt Park. It was because of a stupid tweet.

"You know we're not that kind of business." My dad has so rarely had to discipline me that it's almost funny, how he's straightening his back at the worn-out cushions of the booth as though his clothes don't fit quite right. "I don't even like that we're on Twitter and Facebook at all."

"How else are people going to know about us?" I ask, for about the umpteenth time.

"The same way they always have, for the past sixty years. This is a community, not some . . . internet clickbait."

I don't understand how my dad can look so deceptively young and hip for a dad—all bearded and skinny with a baseball cap that confuses customers into thinking he's our much older brother—and still be such a bonehead about social media. Honestly, our food is so good it *should* be in ridiculous Hub Seed roundups and viral food videos. I have watched literal tears form in people's eyes when they've bitten into our sandwiches. The way the cheese in our grilled cheeses peels apart with each bite is near ungodly in nature. With just a few well-lit Instagrams, a few well-executed tweets . . .

They could be out of the hole they're in right now, that's for damn sure.

But I can't say that to him outright. My parents think Ethan and I don't know we're not doing so hot right now, only dealing with the finances in the back office when we're out of sight—and I'm sure that has every bit as much to do with my dad's pride as it does with protecting us from it. Trying to push my agenda here will only make things worse.

"And besides," my dad says, "that tweet was crossing a line."

"I didn't think freaking Marigold was gonna retweet it."

"Even if she hadn't, it was over the line. I don't want to be provoking other businesses, especially not—" He cuts himself off, shaking his head. "And now it's gone 'viral,'" he says, using actual air quotes, "so we can't even delete it. Especially since they responded."

"They *what*?"

I lunge for my phone, my dad already warning me against the impulse to send something back. But why the hell shouldn't we? A silly *Mean Girls* quote in response to them literally stealing from our business?

"This is the Twitter equivalent of spitting in Grandma Belly's face. You're gonna just take this lying down?"

He presses his face into his hand. "Everything doesn't have to be so *dramatic*."

In all honesty, I'm a little bit stunned. I may be way more of a hothead than he is, but nobody is a fiercer defender of Grandma Belly than my dad. I open my mouth to remind him as much, but he beats me to the punch.

"No more tweeting. The account is off-limits."

"But Dad—"

"But nothing." He gets up abruptly and claps a hand on my shoulder. "You're gonna be running this place someday, Jack. I have to know you're gonna be able to do that with its best interests in mind."

My face burns. His back is turned to me, so he misses the wince I don't manage to swallow down in time—the one that has only gotten more pronounced over the years as his implications that I'm the twin who will stay behind and take charge of the deli have slowly but certainly become less implied and spoken more like facts.

"Anyway, you're on register in the evenings for the rest of the week."

"Seriously?"

It's actually a lot better than I was expecting. It's the fact that my dad can flip from telling me he expects me to run this place and then treating it like a punishment in the next heartbeat that really gets me. To me, it's yet another spoken confirmation of an unspoken thing—that Ethan's the twin destined for greatness, and I'm the one who will stick around and deal with whatever he leaves in his wake.

"Consider yourself lucky. The next time an eighties pop icon retweets you, I'll make it a month."

"They ripped us off," I argue. I know it's not helping or hurting my case, but I don't even care about that anymore. The punishment's been doled out. The anger is still there.

My dad lets out a sigh, then rattles the shoulder he has his hand on and squeezes. He's making one of those *fatherhood is testing me* faces he makes when one of us says something he's not sure how to answer, like asking about the Easter Bunny, or why the college undergrads smell weird when they come in the deli after 4 p.m. on a Wednesday. (Pot, to be clear. It was 800 percent pot.)

"I know, kid. But we've still got something they don't."

"A 'secret ingredient'?" I mutter.

"That. And our family."

I wrinkle my nose.

"Sorry. Had to go full Nick Junior to snap you out of it. Go help your mom."

Which is how I find myself here, tied to the register, taking the orders of the old ladies who have book club every Monday night, half of a little league soccer team, and a group of giggling middle schoolers who paid in quarters. Living the dream.

Okay, okay—the cliché burden of my dad's expectations aside, it's not so bad. I genuinely enjoy being up front. My popularity in high school doesn't extend more than a few inches beyond the dive team, which I've never minded much—probably because here, people know me. If every block in New York had its own block celebrity, I'd probably be ours. Not for any redeeming qualities of mine, but mostly because all the regulars watched me and Ethan grow up, and of the two of us, I am much worse at shutting my trap. I know way too much about the personal lives of the regulars—the frequency of Mrs. Harvel's dog's bowel movements, the messy details of Mr. Carmichael's wedding that led to an even messier divorce, exactly what kind of fruit Annie—who was sixteen when I met her, but is thirty now—is eating so she can "convince her uterus to spit out one of the girl eggs next time."

And they know me too. An engineer who comes in every Tuesday and Friday for his tuna sandwich melt will always help if I'm stuck on something in a math class. The book club ladies are always sneaking me homemade peanut butter cookies, even though I'm surrounded by a sea of miscellaneous baked goods. Annie's been giving me unsolicited dating advice since before my voice started cracking.

So it adds yet another layer of confusion when my dad rolls this out as a "punishment," like he hasn't been pulling me or Ethan downstairs to run the register every other day since we were small. It's not like we're short-staffed or anything—my dad's just always been into the idea of this being a family business, so participation has been less than optional. As early as six, we were yelling orders to the cooks in the back and wiping down tables, mostly because the regulars found it charming and it kept us occupied in the summers. Now, my parents have us doing everything from register to inventory to sandwich assembly.

Well, by "us" I mostly mean me. I'm the one tapped for random shifts when there's a need. And I get it—Ethan's busy with all the student council nonsense and extracurriculars and generally being the prince of our high school. But I resent the assumption that just because I don't have debate club practices or someone to make out with on the steps of the Met, his time is somehow worth more than mine.

In my parents' defense, I guess I haven't told them about moonlighting as a crappy app developer. And in my defense, there's no way in *hell* I'm going to tell them about it now that Rucker is on a witch hunt and Dad is more determined to live in the 1960s than ever.

"Something on your mind?" my mom asks, when there isn't anyone in line at the register.

I lean against the counter and sigh. "Just the infinite, suffocating void of trying to navigate the world without my phone in my pocket."

My mom rolls her eyes and swats me with the towel she was using to rub down tables—which, gross.

"Who have you been texting so much?" she asks, reminding me that just about nothing gets past her eagle eyes. "Oh, let me guess. You're talking on that Woozel app."

"Weazel."

"Ah, yes, *Weazel*."

If Mom's favorite thing is mocking Rucker's emails to the parents, then her second favorite thing is pretending to be hip and cool. Something she can do a lot easier than most parents, because our mom actually *is* cool. She can somehow walk into a PTA meeting full of Upper East Side moms decked out in pearls and giant sunglasses in nothing but her jeans and a Girl Cheesing T-shirt and intimidate the whole room with a look. It's like cool just oozes out of her skin.

Luckily, the coolness is genetic. Unluckily, Ethan stole it all in utero and left me out to dry.

"Should I be very alarmed? Are you kids using it to plot a school takeover and replace Rucker with someone who wears pants from this century?"

"Now *there's* an idea."

She presses her lips into a smirk. "You're welcome."

Sometimes my mom is so antiestablishment that I'm confused about why she insists on us having a private school education in the first place. But I guess it's more for my grandparents' sake than ours—the ones on her side, not Grandma Belly's. They never quite approved of her marrying my dad and co-running a deli, when, as far as I can tell, they had very much primed her to be some hedge fund manager's trophy wife. I think putting me and Ethan through Stone Hall was a way of saying she hadn't completely abandoned her roots, the same way my dad's always been tied to his.

The same way I'm going to be tied to them, I guess.

"As long as you kids are being safe . . ."

I snort. "Really, Mom, it's like—dumber than Snapchat. Just people posting pictures of graffiti in the bathroom and making fun of Rucker."

"So you *are* on it."

I roll my eyes. "Everyone is."

She gives me a look she rarely has to give, as if she's lifted some part of me like the hood of a car and is inspecting it for leaks. A stupid part of me wants to tell her right then. *I made this*, I want to say. *I made it without any help, and it's making people happy.* I want to tell her about Mel and Gina making out in the hallway this morning. I want to tell her how someone was having a total meltdown about chem lab in the Hallway Chat the other day, and at least twenty other students sent encouraging messages to calm them down. I want to tell her that in my own weird way, I made something that's doing *good* in the world, something that feels as if it matters.

It's the look. It's always that damn look. And I start caving and saying all kinds of stuff I shouldn't.

"But yeah, I've been texting a girl from school."

It's out of my mouth before I can think the better of it. As much as I try not to wreck this thing with Bluebird by overthinking it, I keep underestimating just how much space she takes in my brain until moments like this—when I'm staring too intently at a classmate on her phone in the hall, or staying awake until some absurd hour trying to come up with an equally witty response to something she's typed, or apparently about to blurt her entire existence to my mom.

"Aha! Ethan said he spotted you out with a girl." She sees the indignant look on my face and raises her arms up. "Your dad was looking for you, and you weren't picking up, so he called Ethan."

"I'm surprised he came up for air long enough to breathe, let alone pick up his phone," I mutter. Leave it to Ethan to gossip about me to Mom without saying anything about it to me first. "And it was his fault I was with her in the first place. We were talking about swim and dive stuff."

"So you're not dating her?"

"No!"

Mom raises her eyebrows. Okay, that sounded defensive even in my own ears.

"I mean, no. Pepper's, like—not the kind of girl who's into

dating. More the kind of girl who's into wrecking the grading curve in AP Gov."

I'm about to make another quip about her, but for the first time it seems a little unfair. I didn't hate hanging out with her today. I mostly just offered to go rib Ethan as a joke, to get her to lighten up—I didn't think she'd actually want to walk around after the politics of swim and dive were all taken care of. Or that she wouldn't be immediately against the idea of working together. It knocked me so off guard that I actually agreed to take on captaining duties for the rest of the season.

Whoops.

"See? You kids don't even need your newfangled app to make friends."

And then the moment is gone—that weird urge to spill the beans to my mom and tell her about Weazel, about the mysterious Bluebird, about what I've *really* been doing when there's a light under my door past midnight.

The truth is, it feels too much like letting her down. Both of my parents. Like they're counting on me to be the kid who keeps this place afloat, the kid who stays. I'm almost relieved my mom took my phone away before I had to come up with some kind of answer for Bluebird—the issue isn't so much what I want to be, but whether or not I can be it without hurting everyone else in the process.

Pepper

When my alarm clock goes off the next morning, it almost feels like a joke. So does the fact that I may be the first person in human history to have a Twitter hangover.

Just as I predicted, the moment I walked in the door, my mom thrust her laptop in my face and asked for help answering more #GrilledByBLB selfies, undeterred by the backlash we'd gotten for our response to that deli that only seemed to be ramping up by the second. Sitting there and getting all the notifications from people tweeting at the corporate account was the internet equivalent of sitting in a dunce chair and having rotten tomatoes chucked at us all night.

I barely even got a chance to text Wolf back, and my AP Calc assignment looks like a drunk person scribbled on graphing paper. I didn't even get to my college apps. Let that be my mom's big punishment for dragging me into this—as determined as she's been to help me blend in here, nothing will look quite as bad as me not getting into a single top-twenty college because she had me tweeting GIFs at strangers all day.

For a moment, I just lie on my pillows and wonder what would happen. We've never really talked about it—me getting good grades to get into a good school has always been the expectation. I guess it started around the time she and Paige really started going at it. Mom was so stressed about Paige's antics, the arguments and the way she refused to make friends with anyone here and was always wandering around the city, pulling the *I'm 18 now* card like a party trick. But Mom was happy, at least, when I came home with good grades. When teachers were telling her what a delight I was to have in class. When I made varsity swim team.

And when Mom was happy, it was harder for Paige to pick fights—when Mom was happy, it was infectious. I forget, sometimes, that the three of us have good memories in this apartment. That Mom was the one who helped us start our baking blog in the first place. That we watched *Gossip Girl* reruns and flipped out whenever we recognized an exterior. That every now and then, there was this glimpse of how it could be, instead of how it was.

But then something else would make Paige snap. Dad's flight to visit us would get canceled for weather, or she'd have a rotten day at her new school. Then she'd do something to get under Mom's skin, and Mom would push back, and the apartment would go from Hello Kitty to hell on earth in the time it took for me to take out the recycling and come back.

The thing that still doesn't make sense to me is why Paige even came here in the first place. She could have just stayed in Nashville with Dad, finished senior year with her friends, and avoided this whole mess altogether.

If you can even call it a mess anymore. It's been so long since Paige started cold-shouldering Mom that it's more normal than not.

The snooze alarm goes off, ending my pity party. I blearily pull out my phone and see Wolf never got back to me last night. It feels, for an irrational moment, like he knows what I did. Like this is the universe's way of punishing me for aiding and abetting pettiness on social media. Or maybe he's just bored of talking to me.

Or worse—maybe I said something specific enough that he knows it's me, and he's already disappointed.

I'm being paranoid, and even I know it. He's probably busy. Doing stuff like AP Calc homework that *doesn't* look like it was written while hanging upside down from a ceiling fan. Or whatever it is teenagers do when their parents aren't dragging them into Twitter wars.

At least the stupid hashtag is over. Or at the very least it *should* be.

After I finish brushing my teeth, my mom unceremoniously opens the door to the bathroom and shoves her phone screen into my eyeline.

It's a picture of the new Grandma's Special grilled cheese in a BLB wrapper, sitting in a puddle on the sidewalk. tell me i'm pretty #GrilledByBLB, the caption reads. It was sent from that deli—Girl Cheesing—just a few minutes before.

"Got a sec?"

Mom's already decked out in her outfit for the day, a sleek black dress with black tights, and a navy jeweled statement necklace to match her navy boots. Her hair is already blown out, her makeup perfectly applied. Standing next to her in the mirror makes me look like I've stumbled out of a crypt.

"Can't Taffy handle it?"

"Taffy won't be in until nine, and she wasn't built for these kinds of tweets anyway. Not like you are."

I hand her phone back to her, spitting my toothpaste into the sink. "Mom. The recipes are really, really similar."

"It's *grilled cheese*. Don't be silly."

But it isn't silly, really. The recipe alone might have been a coincidence—sourdough bread with muenster, cheddar, apple jam, and honey mustard—but BLB branded it with the exact name as theirs. It's enough to make any copyright lawyer do a double-take, if we're unfortunate enough that this deli really does have some kind of legal position to come at us.

"Who even had this idea in the first place? I feel like you should talk to whoever it was."

She bites the inside of her cheek. "You're right. And I will. But first, let's come up with a response to this tweet."

I shake my head. "The hashtag is over. It was just for the day. It'll be weird if we keep going now."

"It'll take you like two minutes."

Two minutes to draft it, sure, but then an hour of compulsively checking it to see how it's being received, and a day of feeling weirdly guilty about it, and by then, she'll probably ask me to write more tweets that will "take two minutes" and the whole thing will start all over again. A point I have every intention of making to her, except she beats me to the punch.

"And if you see Landon today, could you ask him about dinner? His father and I are scheduling a sit-down here for when he gets back from Japan in a few weeks, and I'd love for him to join us."

My mouth practically unhinges. "Landon can't come here." Not *here*, with my bright pink Pepto-Bismol bedroom and the watercolors of Big League Burger menu items my mom commissioned and hung on the wall. Not *here*, where I'd have even more space and time to make an ass of myself in front of Landon than I already do.

"It'll be good for you. You'll get a front seat to business negotiations." She raises her eyebrows at me conspiratorially.

"With the kind of jobs you'll be fielding after college, you'll need it."

Before I can protest, her heels are *clack-clack-clacking* down the hall, her keys are jingling, and she's out the front door.

I don't tweet right away. The miniature rebellion doesn't count for much, but it's just enough to rub me the wrong way. I take my time getting ready before I send it, so much time that I'm too late to make myself toast and end up digging through the fridge to find my leftover Monster Cake to eat on the way to school.

I notice a bit of it is missing and smile despite myself. Some things, at least, never change.

Pepper

I hit Park Avenue, nodding at the doorman on the way out, and pull the corporate account back up on my phone. It will honestly look stupid for us to respond to this barb. We're already in hot water for the way we responded to the last one. But it's either tweet now or get a bunch of semi-terrified texts from Taffy later.

Big League Burger @B1gLeagueBurger
Replying to @GCheesing
OMG! Finally! The public knows the ~secret ingredient~ grandma adds to your grilled cheese. Thanks for the pro tip guys but we'll pass for now
7:03 AM · 21 Oct 2020

I'm still half asleep by the time I get to homeroom, but not half asleep enough I don't notice Jack and Ethan muttering to each other in heated voices in a corner of the room. I sit at my usual desk, trying to ignore it, but the room is empty enough it's hard not to hear them.

". . . going to *kill* me. He thinks *I* sent that stupid picture."

"So what? I'll tell him it was me. I don't care. It's not that big of a deal."

"He's already texted me like seven times. He told us to drop it—"

"You should have seen the shit people were saying—"

"I did. I *did* see it. And then I logged off."

I pull up the Weazel app, wondering if it's something from the Hallway Chat. But the only recent message in there of note is someone roasting the grammatical correctness of the graffiti someone recently scrawled in one of the stalls of the girls' bathrooms. No pictures that look like they'd set the Campbell twins at each other's throats, which is a weird enough occurrence in and of itself—I've never once seen them fight.

"Just forget it," Jack mutters. And then he's sitting himself right down in the seat next to mine, the same way we were yesterday.

I don't know if I'm supposed to say anything or not. There's no way to pretend I didn't hear their conversation because the three of us are practically the only people in the room. That is, until Ethan says something under his breath to excuse himself and then ducks out.

It's quiet for a moment, then, but knowing Jack, it won't be for long.

"Do you have any siblings?" Jack asks.

He looks antsier than usual, slouching in his seat, his knuckles quietly drumming on the desk.

"Yeah. An older sister."

Jack nods. Opens his mouth as though he's going to say something else, and then thinks better of it.

I pull out my Monster Cake, a little squished in its aluminum foil, and break off a piece to offer Jack. His eyebrows lift, and he looks at me in confusion, like I'm trying to hand him a fish.

"It's not poisonous."

He takes it from me, examining it. A few crumbs end up on his desk. "What is it?"

I hesitate for a moment. I don't think I've actually discussed this unholy mash-up of desserts with anyone aside from my parents and Paige. I wonder if it's some kind of betrayal, sharing it with someone outside of the family.

"Monster Cake."

"*Monster* Cake?"

His lips quirk in amusement, and then I see it again—another shift, another reconsideration. I decide I don't mind it this time.

"It's pretty much a mash-up of every junk food known to man, baked into a cake. Hence the name."

Jack takes a bite. "Holy *shit*."

My face heats up. People are starting to walk into the room just as Jack literally tips back in his seat and moans.

"Jack," I hiss.

"This is the best thing I've ever tasted."

I can't tell if he's making fun of me or not, but either way, he is decidedly making a scene. I wrap up the rest of the cake and shove it into my backpack.

"I mean, this is *obscene*. How did you come up with this?"

"It's just—I mean, it's not like I . . . We were little kids when we made it."

Jack literally kisses his fingers. I stare into my lap, my face burning, a reluctant smile blooming. I haven't had a ton of time to update our blog lately—Paige has been posting on overdrive to make up for it—so I've forgotten how it feels, having someone try some weird dessert I made up and enjoy it. Usually it's just people commenting from some corner of the internet, saying they tried it, or Paige groaning her approval when we meet up and bake together.

But this is different. This is so . . . personal, almost. Having someone outside of the family try something I made right in front of me. Maybe I don't hate it.

"I feel like you may have flown too close to the dessert sun. I've never tasted anything like this, and my parents literally own a—"

"Mr. Campbell, if you insist on eating in my classroom, at least have the decency not to turn my floor into your personal napkin."

I manage to muffle my laugh by turning it into a cough. Just as Mrs. Fairchild turns her attention back to the board, Jack catches my eye and winks.

I roll my eyes, and then his friend Paul comes in, buzzing about something that happened on the Weazel app. He's lucky Mrs. Fairchild is either hard of hearing or very committed to pretending she is, or he'd be screwed right now, considering the no-tolerance policy on the app. That aside, there are narcs all over this place—enough of them that I'm never actually stupid enough to pull Weazel up on my phone at school.

Okay. Maybe sometimes. But I try not to, because whoever Wolf is, he responds so fast during school hours, I'm legitimately worried I'm going to get him in trouble.

And despite Jack's suspicion that I was ratting people out to Rucker the other day, that's pretty much my worst nightmare. If Wolf got in trouble and was kicked off the app, I don't know what I'd do. It's almost scary, how fast I went from not having him in my life to feeling like, Paige aside, he may be the best friend I've got. We're just on the same wavelength on everything. Life at Stone Hall, but more importantly, feeling like the odd one out here.

The likeliest scenario is that Wolf is someone who has a study hall, or a gap in his schedule. Someone like Ethan, who's constantly in and out for student government stuff. Or someone with one of the senior internships where they get to leave school for two hours a day, like—

Huh. Someone like Landon.

By the time homeroom lets out, my stomach is gurgling from lack of breakfast. I pull out the Monster Cake as covertly as I can, planning to shove some in my mouth when I open my locker, but I discover as soon as I unlock it that I have acquired a stray. Somehow Jack has managed to follow me across the length of the entire hallway, his friend Paul in tow.

"Just one more bite?"

I grin into my locker door, so he can't see. "You sound like a junkie."

"I might be one now, and it's kind of your fault. So you have a responsibility to keep supplying. Or I'll go into withdrawal."

"What are you even talking about?" Paul asks, standing on the tips of his toes to look into my locker, even though we're the exact same height.

I rip off another piece for Jack, and then, in a moment of Monster Cake benevolence, hand some to Paul too. I might as well stay on good terms with as many members of the dive team as I can, now that we're apparently sharing lanes.

"Oh my god. You're my new favorite person."

Jack ribs him. "How easily your loyalties shift."

Paul salutes us both. "Gotta head to my internship."

I pause mid-chew. So maybe Landon's not the *only* person I know who ducks out of school regularly.

I try to imagine it. Paul awake late at night by the dim light of his phone, texting me terrible puns about *Great Expectations*, making fun of our chain-smoking PE teacher for her aggressively hypocritical lectures on the dangers of cigarettes. Telling me about his family, listening to my woes about mine.

"Still on for grabbing some grub after practice?"

It doesn't feel quite right, but that's the problem—I can't really imagine anyone being Wolf. Like there's some kind of mental block, every time I try to give him a face. Sometimes he feels more like some bodiless entity than a person.

And sometimes—like yesterday, when he was upset about that thing with his parents—he's so real it's like we're huddled in a corner together somewhere, so close I could reach out and touch.

I blink up at Jack, mentally replaying the last few seconds of whatever he was saying to me. "Huh? Oh. Yeah, I'm good for after practice."

"Ethan said your coach sent you a meet calendar, if you want to forward it to me."

"Oh, yeah." I check to make sure the hallway is clear, then pull the attachment up on my phone and hand it to him. "You can airdrop it to yourself."

Jack fumbles for a moment, trying to hold both our phones at the same time. "Your screen just went black."

My hands are too occupied trying to wrap up the leftover Monster Cake. "The password's just 1234." My dad set up our phone codes for us when we all upgraded last month, and the only reason I tell Jack is because I have every intention of changing it when I have time.

Jack lets out a low whistle. "You realize that's like the phone equivalent of leaving your keys under your mat."

He hands me back my phone, and then the warning bell rings and Jack salutes me, heading off with a Monster Cake–induced skip in his step, and I can't help the slight skip in my own.

Pepper

I spend the next few hours attempting and ultimately failing to ignore the texts coming in from my mom and Taffy. Once the final bell rings, I take a few minutes outside of the locker room to attempt to string together a timeline of Twitter events. It turns out Girl Cheesing's account—which now has a whopping eleven thousand followers compared to yesterday's three digits—responded to my tweet from this morning pretty fast.

Girl Cheesing @GCheesing
Replying to @B1gLeagueBurger
still tastes better than unoriginality though amirite
7:17 AM · 21 Oct 2020

And maybe that would have been the end of it—nobody asked me to respond to that during school. Odds are my mom might have just let Taffy ignore it, and we all could have moved on with our lives and maybe settled this in small claims court instead of on Twitter, the way I just kind of assumed adults did.

Enter Jasmine Yang, famous YouTuber and host of the popular vlog "Twitter Gets Petty." In a three-minute video posted about an hour before school let out, she detailed the few tweets involved in our "feud," essentially narrating the nightmare of the last twenty-four hours of my life.

"I think it's safe to say these two accounts are pretty *cheesed* with each other. So who's it gonna be, Petty People?" she says at the end of the video, addressing her followers with a cheeky grin. "Team Girl Cheesing or Team Big League? Let me know in the comments, y'all. I know who's getting *my* vote."

The video shows a screenshot, then, of her responding to a Big League Burger tweet with the word COPYCAT all in caps, alongside a flood of cat emojis.

And somehow, in the hour between her posting the video and me getting out of school, the idea has taken off so aggressively that *hundreds* of Twitter users are doing the same. Every tweet, every Instagram post, every Facebook announcement that BLB has made in the last few months is just a *sea* of people commenting with the cat emoji.

It would be funny, if I were literally anyone else on the planet. But I just happen to be the person who is going to be chained to a phone until I find some way to fix it.

My brain is practically churning by the time practice is over. I'm so preoccupied with what on earth our next tactical move can be I don't even notice Vice Principal Rucker standing in the lobby of the gym where we hold practices until I hear his unmistakable nasally voice saying, "Excuse me, Miss Singh, but what exactly am I seeing on your phone screen?"

Pooja's back is turned to Rucker, but I have a direct view of her face—or, more appropriately, the look of sheer terror that has replaced her face. I know it can only mean one thing.

"Um—it's, uh—"

"No, no, pull it back up. I'd love to see."

"Is that the phone Coach Thompkins found on the pool deck?"

Pooja is holding her breath, staring at me with traffic-light eyes. It takes her a second to catch on, but then she nods.

"We're trying to figure out whose it is," I explain to Rucker. I turn back to Pooja. "Any luck?"

Pooja hands her phone to me, her face collected but her hands shaking. "Not yet."

Rucker eyes the phone in my hands. I try not to move it too much, knowing if the screen lights up that Pooja has a picture of herself posing with a cut-out of Ruth Bader Ginsburg that will give her up in an instant.

"It looked like it was logged into that Weasel application," says Rucker.

"Yeah," I say quickly, "that's how we know it's someone from Stone Hall."

Pooja nods. "And we'll, uh, definitely tell you whose it is when we figure it out."

I can feel his eyes on me, and then on Pooja, trying to decide whether or not he trusts us. But his eyes are nothing compared to Pooja's, who is staring at me like she's still waiting for me to throw her under the bus. Neither of us really plays dirty—at least not since freshman year—but we haven't exactly played nice either.

But as much of a thorn Pooja has been in my side over the years, the last thing I want to do to shift the playing field is let her go down for something as dumb as chatting with people on an app I could just as easily have been caught using, if I'd walked out five seconds before she did. If I beat her at anything, I want the satisfaction of knowing it was fair and square.

"Thank you, girls, for being vigilant about this. If you hear anything else . . ."

I hold back the urge to swallow in relief. "You'll be the first to know," I lie through my teeth.

Rucker nods, and then he's off, not so subtly trying to infiltrate a group of dive team freshmen who see him coming from a mile off. I turn back to Pooja, whose face looks like there isn't any blood in it.

"Thanks," she breathes.

I shift my backpack on my shoulder. "No problem."

"Seriously . . . you just saved my ass. And like, a dozen other asses. I'm in the middle of setting up the study group times for the history midterm."

"Don't worry about—wait. You're Bunny?"

Pooja nods, almost cautious about it. Then, when I don't end the conversation the way one of us usually does, she relaxes marginally and says, "I mean, not my first choice, but at least I'm not whoever got saddled with Donkey."

Usually I make a point to keep my expression as cool as possible in front of Pooja, but I can't help but stare at her in disbelief. "You're the one who's been setting up all the AP study groups."

Pooja shrugs. "Well, yeah. The app makes it super easy. And this year's got us all whipped."

For a moment neither of us says anything, me just staring at her, and Pooja shifting her weight between her feet, like she can't decide to wait me out or leave.

Because here's the thing with Pooja—maybe, for a hot second, we could have been friends. We were grouped together in World History freshman year, when our teacher divvied us up for a graded in-class quiz bowl. It was late September, so just when I was starting to get into the groove of how to make myself fit in, and when I was more committed to making a good impression and the grades to match than ever—the fighting with Mom and Paige had only been escalating, and it felt like succeeding at Stone Hall was the only power I had to stop it.

At that point I still hadn't really made any friends, but I'd scouted out some potentials. Mel, who seemed to bake a lot, based on some light Instagram stalking, and Pooja, who I'd overheard in the halls talking about trying to make the 100-yard butterfly her event. When we got put into the same group, I was hoping to talk to her about the school's swim team before the season started. I was working up the nerve—it was still new to me, the idea of having to make friends instead of having built-in ones—when immediately I wasn't nervous at all. Pooja was nice, and funny as hell. She kept writing notes in the margins of her notebook to show the rest of our quiz group, some crack about how the code of Hammurabi would apply to Snapchat, or adding "freshmen at Stone Hall" under the bottom rung of a social hierarchy of Mesopotamia.

I was laughing at one of her jokes when Mr. Clearburn called on me. "Miss Evans, if you're not too busy goofing around, maybe you could bother to tell us the modern-day country where most of Ancient Mesopotamia was located?"

Even if I did know the answer, I was so mortified in that moment, I couldn't have told him my first name. I sat there with my mouth open until Pooja whispered, "Syria."

"Syria," I blurted.

"Wrong, and I'm deducting a point from your team for disruptiveness. Miss Singh?"

Pooja gave her answer to the desk. "Iraq?"

"Correct."

The sting of not just looking bad but letting down the other three people on our quiz team was so searing, it felt like I'd been pushed into the fryer at Big League Burger. I glanced over at Pooja, but she wouldn't even look at me. It was a hard lesson, but a lesson learned: everyone at Stone Hall is out for themselves.

The rivalry just kind of grew organically from there. I never forgot what she did, and I certainly didn't forgive. Every time we've come head-to-head since, in class or in swim team or any other school-related thing in between, I've held the embarrassment of that with me like a constant throbbing reminder that this isn't Nashville. That this is a whole new species of human, and its food chain goes so perilously high that there's always someone at your feet waiting to pull you down.

But this—this doesn't add up. Pooja being Bunny, the user on Weazel who's been reserving library times and hosting coffee shop meetups for all the toughest AP classes. Because if Pooja is Bunny, that means she's been pulling people up that food chain right along with her.

Finally I shake my head. "I guess I thought . . ."

The sentence hangs there uncomfortably, because we both know what I thought. Pooja shifts her backpack on her shoulders, looking at her shoes before looking back up at me.

"You should come, you know." The words are hesitant, like she means them but isn't sure how I'll take them. "I mean—not that you need it. But I'm sure it would help some of the others."

I'm so stunned by the offer that I forget I'm supposed to answer.

"Anyway, my brother's waiting for me out front, so . . ." She waves awkwardly. "Thanks again."

"Yeah."

And then she's off—Pooja, Bunny, or whoever she really is—leaving me torn with a new kind of uncertainty in her wake.

Pepper

Once Pooja clears the lobby, my phone pings in my pocket, pulling me out of my confusion and right back into the Twitter maelstrom. I pull out my phone, already bracing myself for the notifications, swiping through them one by one—

And realize there aren't any from Wolf. That there weren't any yesterday around this time either. That for the first time in our correspondence, neither of us has said anything between the hours of three and five, which is our usual peak time for bitching about whatever assignments we got earlier in the day.

Okay. I'm not stupid enough to think that Landon is Wolf just because he happens to not be texting on Weazel during the same times as swim and dive practice. By that merit, any member of the swim team, the dive team, the basketball team, the golf team, or the indoor track and soccer teams could be him too. If anything, this has only widened the ridiculously large pool of people he could be.

But it's just one more thing in a list of already uncanny things that makes me think that maybe, just maybe, it is him after all.

That fourteen-year-old Pepper's crush was fast, but maybe not baseless. That maybe there really was something then, the way there certainly seems to be something with Wolf now.

Another ping comes in, this time from Taffy. U out of practice yet?

I sigh, shaking myself out of my head, and start walking to the bakery where Jack proposed we meet, while attempting to diffuse the Twitter situation on the way. I call Taffy first, an idea forming in my head as I walk down the street, the thousands of cat emojis still swimming in my vision.

"Is anyone from the design team in today?"

Taffy's voice is approximately an octave higher than usual. "Yeah, Carmen's here."

"Okay. Get her to find, like, a stock photo of a cat."

"Any cat?"

"A cute one, I guess. Yeah, any cat."

My life gets more ridiculous by the second.

I wait for the light to change at Eighty-Ninth Street as she writes it down on one of the unicorn-shaped Post-it pads she keeps at her desk. We're so in sync by now, I can sense the exact moment she lifts the pencil from the paper through the phone.

"Then do one of those, like, really corny photoshop jobs so it's holding a Big League Burger grilled cheese. Like so bad that it's funny."

"Got it, got it . . ."

"Then have her do an animation of sunglasses dropping down on it."

"I know that one!" says Taffy excitedly, as if she was not hired for the exact purpose of knowing about memes on the internet.

"Okay, those sunglasses. But no text," I instruct her, feeling like a schoolteacher. "Just the sunglasses dropping down."

There's murmuring on the other end. "She'll have it ready

in a half hour." The murmuring becomes decidedly more distinct, then, and I hear what can only be my mom cutting in, the low, authoritative tone of her voice unmistakable. ". . . She'll have it ready in less than five," Taffy amends.

I'm outside of the bakery, then, and see Jack has already found a table and is quite literally taking a baguette to the face. He looks like the picture of contentment, his hair still damp from the pool and curling at the edges, ripping off the end of the baguette with his teeth in that unselfconscious hungry teenage boy way. I stop for a moment just to watch him, feeling strangely charmed by the whole thing.

He spots me the moment the door opens, waving so I know where he is. I hold up a finger and stand in line to get a cup of tea. At the last moment I peer down at the counter and ask for one of the massive apple pastries, the ones I've passed in this window countless times but always have been too busy to stop and get by myself.

My phone hums in my hand. The GIF of the cat is in, just the way I asked for it. I save it to my drive and pull up the corporate Twitter, hating myself for it but also wanting to get it over with as soon as I possibly can.

"Trade you some baguette for some of whatever that is," Jack offers.

"Deal." I drop off my backpack and my swim bag at the table. "Just one sec."

I wince when I see there are over a hundred notifications piled up on BLB's Twitter, knowing every single one of them is cat-related or worse. I pull up a tweet draft, taking a sip of my tea, as if I can burn the wrongness of it down my throat.

Yuck. I forgot to put sugar in it. I glance around to look for the coffee counter, getting up from my chair and bumping into someone who was coming at me from the left. My tea sloshes onto my shirt, and I back into the table, dropping my phone on it.

"Sorry, sorry—"

"Pepper?"

I blink up into the ice blue of Landon's eyes, so close I can see the distinctive little freckle just above one of them that I memorized my freshman year like his face was some kind of constellation. He cracks a smile just as I swallow down a grimace.

"Sorry," I mutter again, ducking my head down. There's a bread bowl full of mac and cheese on a tray in his hands, the cheese still bubbling. The views are both so overwhelming that I'm not sure which to settle on, the cheese or his face.

"Hey, Ethan—"

"Jack," the two of us correct him at the same time. Jack turns his attention back to his baguette, but not before I see the sliver of a smile on his face.

When I look back at Landon, he is still momentarily disarmed, blinking before the easy smile is back on his face again. "Well, then. My bad. Fancy running into you guys here."

My throat feels dry. I am staring at Landon's uncannily symmetrical face and thinking, of all things, of my mother.

"Yeah," I half croak. "Was just . . . sorry. I was going to put sugar in my tea, and . . ." *Am now narrating every pedantic detail of my life to you for no reason.*

I beeline for the coffee counter, painfully aware that Landon is falling into step next to me. This is it, then—the universe giving me the opportunity I completely missed during practice today. As if it practically is shining a neon light on my mom's ridiculous request.

I steel my entire body like a truck is coming at me. It's a letdown, almost, that I have spent the last four years at Stone Hall trying to be worthy of the Landons of the world—the people who just fit here, the way I used to just fit back in Nashville—but even after all this time, I can't look at him without feeling like the clueless little freshman I was when we first met.

Eventually I force the words out of my mouth.

"So—are you . . . um, my mom says your dad is coming to dinner at our place?"

Landon takes a step ahead of me and grabs me a sugar packet from one of the little containers on the counter. It's the wrong kind, one of the fake ones without any calories in it that make your tongue shrivel, but I'm too busy focusing on not tripping again to care.

"Oh, wow, yeah. My dad mentioned something. Didn't realize it was your place."

I nod, way too vigorously than the situation merits. "Yep, um, yeah. My place." This is social suicide, but somehow still not as bad as letting down my mom. "You should come."

There's a half second where he's still trying to catch up to what I said that I think I may die right there in the middle of the bakery, just lie down on the tiles and let the elements take me.

"Yeah?"

"Yeah."

Landon nods. "Yeah, yeah, I'm—that sounds cool. I've got some deadlines for my internship, but I'm pretty sure I'll be out of the weeds soon."

I better win some kind of Daughter of the Year award for this. "Maybe I'll see you then."

Jack

The really stupid part about the whole thing is, right before it all blows up in my face, I decide I like Pepper. Well, not decide, really—it just kind of sneaks up on me. One second I'm tearing through a baguette, relieved my mom is nowhere within a three-mile radius (consuming bread from other establishments is treason in the Campbell family), and the next I'm looking up, seeing this wry look on Pepper's face as she's standing in line for her tea—the kind of look you give someone you don't just tolerate, but maybe care about. The difference between exasperation and mild amusement, that line of *what on earth is that guy doing* and *what on earth is my friend doing.*

And yeah, maybe it was kind of happening before that. Ethan asked me to meet up with Pepper the first time, but I kind of hijacked it after that. Ethan doesn't even know Pepper and I are meeting to go over swim and dive stuff—not that he'd mind, since the organization of the dive team can roughly be described as "extremely hot mess" and his captainship was more of a formality than anything. He'll still slap it on his resume and call it a day.

He has kind of a bad habit of doing that—overcommitting and pushing stuff onto me. Saying he'll bring day-old stuff from the deli for a fundraising thing at school, and then asking me to do it when his schedule gets too thin. Promising Mom he'll pick up Grandma Belly's prescription, then calling me in a panic when he realizes his student council meeting is running too long for the pharmacy's hours. I know he doesn't mean to do it, but he has a tendency to bite off more than he can chew—and then remember, thanks to me, he has a second mouth.

Funny, though, that as strapped for time as Ethan is, he sure found some to tweet from the Girl Cheesing account this morning and do the one thing our dad told us not to do.

But for once, I really don't mind picking up Ethan's slack. I like spending time with Pepper, with her Monster Cake and the unexpected blunt funniness of her and the way she's always trying to tuck her bangs behind her ear even though they're too short. I like her enough that I don't even hesitate to ask if she wants to swap bites of baked goods. I like her enough that, for the first time in months, I'm not glancing at the phone my mom liberated after last night's shift, waiting to see if Bluebird has responded to my last message.

I like her enough that the minute she bumps into Landon, something unfamiliar and hot coils in my stomach, something that makes me irritated with Landon even though he's done literally nothing to wrong me in his life.

Something happens to Pepper too. Her cheeks are all red, and I can tell she's stammering even with her back turned, even from halfway across the café. I squish the piece of pastry she gave me between my fingers, making a gooey apple-y mess.

I pull my eyes away from them, and that's when it happens. That's when everything goes to shit in one fell swoop. Her phone is on the table. I don't even mean to look. I'm a New Yorker; I pride myself in my ability to mind my own damn business. But there's something moving on the screen, some ridiculous-looking cat GIF, and like a raccoon looking at a shiny thing, I can't tear my eyes away from it.

Then, as I'm leaning back, I take in the rest of the screen. I notice the blue checkmark first. The GIF is part of a drafted tweet. For a second I'm even amused—is Pepper verified on Twitter? Was she secretly in some kind of sports league or singing in a country band back in Nashville?

But the account doesn't belong to Pepper. It belongs to Big League Burger.

My brain doesn't quite know how to communicate the information to my body, so I just laugh. I laugh so hard, the woman attempting to eat a scone at the table next to me looks up in alarm, even though she has noise-filtering headphones on. But it's like something laughs out of me, then, something heavy that comes loose in my chest and lodges in my stomach and instantly starts to calcify.

Pepper comes back, all red-cheeked and wide-eyed, practically stumbling into her seat as if she's forgotten what it's there for. When her eyes finally meet mine, she blinks, snapping out of it so fast, I can only imagine I am projecting every inch of the horror I'm feeling on my face.

"What?"

My mouth opens. Closes. Opens again.

"You have a drafted tweet from the Big League Burger account on your phone."

I don't sound angry. Am I angry? It feels like being a little kid again, practicing tricks on the diving board; like all those first few times I tried to jackknife and ended up belly-flopping into the pool. How the sting of it just stuns you for a few beats before the pain hits; the strange whiplash of how water can be so slippery and welcoming in one second and nearly knock the freaking wind out of you in the next.

"Oh." Pepper grabs her phone, and now her cheeks aren't just tinged, but a bright, flaming red that creeps up her neck and into her cheeks. "Sorry, didn't mean to leave my phone here."

Maybe I shouldn't say anything. In fact, I absolutely shouldn't. I feel like every possible appropriate response I could make just shoved its way into a blender, and whatever comes out now is going to come out all wrong.

Pepper fidgets under my stare, reaching for her bangs again. "It's dumb. My mom—well, my parents founded Big League Burger." She says it with her shoulders hunched, with her eyes flitting between me and the table. "They have me send tweets from the account sometimes."

"Like tweets at Girl Cheesing?"

There's that familiar crease between her brows. "You know about that?"

The baguette feels like it's sloshing in my stomach. I manage to nod.

Pepper shrugs. "It's dumb," she mumbles, picking at the lid of her tea. "The whole thing is . . ."

"It's not dumb."

I don't mean for it to come out the way it does. Even I'm surprised by the sound of myself. Her eyes snap up to meet mine, wide and wary.

I stand from my chair, grabbing my backpack, my coffee, the ridiculously large baguette.

"Wait—are you leaving?" There's an edge of panic in her

voice, a kind of insecurity I didn't think someone like Pepper was capable of feeling. "Are you mad or something? They're just some stupid tweets."

I round on her, forgetting how tall I am compared to her until she has to jerk her neck up to meet my eye. I take a step back. "Yeah? Well, that's my family you're sending those stupid tweets to, that's my *grandma* you stole from."

Pepper's lips part, a little "oh" of surprise breathing out of her. I watch, my fingers curling and my nails cutting into my palms, as she follows my words through to their meaning and her entire body goes rigid.

It takes her a moment to speak. I want to storm out, want to be anywhere other than this stupid bakery that seems to get smaller by the second, but I'm rooted to the spot, rooted by the way she's looking at me. She always seems to have a comeback at the ready, some kind of answer prepared. Right now, she just looks lost.

"Your family owns Girl Cheesing?"

"Since 1963. Which is how long Grandma's Special has been on the menu, by the way."

Pepper shakes her head. "I didn't . . . I had no idea you—"

"Can you imagine what it was like for her? Starting up a business with my grandpa when they didn't have a penny to their name? Coming up with all of those recipes herself and working sixteen hours a damn day for over half of her life to serve them?"

Something flickers in Pepper's eyes. It's not remorse. It's more like understanding.

I don't want it. I'm so angry that anything she projects just seems to slide right off me, into a puddle on the floor.

"It's not—my mom just makes me do it. It's not anything personal."

"First of all, your mom didn't *make* you do anything." I glance to my left and see there's a clear path to the door, but I'm not done yet. I pull out my phone and open the Twitter app to the Girl Cheesing account, shoving the tweet with the crack about the secret ingredient from this morning under Pepper's nose. "And that's my grandma's legacy. That's my entire family's livelihood. Don't you dare stand there and tell me it isn't *personal*."

"Jack, wait—"

"Do whatever you want with the stupid fundraising. I'm sure you'll have no problem coming up with ideas because you can always just rip off someone else's."

Jack

I find out approximately two seconds later that it is very difficult to commit to a heated storm out of a bakery with a giant baguette in your hand. I stalk toward the Eighty-Sixth Street subway station anyway, people looking up at me with alarm that instantly shifts into amusement. I slow my roll just long enough to spot a homeless person who could actually use the baguette I'm wielding, and hand it to him—only to look up and see we're standing just outside, of all things, of a freaking Big League Burger.

I catch sight of my reflection in the window, my hair all whipped from the wind, my face contorted. I don't even have the dignity of being able to look angry. Like Ethan and my dad, I've been cursed with angry expressions that only extend as far as "mildly confused puppy." The worst part is, I've seen my own face on Ethan's enough times to know it's ridiculous.

I'm grateful, suddenly, Ethan busted into the account and kept ribbing Big League Burger all day. So grateful I'm willing to skip into the deli and take the blame with a big fat smile on my face. It'll be worth it. Hell, I'll keep on doing it. Just one more thing to tack to the laundry list of things Ethan has started that I've had to finish.

There are at least six texts from Pepper by the time I emerge out of the subway, and another few from my dad and from Ethan that I've also pointedly ignored. I'm turning the corner when my phone starts to buzz in my pocket—my mom's calling. I brace myself. I can ignore 99 percent of the people who have my phone number, but I can't ignore her.

"Where *are* you?"

"Down the street, why?"

The words come out in a rush, as if I've been running. And granted, I have basically been power walking like I'm on fire, but it's more than that—I'm terrified in that moment that the shoe we've been ignoring just dropped. That something happened to Grandma Belly, and not only was I not there, but I was cavorting with the enemy when it happened.

"Get here. *Now.*"

Okay, scratch that. I'm just in a volcanic amount of trouble. And the only thing worse than my dad being upset with me is my mom being upset with me.

I'm about to open my mouth and tattle on Ethan like the total yellowbelly I apparently am, but my mom beats me to the punch.

"The place is *packed*. We have customers out the door and not enough hands in the world to serve them. Wherever you are, Jack, RUN."

For a moment I'm certain it's a prank. And then I round the corner and see it with my own eyes: a sea of people, so far down the block they're waiting past the old bookstore, past the bodega and the locksmith and the hole-in-the-wall sex toy shop that doesn't open until eight o'clock. People of all ages, with backpacks and briefcases and strollers, all of them craning to get a glimpse at the door and how many people are in front of them.

I haven't seen this many people clustered outside of a shop since the damn cronut.

I take off at a sprint, the anger completely stunned out of me. Some people grumble about me cutting the line—"I *work* here," I mutter, which perks a few impatient customers up—and by the time I get up to the counter, I see my mom beaming an almost-manic grin at the register, and we've even opened the second one, which is something I don't think we ever do outside of big events like Pride spilling in more customers, or that summer a Groupon tour ended on our block.

"What *happened*?" I demand, diving for an extra apron. If Ethan and Mom are already up front, that means I'll be joining Dad in the back for prep. Thank god this insanity will spare me from parental wrath for at least as long as it takes to get all these people fed.

"Ethan's tweets!" Mom chirps. Before I even feel my face start to pinch, she adds quickly, "Both of your tweets. After they went viral, I guess . . ."

I blink. "Wait, so—I do one shady tweet and get in trouble, and Ethan tweets a whole bunch of *wildly* rude things and—"

My mom leans forward, grabs my chin, and steps on her tiptoes to kiss me on the cheek. "We'll talk disciplining later. Sandwiches now. Go, go, go."

For the next three hours until closing, I am barely able to come up for air. I can make any of our sandwiches with my eyes closed, and by the time eight o'clock finally rolls around, I practically am. The line only seems to get longer, and the shenanigans more absurd—there are bloggers taking pictures, a man dressed in a shirt with printed grilled cheeses on it who calls himself a "grilled cheese authority," teens much trendier than I am taking side-by-side pictures of our Grandma's Special with Big League Burger's for their Instagram stories.

And more importantly, a *shit ton* of cash going into the register.

At the end of the day, when we finally close the door on the last customer and lock it, we all collapse in the Time-Out Booth, wheezing as though we've just run the New York marathon.

"I can't feel my feet," my mom groans.

I lay my head down on the table. "My entire body is covered in brie and honey mustard."

I can hear the smirk in Ethan's voice even with my arm covering my eyes. "Two girls asked for my number."

"You already have a boyfriend," I remind him, poking one eye out to glare.

"And I told them that."

"But you didn't think to mention you have an *identical twin*?"

"Okay, we need to strategize," says my dad, clapping his hands together. "If the rest of the week is going to be anything like this, we need to have all hands on deck. Hannah, if you want to check on stock, I'll start calling all the day shifters to see if anyone wants overtime. Boys, if you could scrub down and close up shop for the night—"

"Wait. That's it?"

My dad pauses, halfway up from his seat. "What's it?"

My face is volcanically warm. I'm not a narc. I'm *really* not. If I were, Ethan's golden-child status would have been knocked down more than a few notches years ago—he's been sneaking beer out with friends in the park and even smoking the occasional joint since we were fourteen.

But the double standard has never been more unfair than it is right now.

My mom gets it before my dad does because she is all too aware of the quiet way I keep score. She puts a hand on my shoulder and squeezes. "Your father already had a talking-to with Ethan before the huge rush of people. No more tweeting. At least, no more like the ones you sent today."

I have to bite my cheek to stop myself from saying anything else.

"Agreed," says my dad. He hovers at the edge of the table, for some reason fixing a look at me instead of Ethan. After a moment, he sighs. "You have my permission to tweet from the account again. But I need it reined in. Ethan, if you're going to tweet from it, you have to run it past Jack first. Understand?"

I blink up at him, not sure I've heard correctly.

"Run it past *Jack*?" Ethan protests.

"Jack managed to keep it somewhat tone-appropriate. Besides, he's on the Twitter account more than you and spends more time on the floor. I trust his judgment."

Dad claps me on the back as he walks away, and Mom smirks as she gets up to follow him. I can't help but feel a little smug about the whole thing—at least until I look up and see Ethan's face, and the flicker of hurt on it that passes so fast, I almost miss it.

"Okay, then," he says, holding up his hands in surrender. "It's all you, bro."

I lean back in the booth, trying to dial down my satisfaction.

"We'll do it together," I offer.

Ethan shakes his head. "You heard Dad. You're the one they trust." He says the words like they're only the edge of something he really wants to say. But before I can press him, he says, "Just make sure to give 'em hell."

And then, like someone dropping a hammer into my stomach, the afternoon comes rushing back. "About that."

Ethan leans forward. "What is it?"

Ethan's my brother and I love him and all, but we don't have one of those psychic twin vibes. When he sprains his ankle in soccer practice, I don't feel some phantom twinge across the field, and when one of us is upset about something, the other one usually doesn't notice until we say something point-blank. Which is how I know my face must look like a real mess if Ethan's asking me that.

I consider for a moment not telling him. There's this strange tug pulling me back, some misplaced loyalty to Pepper that I guess even finding out the truth about her didn't quite knock out of me.

But even if I wanted to keep this to myself, I couldn't. Not with Pepper as captain of the swim team. Whether I keep doing Ethan's captain duties or not, one of us will be dealing with her until the end of the season, and I can't just send him in blind.

"Big League Burger—Pepper's parents are in charge of it."

It takes Ethan a moment to place her, and for some reason I feel a flash of annoyance. "Pepper Evans?"

I nod. "And . . . it looks like Pepper is running their Twitter. Or at least, it looks like she's a big part of running it."

Ethan's eyes widen in the same dumbfounded way I know mine must have three hours ago. "That's—there's no way."

"That's what I thought. I only found out this afternoon."

"The world can't be that small."

I prop my elbows on the table and lean my head into my hands, suddenly feeling like I haven't slept in years. I'm past surprise, past disappointment. I just want to throw my body onto my bed and sleep until the end of time.

"Apparently it is," I mutter.

Ethan lowers his voice. "Are you gonna be able to keep at it? I mean—you're friends, right?"

"No." Ethan pulls back, and I realize I've said it through my teeth. I sag forward, sinking deeper into my hands, my elbows aching against the table. "At least not anymore, we're not."

Ethan levels with me for a moment, and then nods. "Maybe it'll all just . . . blow over after this." He knocks his knuckles on the table as he gets up. "Anyway, let me know if you need any help."

I wait for a few seconds after everyone's left to reach into my back pocket and grab my phone. Three messages from Bluebird, but no more texts from Pepper. Somehow I already know what I'm going to see before I open Twitter, but I can't stop myself—and there, sure enough, is a tweet from Big League Burger. The stupid cat GIF, with its sunglasses and its grilled cheese. I don't know what part is more stupid—being disappointed about a GIF of a cat, or that there was even a tiny part of me that thought she might not post it at all.

Pepper

Bluebird

So you never told me what it is you want to do with your life.

Bluebird

I mean, no pressure or anything, it's just the rest of forever

Bluebird

It's okay if you want to be Rucker's protege. I mean, I'd stop being friends with you, but who needs friends when you have a 401k and 16 pairs of patterned pants

Great. That makes six unanswered texts to Jack, three unanswered texts to Wolf, and several SOS texts to Paige, who I know is either in class or sucking face with a fellow coed. I hope it's the former, because I'm really not up to getting a play-by-play right now.

In fact, I'm probably not up to any kind of play right now. My mom's going to be home any minute, and the kitchen looks like Keebler elves threw a rave in it.

I didn't mean for it to escalate to the extent it has—a pot of browned butter remnants on the stove, cocoa powder on the marble counter, leftover dark chocolate sauce congealing in a bowl in the sink. After the incident with Jack, I'd walked straight home, reeling from the surprise of it all, the complete absurdity, and convinced myself I could take my mind off it if I just pulled out my AP Gov textbook and buried myself in it.

It turns out no amount of learning about the ins and outs of federalism is enough to distract me from the gnawing guilt, or the unwelcome weight in my chest every time I think of Jack's face just before he walked out of the bakery's front doors.

If I couldn't escape the guilt, there was nothing left to do but lean into it. And leaning into it is what led me to grabbing the forty dollars my mom leaves out in the front to order food if I ever need it, schlepping miserably down to the bodega, and collecting everything I needed to make Paige's infamous So Sorry Blondies from the summer before she left for college.

I pull them out of the oven now, the smell wafting through the kitchen—the brown sugar and butter and toffee against the richness of the dark chocolate chips and pockets of dark chocolate caramel sauce. A little bitter and a little sweet. I set them on the stove to cool and lean back on the counter, looking at the horror I have wrought upon my mom's spotless kitchen.

I whip out my phone (no texts from Jack; just a few from my dad, asking which pies to preorder for Thanksgiving) so I can take a few pictures of it for the blog. Paige and I have been playing phone tag all week, but that hasn't stopped her from nagging me to update. To be fair, she's had the last three posts, with impressive pictures of Rainy Day Pudding, Unicorn Ice Cream Bread, and a recent addition I'm too scared to ask about called Help Me Hangover Cookies. Meanwhile, I haven't posted since I made our Trash Talk Tarts in September—courtesy of the thinly veiled comment I found in the Hallway Chat on Weazel, where someone bitched about a "certain blonde android making the rest of the AP Chem class look bad." While we're all too stressed out and busy to bully each other beyond the occasional snide remark, I don't think it's too presumptuous to assume they meant me.

Just then my phone rings, and my dad's face dressed up as the Big League Burger mascot for Halloween pops up on the screen.

"What's up?"

"Pies," says my dad. I can recognize the background noise from our old favorite bakery in Nashville—the bells on the door, the chime of the register. The place is always packed. "Your mom says apple. Paige says pecan. If you have a third one in mind, open your pie hole and speak now."

My mouth waters just at the thought of those pies. Ever since we moved here, we always do major holidays in Nashville, since all the grandparents are out there. Sometimes I see old friends. Mostly I just hang out with Paige and tear up Dad's kitchen the way I tear up Mom's.

And, of course, run point with Dad to do everything and anything we can to keep Paige and Mom from going at it—which is easier to do these days, since during the holidays they seem to barely talk at all.

"Chocolate," I tell him. "The pudding one."

"Chocolate it is," he says, just as the oven timer goes off on my end. He must hear it, because he says, "Does this mean *P&P Bake* is getting an update today?"

"If I manage not to burn these blondies like I did with last week's cake."

"So Sorry Blondies?" my dad asks. He's not a big worrier—he's one of those parents who is more into listening than prying—but even he knows these particular blondies have notorious origins.

The way my parents' divorce happened was . . . anticlimactic. They sat us down one day over dinner and told us it was mutual. That they loved each other, but thought they were better off as friends. And as stunned as Paige and I were, it didn't really rock anyone's worlds. We were still in Nashville. We all still lived in the same place. My dad just started sleeping in the guest room, and that was that.

Or at least, it was for a few months. It was around that time that Big League Burger was getting too big for them to manage alone. The options were to sell parts of the franchise, or fully take the reins of the whole thing. My dad waffled—his heart was always in the original location, not the others that followed—but my mom didn't hesitate. She loved every part of it, big and small, and didn't want someone outside of the family in charge. If he didn't want to take those reins, she would. And she'd head to New York and open the corporate office there to do it.

Even though our dad was in full support of the idea, it was around then, I think, that Paige conflated everything that happened with BLB with the divorce and started blaming Mom. And for a little while, when Paige wanted me to be on her side about that, I wondered if I should too. After all, she seemed to be the one in motion, instigating the change.

But it wasn't her so much as it was BLB itself. I think it honestly shocked my dad, how fast we grew. Mom embraced it, pushing outward to the wind, and Dad seemed to cave in on it, becoming more and more invested in the goings-on of our original locations, as if he could just put up blinders and pretend the world ended right there.

So really, it's not fair to blame one of them. I think, in the end, it punctuated something they knew all along, but the day-to-day of our old lives always shielded them from. Mom is someone who likes adventure, and taking chances, and asking questions. Dad is someone who is perfectly content with what he has and where he is, and doesn't especially love change. And Big League Burger was nothing if not changing.

And so were we. Mom asked me to come to New York with her, and I couldn't imagine saying no. I was always her mini-me, always nipping at her heels. She made it sound like an adventure—and maybe it would have been, if Paige hadn't decided at the last minute that she was coming too.

Enter the So Sorry Blondies. It was a few weeks after we'd moved here, and the first of Paige's many blowups with Mom, accusing her of all kinds of things—saying she didn't love Dad at all, that she'd ruined everything, yelling loud enough that it's a miracle our neighbors' ears didn't bleed. Once it was over, Mom left to run in the park, and Paige left to go to the grocery store down the street, and I stayed in the too-big, too-unfamiliar apartment, wrestling with the strange feeling I had to take sides and not knowing which side to take.

Once she'd calmed down, Paige employed my help in making the So Sorry Blondies. We even Skyped in Dad, who didn't have very strong dessert opinions, other than to make sure the edges were crispy. Mom accepted them with a conciliatory smile, and that night, we all ate them for dinner. It was one of those bright spots that punctuated a grim year; a weird little pocket in the timestream I remember with an equal amount of affection and regret. It hurts to remember, but sometimes I have to, or I'll forget the way we used to be all together. Like the blondies themselves—the bitter and the sweet.

All this is to say, I know these blondies aren't magic. It's not going to make some bridge between me and Jack for all the water to go under. But I can't think of anything else I can do.

"They're for—a classmate," I tell him, just barely stopping myself from saying they're for a boy.

Mom's key turns in the door.

"A classmate, huh?" my dad asks. I can hear the relief in his voice. The last thing either of us wants is another family feud. "What kind of teenage drama merits the full blondie?"

Mom waves as she comes in, dropping her briefcase on one of the kitchen stools and offering me a weary smile as she pulls off her sunglasses.

"It's Dad," I tell her.

She perks up. "Ask him how the new menu has been doing." Even though we're sprouting new locations every other week, she still loves to hear Dad's day-to-day at the original spot.

"Tell her it's going well," says Dad, hearing her from the other end. "The Twitter, though—well, I'm at the front of the line, so I gotta order now. I'll call you both back in a jif."

"Chocolate pudding," I remind him.

"On it, hon. Love you."

"Love you too."

I hang up and see my mom looking at the So Sorry Blondies, a wistful expression on her face. It makes my throat ache, like the space in the room where Paige should be has never been quite as big.

"Everything okay, Pep?"

No. And I'm not even really sure why. Only a few days ago I was about as attached to Jack as I am to the guy who delivers our mail.

I tuck my bangs behind my ear. If I get into it like I almost did with Dad, I'll have to tell her about Jack, and given the circumstances, I don't especially want her to know. "Yeah, just . . . doing a post for the blog."

"Paige is still posting too?"

I bite the inside of my cheek. It's weird that most of the information Mom gets about Paige these days comes from me or from Dad.

"Yeah."

She closes the fridge and leans there against the door for a moment, biting her cheek the same way I am. No matter what evolution of my mom I'm looking at—the barefoot, back-porch-singing Nashville one, or the high-heeled, power-walking one—there are always these uncanny moments when we're both thinking the same thing or feeling the same way, and our bodies seem to mirror each other's, like two halves of a coin.

She blows out a breath, reopening the fridge to grab the jar of tomatoes she's always snacking out of, and then props herself on the other kitchen stool. "Taffy had trouble reaching you toward the end of the day."

"I had practice. And homework." And apparently two hours of guilt-induced baking, although that goes without saying.

My mom nods. "There are a lot of eyes and ears on that Twitter feed, you know. I know you're juggling a lot right now, but we could really use your help."

"I did." Not necessarily on purpose; after I ghosted on her, Taffy must have sent out the GIF of the cat herself. It had ten thousand retweets last I checked. "And now that the whole thing with that deli is winding down—"

"Winding down?" My mom laughs. "It's just getting started."

"What do you mean?"

She pulls out her phone and opens Twitter, where there's a new tweet from the Girl Cheesing account.

Girl Cheesing @GCheesing
Anyone who unfollows Big League Burger on Twitter gets 50 percent off their next grilled cheese! And, y'know, the relative comfort of knowing they're eating something that doesn't suck
6:48 PM · 21 Oct 2020

"So? Got any ideas cooking?"

The thing is, I always do. Within seconds, usually. Sometimes before I even finish reading a tweet. But right now, my mind just draws a giant blank. Right now, I'm looking at this tweet, but the only words I'm really hearing are Jack's on his way out the door: *Don't you dare stand there and tell me it isn't personal.*

"Actually, I was thinking—I had some other ideas for things we could post, memes or some funny quote retweets we could do—"

"Sure, of course, we can do those later. But how are we going to respond to *this*?"

I've been smiling this uneasy smile, but I can feel it starting to tilt on my face. And that's not the only thing tilting. Something is off here, something I don't fully understand.

"Should we?" I ask. I keep my voice bright and noncombative. "I mean, they're such small potatoes. We can do better than that, right? The McDonald's Twitter account posted some promotion about their new McCafé flavor this morning, and I bet I could—"

"Maybe you could sleep on it? We can loop in Taffy in the morning."

She pops another tomato into her mouth.

"Actually, Mom, um—I'm really busy this week, and I don't think I should tweet at that Girl Cheesing account anymore."

She shrugs. "So give Taffy some jumping-off points."

I turn my back on her, pretending to wipe some crumbs off the counter so I can pinch my eyes shut for a moment and brace myself. Unlike Paige, I'm not so good on the whole rebellion front.

"What I mean is, I think we should just . . . full stop. No more tweeting at them at all."

The tomato crunching stops for a moment. "You can't just let him *win*."

My ears snag on the word, my heart lurching.

"What do you mean 'him'?"

There's a beat, and then my mom waves her hand dismissively. "The owner's probably a *he*."

"It's called *Girl* Cheesing."

Not to mention, assuming an owner of a business is a guy is just not my mom's MO. Long before she dreamed up the idea for Big League Burger and helped build it up to the veritable empire it is today, she was almost *too* progressive a feminist for a place like Nashville, where she jokingly but not-quite-jokingly would clamp her hands over our ears anytime a line in a country song said something about girls with painted-on jeans or sitting on tailgates, saying it would make us "the complicit kind of cowgirl."

"You know what I mean."

But now she's the one having trouble looking at me.

I could tell her, I suppose. About Jack. But I already know

what it'll look like—that I have a crush on him or something, and I'm backing out of something that matters to her over a dumb boy.

"I'm going to lie down," says my mom, getting up from the table so suddenly she leaves her briefcase and her sunglasses behind. "There should be leftovers in the fridge if you're hungry."

I can't stand the idea of her being upset with me. I feel it all over again like some phantom force—that tug between her and Paige, except this time, of all people, it's between her and Jack.

"I'll queue up some ideas," I tell her retreating back.

Which isn't a lie. I will. They just won't necessarily have anything to do with our Twitter feud. This has to be where it ends. It was embarrassing enough when it was a tiger against an ant; it's another thing entirely when it's a tiger attacking a family. And as determined as Jack was not to hear me out, the truth is, I understand that—the pride. The loyalty. The ridiculous lengths you'll go to when it comes to protecting your own.

We used to have that, once upon a time. Now, I guess, the front lines are just me and 280 characters on a phone screen.

Jack

Wolf

This. Has been. The longest day. Of my entire existence

Bluebird

Oh hey look who's alive!

Wolf

Barely, though

Wolf

Sorry I've been MIA

Wolf

And to answer your question: be Spider-Man. That is what I want to do with my life

Wolf

But since that is a biological impossibility I have

turned my attention to slightly more realistic pursuits

Bluebird

Disappointing, but go on

Wolf

Honestly? What's probably going to happen is I end up in the family business

Bluebird

Maybe don't go on. This is starting to sound like the opening to a Godfather movie

Wolf

Believe me, I have made PLENTY of offers people have no problem refusing

Wolf

But family business aside, I guess I like working with apps

Bluebird

Like making them?

Wolf

I guess, yeah. I mean I'm obviously not a pro at it but it's fun to tinker with

Bluebird

Well? Have you made any?

Wolf

REALLY dumb things

Bluebird

Show me

Wolf

You might not like me anymore

Bluebird

Who says I like you now?

Wolf

Um OUCH

Bluebird

How about this? If you don't show me I won't like you anymore

Wolf

That logic is cruel but sound. You asked for this

Wolf

macncheeseme.com

Bluebird

Is this . . . is this an app for finding emergency mac and cheese

Wolf

Like Spider-Man, I am only looking out for the citizens of New York

Bluebird

Oh my god it says there are 203 places within a three-mile radius of me where I could get mac and cheese RIGHT NOW

Wolf

Really though is there any other reason for people to live in this city

Bluebird

I AM SO OVERWHELMED

Wolf

Mac and cheese fan?

Bluebird

You should do another one of these but with cupcakes

Wolf

Your feedback is noted and appreciated

Bluebird

Really though, this is super cool

Wolf

Thanks. You're like one of two people on the planet who has the access link, so be honored I guess

Bluebird

WHAT? You should be sharing this shit with the world. It's your moral responsibility

Wolf

With great power . . .

Bluebird

Comes delicious responsibility

Bluebird

I think I'm gonna get mac and cheese, I'm not kidding

Wolf

This is my legacy now, huh?

Bluebird

And hey your dreams technically didn't NOT come true

Bluebird

Since you're posting your app on the world wide . . . web

Bluebird

Get it?

Wolf

I'm blocking you.

Bluebird

WEBS. Like SPIDER-MAN'S!!!!

Wolf

B l o c k e d

Bluebird doesn't answer me for a few moments, then. I assume she's just hustling her way out the door like I am, until I reach the 6 train platform and see another notification come in that makes my stomach drop.

Bluebird
Do you think it's weird that the app hasn't outed us yet?

Bluebird
Like maybe we are lab rats in this app's experiment or something

Wolf
IDK. It is weird though

Bluebird
Are we going to do something dumb like not tell each other who we are until graduation

Wolf
Do you want to know?

Bluebird
Sometimes

Bluebird
You?

Wolf
Sometimes

Wolf

I feel like

Wolf

Ah sorry that sent too soon

Wolf

I don't know. What if you think I'm someone I'm not and you're disappointed?

Bluebird

I feel the same way

Bluebird

Just kidding. I'm embarrassingly hot. I'm actually Blake Lively

Wolf

Well this is awkward because I'm sitting with her right now, so

Bluebird

SHIT. Not again

Wolf

XOXO gossip wolf

I spend the rest of the ride to the Upper East Side typing and deleting messages back, wondering if I should just leave it at that or say what I want to say. The trouble is, I don't know what I want to say. If I want us to stay in the dark, or if I want all our cards out on the table.

But if I've learned one thing from occasionally being too impulsive for my own good, it's that once you open a door like that, you don't get to close it again. Right now, Bluebird is nobody and everybody at once—but right now, Bluebird likes me. And I'm worried that in changing that first bit, the second one might change too.

Apparently that worry is intense enough that I forget my breakfast. My family owns a *deli* we *live on top of*, but somehow I not only forget to grab one of the infinite delicious options I have at my disposal, but I don't realize it until I'm standing outside of homeroom, five minutes to the bell, with no other options but to eat the ridiculous red tie they make us wear as part of our uniforms.

My stomach gurgles like a sentient being. This is it, then. I'll die before noon.

It doesn't help I got next to no sleep last night. After that shift, I should have slept like a dead person, but every time I did, my dreams were all tangled, like someone rattled the synapses in my brain. I kept waking up to different jolts to my system—my anger at Pepper. The irritation of Ethan getting off scot-free, yet again. The worry of wondering whether I'd shown the mysterious Bluebird too much by sending her the link to that old app I made last year, and the gnawing guilt of knowing even by sending it, the situation just got a little more complicated than it was before.

I scan the hallway for Paul. There's *one* friendship I know I haven't screwed up. A friendship that comes with a free CLIF Bar, if I'm lucky, because Paul seems to be carrying an absurd amount with him at all times, as if the apocalypse is going to hit while we're in class.

Apparently my luck has really and truly run out this morning, because the person whose face I spot instead of Paul's is the last one I want to see right now.

"Can I talk to you?"

I had a plan for this. I rehearsed it in my head last night like a total loser, which I had plenty of time to do, thanks to the not-sleeping thing. And the plan was simple, because the plan was this: ignore Pepper. Don't acknowledge anything she says, and walk away.

The thing I did not factor into that equation, unfortunately, was Pepper herself. Or the fact that she seems every bit as miserable as I do, with her bangs slightly off-kilter and her blue eyes earnest and overtired, as though she spent most of last night awake too. Still, I'm determined not to acknowledge her—that is, until I see that she appears to be holding a container full of the most obscenely gooey blondie situation I have ever laid eyes on in my life.

I shift my weight between my feet, my resolve and bravado as absent as my breakfast.

"The bell's about to ring," I say.

"Just for a second?"

It's more than her eyes. There's this openness to her. Not like there's a crack in the mask of Robot Pepper, but like the mask is off completely. Somehow in this moment that she's never looked more different, she's also never seemed more familiar—and just like that, I realize she's already become someone I can't just dismiss, even though by all accounts I should.

"Fine."

Ethan passes us in the hallway, raising his eyebrows at me as he does. Pepper's face is on fire by the time he slips into homeroom.

"I know I said it, but—I really am sorry. I had no idea it was you on the other end of that."

"But you knew it was someone."

"Yeah. And I felt gross about it. But my mom . . ." She shakes her head before I can even pull a face. "It's a whole thing. But what I wanted to say was that I get it. I mean, I know it doesn't seem like I would, but—we were smaller, once."

I can't help it—it's coming out of me before I can do anything to clamp it down. "You think we can't hold our own because we're *small*?"

"No, no, that's not what I—sorry. That's not what I meant at all." She takes a breath, and I realize she's actually flustered. Pepper, the girl who was one time challenged to argue *against* global warming for a debate club event in front of half the school, is flustered talking to me. "What I mean is, back when Big League Burger started, it was just us. My parents and my sister and me. And it was like that for a while, before we . . . well, you know. So I get it."

There's this uncertain lilt in her voice, in the way she is looking at me. Like she isn't expecting me to accept her apology. To be fair, I wasn't either.

But that's not the reason why, for a few moments, I don't say anything. It's that there's something else hovering on the end of that last bit, like there's more to the story. Something else that fractured between the Big League Burger then and whatever it's become since.

I want to ask, but then Pepper is shoving the Tupperware under my nose. "Also, these are for you."

I may have my pride, but my stomach sure doesn't. I already know I'm going to take them, probably already knew before Pepper opened her mouth and swayed me with her speech.

"What are they?" I somehow manage to ask, despite the saliva pooling in my mouth.

"An apology. They're literally called So Sorry Blondies."

"Another Evans sisters invention?"

She lets out a huff of a laugh, like she's been holding her breath. "Yeah."

I take it from her, partially because she looks like she has no intention of putting her arms down otherwise, and partially because I'm so hungry, the janitor might have to come peel me off the floor if I don't eat something soon. She watches me nervously, as if she can't tell if she's actually been forgiven or not.

"Look." I glance into the classroom, where Ethan is thoroughly distracted by Stephen and no longer keeping an eye on us. "I may have . . . overreacted."

Pepper shakes her head. "I told you. I get it. It's your family."

"Yeah. But it's also—well, to be honest, this has been kind of good for business."

Pepper's brow furrows, that one little crease returning. "What, the tweets?"

"Yeah." I scratch the back of my neck, sheepish. "Actually, we had a line out the door yesterday. It was kind of intense."

"That's . . . that's good, right?"

The tone of my voice is clearly not matching up with the words I'm saying, but if I'm being honest, I'm still wary of this whole overnight business boom. And if I'm being honest, I'm even more wary of Pepper. If this really is as much of a family business as she claims it is—to the point where she's helping run the Twitter handle, when even I know enough about corporate Twitter accounts to know entire teams of experienced people get paid to do that—then she might have had more of a hand in this whole recipe theft thing than she's letting on.

The fact of the matter is, I can't trust her. To the point of not knowing whether I can even trust her knowing how our business is doing, or just how badly we need it.

"Yeah, um, I guess." I try to make it sound noncommittal.

My acting skills, much like my breakfast-packing skills, leave much to be desired.

"So . . ."

"So."

Pepper presses her lips into a thin line, a question in her eyes.

"So, I guess—if your mom really wants you to keep tweeting . . ."

"Wait. Yesterday you were pissed. Two minutes ago you were pissed."

"I *am* pissed. You stole from us," I reiterate. "You stole from an eighty-five-year-old woman."

"I didn't—"

"Yeah, yeah, but still. You're them, and I'm . . . her. It's like a *choose your fighter* situation, and we just happen to be the ones up to bat."

"So you're saying—you don't *not* want me to keep this up?"

"The way I see it, you don't have to make your mom mad, and we get a few more customers in the door too."

Pepper takes a breath like she's going to say something, like she's going to correct me, but after a moment, she lets it go. Her face can't quite settle on an expression, toeing the line between dread and relief.

"You're sure?"

I answer by opening the container she handed me. The smell that immediately wafts out of it should honestly be illegal; it stops kids I've never even spoken to in their tracks.

"Are you a witch?" I ask, reaching in and taking a bite of one. It's like Monster Cake, the Sequel—freaking Christmas in my mouth. I already want more before I've even managed to chew. My eyes close as if I'm experiencing an actual drug high—and maybe I am, because I forget myself entirely and say, "This might even be better than our Kitchen Sink Macaroons."

"Kitchen Sink Macaroons?"

Eyes open again. *Yikes.* Note to self: dessert is the greatest weapon in Pepper's arsenal. I swallow my bite so I can answer her.

"It's kind of well-known, at least in the East Village. It even got in some Hub Seed roundup once. I'd tell you to try some, but you might steal the recipe, so."

Pepper smiles, then—actually smiles, instead of the little smirk she usually does. It's not startling, but what it does to me in that moment kind of is.

Before I can examine the unfamiliar lurch in my stomach, the bell rings and knocks the smile right off her face. I follow just behind her, wondering why it suddenly seems too hot in here, like they cranked the air up for December instead of October. I dismiss it by the time I get to my desk—probably just all the Twitter drama and the glory of So Sorry Blondies getting to my head.

"One rule," she says, as we sit in the last two desks in the back of the room.

I raise my eyebrows at her.

"We don't take any of it personally." She leans forward on her desk, leveling with me, her bangs falling into her face. "No more getting mad at each other. Cheese and state."

"What happens on Twitter stays on Twitter," I say with a nod of agreement. "Okay, then, second rule: no kid gloves."

Mrs. Fairchild is giving that stern look over the room that never quite successfully quiets anyone down. Pepper frowns, waiting for me to elaborate.

"I mean—no going easy on each other. If we're going to play

at this, we're both going to give it our A game, okay? No holding back because we're . . ."

Friends, I almost say. No, I'm going to say. But then—

"I'd appreciate it if even one of you acknowledged the bell with your silence," Mrs. Fairchild grumbles.

I turn to Pepper, expecting to find her snapping to attention the way she always does when an adult comes within a hundred feet of disciplining her. But her eyes are still intent on me, like she is sizing something up—like she's looking forward to something I haven't anticipated yet.

"All right. No taking it personally. And no holding back."

She holds her hand out for me to shake again, under the desk so Mrs. Fairchild won't see it. I smile and shake my head, wondering how someone can be so aggressively seventeen and seventy-five at the same time, and then I take it. Her hand is warm and small in mine, but her grip is surprisingly firm, with a pressure that almost feels like she's still got her fingers wrapped around mine even after we let go.

I turn back to the whiteboard, a ghost of a smirk on my face. "Let the games begin."

PART TWO

Jack

"Should we have a signal?"

I pull my goggles off my face. "Why would we need a signal?"

"I dunno," says Paul, shifting his weight between his feet so rapidly, I'm a little worried he's going to slip on the pool deck. "Just in case I forget? You said 4:15, right? Sometimes I just get so in the *zone* when we get to play water polo, man, and I might just—"

"If you forget, I'll just . . . swim up and nudge you or something."

"That's not much of a signal."

I hold in an almighty sigh. I'm lucky Paul is helping me in the first place. This is kind of above and beyond the best friend call of duty. "Fine. I'll—hold up three fingers, I guess."

Paul's face bursts into a freckly grin. "*Sweet.* I'm on it. This is gonna go *so great.*"

Somehow the more times Paul has said some variation of that in the last twenty-four hours—which I think is a number in the dozens by now—the *less* likely it seems that it will. The good news is, as usual, if this doesn't work, I have more than a few backup ideas in my arsenal. In the last two weeks, I've learned that staying a step ahead of Pepper means you're already three steps behind.

We agreed not to go easy on each other, but I suspected for the first, say, four hours or so, maybe she was anyway. Apparently she was just waiting for lunch to quote retweet the deal I posted to our Twitter page:

Big League Burger @B1gLeagueBurger
Anyone who unfollows Girl Cheesing on Twitter gets 50% off our grilled cheese too! All three and a half of you are welcome anytime

> **Girl Cheesing** @GCheesing · 1d
> Anyone who unfollows Big League Burger on Twitter gets 50 percent off their next grilled cheese! And, y'know, the relative comfort of knowing they're eating something that doesn't suck

12:35 PM · 22 Oct 2020

Before we'd hit the pool deck that day, I'd been scrolling through Twitter and decided to go another route. Some video was trending, with the headline:

Big League Burger May Start Testing Delivery in Several States

I quote retweeted it from the Girl Cheesing account, writing:

Girl Cheesing @GCheesing
oh god is nowhere safe

> **Boostle** @boostle · 1d
> cool never putting on real pants again
> boostle.com/p/big-league-burger-may-start-testing-delivery-in-several-states

2:42 PM · 22 Oct 2020

It hit a thousand retweets before practice even started. I realized, then, the notifications that had been rolling in weren't just comments and likes and retweets—people were starting to follow our account too. Thousands of people. People who seemed every bit as invested in this Twitter spat as Pepper and I were ourselves.

After practice that day she'd offered me a breezy wave, then walked into the locker room, where she'd promptly responded to my tweet with an image of a bike messenger posing outside of Girl Cheesing, holding up a giant Big League Burger bag. The tweet read: Apparently not!

By nightfall, Jasmine Yang released another vlog update on "Twitter Gets Petty," breaking the whole exchange down with screenshots and even analyzing all the unrelated likes and replies both accounts made in between.

"Stay up-to-date with all things in the #BigCheese war by tuning in to my page, where you can decide in real time who's in the lead." She pointed down to the bottom of the screen.

"Comment with the cheese emoji for Girl Cheesing, and the burger emoji for Big League Burger. Ta-ta for now, Petty People!"

And just like that, our Twitter war had a hashtag, we had a rabid new fanbase, and I'd learned a valuable lesson: I was better off not provoking Pepper into responding to something, because she had home-court advantage and knew how to use it.

I catch sight of her now, somehow ridiculously easy for me to spot in the sea of swimmers even though she's wearing the same black Stone Hall swimsuit and cap as every other girl in the water. They're doing some kind of sprint drill right now, switching back and forth between butterfly and freestyle every other lap, while their coach hollers vaguely motivational things from the bleachers. It looks like hell, but for me, it also looks like salvation—when Pepper's submerged for two hours, it's the only time she isn't a few buttons away from the Big League Burger Twitter page, poised to strike.

And boy, has she ever. So that evening I didn't tweet at all. Well, couldn't, really—the deli was packed to the gills again, with a line so far out the door that when Grandma Belly saw it from the window of the apartment, she asked if people were waiting to get raptured.

"They're here for your grilled cheese," I told her.

She fixed me with a look, crossing a leg on the massive armchair she spent most of her time in and raising a single eyebrow at me. "Not unless you changed my secret ingredient to cocaine, they're not."

I swear she only ever rolls out her most crass lines when it's just her and me. I guess that's the price Ethan pays for being so busy all the time.

When I didn't respond right away, she added, "Back in my day, it was more than my grilled cheese bringing in customers, if you know what I mean."

"*Grandma.*"

"What?" she asked innocently. "I also make a mean toscakaka. Best you can get this side of Sweden."

I don't know about the whole Sweden thing, since I've never actually left the East Coast, but I couldn't deny the deliciousness of the toscakaka. It wasn't on the menu anymore, since Grandma Belly's version trumped all others, but that almond caramel cake was one of the things she'd taught me how to make on rainy Sundays when the deli was slow and she had the energy for it. I have a whole arsenal of mismatched Swedish and Irish dishes in my back pocket, courtesy of her and Grandpa Jay, who died when we were in middle school. My dad keeps saying we'll bring some of them back once I graduate—assuming, I guess, that I'm not going anywhere, and I'll have the time to make them, then.

"Seems to me like the grilled cheese isn't the whole story, hmm?"

I hadn't turned around because Grandma Belly can sniff out a lie faster than she can sniff out Kitchen Sink Macaroons cooking in the oven. Instead, I shrugged, still staring out the window. There was no reason to stress her out with the Twitter thing—I had it under control.

"Yeah, well. Good press," I said.

Good press that had only gotten more aggressive by the day. That night, I waited for the Big League Burger corporate account to tweet, and it was deliciously generic—clearly something scheduled that Pepper didn't have anything to do with. Customers who come to Big League BOO-ger on Halloween get a free junior milkshake with every Big League Meal purchase!

It was too easy. I responded to the tweet within five minutes of it with a picture of Big League's version of the Grandma's Special I screenshotted from their Instagram.

Girl Cheesing @GCheesing

I'm thinking about this for my costume, but I don't know. Too scary for the kids? Don't want to give anyone nightmares

8:45 PM · 22 Oct 2020

The next morning I woke up to another two thousand followers on the Girl Cheesing account, courtesy of write-ups on a few viral websites and another vlog from Jasmine. I walked into homeroom that day half expecting Pepper to go back on her own word. I thought maybe she'd be frosty with me or avoid me entirely.

Instead, she waltzed right up to my desk and said, "Pie?"

I narrowed my eyes at her, and then down at the container in her hands, where there were chocolate hand pies lined up in neat rows. The So Sorry Blondies were all gone by then, devoured between me and Paul and the rest of the dive team, and the memory of their deliciousness was too fresh for me to resist another Pepper Evans creation. I took one of the mini pies with a wary hand, just as she pulled out her phone, tapped it a few times, and smirked.

I stopped chewing. "Did you just tweet?" I asked, my mouth full of chocolate.

Pepper swept her bangs back with her fingers, and this time the gesture was calculated and breezy. "Did I?"

I scowled into my phone screen, lowering it under my desk so Mrs. Fairchild wouldn't see. This one was just a GIF of Regina George from *Mean Girls*—"Why are you so obsessed with me?"

"At least your pie is better than your tweets," I mumbled.

But the smirk on Pepper's face only deepened. "Those are from the Big League Burger bargain menu, by the way."

My mouth dropped open. Pepper turned her eyes back to her textbook, burying her smirk in it. "Enjoy."

But that, as it turns out, was child's play. Two weeks have passed since then, and I don't think I've gone a full waking minute without thinking about our Twitter war since. I've started *dreaming* in memes. It's a miracle if anything that comes out of my mouth isn't unconsciously accounted for in 280 characters or less.

By then, the Girl Cheesing account had a whopping seventy thousand followers, and we had to install a ticketing system to stop the line from getting too out of control outside. We even put up the old HELP WANTED sign I hadn't seen since freshman year. It was a brand-new Girl Cheesing, a new era, a charge in the air nobody was impervious to—Dad was running around like a teenager, Mom was smiling so hard, it looked like her face might hurt, and even Ethan started spending more time downstairs in the deli instead of always begging off to hang out with his friends.

But two weeks in and we're both ready to drop. This morning, I fell asleep in English. Yesterday, I'm pretty sure I saw Pepper take a micro-nap while hanging on the pool wall waiting for a set to start. So really, as desperate as my next move seems, I'm doing it just as much for her benefit as mine—I don't need Pepper drowning in the shallow end of the city's ugliest community pool on my conscience.

And the only way to make that happen is to make Twitter go away. Short of hacking into whatever satellite keeps the internet running and pulling the plug on the whole thing, the only feasible way to do that is to shut down Big League Burger's Twitter.

Hence, this ill-fated plan—one that hinges precariously on Paul, the general dismissiveness of our coaches, and Pepper trusting me not to be a complete and total ass.

"Okay, since this is the first Friday water polo game of the season, a refresher on the rules."

Landon's standing on the high dive board, like a king addressing his people. He kind of looks like one, with the heads of everyone on the swim and dive teams turned up to him, his hand raised with the moldy soccer ball we use to play water polo like some kind of scepter. Vice Principal Rucker would kill to command this kind of attention.

"The rules are: no drawing blood. And . . . that's pretty much it."

A few of the more nervous-looking freshmen cut glances at our coaches, who are, predictably, deep in some hushed argument about something I know for a *fact* has nothing to do with sports and everything to do with the rumor circulating on Weazel that someone saw them making out in the park over the weekend. But hey, at least it got Coach Thompkins to show up for practice for once.

We divide up into the same teams we've had since my freshman year, give or take a few new recent additions of underclassmen. Since the dive team is significantly smaller than the swim team, each of our water polo "teams" is a mix of both. Much to the annoyance of literally everyone in the pool, Ethan and I are on separate teams—a condition we abuse liberally, because more often than not some sucker from the wrong team will pass one of us the ball and give us an unexpected advantage.

Well, suckers who aren't Pepper, at least. Who happens to be both ruthless and on Ethan's team.

The game starts out the way it usually does—with Landon chucking the ball into the middle ground of the pool and everyone swarming it like piranhas, dunking each other by grabbing onto heads and shoulders, barely avoiding elbowing each other in the face. I steer clear of the madness, swimming out closer to our goal, hoping one of the six sets of hands currently clutching the soccer ball that's half submerged underwater will throw it in my vague direction.

"Been a few hours since your last tweet. You losing steam there, Campbell?"

"Oh, trust me, Pepperoni, my next move will be worth the wait."

She treads a few inches closer to me, close enough I can see the strands of hair poking out of her cap. Her hair isn't particularly wild, but I've noticed anytime the swim coach puts them through an intense set, her cap can't stay fully on her head to save its own life.

"Judging from what I saw of the dive team's lap swimming today, you're an *expert* at making people wait."

I grin into the water. "Been watching me swim, huh?"

Pepper's eyes are still on the mayhem ahead, unfazed, but I see her lip twitch. "If you can call that swimming."

"Please, I could take you in a race in a heartbeat."

She laughs out loud. "Wanna bet?"

"Sure. Let's go."

She follows my eyeline to the edge of the pool like she might actually race me, but then I reach forward and tug her cap off her head in one swift motion, her blonde hair spilling into the pool in wet tangles around her face and shoulders.

"Foul!" Pepper crows, yanking it back from me.

"You know, for someone named Pepper, you're pretty salty about losing."

She groans at my pun as she shoves her hair back into the cap, but then counters, "For someone named Jack, you're pretty bad at knowing when to hit the road."

"Wow, Burger Princess, sick burn."

And *damn it* if she hasn't gone and done it again—distracted me right at a peak moment for me to most fully make an ass of myself. The soccer ball is sailing over our heads, and Pepper's already plowing through the water with the focus of a shark, halfway to where it's about to smack into no man's land.

Not on my watch.

I reach out and grab her ankle and yank her back the way she's done to me too many times to count, but unlike me, she seems to be expecting it—expecting it so readily, she snaps her body through the water like a rubber band, using *me* as an anchor for momentum, and before I know it, she's got a palm squarely on top of my head and is dunking my entire body underwater.

I let out a glugging cough of surprise before breaking the surface, just in time to see Pepper scooping the ball out of the water and chucking it to Ethan halfway across the pool in a motion so fluid and seamless I might have dreamed it.

"What—*how*—"

She swims back over to me, her strokes dainty and smug. "You were saying?"

I set my pointer finger and my thumb on the surface of the water and flick some at her. She responds by full-on splashing me.

"Jack! Oy!"

It's Paul, being about as subtle as a gun, yelling across the pool to indicate he's going to pass to me. I kick myself away from Pepper so I might have a Klondike Bar's chance in hell of actually catching it, but I'm not fast enough—her hand is already resting on my shoulder.

It's a basic defensive move in water polo, but for one weird, weightless blip, it isn't. She takes her fingers and squeezes them, tightening them around the muscle of my shoulder, not enough to be aggressive or competitive. Just enough that I'm not sure if my heartbeat is from the adrenaline or something else.

It's weird—I think, guiltily, of Bluebird. Of the near radio silence between the two of us lately. As soon as we got on the topic of each other's identities a few weeks ago, I panicked and pulled back—the less we talked, maybe, the less room she'd have to wonder why the app hadn't revealed our identities to each other.

So I bizarrely feel like I'm cheating on her. With Twitter, not Pepper, of course. But I'd be lying if I said there weren't a kind of relief to the switch. Pepper, at least, I don't have to lie to. We do all of the backhanded stuff right out in the open, where everyone can see.

The ball is sailing over the other players, headed straight for me. I pull myself out of Pepper's grasp, but she's launching herself out of the water too, using me as leverage again. The ball smacks both of our hands at the same time and then skims right past us, but not before we look at each other in surprise.

For a second our faces are *alarmingly* close, close enough that she gasps and I forget to breathe altogether, and then *wham*—our foreheads smack right into each other's.

"Um, *ow.*"

"*Jesus.*"

And then, at the same time: "Are you okay?"

There's a beat where we look at each other, not fully processing what just happened—no doubt courtesy of the mild concussion we might have just given each other—and for a second, I forget where we are entirely.

"Jinx," I say. Jack Campbell, moment killer.

Pepper laughs, looking relieved. "Oh, good. I was worried I'd killed your last brain cell, but you seem okay."

"Hey. Jinx means you're not allowed to talk. Did you *have* a childhood?"

"I actually came out of the womb a Twitter bot."

"Must have been one heck of a shock for your parents."

"Yeah, but at least there weren't two of me."

"When you're this good-looking, it only makes sense to have a spare."

"Campbell! Evans! Are you going to keep flirting over there or actually make yourselves useful?"

It's Landon, yelling from the other end of the pool. Pepper immediately takes off, but not before I see that her face has gone so red, it actually *looks* like a pepper. She all but leaves me in the dust, not even looking back.

"Now?"

I blink. Somehow Paul has swum up right behind me without making a sound and is holding three anxious fingers in front of my face. I check the clock by the pool and see it's almost 4:15, glance farther up the water and see Pepper and Landon laughing at whatever Ethan just said.

"Yeah. Now's good."

And so starts a performance so stilted and awkward that somewhere up the street, our classmates rehearsing for the school's production of *Seussical!* just shuddered without knowing why.

"Oh, man. I feel quite ill," says Paul. Loudly. And in what appears to be a slight British accent.

I hold in a sigh. "Oh no, that sucks. Want me to walk you to the nurse?"

"Yeah. Because I'm sick. Like in a stomach way," Paul continues.

One of the sophomores on the swim team cringes from behind him, and she and a few of the others swim in the opposite direction. I figure they'll spread what Paul said fast enough nobody will question us when we get out of the pool and don't come back for an inordinately long time. Sure enough, the coaches don't even bat an eye as we get out and Paul makes another declaration about his mysterious illness, which is starting to become a *lot* more dramatic than originally scripted.

"How'd I do?" he asks excitedly, the moment we make it to the locker rooms.

"Academy Award–worthy," I deadpan, pausing outside of the girls' locker room. I knock and crack open the door, calling, "Maintenance," and waiting a beat.

No answer. Perfect. I find the TEMPORARILY CLOSED FOR CLEANING sign propped against the wall and Velcro it to the door.

"I'll be right back," I tell Paul, who salutes me as I take one last glance over our shoulders and sneak into the girls' locker room.

It doesn't take long to find Pepper's backpack in one of the lockers—it may be the same nondescript navy Herschel bag that half the people in our class have, but there's a tiny little keychain that says "Music City" on her zipper. I find her phone in the front pocket where I always see her sliding it out before and after class and type in 1234, hoping against hope that she never got around to changing it.

Boom. I'm in.

It's almost *too* easy.

I pull up the Big League Burger Twitter account, and it occurs to me that I could do some major damage right now. Like, *get someone fired* kind of damage. Send a tweet that says *We confess to ripping off a defenseless old lady's grilled cheese recipe because we're all corporate assholes* kind of damage.

But even I'm not that much of a tool. I pull up the settings to the account, change the password, and lock her out.

I'm about to quit the app and shove the phone back into her bag when it buzzes in my hand. It's a text from "Mom."

Text me when practice is over—that last tweet was good, but I think we can do better

I don't mean to read it, it's just *there.* And very quickly followed up by another one.

Also Taffy's leaving early tomorrow, do you mind checking the tweets she queued?

My thumb grazes the screen and accidentally taps the text, opening it up to a whole string of them. I move my finger to close out of it, but not before I've managed to skim some of the recent messages—Can you just send Taffy a tweet idea real quick if you get a chance? It's been hours, says one of them.

Paul coughs noisily from the front door.

"*Shit.*"

My signal to leave. I shove Pepper's phone back into her backpack and zip it up, then race to the exit on the other side of the girls' locker room, barely making it out before someone walks in from the original one.

And then that's it. The deed is done. I slink back into the boys' locker room, where Paul is already waiting for me, his expression manic and gleeful. He claps me on the back a few too many times, a hyper parody of something the Landons or the Ethans of the world might do. I smile back, but it feels a little less like a victory and a little too much like that moment Pepper stuck her hand on my head and dunked me.

This whole time I'd rolled my eyes about her mom whenever she came up. I didn't believe a grown adult could be this invested in their kid doing something this objectively dumb—not even my parents, who joke about all the business it brings in, but probably wouldn't do more than shrug if I swore off it forever.

I feel a weird pinch of guilt as I walk out of the locker room, but not necessarily for locking Pepper out of the account. For the reminder that, fun and games aside, this whole Twitter thing means a lot more than either of us want to admit.

Pepper

"Please don't make us do this," Pooja moans.

Landon puts a hand on her shoulder, jostling it slightly. I still have my eyes peeled on it as he takes the hand away. "Rules are rules," he says with an easy grin. "And you guys lost fair and square."

"At least it's not pool water Kool-Aid this time," says Ethan.

I glance up the pool deck, toward the locker rooms, not even realizing I'm looking for Jack until I come up empty of him. It's not like it matters where he is, but I can't stop myself from compulsively checking, like he's become some kind of shadow I feel weird without. That, and his team lost—and the terms of this particular water polo war were that everyone on the losing team had to do 100 yards of butterfly, nonstop. There are very few things in this world I would pay good money to see, but watching Jack flounder at the hardest stroke after years of acting all cocky about doing flips into the water is decidedly one of them.

"Ugh. Say nice things at my funeral."

"C'mon, Pooja," says Landon, "you could swim this in your sleep."

I shouldn't care. And I don't. Or I wouldn't, if it weren't for something I'm getting a little more sure of by the day, something I can't decide whether I want to be sure of or not.

I might be right about Landon. It all checks out. Him texting during the day, when he would be off-campus. *Not* texting during the exact same times as swim and dive practice. And there is nothing quite so damning as the app Wolf sent me, the mac-and-cheese locator—Landon's the only senior this year interning at an app development startup, and the smell of that mac-and-cheese bread bowl he was sporting the other day is so burned into my memory that I'll probably be telling my grandchildren about it.

I'm going to ask him. Tonight. Point-blank. He'll already be in our apartment for that dinner with his dad. The second most embarrassing scenario will have already occurred, so I might as well just lean into the first. And if I don't ask him then, when I actually have him alone for the first time in four years, I don't think I ever will.

I head into the locker room, overly aware of the fact I'm going to have to hustle home to get my hair and my outfit in working order before Landon and his dad get to our place for dinner. Naturally, by putting a desire into the universe *not* to waste time, I run smack into Jack.

"Ah. Sorry, Pepperoni," he says, touching the spot where his shoulder brushed mine. He looks unsettled, his eyes a little wide. "Good luck keeping up with me tonight."

He moves to walk away from me, but I stop him, grabbing the crook of his arm. For a dive team slacker who probably couldn't remember the order of strokes in an individual medley to save his life, it's surprisingly firm.

"If you think I'm out for the count just because it's Friday . . ."

Jack takes the hand I have on his arm and presses it between his with mock solemnity. Mine is still wet, so our palms and fingers slick against each other's in a way that would be weirdly intimate if his grin wasn't at the exact half tilt it always is before he makes fun of me.

"Oh, don't worry. I figure you'll be free as a bird."

I narrow my eyes. He looks more pleased with himself than usual.

"See you Monday," he says, letting go of my hand and striding down the pool deck to his brother.

I'm still shaking my head as I walk into the locker room, coming out of the fog of being in the pool and back into the laser focus of everything beyond it. There's not just the dinner to think about, but homework, and *Twitter*, and calling Paige back, and that college essay prompt I haven't even started on—

"What the hell?"

The Big League Burger Twitter account has logged me out. I type in the password, but nothing happens—it just prompts me to type in something else. I'm about to call Taffy and ask if the password has changed, but she beats me to it with a text.

Did you change the twitter password?

Shit. We've been hacked.

And the irony is, I don't even have my *own* Twitter account to log into so I can see what the person who hacked us is doing to the account.

No. I'll hit "forgot password" and get us back in. Anyone from the tech team around?

I've never met anyone on the tech team, but judging from my mom's less-than-veiled complaints about them, I'm guessing they're not going to be very quick about this. Which means whoever out there in the world just turned my Twitter account into their personal tweeting playground might just as easily be able to hack back in and do it again.

I look away from the phone for a moment. *My* Twitter account?

There are texts from my mom too, that I must have opened without realizing when I tried to get into Twitter. I wonder how many seconds it's going to take for her to catch wind of this.

And naturally, no texts from Wolf either. Just a whole stream of people in the Hallway Chat bitching about the administration cracking down on Senior Skip Day. I obviously wasn't going to participate in that anyway—we have weekends to do whatever stupid teenage nonsense we need to do, not to mention an entire summer before college.

And no doubt whatever Ethan and the rest of the kids who usually lead this kind of thing will want to do is downtown, and I, being the loser that I am, have yet to go unchaperoned below Seventy-Fifth.

I have half a mind to post something in the Hallway Chat. Something about needing a good idea for a low-key place to take a date, or maybe something about prom. Some ridiculous thing that *Bluebird* can post, so Wolf can see it in the open forum and remember I am, in fact, still alive.

Jesus. I'm trying to play head games with someone I haven't even technically met.

Another text, this one from my mom.

Did you let anyone touch your phone?

"Oh, for god's sake," I mutter.

"Everything okay?"

"*Yes*," I snap.

Pooja takes a step back, looking stunned, still a little breathless from her swim. I realize half a dozen heads have swiveled to look at us, and my teeth are gritted like an animal poised to attack.

"Sorry—I didn't mean to butt in," she says.

"No, I'm sorry. I shouldn't have—I'm fine. Sorry."

Pooja nods and goes back to her locker without saying anything. I change as quickly as I can back into my uniform, desperate to get out of there—but to go where? To the apartment, where I'll have to sit like an animatronic puppet and smile at Landon's dad until my cheeks hurt, until I think I might actually explode into molten lava from the embarrassment of what I'm about to ask him?

Maybe I just won't. Maybe it's better if I just let the whole thing go, Landon and Wolf with it. Because what's on the other side of it, if it really is him? If Landon liked me as Pepper, he had plenty of chances to show it in the last few years.

Or he would if I hadn't avoided him like the plague for the first two of them, afraid of humiliating myself.

But maybe I owe it to that girl—to the freshman me who was too scared to talk to him. There must have been some reason I felt that way, even if it doesn't quite feel that way now.

I turn to leave and end it right there, but then Pooja walks past.

"I really am sorry," I say, following her out. "I didn't mean to snap."

I'm expecting her to brush it off again, but then she tilts her head at me and says something that stops me in my tracks.

"It's Jack, isn't it?"

Something tightens in my chest. "Huh?"

She smiles at me, this guarded little *oh, c'mon* kind of smile. It's weird, but I spend so much time deliberately *not* meeting Pooja's eye, I'm surprised to see the warmth in them. Surprised, and then profoundly uncomfortable—because I don't need her being nice to me. I don't want to owe her anything, don't want to tip the scale that's been teetering between us since the great Mesopotamia mishap of freshman year.

But before I can even parse through that, I have to figure out how the hell she found out about Jack. As far as I know, we haven't spoken a word about the Twitter war to anyone outside of Ethan at this school.

"I mean, you guys *are* dating, right? Or like . . . kind of seeing each other?"

My laugh is so sharp, it pierces through the now-emptying locker room. "Dating?" I manage. "Me and *Jack*?"

Pooja's expression doesn't change. "You guys are around each other, like, all the time."

"Yeah, because—" *Because we're destroying each other in a virtual battlefield armed with memes and snark.* "Because he's helping Ethan with captain stuff. You know how busy he is."

Pooja shrugs. "Okay." She adjusts her backpack straps, still staring at me in this way that lets me know she's not done talking. "I just . . . well. If you want to talk to someone about it, I'm probably your best bet, all things considered."

I let out a huff of a laugh before I can think better of it. Pooja's lips set in this grim line, like I've brought something out into the open, something we both know. Which is why I end up asking, "Wait, what do you mean?"

"Oh, please. Everyone knew about my big crush on Ethan two years ago."

"I didn't."

Pooja flushes. "Oh. Well. I made some very public declarations about it, which was pretty stupid of me, because he was out by then. You'd think I'd know him well enough to know that before I decided to have a massive crush on him, but . . ." She shrugs.

"Oh." It's all I can manage. I feel stupid for not having known, but then again, I guess I haven't exactly been a social butterfly these last few years.

Pooja waves a hand at me. "Water under the bridge. We're actually good friends now because of it."

"Well—that's good."

I don't know what else to say. It occurs to me that, Paige's antics with undergraduates aside, I've never really talked about crushes with anyone before. There hasn't been much to report on my end, and everyone else already had built-in friends to talk to about it with when I got here.

"Yeah. He's been using the student council to help me organize the study groups too."

When she says it, I can hear that same detached caution we usually use around each other starting to creep back in. It feels like there's some kind of gate starting to close back up again. At the last second, I shove a hand through to stop it.

"Those are going well?"

"Yeah, I think so," she says, brightening a bit. "It's sort of getting people to—I don't know. Band together. Us against them, instead of us against each other, you know?"

I do and I don't. "But—aren't we?" I feel stupid for asking, but it doesn't change the fact of college admissions. "Against each other?"

Pooja's lips crease. "See, I hate that. And I think it's making us all a little dumber, in the end. What's the point of learning if you're just doing it to beat someone, you know?"

I blink at her. Because that's the thing—that's kind of always been the point. At least, it has been since I moved here.

"I actually remember stuff we learn when we all meet up to study. So I think it's good. For grades, and for the long run." She opens her mouth and hovers for a moment, hesitating. "You know—Ethan was supposed to lead the calc study group on Tuesday, but he can't make it. And I know that's one of your best subjects, if you wanted to maybe . . . I mean, if you have time."

I open my mouth to dismiss the idea, but then I surprise us both. "Yeah. I'll check it out."

Pooja's smile is bright enough to compete with all of the fluorescent lights in the girls' locker room combined, and for an absurd moment, I almost want to tell her everything. The stupid Twitter war. The chats on Weazel. The way I haven't slept through a full night in so long that every now and then, I feel like I'm about to crack. It's stuff I can't talk about with Paige because it would just make her angry with Mom—and stuff I can't talk about with anyone else, because it feels like giving too much of myself away.

But Pooja just gave me a piece of her, whether she meant to or not. Maybe it really is that easy. Maybe I really can just talk to her, and not just to some faceless boy in an app.

"Pooja, your brother's waiting for you!"

I let the breath I was holding go, and Pooja waves and heads out of the locker room, taking my urge to spill everything with her.

Pepper

The dinner is nothing short of a disaster.

First off, Landon is a no-show. A bit after six o'clock, my mom ushers his father into the dining room, where I'm already waiting in my blue sweater set and a pair of khakis like a Stepford child. She raises an eyebrow at me. The displeased eyebrow. More specifically, the *I thought you told me your friend would be here* eyebrow.

I don't know what's worse—my mom's disappointment or the crush of embarrassment that immediately follows it. It's so quick and so searing, it feels like he stood me up on an actual date.

"Where's Landon tonight?" my mom asks, taking Mr. Rhodes's coat.

"Oh, you know. Homework. Swim team stuff," his father says.

I bite my tongue before I give in to the reflex to say I'm on the swim team too. My mom offers me the subtlest of nods as a thank-you. The last thing she wants to do is make him uncomfortable.

And maybe that would have been the end of the awkwardness, if my mom could just relax. She's saying all the right things—hyping up the universality of Big League Burger, citing comparable successes from companies that expanded overseas, talking about emerging markets in countries that haven't had a lot of chain expansions in them yet—but she cannot for the life of her stop checking her phone.

"Is something wrong?" Mr. Rhodes asks.

"Hmm? Sorry," says my mom, putting the phone down with a smile that's all teeth. "We're having a slight issue with the company's Twitter page."

"Oh?"

"We had a security breach. Our team is still trying to figure out how." My mom stabs at a piece of her parmesan roasted broccoli with more gusto than necessary.

I've been doing my best all night not to make eye contact with anyone and say the bare minimum required of me, so I can enjoy this fancy meal and start outlining my French essay in my head in peace. But even I'm not immune to the sudden shift in the room, to the way Mr. Rhodes's lips press into each other and his eyes briefly go to his plate.

"That's actually something I wanted to talk to you about—the Twitter account." He straightens up a bit, firm but apologetic at the same time. "You talk a lot about this being a family company, and I just don't see those values reflected in the company's social media presence."

The air in the room seems to come to a complete standstill. For some reason, my mom's eyes sweep over to me—like she needs me to toss her some kind of lifeline.

I look down at the table and refuse to look back up.

"Well—of course, of course, I understand your concerns." I can hear the slight edge in her voice. That nervous lilt I used to hear growing up when she had to talk to the landlord about rent being late that month, or prep herself in the mirror to talk to someone at the bank about business loans for Big League Burger with my dad. "But you know how it is with social media these days. The more of an impression you can make, the better for business."

"You aren't afraid the impression you're giving might alienate some of your customer base?"

As pissed as I am at Landon right now, I could hug the life out of his father for this.

Because as much as my mom refuses to believe it, this whole thing has been a bad PR move for us. Most of the replies to tweets sent by the account are still either cat emojis, people who are up in arms about the protection of small businesses, and straight up trolls. I was almost relieved when Girl Cheesing started to rack up tens of thousands of followers—at the very least it evened the playing field so we didn't look like total bullies.

I can tell my mom is trying to answer carefully. Despite everything, I wish, in that moment, there was something I could do to help her.

But it turns out, she can't even help herself. I'm expecting her to concede. To smile and tell Mr. Rhodes that rerouting the social media strategy is certainly a consideration she'd be willing to make, especially given what's at stake here. The idea of an international expansion is all she has talked about since she moved us to New York in the first place.

"If anything, I think it will make our brand even more recognizable overseas."

Mr. Rhodes smiles one of those smiles that doesn't reach his eyes. "Well. Maybe."

Whatever my mom was hoping would get set into motion tonight falls so flat, there is no mistaking it. I basically tune them out after that, all but running into my room and shutting the door as soon as my mom ushers Mr. Rhodes out. I brace myself, waiting for her to knock—we'll talk, maybe, and decide to drop the Twitter thing. And then we'll go into the kitchen and bake something, the way we used to when things didn't go our way. International Funding Rejection Pie. Something ridiculous, something that will make us both laugh.

But she doesn't knock. I hear the door to her room click shut, and that's the last I hear from her for the rest of the night.

I wish I could call Paige. But instead, I find myself opening the Weazel app, hovering over the chat between me and Wolf.

Bluebird

You know that whole thing about parents wanting stuff for you that you don't know if you want?

Bluebird

Well, I get it.

I set the phone down, not expecting an answer. Almost hoping I won't get one. I'm angry at Wolf for ghosting me, angry with Landon for standing me up, angry with myself for caring as much as I do.

Wolf

Yikes. Going full teenage angst on this glorious Friday night, huh?

I startle at the sound of the notification coming in. The relief is crippling, almost humiliating. Like I've been in solitary confinement and someone has finally poked their face in through the bars to say hello.

Bluebird

Let me guess. You're out drinking and partying with the rest of the reckless youth

It's not meant to sound passive-aggressive, but I suppose it does. I wonder what Landon is doing right now that was so much more important than sucking it up and coming over here for two hours. Maybe this way I can find out.

Wolf

Nah. Much dweebier than that. Mostly messing around on the computer

My throat is tight. So, not important at all.

Wolf

How about you? Getting wild and reenacting Gossip Girl plotlines?

Bluebird

Yeah, I'm blowing through my trust fund as we speak

Wolf

Anyway, sorry the 'rents are giving you trouble, birdie. What do they want?

It occurs to me, in that moment, I'm not even really sure *what* my mom wants for me. I know all the immediate things—come up with tweets. Get good grades. Get into a good school. But beyond that, I have no idea what she wants me to do.

Beyond that, I don't really have any idea what *I* want to do.

Bluebird
The usual, I guess

Bluebird
You've been busy, huh?

I think for a moment that'll scare him off again. That the texts will peter out the same way they did before, and we'll go back to the odd silence between us.

Wolf
Kind of, yeah

Wolf
But I've missed this

It's not quite *I missed you,* but it's close enough that just like that, the anger evaporates. Just like that, I forgive the murkiness of the last week with a kind of swiftness that should maybe alarm me. I don't care. It's nice to have someone in my corner again, even if that corner is one I can't see.

Bluebird
Yeah, me too

Bluebird
Even though you have not made a cupcake locating app yet, which to me is a clear sign of disrespect for the institution of dessert

Wolf

Shit. Am I gonna wake up tonight with Cookie Monster two inches from my face holding a knife?

Bluebird

Sleep with one eye open

Pepper

It turns out all of Mom's panicking is for nothing. Whoever hacked the Twitter account didn't do anything to it, and didn't bother trying to get in again over the weekend either. The tech team promises to keep an eye on it and try to trace the breach when they all get back into work on Monday.

I spend the weekend alternating between the homework I've neglected and battling Jack on Twitter. On Saturday morning he posts a tweet reading: finally tried BLB's "grilled cheese." video review below! with a link to a compilation of animals making scream noises in the wild that goes on for a full ten minutes.

"Have you noticed that the BLB Twitter page is off its rocker lately?" Paige asks when I finally manage to call her on Sunday morning. "It looks like they're in some kind of tiff with a deli?"

I wince. "Yeah . . . I guess it's all . . . part of the strategy, or whatever."

"I can't believe Mom hasn't shut that the hell down. Even Dad's noticed. He called me all stressed out about it."

I talked to our dad just the other day, and he didn't mention it to me. I think he must know I've been recruited into this Twitter madness. He's pretty quiet, but not a lot gets past him either. Especially not when it comes to Mom.

"I mean, do we even know these people?"

Yes. A little too well. So well that I can, all too easily, picture the exact tilt of the smirk on Jack's face when he posted the screaming tweet.

"I dunno." I make a quick move to change the subject. "Wanna explain the Fuck Your Midterms Meringue recipe you just put on the blog, or . . ."

Paige laughs. "Buckle up, kid, cuz you're about to get an *earful* about my Greek History professor."

After I get off the phone with Paige, Mom and I go down to Bloomingdale's to look at couches for the new corporate office expansion, which is renting out another floor in their Midtown building. We stop for lunch at a little café, and we talk about school and all the clothes I'm going to wear when I get to college and don't have to wear a uniform and Taffy's new puppy, which she has been Instagramming so enthusiastically, I feel like I'm half raising it with her.

Nobody mentions Twitter, or college apps, or the veritable disaster of Friday night. The day ends with a shine already on the memory of it. It reminds me of the way Mom would, once a year, let me and Paige play hooky from school—she'd drive us all the way there and then just pass the school and keep driving, and we'd get pancakes at IHOP or take pictures on the bridge or drive into Belle Meade and stare at all the mansions. A stolen day. The kind of day that ends too fast but stays with you much longer.

I should have known the universe would find some way to balance it out.

Jack is particularly smirky during Monday's practice, for reasons beyond me—he has yet to respond to the latest volley in our tweets, so the ball is in his court.

"Seemed a little quiet on Friday night," he says, as the swim team is getting out of the pool to give up the lanes for the divers. "Fall asleep on the job?"

And then the meaning of the smirk becomes all too clear. "Did you . . ."

Jack tilts his head at me. "Did I what?"

Landon calls over to me to help pull out the stretch bands for dry land exercises, and before I can turn back around, Jack has already jumped into the water and started swimming away. I go through the next twenty minutes trying to decide just how angry I'm going to get about this, or if I'm really even allowed to get angry at all. We said we wouldn't let it be personal. We said we wouldn't hold back.

But nobody said anything about *hacking into a corporate-run Twitter account.*

I guess he didn't really do anything, though. In the grand scheme of things, he just minorly inconvenienced the tech team on a Friday night.

Or at least, that's all I think he's done, until I get into the locker room and see five missed calls and a voicemail from my mom.

"So the tech team finished their little investigation. Turns out whoever changed the password on the account did it from *your phone.*"

I freeze, the phone poised on my ear, my blood running cold. That's impossible. If someone were going to access the account from my phone, they'd have to know my passcode first. And nobody would know that, unless—

I'm going to kill him. I'm going to *maim* him.

"Call me as soon as you get this, and come straight home after practice. We need to talk."

I set the phone down and just stand there. Jack has jokingly called me a robot more times in the last few years than I can count, but in that moment, I genuinely feel like I'm short-circuiting. There is too much of me happening all at once, and my body doesn't know what to settle on—the anger at Jack, the indignation at my mom, the fact I've been juggling so much in the past few weeks that I'm tired enough to sleep on the floor of the locker room with everyone gossiping and changing over my head.

Naturally, it eventually settles on the least convenient option, which is to burst into tears.

I feel someone's hands on my shoulders pulling me away from the lockers, and only vaguely process they belong to Pooja, who manages to pull me over to the handicap bathroom stall and lock the door on us before the snot starts flying. I have the blessing and curse of being the kind of person who only cries twice a year, so naturally, when it happens, it happens in the most volcanic, disgusting way possible—red eyes, gushing nose, splotchy face, and all.

I manage to pull myself together after a minute or so, and blink at Pooja, who's leaning against the plastic wall on the other side of the stall.

"Thanks," I say, my voice clogged with snot.

She unrolls some toilet paper, bunches it up, and hands it to me. "You wanna talk about it?"

I shake my head, but in that same moment I take this ridiculous, hiccupping breath, and *whoosh.* It's not just the snot floodgates that are open, but the verbal ones too. Before I even realize what I'm doing, I'm telling her everything—about tweeting for Big League Burger, about Jack and Girl Cheesing, about my mom breathing down my neck and about me being stupid enough to tell a teenage boy my phone's terrible passcode and not immediately change it.

For a few moments, all Pooja can do is blink at me.

"Okay, first of all, this is possibly the weirdest thing I've ever heard. And we live in New York City, so that's saying something."

I let out a wet laugh.

"And second of all . . . well. I don't really know anything about sending good tweets or what exactly the extent of this bizarrely flirtatious war between you and Jack is."

"It's not—nobody's flirting—"

"But," says Pooja, pointedly ignoring my protests, "I *can* think of a way to get Jack back."

Pooja may think the whole Twitter thing is weird, but to me, it doesn't quite get any weirder than this—Pooja extending an olive branch, after four years of being just short of an archnemesis. I should be suspicious of this, maybe, but that's the thing—despite never actually being her friend, I know Pooja. Alarmingly well, in fact. I know her motivations, know the exact expression she makes when she is calculating a next move, know her weaknesses and strengths almost as well as I know my own. The same way I know, for whatever reason, she is being sincere right now.

Plus, it means getting payback.

"I'm listening."

Jack

I should know something is out of order with the universe the moment I see Pooja and Pepper huddled by her locker Tuesday morning. It is a known and established fact at Stone Hall that the two of them are neck and neck in just about everything; there are battle scenes between Gamora and Nebula in *Guardians of the Galaxy* less brutal than their ongoing competition with each other.

But I figure, in the way all unsuspecting idiots do, that it has nothing to do with me. The same way I figure, the way all unsuspecting idiots do, that I've gotten away with something, when in fact it's about to go terribly wrong.

Enter: one very skittish-looking Paul. Emphasis on skittish, because Paul is already baseline about as nervous as a chihuahua at any given time. He walks into homeroom and slides into the desk next to mine, leaning in close and talking out of the corner of his mouth.

"Is it you?" he asks.

"You're gonna have to be more specific."

He glances up at the front to make sure Mrs. Fairchild is still absorbed in the Fiber One bar she's consuming, then slides his phone screen over to me. I skim the text, my stomach dropping a little more with each line of the email.

Dear eager beavers of Stone Hall,

After an investigation into the "Weasel" app, it has come to the attention of the school that its creator has limited access to the app to student email addresses at Stone Hall, and that the app originated under one of those addresses. We have concluded that the creator and distributor of this app is a student. I urge anybody with information about the app's origins to come forward, so we may have a reasonable discussion with that person about next steps.

Vice Principal Rucker

"It's not *dangerous*," I say through my teeth. "That's bullshit. Literally last week a whole bunch of people made plans in the Hallway Chat to put all those nice Post-it notes on people's lockers. What the hell?"

"So . . . it was you?"

I unclench my jaw. Paul's eyes are wide, as if he has just become the unwitting accomplice to murder.

"What makes you say that?" I ask carefully.

"Uh, the ten other work-in-progress apps you've talked about on and off for the last few years?"

Well, he's got me there. Paul is one of the very few people who even knows I've been messing around with app development—mostly because at some point or another, Paul has been the reason for them. I once made an app whose sole purpose was to send him a random GIF of someone sneezing every time the pollen count hit a certain threshold, so he'd remember to take his allergy meds before class.

"Look, man, it's not like I'm gonna rat you out." There is something close to a whine in the back of his throat, the way it was when we were kids and he suspected he was getting left out of something (which, to be fair, he usually was). "You can tell me."

It's not that I don't trust Paul. It's just that I don't want *anyone* knowing. The whole magic of the app is its anonymity, the safe space it's created to just *be.* In a way, if I tell Paul I made it, I'm taking that away from him too.

But then enough seconds pass and Paul starts to deflate, looking even more like a kicked puppy than usual.

"Fine. Okay. I made it."

"I *knew* it!"

"For all of a few minutes, yeah," I grumble, making note of the time stamp on the email.

"This is *so cool*, Jack."

"Keep your voice down," I remind him, shooting a cautionary glance around the room. "Nobody knows about this."

"Not even Ethan?"

I barely suppress an eye roll. "Especially not Ethan."

Paul sits in his chair for a moment with his eyes all glassy, like he's absorbing something too profound for his brain to accept. "*Wow.* You're basically like—the secret god of Stone Hall."

My face goes hot. "I just made some stupid app. All I do is make sure people aren't being dicks."

"Do you talk to people on it?" Paul asks. "Do you control when people get outed to each other? Do you know everyone's aliases?"

"No, no, and absolutely not."

Well, that's a lie and a half, but I'm sticking to it. I don't want him fishing around the aliases in the Hallway Chat and trying to guess which one is me. Or worse—ask me to out someone else.

"Oh, come on. You can't check?"

And whoop, there it is. "No," I say, firmly enough that Paul flinches a little bit. I try to relax, try to level with him so he'll get it. "It's—that's the whole point of it. You know? Everyone's anonymous. Everyone can feel comfortable. So no, I don't check. I don't even know if my own twin is on it."

Paul considers this. "Shit. That's hardcore."

I shift uncomfortably in my seat. "Yeah. I guess it is."

The warning bell rings, and in comes Pepper. If I'm expecting any kind of reference to my handiwork on Friday, she makes it immediately clear I'm going to be disappointed. She lifts her hand and wiggles her fingers to wave at me, with a sly expression on her face. I know her well enough by now to properly dread whatever is on the other end of it.

But the rest of the day is eerily quiet. The only tweets that come out of the Big League Burger account are about a charity they partnered with and a stop-motion GIF of a hamburger doing a little dance. The only other notifications on my phone are from Bluebird, making some crack about the pattern of birds embroidered on Rucker's pants today.

It's a relief, having her back, just as much as it was a relief not to be talking to her.

I know at some point or another I'm going to have to come clean. We can't exist in the bubble of Weazel forever. But for now—for now, it's nice to have someone who isn't tied up in the rest of the mess that is my life. Someone who isn't either waiting for me to tweet or ready to jump the second I do. Someone who doesn't think of me as Ethan's brother before they think of me for *me*.

It's different, in a way, now that someone knows. Maybe even more traitorous, now that I've told Paul and not the person I've been talking to on it for months now. It also takes away my coward's way out—just triggering the app to reveal ourselves to each other, and never telling her I was the one who created the app. Now Paul knows. And the only thing bigger than Paul's heart is his mouth.

Maybe it was meant to happen like this all along. Maybe there was no scenario where I didn't get in trouble for it. Maybe this is just one of a slew of countless things I have managed to sabotage right from the get-go—only this time, I can't even blame the Ethan-shaped chip on my shoulder. I did this all on my own.

It's weird, the way the guilt of it follows me around, but doesn't quite hit me. I still haven't done a good job of narrowing her down. Presumably she is not lactose intolerant and isn't absent today. She seems not to come from a super wealthy family either, but it's hard to tell who falls into that category anyway since we all wear the same school uniforms. Maybe if I were on Instagram, I could rule the richer kids out, but it seems creepy to obsess too much.

So instead, I just walk around feeling vaguely apologetic at every girl I pass in the hallway, making way more eye contact than I intend to, until the female half of the school probably thinks I need glasses.

Pepper, on the other hand, doesn't even acknowledge me on the pool deck, but the ghost of that smirk of hers seems to be on her face whenever I'm within ten feet of her. It isn't until I'm walking out of the locker room after practice that I know why.

"Dude. I thought you said you were on top of this."

I scowl at Ethan, who has shoved a screen with the Big League Burger Twitter page so close to my nose, he nearly squashes it.

"Who says I'm not?" I ask. "Besides, shouldn't you be frenching on some concrete steps about now?"

"I would be if it weren't for *this.*"

I sigh, taking the phone from Ethan's hand. "What could possibly be so—"

Oh. As it turns out, it's not Big League Burger's page I'm looking at. It's Big League Burger's branding on the header image, and a picture of Big League Burger's "Grandma's Special" on the profile avatar, but it is very much the Girl Cheesing Twitter handle. Well, what's left of it—the name on the page has been changed to #1 BLB Stan.

"*Pepper.*"

"You better fix this before Dad sees."

My fingers clench around his phone. "It's not like we're locked out of the account. You could have just fixed it yourself."

"This is *your* job, remember? I'm not supposed to touch the precious account without your permission."

And then, just like that, a table I never thought was capable of turning has shifted. Ethan's not angry because of Pepper's little prank. Ethan's *been* angry.

It should probably strike some sort of empathetic chord in me, but it doesn't. For seventeen years now, I have stepped to the side for him and never once made him feel bad about it. I can't believe he won't do the same for me over something this stupid.

"What's your problem?"

Ethan's nostrils flare. "I don't have a problem," he says, with an edge that says he very much does.

The irritation surges up in me like a live wire, like something I have spent too much time trying not to ignite. "You're really this pissed off because for once Mom and Dad are counting on me for something instead of you?"

That stuns the anger right out of him. His mouth drops open. "Are you kidding?"

There are people walking past us. Classmates, probably. But if Ethan isn't going to budge, then neither am I. "You can't stand it, can you? That for once, you're not the *golden child*."

Only after I say it do I realize I've been waiting to say it—not just since this whole Twitter thing started, but for years. Years of Ethan and his academic awards and his student government nominations and being surrounded by friends on all sides, years that pushed the two of us to where we are now: Ethan, poised to leave the nest, and me, tethered to it with a rope.

Especially because this Twitter war ultimately means the same thing it always has: my parents still have way more faith in Ethan than in me. The only reason I'm the one running the account is because we all know I'm the kid who's going to get left with the deli while Ethan takes over the world.

But then his anger is right back, twisting into something ugly in his face, something more immediate and deeper than I ever expected. "You think *I'm* the golden child?"

I don't think he is, I know he is. I open my mouth, but suddenly my throat is too tight to say any of it—all the things that have been brimming under the surface are all coming up at once, fighting each other on the way out.

In my head I've had this conversation with Ethan a thousand times. In my head I've been angry, indignant, and firm. In my head I've rehearsed it so many times that I should be more prepared to defend myself than I have for anything in my life.

But of all the things imaginary Ethan said to me, it was never that. And of all the times imaginary Jack confronted him, I never felt as conflicted as I do right now.

In the end, I swallow it all down. I don't understand the look on his face, and I don't want to. My own hurt is too much to take on his too. So I hand him back his phone, with a little more force than necessary. "Don't worry about it. It's under control."

Ethan lets out a snort and stays rooted to the sidewalk, looking at me like he's waiting for one of us to take one last shot. After a moment we both turn away at the same time, with identical scowls, stalking off in opposite directions. But I'm still seeing his twisted expression long after he walks away—not just because I've never seen it on his face like that before, but because I think I saw more of myself in it than I ever have.

Jack

I assume I won't get to see Pepper gloating about her handiwork until tomorrow morning, but when I walk out of the community center, there she is, leaning against the wall and oh-so-casually drinking from an enormous Big League Milkshake Mash. She turns her head so slowly to look at me that for a moment I am stricken with the weird unfamiliarity of being seen—no, not seen. Recognized. It's rare enough someone knows I'm me and not Ethan without getting a good look at me. It's straight up *weird* when someone can tell without fully turning around. The only person I know who can do that is Grandma Belly—my parents still mix us up so frequently that there's about a 50 percent chance I *am* Ethan, and someone switched us along the way.

In any case, her swivel of a stare hits its mark with an impressive landing, her eyebrows raised just so and the straw still puckered between her lips. The effect of it is absurd enough that it pierces through my bubble of self-pity.

"Did you—did you *sprint* to the Big League Burger on Eighty-Eighth and come back, just so you could wait for me here with that?"

She answers by lifting her other hand, which has another massive milkshake in it. "Cookies and cream?"

I'm starving, but I have principles. "How'd you do it, Pepperoni?"

She takes a noisy slurp of her shake. "Do what?"

I walk over and lean on the wall next to her, kicking my foot onto the brick with the same faux-casual pose. "You know what."

She presses the milkshake into my hand, and I take it on reflex. "Same way you did."

"You took my phone."

That wipes the smug look off her face. "So you *did* steal mine."

"Uh—wait, what? No."

Pepper narrows her eyes at me.

"For like, a second," I concede.

I didn't know it was possible for someone to angrily sip a milkshake, but then again, making the impossible possible is kind of Pepper's MO. "What the *hell*, Campbell?"

It would be easier to take her seriously if there weren't ice cream on her upper lip. My hand flinches just before I realize I'm lifting it like I'm going to wipe it away or something.

"That's crossing a line. I wouldn't go into your phone."

If we're talking about line-crossing, I could argue that she had me squarely beat on that the moment Big League Burger ripped off my grandmother. But she had nothing to do with that. I may not have fully believed her two weeks ago, but I do now.

"Sorry."

She lifts her eyebrows in surprise, then sucks on the inside of her cheek and stares out at the traffic like she's trying to decide whether or not to accept the apology. "Well, I get it. It's hard keeping up with me. You clearly needed the break."

I let out a huff of a laugh, my chest untightening. "Please. I'm tweeting circles around you."

"Then why don't we up the stakes?"

"What, you want this war to bleed into Instagram?"

Pepper snorts. "Please. I have no interest in embarrassing you *that* thoroughly."

"Embarrassing me, huh?"

Somehow in this back-and-forth snark we've gravitated so close to each other that my shoulder is grazing hers. Her eyes flicker to it for a moment, but neither of us moves.

"My staged food pictures put Martha Stewart to shame."

"Yeah? Well, people are too busy actually *eating* our food to 'gram it, so."

She responds with another slow slurp of milkshake, not breaking eye contact.

"Okay, fine. How do we up the stakes?"

I hear the smirk in her voice before it fully curls on her face. "Sudden death. Retweet war. We both tweet pictures of our grilled cheeses at the same time, and whoever has more retweets by the end of the week wins."

I'm dismissing this before she even finishes the sentence. "You have way more followers than we do."

"And you have way more engagement per follower than we do," says Pepper, with the bored air of someone who is anticipating this argument, of someone who has done their research and then some. "But I have a solution. We get a neutral third party involved."

"Is there anyone in the world who doesn't have an opinion on our grilled cheeses right now?"

"Unlikely. Which is why I think we should approach an outlet. Isn't one of the cofounders of Hub Seed a Stone Hall alum?"

"You think you can get the *Hub* involved in this?"

Pepper shrugs. "They've already reached out to Taffy about writing an article on the Twitter spat between the brands. I'm guessing if your parents have checked the deli's email lately, they've gotten one too."

It's a true testament to how deep we've sunk into this that I not only know who Taffy is, but that she and her dog have been popping into my "suggest following" so much on Twitter, I know which sparkly outfit she dressed Snuffles in yesterday.

"So . . . what? We ask them to tweet images of both of our grilled cheeses?"

She nods. But she's dreaming. The Hub might be interested in our shenanigans for a quick one-off story, but they've got over five million followers on Twitter. That's the kind of social media real estate you don't waste on two teens in a grilled cheese fight.

"I'll propose it to them over email. They'll send a tweet explaining the stakes and tweet two pictures: yours and mine." She pauses for a moment, raising her brows. "And to really make it fair—we'll ask them not to say which grilled cheese is which."

"Won't it be obvious when yours looks like flash-frozen garbage someone stuck in the microwave?"

Pepper doesn't bat an eye. "So, are you in or what?"

I slump back farther on the wall, making myself her height so our eyes are level. Up this close, I can see the faint spray of freckles on her nose that must be more visible in the summer.

"Depends. What happens if I win?"

As usual, Pepper is all too prepared with an answer. "Loser

concedes to the other from their account. A humble tweet of acknowledgment, once the people have spoken."

"You seem eerily confident for someone who's about to go down."

"So you're game?"

I consider her for a moment, with her tangled, wet bangs fringing her face and her eyes so steady on mine, and suddenly I can't resist.

"Let's sweeten the deal."

"What are you thinking?"

"If you lose, you have to jump off the high dive."

I'm expecting Pepper to freeze, or at least have a reaction half as visceral as the last time I brought up that little incident in freshman year when she scrambled off the high dive so fast her butt might have been on fire. Instead, she doesn't break eye contact with me for even a millisecond as she gives me a nonchalant shrug.

"Fine."

"Fine?"

"But if you lose, you have to do that hundred-yard butterfly you skipped out on the other day." She pauses. "*And* give back the dive team's time in the lanes."

The idea of losing with Grandma Belly's grilled cheese on full display is so unfathomable I don't even hesitate. "You've got yourself a deal."

This time, I'm the one who extends my hand out to shake. Pepper smirks, and when she takes it, she squeezes my fingers hard enough I'm half expecting them to be stuck together when she pulls away. Instead, there's this strange tingle, like we've forged something, made a pact in this second with more weight to it than anything we could put on paper.

Then suddenly she's laughing at me. I don't even realize it's because I've started drinking her stupid milkshake until something unfamiliar hits my tongue.

"This isn't cookies and cream. You did something to this."

Pepper takes another slurp of hers. "Salted caramel sauce," she says.

I take another sip against my will, which has apparently disintegrated in the few seconds between the first sip and right now. *Jesus*, this is good. It feels like my taste buds just woke up from a long nap.

"That's not even on the BLB menu," I protest. I would know—I've been researching it with an absurd amount of dedication, to find things to mock on Twitter when the time is right.

The look she shoots me is patronizing. "I carry my own."

"You *what*?"

She kicks herself off the wall and starts walking away.

"Get the picture sent to me by tomorrow night."

"You can't just casually tell someone you carry caramel sauce around and walk away like that's a normal thing," I call at her retreating back. "What *other* emergency dessert condiments do you have stashed in your bag?"

She deigns briefly to look over her shoulder at me. "Tomorrow night!"

I'm shaking my head and laughing as I head down the street in the opposite direction, still feeling the ghost of the smirk she aimed in my direction like it's something I've accidentally carried with me. It's not until the 6 train finally rolls up to collect me a few minutes later that I realize I've not only forgotten to restore the Girl Cheesing Twitter account back from its newly hacked glory, but that somehow my stomach has committed a crime against nature and managed to devour an entire sixteen-ounce Big League Milkshake Mash, possibly without even pausing to breathe.

I toss it into a trash can with a sigh. Twitter, I can deal with. Pepper, on the other hand, has a way of sneaking up on me I'm not so sure about.

I pull out my phone again, stricken with this not entirely unwelcome urge to text her, to keep the banter volleying back and forth in that easy rhythm it always does. But I have to remind myself that Pepper is still the enemy, insanely flavored milkshakes and memorable smirks and lingering handshakes aside.

And I've got a Twitter war to win.

Pepper

By Saturday, everything is back in order, and so am I. My uniform is perfectly pressed, my college admissions essay polished, my tweets queued for the weekend. Pooja's brother's handiwork hacking into Girl Cheesing's Twitter has been undone. The photos of both grilled cheeses have been sent to Hub Seed, and both will be sent from their main Twitter account today at two o'clock.

Which happens to be the exact time I will be settling into my chair for my first college admissions interview with a Columbia alum named Helen.

"You look nervous, Pepperoni."

I cut a side glance when I hear Jack approach, determined not to look at him. It's weird enough, seeing him on a Saturday. But even in the side glance, something seems off—he's standing up a little straighter, wearing his school uniform with a little more care. Even his usually unruly hair seems to have been tamed to some degree, looking very much like some well-meaning parent ran a comb through it. I can't help but look him up and down because it's uncanny how much he looks like Ethan.

He catches me looking, and I brace myself for the snarky remark that's sure to follow. But instead, his cheeks redden like he's more embarrassed to be looked at than I am to be caught looking.

I clear my throat, shifting my weight onto my other foot. "For a college admissions interview? Please. I could do these in my sleep."

Jack stretches one of those wide, tall boy stretches, looking more like himself again. He loosens the tie on his school uniform and stares down the hallway at the rooms where other students are coming and going.

"Well, your resume is longer than a CVS receipt, so I don't doubt it."

"Did you just get out of yours?"

"Yeah. I'm all set. Headed straight for the Ivies." His eyes cast off to the side, and there's this edge to his voice that doesn't match his words. Before I can ask, he blows out a breath and says, "So, who are you meeting with? Yale? Harvard?"

He says their names with a faint mockery, emphasizing it with a click of his heel. I wonder what his deal is. He goes to this school too, and he's clearly interviewing—it's not like he isn't every bit a part of this.

"Columbia."

Some of the bravado seems to leak out of Jack's expression.

"What?" I ask, off his look.

He hesitates for a moment. "You know Columbia's interviews are on their campus, right?"

My blood turns into ice. "What?"

And then, suddenly, it makes sense: why I don't see Pooja or the other Columbia hopefuls here. Why there isn't a sign-in for the Columbia rep yet. I just assumed it was because I was here absurdly early, the way I always am. It didn't once occur to me it was because I'm an *idiot*.

How could I have let this happen? Instead of doing anything productive that might help the situation, my feet are rooted to the floor, my brain pressing back and back and back, into the haze of the last few weeks. The homework that barely got finished before sunup. The endless texts from Mom and Taffy. The color-coded pages of my planner looking like someone puked a rainbow onto it. And somehow, despite every precaution, I let one of the most important things fall through the cracks.

Oh my god. I've been so wrapped up in tweeting I might have just blown my chances at *college*.

Jack's hand is on my shoulder. I don't know how long it's been there, because suddenly he is very close to my face.

"What time is your interview?"

"Two."

"Okay. It's one-thirty. You should still be able to get a taxi."

It feels like the space between my ears is roaring. "I don't have my wallet." The interview was only a few blocks away from home; I didn't think I'd need it. And now if I go back, my mom will *know* I screwed up, she'll see it all over my face, and then she'll be disappointed, and I think I'll maybe just snap. I think I'll maybe come completely unglued. It's all bubbling to the surface all at once, the last few weeks of doing her Twitter bidding, the last few years of this stupid city and this stupid *school* and this interview for a college I don't even know if I want to go to—

Jack is pressing something into my palm. A MetroCard. "It's a spare. You can give it back on Monday."

I'm still shaking my head, half of me here and half of me in the living room, where this imaginary fight is happening with my mom.

"I can't believe I screwed this up."

"Pepper, it's fine. Just take the M4."

"The what?"

"The bus."

And then, senseless with the kind of panic only academia can incite, I am blurting for the entire hallway to hear, "I've never taken the bus in New York."

Jack opens his mouth like he's going to make a remark, but then thinks better of it. "Okay. That's—well, this one's easy. The stop's like two blocks from here, and it's a straight shot to the main campus, thirty minutes tops."

I open my mouth, but nothing comes out.

"What?" Jack asks. Not unkindly, not impatiently. Which is why, before I make a conscious decision to, I'm admitting the second, far more embarrassing truth.

"I've never left the Upper East Side by myself."

Jack laughs, the way you laugh at a friend who just rolled off a good one-liner. A beat passes. I can't even make my face move.

"Oh. You're serious?"

The word comes out in a croak. "Yeah."

Jack yanks his sleeve up and checks his watch again, seeming to weigh something he decides on a moment later, when his eyes lift and immediately meet mine.

"Okay. Let's go."

He starts walking down the hallway to the front exit of the school, his legs so long, I have to scramble to catch up.

"Wait, you're—you're coming?"

"Yeah. But you owe me."

I'm too relieved to protest.

"No more tweeting on Sundays," he says. "We both lay down our keyboards for a full twenty-four hours. Those are my terms."

"Done."

I wait for him to list off whatever the rest of the terms are, but that seems to be the extent of them. A few moments and some extreme power walking later we're on Madison Avenue, Jack cutting the corner before I do and yelling, "Run!"

I take off just behind him, my hair whipping out of its perfectly coiffed ponytail, the Oxford shoes my mom bought for the occasion scuffing on the pavement. He barely reaches the bus as the doors shut, banging a hand on the glass with that endearing, sheepish Jack grin, just as I skid to a stop and half stumble into him from behind.

"Sorry, *sorry*," I blubber at his back, nearly tripping as I try to pull myself off him.

Either because of Jack's awkward charm or because the two of us make quite the pathetic pair, the bus driver rolls her eyes and opens the door. We're still stumbling as we pile on, trying and failing not to crash into each other as the bus starts back up again, until Jack practically falls half into my lap when we finally find two spare seats.

He opens his mouth to apologize, but before he can, I start to laugh.

"Oh, god," says Jack, leaning back into his seat and taking a quick glance to survey the other passengers on the bus. "Is this it? Did you finally crack under the pressure?"

"I just—oh, man." I'm so out of breath from running, I'm on the verge of wheezing. "I remember one time—in Nashville—my sister and I were running, and we beat my mom to the bus, and it just . . . took off. Without her. We were like, five and eight, probably."

Jack's eyebrows knit like he's not sure whether or not he should laugh too. "That sounds . . . hilarious?"

I'm remembering that day so vividly, it feels like I've restored some color to it, like I'm living it more fully now than I even was then.

"She had to chase the bus for like a mile in her sandals. We were such little assholes. We didn't even look out the window—we were already planning our new lives like we were orphans in a book series or something."

"Were you going to live in a boxcar?"

"Nah. We were going to bake. Paige was really big on wanting to grow up to be a baker then. Open up her own place right next to Big League Burger. I think it was gonna be called Paige's Pancakes. Clearly the branding needed some work."

"Where is your sister?"

I blink, and suddenly I'm back on a bus on a street lined with buildings and traffic and too many people.

"UPenn."

Jack's eyes are teasing. "How come she's not fighting me on Twitter?"

I raise my eyebrows at him. "How come Ethan isn't fighting me on Twitter?"

The smile falters on his face for just a split second. "Touché." He leans even farther back in his seat, stretching out his legs once a few people get off at the stop. "And because he kind of sucks at it. That was him on day two, you know. He tweets like he's out for blood."

"And you go easy on me, is that it?"

He knocks his shoulder into mine. "Hell no. I just don't make the company look bad." He turns his head to look at me, his eyes disarmingly close. "I take it your sister didn't inherit the Evans family snark?"

"No, no, she did." My cheeks are hot. I turn my head to the window, toward the cool air of the street. "She and my mom are sort of—well, I don't know."

Jack is uncharacteristically still, like he's waiting. Like he thinks there's more I'm going to say. And then, just like that, there is.

"After the divorce she came here with us for a while—before she headed off to school, I mean. And she and my mom had a falling out."

"'Falling out,'" Jack repeats, like he's testing how it sounds. "That's like something someone would say in a soap opera."

I shrug. "Yeah. I don't know what else to call it. I didn't think it would last this long. I mean, I thought it was just delayed teenage rebellion or something. But then it stuck."

"And your dad?"

"He's still in Nashville. We go visit him on breaks." I can tell he wants to ask, or maybe it's just I want to explain—why he isn't here, when my mom and I are. "I think he never quite got used to the idea of Big League Burger not being his baby anymore. So he stayed home."

Home. Only after I've told the whole truth of it does it feel like I've put too much in the air, like it just slid out of me and into this bigger, scarier space where Jack can see it, and I can see it too. That I don't belong here. That even after all this time and everything I've done, the things I've pressed and organized and pushed into myself to fit into this place, *home* is still somewhere a thousand miles away.

Farther than that, even. Because that version of home doesn't exist anymore.

Jack points out the window, and I follow his finger to yet another Big League Burger location we happen to be passing.

I'm so relieved to have something else to focus on that my

voice comes out too loud, too fast. "See? That's weird! There used to just be the one, and now we're everywhere."

Jack tears his eyes away from it to look back at me. "Do they all know who you are? Are you the Burger Princess of the Upper East Side?"

This time I'm the one who ribs him, with an elbow into his side. "Yeah. They all have to curtsy when I walk in."

Jack does an exaggerated bow with his chin, never breaking his gaze. I roll my eyes.

"Actually, nah, it's weird. I know everyone at the corporate office, but not any of the people in the actual restaurants." I'm nervous. That must be it. I'm nervous and I can't shut up, and Jack is just sitting there and *letting* me not shut up. "Which is just sort of wild, since I watched the first one get built and basically grew up in it. Everybody knew everybody."

"Yeah. That's how it is down at our place."

The unwelcome ache is back again, but now, I think, I'm starting to understand the root of it.

"It must be nice—growing up here, I mean. Staying in one place. Knowing everyone."

Jack doesn't do that teenage boy thing where he shrugs it off. Instead, he seems to come to life even more, with an openness I usually only see in him from a distance, talking to Paul or goofing around with other kids on the dive team. He leans forward in his seat, his eyes conspiratorial when he answers, like he's sharing something special.

"Yeah. It's cool. We have a bunch of regulars. Some old ladies who all make me call them 'Aunt,' so I don't even know their real names. Some NYU professors, a bridge club, one of those run-and-chug running clubs that mostly runs a mile around the neighborhood so they can all get drunk after. Everybody knows everybody. I was practically raised on that deli floor." He laughs a little ruefully, scratching the back of his neck. "Can't get away with shit."

"You're an identical twin. You can't just tell them Ethan did it?"

"Nah. Ethan's too smart to get caught. Or maybe just too popular." He deflates almost imperceptibly, blowing out a breath. "Which still does nothing to stop our classmates from mixing us up after twelve solid years."

I peer into his face—the distinctive way his brow furrows, the unruliness of his hair already out of the confines of the style someone put it in, the way he seems to just fit in anywhere he goes with an understated kind of ease. He objectively is Ethan's match in every way except for minor ones, but in my head they're practically different species.

"I don't get it. You two couldn't be more different."

Jack snorts. "Yeah. Thanks."

"What?"

Jack extends his arms out to some invisible audience, his voice taking on a completely different pitch. "'You're nothing like your ridiculously popular, wildly successful brother everyone fawns over and adores.'"

"Whoa. That's not what I meant." My irritation at being misunderstood is instantly dampened by this *look* seared across his face, one he can't hide because there's really nowhere to hide it. Being on a bus is kind of like being on a stage. "Hey. I didn't mean it like that. I meant—you guys are in your own worlds, you know?"

Jack nods. "Sorry. Just feels like—it's dumb, but it just feels like everyone likes him better, you know?"

I wait for a second for a punchline, for him to soften it with something else. An excruciating few seconds pass, and then it's all too clear he won't.

"Well, for what it's worth, I don't." And then, because the tips of his ears are suddenly visibly red, I add, "I mean, you're both pains in my ass, so it's really not worth *much* . . ."

"Aha," Jack deadpans. The *look* is gone, replaced by the half grin. "I think you like me."

I cross my arms over my chest. "I just said as much, jerk."

"I think we're even *friends*."

I'm about to shoot another well-aimed crack at him, but it stops halfway up my throat. "Thanks for doing this," I say instead.

The half grin softens. Jack rubs a hand on the back of his neck. "Yeah, well. The longer you're knocking someone's socks off in that interview, the more time I have to undermine you on Twitter, so—win-win."

My smile only falters for a second, only because for the first time in weeks, I forgot about the Twitter war altogether. The moment feels like a stolen one, until it isn't. Jack leans back and so do I, and the moment goes on for just long enough that I almost wish I could stay here instead of having to face what's on the other side of our stop.

Pepper

We make it to Columbia with a truly miraculous two minutes to spare. Jack knows exactly where to go, sprinting up ahead of me so I'm clunking behind him in my too-tight shoes, eventually admitting off my confused look he'd done a round of interviews with Columbia the week before.

"*What?*" I wheeze. "And you're only just telling me *now*?"

"It's not like I'm going to get in. What's there to tell?"

"Everything they asked you in the interview!"

Jack gives me a quizzical look. "Well, that's easy," he says. "Brag about your grades and just tell them what you want to do. What you're passionate about. That's it."

I open my mouth. Shut it again.

"Books. Wrecking grade curves. Tweeting mean memes," Jack supplies for me.

"Right."

Jack tilts his head to the side, his eyes searching my face before creasing into a frown. "These are the Ivy Leagues, Pepperoni. If you don't know what you want to do, you'd better at least come up with a decent lie."

"Patricia Evans?"

My ears perk at the sound of my full name, which I only ever hear once in a blue moon. It's the interview coordinator, who has just stepped back into the lobby and, by the grace of whatever gods are in charge of college admissions, did not just see me sprint in here like a total doofus.

That small mercy was *not*, apparently, extended to Jack's mockery.

"Patricia?"

I lean in close to him while the coordinator's still out of earshot. "Utter that name one more time and you're dead meat, Campbell."

The grin is slower and softer than I've ever seen it, and this time more than a half. He nods at me, somehow both impetuous and sweet at the same time, and says my name the way I've never heard it before: "*Patricia.*"

My heart stutters under his eyes, cuts me off before I can even think of something to retort.

Then Jack's eyes go wide and he gestures down the hall, where the coordinator has already taken off. "Go!"

I hustle down the hallway, feeling like there's a strange aftertaste in my mouth. *At least come up with a decent lie.* It was the most helpful thing he could have said to me walking into this, because of all the things I've prepared and overprepared for to the point of exhaustion in the last four years of trying to keep up with the madness of this school, I have no idea what I'm going to say.

And more to the point, I have no idea what I want to do.

It shouldn't be a surprise. I've had years to think about it.

That, and just the other day I was pestering Wolf about what he wanted to do—talk about the pot calling the kettle black.

But that's just it, I guess. I've never *had* to think about it. I have very diligently kept all of my options open. The AP classes, the killer GPA, the SAT scores in the 99th percentile, the varsity letters from swim team, the debate club, the fund-raising . . . I've taken on everything and succeeded at it. There is not one weak spot that can be pointed to in my resume, not a single thing that would make an administrator say, "Yes, but what about her . . ."

Except maybe this. Except the part where it's suddenly clear to me why I've been struggling so much with my college essays, with articulating who I am in so few words. How can a person even know who they are if they don't know what they *want*?

"She just needs a few minutes to grab some water and freshen up," the coordinator tells me. We've reached the end of the hall and are standing outside of an office door. "She'll let you know when she's ready."

The door opens, then, and out comes Landon. He looks every bit as unfazed as he always does, as if he's walking out of practice instead of out of the office of someone whose thumb is basically on the pulse of our entire futures. He smiles when he sees me, like it's a reflex, and the smile immediately falters.

"Pepper. Oh, man. I meant to—I meant to apologize."

I'm just rattled enough that I can't keep the skepticism off of my face until it's already there, furrowing in my brow. Landon doesn't miss it.

"It's just—uh." He glances at the office door, which is still shut behind him. "My dad's so—he's always trying to drag me on these business things with him. He's so pissed I'm going into app development."

To be fair, I didn't make it easy for him to apologize. Even though we've crossed paths at practice, I've spent the last week avoiding him, trying to convince myself he isn't Wolf. I couldn't let myself believe a person I'd shared so much of myself with would ditch me in real life. It would only confirm the worst fear—that the person who likes me as Bluebird wouldn't like me half as much as the person I actually am.

But I haven't stopped wondering, even if I stopped trying to connect the dots.

"And—and you want to go to Columbia for that?" I ask, because it's subtler than, *Are you the reason I've been having stellar mac and cheeses at every place within a five-block radius of my apartment the past few weeks?*

Landon relaxes, assuming he's been forgiven. "No. I'm just interviewing because he's an alum." He doesn't even bother to keep his voice down—I wonder what it's like, being that sure of yourself. Knowing what you want so definitively you don't even *care* about keeping doors open. "Truth is, a few buddies and I are gonna launch a startup as soon as we're out of here."

I feel faint. "Sounds . . . risky."

"Yeah, well. The internship's been a real help. I think we've got a shot." Landon rolls his eyes. "Either way, it's better than all the money-pushing my dad does, that's for sure."

Wolf develops apps. Wolf talks about his parents trying to pressure him into the family business. Wolf never chats me during swim practice.

"Anyway—let me make it up to you. I'll buy you dinner on Senior Skip Day."

"Oh, uh—you don't have to . . ."

Is this a date? Should I tell him I know who he is before I agree?

Do I know who he is?

"A bunch of people on the swim team are hanging," says Landon. "You in?"

I'm expecting the air that blows out of me to be disappointment, but instead, it feels a little too close to relief.

"Yeah. Yeah, sounds fun. I'm in."

Landon smiles, and the door opens, and I snap myself back into Studious, Goal-Oriented Pepper so fast, it's like the encounter never even happened. I walk into the room so composed, the interviewer immediately smiles at me in that satisfactory way adults always smile when I put on my game face. I shake her hand, I make small talk, and I lie to her face—tell her I'm interested in studying world affairs, and basically parrot everything Paige has been telling me about her studies at UPenn. By the end of the interview, I can tell I have won her over the same way I've won over every teacher, every administrator, every object of my people-pleasing for the last four years.

I walk out, expecting to be buoyed by the same satisfaction I usually feel, but I'm completely spent. That, and a little terrified—it occurs to me as I walk down the long hallway back to the lobby that I have no idea how to get back home. The same bus that brought me here isn't going to take me back.

I'm being ridiculous. I can easily walk. The city is a grid up here, numbers and columns and rows. Just because they're not the rows and columns I'm used to walking on doesn't make it mystifying.

My chest feels tight as I walk out, looking around like Jack is going to be standing there when I know nobody in their right mind would be. I pull out my phone in an effort to distract myself, remembering as I unlock the screen that Hub Seed's tweets are probably up. I pull up their page, and sure enough, at the top of their feed is a tweet explaining the terms of the bet, and another tweet below it with a picture of Big League

Burger's grilled cheese styled on a plate, without any other context to explain whose it is.

I scroll down to the second picture, and all my anxiety is swiftly and brutally replaced with rage.

Because the photo that Hub Seed's Twitter account ended up tweeting was *decidedly* not the one Jack sent me. The one Jack sent me fit the bill: high resolution, well-lit, a respectable shot of what was, admittedly, a delicious-looking grilled cheese. Crisped to perfection, cheese spilling out of the edges, a sliver of apple jam gleaming from the sides—

Anyway. It was appropriate, for the terms of what we were agreeing to. What is markedly *less* appropriate is the image the Hub ended up tweeting instead, which features Grandma's Special all right—Grandma's Special, with Ethan holding it up on the plate and beaming into the camera with his best "Vote for Me for Student Council and I'll Get Back Pizza Wednesdays" smile.

Naturally, the Twittersphere is in love.

I don't even have to click to know the comments on it are already flooded with heart-eye emojis, but I do anyway, and sure enough—that grilled cheese looks delicious but that boy's the REAL snack, reads one tweet. uh tell me he's on the menu, reads another. I full-on cringe at the last one: WOW looks delicious . . . grilled cheese looks pretty good too. ;)

It's dirty on two counts: one is that everyone and their mailman will know that's Girl Cheesing's grilled cheese. Ethan's whole *look* screams hometown boy. And another is that people are definitely not retweeting that picture for the sandwich's sake.

They're going to slaughter us. And my mom, in turn, is going to slaughter *me*.

I'm fuming by the time I walk out of the front doors, and sure enough, as if the universe materialized him there for me to funnel the rage straight into, there's Jack. His back is turned to me, and he's on his phone, hunched over, talking faster than usual. I lift an arm to tap him on the shoulder, imagining the way the air will puncture right out of him when he turns around and sees the look on my face, but I'm thrown off by the tone of his voice.

"—wasn't what we agreed to. Mom and Dad said *I* was running the account; you had no right to get involved." He runs a hand through his hair. "I don't care. You knew better. You *knew* that would break the terms of the whole agreement, and why? So you could get your stupid face tweeted out?"

All of the anger leaks out of me, leaving me on the sidewalk with my fists clenched and my body stiff and nowhere to put any of it.

"Yeah, I do care. Jesus. We're better than this. And Mom and Dad *clearly* didn't know what the rules of the agreement were, or they never would have sent that, which means you lied to them."

I back up on the pavement, wishing I hadn't just charged up to him. He obviously doesn't want me hearing this.

"No, Ethan, it's not about that. It's about one more thing you just have to *beat* me at, you can't even let me have—"

He turns, then, too quickly for me to anticipate it. Our eyes lock, and he looks so stricken to see me there that I want to look down, look at the street, look anywhere other than at the way he is trying and failing to wipe the hurt off his face.

"I gotta go."

Jack

I hang up the phone, Ethan's piss-poor excuses still ringing in my ear as I look up and see Pepper, standing there like a deer in headlights, looking like she wants to disappear.

No, worse. Looking like she feels sorry for me. Like the gears are turning in her head, and she's trying to think of the right thing to say to make me feel better—the second twin. The lesser one. The one everyone only bothers to talk to when they're trying to get to the other.

I was worried when I saw that stupid picture that she was going to be furious. That it would wreck this shaky friendship we had now, and the even shakier something else—that weird current between us on the bus when she ribbed me, or the way she almost seemed paralyzed in the moment after I said her full name.

It's worse. Anger, I can handle. Pity, I really can't. Especially not over this.

"Jack—"

"There's a bus stop across the street. It's another straight shot back to Stone Hall."

Pepper takes a cautious step toward me. "Are you okay?"

I keep my eyes trained on the cement. "I'm sorry about the tweet."

"It doesn't sound like it was your fault," she says, her voice low.

So she did hear everything. Of course.

"Your brother's just being an ass."

"Don't," I snap. "Don't talk about my brother."

I'm waiting for her to rile in that way she usually does, waiting for her to rise up to meet me. But she's too steady, standing on the sidewalk with a mortifying kind of empathy.

"I have to go home."

She nods. Tilts her head toward the bus stop across the street. "Just over there?" she asks.

"Yeah."

She waits for a beat, like she thinks I'm going to say something else, but there's nothing in me. I know it's ridiculous to be this upset over a stupid picture, but it's not a picture. It's the tip of the goddamn iceberg. It's every sport Ethan had to beat me at, every stupid project of ours he'd be so excited to start and leave me to finish, every afternoon he left me alone in the deli to live his stupid perfect Ethan life with his perfect Ethan friends and make me lie to our parents' faces about the times he wasn't doing any of that, and smoking stupid *pot*—

It's like I've been watching the shadow of some moon cross over me my whole life, and now it's just a full eclipse.

Pepper walks toward the intersection to get to the bus stop, and without consciously deciding to, I follow her.

She slows her pace down so we're walking side by side, not

saying anything, letting me brew in whatever this is. I don't know how it's possible to want to get the hell away from someone and actively follow them like they're a magnet at the same time, but Pepper seems to take it in stride, glancing over at me every now and then as she comes to a stop in front of the bus stop.

"I'll be fine to get back," she says.

"You're sure?"

She nods. "I'll get you back your MetroCard on Monday."

I rock on my heels, not quite leaving and not quite *not* leaving. We both spot the bus coming down the street, and it makes the decision for me.

"You're super sure?" I ask, just in case.

"Yeah," says Pepper. "And—thanks again."

I don't say anything, just watch her get on, watch the bus pull away and her with it. I suddenly feel like an asshole up here in Morningside Heights, in my spiffy school uniform, my hair still slicked back in the style my mom made me brush it into on my way out the door. The style that screamed *Ethan* so much, it couldn't not feel like a total kick in the pants when I looked at the end result in the mirror.

I shake it out of my hair now and walk over to a 1 train stop. I hope the walk across town to the east side when I get off the subway will do something to calm me, but if anything, I'm even more aggravated by the time I get to the deli—the weather's nice for November and the streets are full, and I'm just the kind of invisible on my own that nobody thinks twice before nearly barreling into me.

Once I actually get home, the deli is packed. Ethan is manning the register. Through the window I can see him taking a selfie with a group of giggling junior high girls. My mom is fluttering around the floor, restocking the napkins and the condiments and the straws, which can only mean my dad is in the back helping out with the cooks or in the office making calls.

Basically, nobody has the time to listen to me bitch.

I do something then that I've never done in my whole life—walk away from the packed deli and head straight up the stairs to the apartment instead. I shut the door, and it feels like a vacuum, the noise of the deli and the street and the cars *whooshing* out of my ears.

"How was the interview?"

I startle at Grandma Belly, who's in her usual chair, her laptop propped on her lap and a game of solitaire pulled up on the screen. She looks close to winning it. One of my favorite things as a kid was to watch that *flip flip flip flip flip* of the animated cards cascading whenever she won; even now she'll call me into the living room to see, will even let me click the last card to win it.

"Okay," I say, shrugging off my backpack and dumping it on the couch in the way my dad hates. "How was your morning?"

She gestures out the window. "Good. It's nice, hearing all that racket from downstairs."

I smile despite myself. "Yeah, it's pretty crowded down there."

"And yet you're up here with me."

Her eyes are more teasing than scolding.

"I could take you down, if you want."

She likes sitting in the booth right by the window. All the regulars know her, obviously. She's something of an icon in the East Village—she's been in business here longer than a lot of people have been alive. But ever since she's been slowing down, she gets too tired to stay down for long and doesn't want to go unless she's got someone else in the family sitting with her.

But she shakes her head and pats the arm of the couch next to her chair for me to sit. "I've got plenty of good company right here."

I take a seat, flopping onto the couch, knowing what's about to come before it does. Nothing gets past Grandma Belly.

"What's on your mind, small fry?"

I'm not going to tell her. It's not like I'm lying to her about the whole Twitter thing—she doesn't understand or care about the social media accounts, so really, there's been nothing to tell. And there's no point in stressing her out about this.

"Oh, come on. You walked in here looking like you dropped an ice cream cone on the sidewalk."

I snort. "Nah."

She raises her eyebrows at me.

"It's stupid," I mumble.

Her eyes are just as steady on me as ever, only seeming to get sharper with each passing year. "I'll be the judge of that."

I glance behind me, as if Mom or Dad or Ethan are going to come out of nowhere and stick a pin in this whole conversation. It's nothing I could ever say in front of any of them. Nothing I even want to admit to myself.

Grandma Belly is still fixing me with one of those looks of hers when I turn back; it's impossible not to spill the beans.

"I just . . . sometimes . . ." There's no way to say it without sounding like a total ass. "Sometimes it feels like I'm—not as—I don't know." It's hard to admit to myself, and harder to articulate. "You know, it's like, everyone goes *nuts* over Ethan. At school. At the deli. He just . . ." I gesture vaguely, as if I can fit seventeen years of mild inadequacy into the air in front of me.

"Honey, I don't know how to break this to you, but the two of you have the exact same face."

That face almost crumbles when she says that, because that

is the crux of the whole thing. I can't blame it on anything. I can't say it's because he's taller, or better-looking, or older, or any of the other things a brother could say when one outshines the other. We got all the same tools. He's just better than I am at using them.

Grandma Belly seems to see it written all over me. She reaches forward, toward my head, and I duck down to let her mess up my hair. Even after all this time, it's weird to me that I'm this much taller than her, even though it's never felt weird with anyone else.

"Don't you worry about what Ethan's up to," she says. "You are going to come into your own in a big way. When you get out of this place."

I blink at her in surprise. "Grandma Belly, I think we both know I'm not getting out of this place."

She smiles at me. "You're a homebody. You might stick around for a bit. But you've never been the kind of person who can stay in one place for too long, not since you started to crawl."

I look across the living room, at the shelves crammed with video games and DVDs and the seashell collection Mom keeps adding to every time we go to Coney Island. At the old rug still stained from Ethan's Hawaiian Punch he spilled ten years ago, at the pictures of me and Ethan my dad takes every summer and hangs sequentially on the walls, at the basket where Grandma Belly keeps her knitting needles, making little hats for the babies of regulars.

I look everywhere except at Grandma Belly, because these are the things that tether me, the things I've always been and just assumed would always be. What she's saying right now feels a lot like permission to leave it behind, and it scares me every bit as much as it relieves me.

But we both know it's not her permission to give.

"I don't know if my parents think that."

Which is to say, I know they don't. The assumption that I'll stay behind and help run this place, that I'll eventually take it over, is so ingrained in them, we've never actually talked about it. It just is. Like it was set in stone before I even knew how to read the words.

She pats my knee. "You should talk to them about it. Graduation will come faster than you think." She rests her hand there for a moment and says, "I love the hell out of that deli and everyone in it. I hope whoever runs it someday loves it that much too. But, small fry, it doesn't have to be you."

I'm not used to having serious conversations. Not with Grandma Belly, or with anyone, really. At least not the kinds of conversations that have so much riding on them like this. It suddenly feels like I skipped ahead ten years, like I'm talking for myself and whoever I'm supposed to be on the other end of it.

Still, the words come out in barely more than a mumble. "I don't want to let them down."

Grandma Belly tilts her head at me and narrows her eyes, her classic no-nonsense look. The problem is she always looks slightly ridiculous doing it, so it's hard to clamp down a smile, even now.

"You could never."

It still helps to hear, even if I'm not sure if it makes it true.

Jack

I sit with Grandma Belly for a while after that. We eat the day-olds from the deli that Dad stashed in the fridge, chocolate pie and Kitchen Sink Macaroons, and watch a few episodes of her beloved *Outlander* on the DVR under oath that we don't tell Mom we watched it without her. Then the clock strikes eight and I slink into my room, conveniently just before I know Mom and Dad and Ethan will be trudging up from downstairs.

Nobody says anything to me, or even knocks on the door. I'm grateful and disappointed at the same time. I bury myself in my laptop screen—I've been working on something to surprise Bluebird—but the more I try to distract myself, the more restless I am. I don't even realize I've started *tap-tap-tapping* my foot on the wall until Ethan bangs his hand on it from the other room to remind me to stop.

I'm too stuck in my own head. I pull out my phone reflexively, the way I have too many times to count in the last few months—talking to Bluebird has been like touching base with something outside myself, as if we're just close enough to ease each other's minds but far enough away it never feels as scary as it should.

I open Weazel and glance briefly at the Hallway Chat. A few people are swapping contact information for different organizations that are looking for volunteers, since the Honors Society kids have twenty-five hours due at the end of the month. Other than that, it's a pretty slow night.

I hear footsteps in the hall and pull off my headphones, wondering if one of my parents is going to knock. I hear my mom's voice, though, and realize she's talking to Ethan.

". . . nothing to do with this Weazel app we're getting all these emails about?"

"I'm not even on it. Don't have the time. Why?"

"Oh, I don't know. They're saying a student made the app. And I know you're good with computers . . ."

"Mom, I fixed the Wi-Fi, like, two times. I can't develop entire apps."

Whatever they say next, I don't catch. I shove my headphones over my ears and blast the music loud enough to make them go raw. It's the kind of feeling that transcends hurt or anger or any of the things I try not to feel when they do this, over and over and *over* again—always assume the best in Ethan, and just plain forget about me.

Okay. That's not fair. They don't know I'm in here teaching myself to make apps, and they certainly aren't asking Ethan because they're *proud* of the idea of him making my unfairly maligned creation. But it doesn't stop my hands from curling and uncurling, doesn't stop my teeth from grinding together, doesn't stop me from wanting to open the window and scream out into the street like the New York cliché I've probably been destined to become from the start.

I click out of the Weazel app, then, and pull up Pepper's number.

Did you get home okay?

I'm not expecting her to answer so quickly.

Yeah—thanks again. You were a real lifesaver

I'm weirdly nervous texting her, like it's somehow left me more exposed than actually talking straight to her face. And I guess in a way it has. Every time we interact, it's because we have to—whether for the swim and dive teams, or Twitter, or ill-fated college admissions interviews. This is voluntary. Personal. Like anything she writes or doesn't write back can affect me twice as much as it would otherwise.

Today 7:21 PM

Sorry for being a dick.

You weren't

. . . But Ethan did TOTALLY screw up our bet.

Yeah. I'm less than pleased with him at the moment

Pepper's typing, and then not typing, and then typing again. I wince, watching the little ellipses come and go. I can almost picture the exact look on her face on the sidewalk this morning, in the beats where she was trying to decide whether to speak or leave it be.

But he's still your brother

My throat feels thick. It hits the nail on the head, in so few words—I can't really hate Ethan any more than I could hate myself.

Today 7:27 PM

Yeah. Even if I want to scream at him sometimes

Hey, that's the whole point of having siblings, isn't it?

Do you and your sister fight?

Physically. In cage matches.

I snort. She's still typing.

Today 7:28 PM

No, not really. But I'm mad at her sometimes. You know, sister stuff.

Like—the divorce happened, and everyone else found a way to get used to it. She's the only one who won't

Stubbornness must be another Evans virtue

Then breaking the rules of Twitter wars must be a Campbell one

I've stopped fidgeting, at least, but I only realize this because I've started chewing a hole into my cheek. The truth is, I haven't even opened Twitter since I saw the picture of Ethan on the Hub's timeline. I know we're winning, and I wish we weren't. It sucks all the fun out of it.

And for a little while, it *was* fun. Waking up in the morning to see what Pepper had cooked up the night before. Waiting to see the indignant look on her face when she opened up a response, and waiting to see the sly one that replaced it when she came up with something else. At some point, it stopped being a war and started being a game.

Today 7:35 PM

Are we maybe going too far with the Twitter thing now?

TBH, BLB has been going too far since the beginning. Thank god you guys got more followers or we'd really look like assholes

Eh, you don't need our help to do that

But I mean more with the . . . phones and the hacking and stuff

Well, that was super shitty. And my mom was not pleased

But you know what's weird is that
Pooja and I are kind of friends now
because of it?

Wait, what? Did I stumble into a
parallel universe?

I'm part of her study groups now.
We're getting lunch tomorrow
afterward

WOW. From frenemies to study
buddies

This is going to turn the whole school
upside down. Like, full on dancing
in the cafeteria, "stick to the status
quo" upside down

Yeah, it's nice.

If you think you got away with making
a High School Musical reference
without me mercilessly mocking you
for it, you're wrong. I'm saving it for
later

Noted. And I guess Paul had fun with
the whole espionage thing

Just how pissed is your mom,
though?

Eh. She's mostly annoyed

I may have made a colossal mess stress-baking in the kitchen though, and have been banned from baking in the apartment for the rest of the week

Oh, shit. That sucks

Yeah, for you. No more random baked goods

I start to type and then stop. This could be a mistake. Like, the kind of mistake with a consequence as small as Pepper laughing in my face or as large as my parents tearing me a new one.

But I can't imagine my parents not liking Pepper. Even Ethan remains somewhat endeared to her, despite disrespecting our Twitter rules.

So I send the text.

Today 7:47 PM

You could always come use our ovens

And step foot in the enemy camp?

It's not a no.

Today 7:48 PM

We'd only poison you a little bit!

Seriously, though . . . you think after
this we should just call it quits?

On the Twitter thing?

It occurs to me she thinks I might mean something else—namely, the whole friendship thing that seems to have inadvertently bloomed out of the Twitter thing.

Yeah. I think it's run its course, probably

It takes Pepper a bit longer to respond.

Today 7:55 PM

Agreed

After the Hub thing is over?

It was my idea, but suddenly I'm reluctant to agree. No more tweeting means a whole lot less of Pepper, something I didn't even know meant anything to me until right now—right now, when I'm every bit as annoyed about the Ethan thing on her behalf as I am on mine. Right now, when I'm actually upset over something as dumb as her getting grounded from baking.

Right now, when I realize I'm going to miss these barbs after it's all over.

But we still have swim and dive, for another month and a half. And homeroom. It's not as though we're moving to other planets.

Yeah. After that we lay down our keyboards

Which means this will all be over by the end of this week.

I put my phone back down on my mattress, assuming that's the end of our texting for tonight. It's weird enough I texted her in the first place. Like nudging some kind of boundary, turning us into *that* kind of friend.

But then her next text pushes it further than I did.

Today 8:02 PM

It's weird to me that it took four years and a Twitter war for us to be friends

Aw. So you do admit it?

Begrudgingly

But really. I know you have this thing about Ethan, but you shouldn't. I feel like you've kind of been hiding because of it

Pepperoni. I'm the loudest person in our class.

And if we're talking about hiding, it's really Pepper who is probably guilty of it most. She chameleoned into Stone Hall so quickly, sometimes it's hard to remember we didn't grow up with her, like she was always there in the periphery, setting the bar annoyingly high for the rest of us.

Yeah. I think that's a version of hiding, sometimes

I set the phone back down, my eyes flitting up to the window, feeling so absurdly exposed that for a moment I half expect someone to be peering in from the other side of it. I shut my eyes and try to rein myself in, the way my whole body wants to reject the thing I just read.

I don't know what's worse—that she might be right, or that she figured it out before I did.

Today 8:10 PM

Anyway, loudmouth or not, you're fine the way you are.

But burn that text so nobody can hold it against me later.

I grin.

Yeah, well. Ruthless overachiever with a bloodlust for crushing other people's GPAs aside, you're fine the way you are too.

We both know that's the end of our texting for tonight, as if someone gently closed a book before going to sleep. I sit there on my bed, almost in disbelief it happened in the mere span of an hour when it feels like it wasn't in the bounds of normal time—the kind of conversation you already know is going to stick to your skin long after it's over, long after the person you had it with is gone from your life.

I bite the inside of my cheek. I wonder where Pepper will end up when we're all done here. Wonder in a way and with an ache I haven't even wondered for myself.

In the end, it's Pepper's fault I do the thing I've been alternately trying to do and trying not to do for months now. I pull up the Weazel app and tap on my conversation with Bluebird.

Wolf

Okay, so it's clear the app isn't going to tattle on us anytime soon.

Only kind of a lie, since I'm the one who stopped it from triggering. But the response is almost immediate.

Bluebird

Are you suggesting we take matters into our own hands?

Wolf

I am.

Bluebird

When?

I glance up at the calendar I have hanging on my closet, the one my mom dutifully changes the months on when I forget. On Thursday the tally will be in for our retweet war on Hub Seed. The next day is Senior Skip Day.

Wolf

Friday?

Bluebird

Works for me.

I take a breath, feeling the familiar swoop of anxiety in my gut. But it feels anchored this time. *You're fine the way you are.* It's almost nothing, but in this moment, with this one choice, it makes all the difference.

Wolf

Cool. The seniors are all hanging out around town that night. We can figure it out then

Bluebird

Excellent. Gives me just enough time to come up with an alibi

God, this is gonna be fun.

Pepper

I lied to Jack. My mom wasn't annoyed about Ethan's picture. She was pissed.

"We need to get Hub Seed's social media manager on the phone," she said to me the instant I walked through the door.

I was oddly unfazed. "That's Taffy's job."

She was standing in the kitchen, leaning over the counter, staring into the remnants of A-Plus Angel Cake—Paige's recipe, not mine; apparently she'd aced her French midterm, and I couldn't resist replicating her recipe after she posted it on our blog. Now, though, a good chunk of it was missing, and there was a fork propped in my mom's hands.

"It's a Saturday," she said.

"So it can wait until Monday."

"Weren't you the one who arranged this whole deal?"

Despite Jack stealing my phone, I don't think Mom has any idea I go to school with the sons of the people running Girl Cheesing. She just thinks I got hacked through the cloud or something. So she can't know Jack exists, or that we've been toe-to-toe in person as often as we have been on Twitter. As far as she knows, my hands are completely clean of this.

"Hub Seed reached out to *us*," I reminded her. "And yeah, the retweet showdown was my idea, and we set the terms. They broke them. That's not my fault."

She stabbed her fork into the angel cake, her mouth twisting into a frustrated line.

I stood very still, watching her mull it over and feeling more unsettled by the second. "The tweet's already up, and there's nothing we can do about it. And for what it's worth, I said we should quit doing this weeks ago."

"Well, that's not your call."

"It is if you're going to keep me up all night sending out stupid tweets."

My mom looked up at me sharply. Then her brows deepened into a scowl, and her body postured like she was suddenly anticipating a fight.

Like I was challenging her. Like I was Paige.

But this had escalated far enough. If nobody else was around to challenge her, it would have to be me.

"Is there something about this you're not telling me?"

She wouldn't meet my eyes. "What's that supposed to mean?"

"This whole Twitter thing. It's insane. Dad and Paige and half the internet thinks we're losing it."

"Half the internet is seeing a ton of press about us."

"And thinks we're *jerks*," I emphasized. "Which we are."

"For defending ourselves?"

"If we'd just let it go, it would have been like—like a baby bird trying to attack a mountain. But now it's a *thing*, and it's a thing because we made it one, not them. The further we take this, the worse we look."

"I'm the CEO. I'm the one who built this place up—the one

who turned this operation from a backyard grill to the *force* it is today—"

She stopped, then, because the tears sprang into my eyes so fast it stunned us both.

"Pepper."

I blinked them back. "I miss that backyard grill."

There were a few beats of silence, then, when one of us was clearly going to wave the white flag. I knew if I waited, it would be her. I knew it could just as easily be me.

Instead, I said, "We had integrity, then."

My mom thinned her lips, glaring down at the angel cake. "I didn't steal anything from that deli."

"Then why won't you let this go? We're going to be the laughingstock of—"

"Go to your room."

It was the first time anybody had said that to me since elementary school. I almost laughed.

And maybe it was funny. I'd spent my whole life in constant fear of rocking the boat, of making anybody angry. Jack had probably forgotten the Pepper People-Pleaser moniker he'd briefly given me sophomore year, but it applied then and certainly had up until now.

But nothing terrible happened. The earth didn't pull out from under my feet.

I didn't feel good, exactly, but I didn't feel bad either.

And it was in this weirdly grounded mindset that Jack texted me out of the blue, and I found myself being more forthright with him than I ever would have been even a few weeks ago. It was in that same mindset that, not too long after, Wolf chatted me on the Weazel app and asked if we should finally meet.

It seemed stupid not to say yes. Especially since I would be out with Landon and the other seniors anyway. Now, hopefully, we could do it with all the air cleared between us. It would be different, then—Landon would snap back into the self he is with me, the self he is when everybody isn't watching, and it would all make sense. I had to believe that.

So I said yes.

And it's all I've thought about since—through the frosty breakfast with my mom the next morning, when we barely spoke to each other even though she was on her way out the door for a business trip; through my study date with Pooja, where we split a sandwich and a salad at Panera; through the phone call I had with my dad that night, when he near bored me to tears recounting something Carrie Underwood's husband did in a hockey game.

All I've thought about until suddenly there was a much, *much* larger thing to think about in my immediate line of sight: the article that Hub Seed published about us.

And I mean *us.* Not us as in Girl Cheesing and Big League Burger—us as in *me* and *Jack*.

Pepper

It happens the moment homeroom lets out on Monday. Jack and I link eyes and open our mouths like we're poised to rib each other like we normally do, but there's nothing really to say—we've both stayed off each other's respective Twitter feeds since our run-in on Saturday. Instead, we blow out the same breath and smile sheepishly at each other.

"So," he says, walking up and drumming his knuckles on my desk.

I expect him to brag about the fact Ethan and his grilled cheese have racked up at least five thousand more retweets than we have, but somehow I know from the shape of the half grin that he isn't.

"So," I say back.

He huffs out a laugh. "Well—now that this is all winding down—we should probably . . . I don't know. Actually do our captaining duties?"

I finish shoving my books into my bag. "Oh, those?"

"Let me guess. You already did everything and then some."

"No, no." Truth is, outside of talking to Jack and going to actual practice, I've barely had the time to do anything. "I wanted to save all the dirty work for you."

"Well, in that case, we should probably figure out what we're doing for fundraising. Since the bajillion dollars they bleed out of us for tuition isn't enough."

This time his tone isn't bitter, but knowing—an acknowledgment that I get it. That I come from a background like his, even if I'm well displaced from it now. Like at the end of all of these shenanigans, we've finally landed on common ground.

"Actually . . . I was thinking maybe a bake sale."

Jack's eyebrows lift in surprise. "How old school of you."

I shrug. "Between your deli and my baking prowess, we might actually make it, y'know, not suck."

Jack considers this. "Huh. That isn't a terrible idea."

"I have a good one every now and then."

"You should actually come to the deli."

He made the offer last night, but only in person can I tell he's actually serious about it.

"You guys are in the East Village, right?"

I must sound nervous because Jack pats me on the back. "It's a straight shot down on the 6 train."

"Right."

"It'll be good for you, Pepperoni. See some more of what this great big city has to offer."

The idea of it somewhat terrifies me. It's all well and good to say *straight shot on the 6 train*, but it's so much more complicated than that. There's wrangling a MetroCard, and making sure you don't get on the wrong train, and making sure you get on one going in the right direction, and I've heard sometimes they just decide to go express, and if you're not paying attention, you can end up in the middle of Brooklyn, and *then* what on earth happens to you?

"We can smuggle you in if you want," says Jack. "I think I have a wig leftover from when Ethan was the Joker for Halloween."

I'm being ridiculous. The subway isn't going to swallow me whole. I'll be eighteen in a few months, and in this city for at least seven more—I can't be totally helpless forever.

"What day do you think we should—"

"Did you *see* this?"

It's Paul and Pooja, blurting the exact same words at the same time on either side of us. They pause and look up at each other in alarm like they just ripped a hole through the matrix, and then they're shoving phone screens into our faces, without any caution for Mrs. Fairchild five feet away on the other side of the door.

I take Pooja's phone from her. I'd recognize the Hub Seed logo anywhere—what I'm having trouble processing is the picture of my *face* on it.

"Oh my god."

Twitter's Most Iconic Brand War To Date Is Being Spearheaded—Fittingly—By The Teens

"*The* teens?" Jack is muttering next to me. "I didn't realize we spoke for all of Gen Z, but okay."

"How did they get my picture?"

"Your mom?"

"Oh, hell no."

It had to have been Taffy. My mom would never have sanctioned this. Hell, *I* wouldn't have sanctioned this. And yet there I am—identified as "Patricia," dear God—in my yearbook photo from junior year with the massive zit on my chin, and there's Jack, cropped badly out of a shot of the dive team from last season.

> If you're a breathing human with a Twitter account, there's no way you've missed #BigCheese, this month's epic battle between fast-food chain Big League Burger and their unexpected adversary, a locally beloved deli by the name of Girl Cheesing.
>
> Their respective tweeting has hit an internet already accustomed to the snarky, audience-targeted kind of tweeting we've seen from plenty of brand accounts in the past few years, from Wendy's to Moon Pie to Netflix.
>
> Those accounts may have just laid the groundwork for the kind of war that BLB and GC are waging—a war that has earned a small-time deli a whopping half a million followers and counting, and launched more hashtags than there are things on their menus. But the most surprising thing about this year's #GrilledCheeseGate?
>
> It isn't being run by social media managers. This is a war waged by teens.

Embedded in the article is another video of Jasmine Yang, who seems to have done most of the sleuthing before the Hub Seed reporter wrote about us. Apparently a new vlog of hers went live late last night, and the amount of stalkery involved in it puts any research I've ever done for the debate club to shame. It introduces Jack first, with a smattering of information from his Facebook account and Ethan's. Her bit about me is much shorter, but anyone who knows me would recognize me on sight—in addition to the yearbook picture, there's an old one of me, Paige, my mom, and my dad, posing in front of the first Big League Burger in Nashville, some ten years ago. All four of us are holding burgers. Paige is beaming from behind a pair of braces, and my hair is pulled into astronomically high pigtails.

Any teenager in their right mind would probably be humiliated. But I can't stop staring at the four of us, at the proof I didn't just gloss over the memories in my head—it really was this simple, once upon a time.

The article mentions we live in New York, even says we go to the same school, although it does us the small mercy of not mentioning which one. The article pivots then into a summary of everything Jack and I have tweeted at each other so far, a weird little digital scrapbook of our clashes. I see the first ever tweet he sent, the quote retweet about our new menu items, and see he's paused to look at it on his screen too.

"The tweet that launched a thousand other tweets."

"To think we were only *mildly* sleep-deprived, then."

The article shifts into all the repercussions of our tweets, some of which I am already aware of, and others I decidedly am not. For instance, I'd seen the hashtags, even responded to a few of them—but I had not seen the literal *fan art* depicting Girl Cheesing's and Big League Burger's mascots fighting each other in comic panels, the freckled little girl and cherubic little boy fighting by chucking food at each other.

We get to the line about the joking-but-not-quite-joking fan fiction shipping an older version of the mascots and both of us react so viscerally, several heads swivel to stare at us in the hallway.

"They're *shipping* them?" Jack blurts.

I shake my head. "They're *minors*, for god's sake. This is unholy."

"Forget shipping *them*," says Pooja, taking her phone back from me and scrolling down to the comments section. "Now they're shipping you."

My face is burning before my eyes even land on the first few of them.

lilmarvin 4 minutes ago
Omg, TELL me they're dating!

kdeeeeen 11 minutes ago
Okay but I need ALL the AUs about this on tumblr, stat

SuzieQueue 14 minutes ago
Sry shakespeare twitter is the new r&j

And then, as if she were the moon controlling this new internet tide, I finally see what Jasmine Yang titled her video about us: "Cheese-Crossed Lovers."

I can't look at Jack. I can't look at *anyone*. I don't even know what this feeling is—not embarrassment. No, it's more all-encompassing than that, something I can feel burning from the tips of my ears to the bottom of my heels. It feels like there's a spotlight on all 360 degrees of me, like there isn't a single part of me that isn't exposed.

"Pepper?"

My voice sounds strange even to my own ears, like it's underwater. "This is . . . wow."

The bell rings. Neither of us moves. Pooja and Paul collect their phones and hover for a moment, before giving us harried, sympathetic goodbyes and taking off down the hall with the rest of our classmates.

Jack's the one to break the silence: "Are we gonna make this weird?"

I let out a relieved laugh. "Oh, definitely."

"Cool, cool. In that case, I better get ahead of the rumors that are going to spread about us by telling everyone you have cooties."

"In that case, I'm definitely telling everyone you sleep in Hello Kitty pajamas."

Jack's half grin is curling. "I'm going to tell everyone you chew raw garlic after every meal."

I can feel the laughter bubbling up my throat. "I'm going to tell them you drink pool water. Oh wait! You *did*."

Jack shakes his head. "You're just *neeeever* gonna let that one go, are you, Peppero—"

The bell rings, and we startle at the sound. We've leaned in so close to each other laughing, it's a miracle we don't end up knocking our heads together, our eyes both going comically wide like we've never heard a bell before, like they haven't spent years dictating every second of our teenage lives.

But then for a beat, neither of us moves, staring at each other like our eyes are snagged there.

"Class." The word comes out in a blurt; like it's not a real word, but some gibberish I made up.

"Oh, yeah, that," says Jack. He falls into pace with me. "Wait, no, I've got independent study this period."

He turns and heads abruptly to the other end of the hall. I watch him go, all tall legs and long strides, and realize just before I turn back that I'm still smiling like an idiot. Somehow, though, I don't have it in me to stop.

Pepper

I miss my mom when she's gone, but it is perhaps the biggest mercy the universe has ever bestowed upon me when she calls to let me know she'll be extending her time in California, where she's overseeing new BLBs opening in Los Angeles and San Francisco.

"Listen," she says, "I'm sorry things have been so . . . tense lately."

I don't say anything, aching at the sound of her forgiveness, not understanding just how badly I wanted it until she is giving it.

"I'm sorry too," I say. I don't elaborate—I figure if she's letting the whole Hub Seed article thing fly, then there's no reason for me to bring it up so she can be annoyed about it all over again.

"When I get back, let's . . . have a weekend. Just for us. We'll go upstate. Hang out on a lake."

I open my mouth to tell her that's basically impossible—I have swim meets every Saturday, and she's always catching up on emails and taking calls on Sunday. And even if we could steal away for a weekend, I don't want to go upstate. I want to see Dad and Paige.

But Thanksgiving is right around the corner. At least I have that to look forward to, even if it's bound to be so tense when Mom and Paige finally end up in the same room that three kinds of pie won't be enough to ease it.

"Yeah," I say instead. "That sounds good to me."

I don't hear from her much for the rest of the week, which isn't all that surprising. When Mom gets engrossed in a project, she's like me—she's all in and can't split her focus. But I am surprised I haven't heard a word about the latest Twitter debacle, especially when a final tally of the retweets declares Girl Cheesing the winner, with a whopping twenty thousand more retweets than ours.

Jack's waiting for me Thursday morning, earlier than he usually is. There's a to-go box propped on his desk, a sight I'm not unused to seeing—he and his brother are constantly bringing sandwiches and leftover salad they podged together from the deli. Only this time when he opens it, it looks like the candy aisle of Duane Reade threw up into it.

"What . . . is that?"

"Kitchen Sink Macaroons," says Jack.

They're crumbled either from getting roughed up on the way here or because of their very makeup, but I have to admit—however begrudgingly—they look delicious. Like the Monster Cake version of macaroons. He holds out the box to offer me some.

"Oh, man. Are these Feel Sorry for the Loser Macaroons?"

"More like Waving the White Flag Macaroons. Also Sorry I Got You Banned From Baking Macaroons."

I take one. "Well, you did win."

"Unfairly." He scratches the back of his neck. "So, listen—you don't have to . . . send a tweet acknowledging it. I mean, we already won. No point in rubbing anyone's face in it."

I take a bite of the macaroon, studying him carefully. It's *good*. And I am a person with extremely high baking standards. It's just the right amount of crunch, balanced with just enough gooeyness, courtesy of the chocolate and the caramel and a whole host of other flavors I'm still trying to identify.

"Are you sure?"

Jack shrugs. "I supposedly call the shots on our account, so yeah, I'm sure."

He's not finished, though. I pause mid-chew, waiting for whatever is about to bloom on his face to take shape. Sure enough, he's smirking into his desk before he finally looks up and aims it at me in full force.

"But if you think I'm letting you off the hook about the high dive . . ."

I swallow, hard.

He raises an eyebrow.

"Oh, that old thing?" I say, dusting a few crumbs off of my skirt.

"Yeah." His eyes are suddenly focused on mine. I can't look away. "Don't tell me you're still scared."

I lean in close to his desk, propping my palms on it. "Jack, last night I went on the Tumblr tags for Big League Burger and Girl Cheesing. If that didn't scare the ever-loving crap out of me, *nothing* will."

Jack blanches. "We're on Tumblr tags?"

I lower my voice. "I've seen things I can never unsee."

"God, I wish this were not my legacy."

I doubt he really means that, though. While I got a few weird looks in the hall and during study group and a *ton* of jokes from Pooja about the shipping, our classmates are weirdly into Jack being the underdog of Twitter. Yesterday at practice, a group of freshmen on the swim team practically cornered him in the pool, asking for his "real life" Twitter handle. I nearly choked on chlorinated water when he had to confess that, despite our shenanigans, neither of us has one.

I pop another bite of macaroon into my mouth. "This is actually delicious."

"Why the surprise?" And then, before I can answer: "You know, you've never tried any of our stuff."

"Pretty sure I would burst into flames if I tried to walk through the door at this point. Especially now that my face is plastered on those tweets, and I've basically become public enemy number one."

The smile drops on Jack's face so fast, I almost turn around, wondering if something happened behind me.

"Nobody's actually bothering you about that, are they?"

"What? No." The article, at least, didn't use our last names, and didn't mention I'm related to my mom. Taffy didn't throw me under the bus so much as she lovingly, with the best of intentions, nudged me under one. "I'm so far off the grid even Jasmine Yang couldn't fully blow up my spot. Nobody could find me if they wanted to."

Jack relaxes, marginally. I can still see his foot tapping under the desk. "Yeah, well. Be careful, I guess."

"You too. You have quite the fan club now."

Jack shakes his head. "I'm a flash in the pan."

"In the grilled cheese pan, maybe. In real life . . ."

Jack's cheeks redden. There's a beat where I think maybe

I've gone too far, or that my face has given away something my words didn't quite mean to. But then he punctures the moment, pointing a finger at me.

"If you think you can sweet talk your way out of the high dive, think again. You're in for a reckoning, Pepperoni. Five o'clock. Bleachers."

I roll my eyes. "We'll see."

Pepper

But that is exactly where I am at the precise time, at the precise place, all of the bravado from this morning leaked out of me like a balloon.

I haven't thought about the high dive since freshman year. It's a symptom of a larger problem, maybe: if I'm not immediately good at something, I drop it. As a kid I took piano classes for a month, ballet classes for a year, even soccer for one ill-fated practice that ended with me hauling ass across the field and leaping into my dad's arms when the ball came within five feet of me. I'm a perfectionist, through and through, and even at five, I had no interest in embarrassing myself.

Swimming is something I'm good at, something I don't even remember having to learn. It's probably why I stuck with it so long, even when there were other, more impressive things I could have put on my resume. But diving . . .

I didn't have to try it to know I was terrible at it. There is *nothing* intuitive about leaping that high up from the ground, in twisting your body into ridiculous shapes, in praying you time it down to the split second so you end up slipping into the water instead of face-planting into it. And having a front-row seat to the dive team's practice sessions means I have seen plenty of face-planting in my day.

Jack is waiting at the top of the high dive, grinning down at me.

"How's the weather down there, Pep?" he asks, shifting his weight on the board so it creaks up and down and up and down. Just watching him is enough to make me nauseous.

I glance over my shoulder to make sure most of our teammates have headed into the locker room. Pooja pauses at the door and shoots me a look, but I wave her off.

"Okay," I mutter. "Let's get this over with."

Jack laughs. "It's really not that scary."

"Easy for you to say. You're so tall, the world is like your high dive."

"It's not like you're exactly short."

My heart is in my throat. I swear to god he's tilting on purpose, walking right up to the edge like he's daring the slightest gust of wind to topple him.

"No, but I clearly have a much stronger respect for gravity than you."

"Then just pretend it's the deli's Twitter account. We all know you don't have any respect for *that*," he says cheekily.

Before I can respond, he straightens up and propels himself toward the water, contorting his body so fast, I could blink and miss it. In fact, this might be one of the first times I *haven't* missed it. The dive team makes me so nervous that as a general rule I try not to look at them during practice or meets, in constant fear of watching one of them belly flop or smack their heads on the board.

But I couldn't look away from him if I wanted to. It's mesmerizing, like his body isn't his own for those brief few seconds. I'm used to Jack being all in motion at once, all foot-tapping six-foot-something of him. But I'm not used to motion like this: smooth, seamless, practiced. He projects himself off the board and somersaults in the air and twists and then glides into the water with an almost soundless kind of grace.

I forget to breathe until he's poking his head out of the pool, shaking his hair out of his face.

"Your turn."

My jaw drops.

"You don't have to do anything fancy. Just jump." He mimes it to me, treading water as he holds a flat palm up and pretends his finger is me, leaping off of it.

I'm still replaying Jack's dive over and over, reeling from it. I always thought it would be so scary to watch, but it was exhilarating. So fluid and over so fast, I didn't even have a chance to be worried something would go wrong.

That confidence does not, however, extend to my own abilities. "Yeah. Yep. Sure."

"Five-year-olds jump off this board, Pep."

"Five-year-olds don't understand mortality."

"Y'know, the longer you wait, the worse it's gonna get."

He's right, of course. He swims over to the edge of the pool, and I inch to the ladder, propping my arms on it and taking a deep breath before hoisting myself up a few rungs.

"How'd you even learn to do that, anyway?"

Jack's voice calls up from the bottom of the ladder. "You're stalling."

I climb up another rung to satisfy him, but I'm genuinely curious. "How does a person just like—know that they can *do* that? And not die?"

"I mean, same way you got fast at swimming, I guess. Practice."

My palms are so sweaty, I can't stop myself from imagining what would happen if I slipped right now, just went *splat* on the pool deck. It seems kind of stupid that it's full concrete down there. Shouldn't there at least be some kind of padding around the high dive?

"Seriously though."

"Well—I don't know. We did a lot of silly little-kid dives. Then my mom would take us to a trampoline place downtown, where we'd practice flips and stuff."

"And instead of joining Cirque du Soleil and becoming their latest freaky twin act, you decided to slum it here?"

"As flattered as I am in your faith in us, I'm not *that* good of a diver. I've eaten it more times than I can count."

I shut my eyes for a moment, just before I reach the top. "Don't tell me that."

"Pep. You're gonna be fine."

There isn't a trace of mockery in his voice, not even the usual light teasing. The words are so steady that for a moment, I feel like I'm on the ground again, instead of way too many feet away from it.

"In fact, I think you're gonna like it."

I open my eyes again and ease myself to the top. The board is thick, but it's still slick with water from the dive team's practice. I pinch my toes to feel the roughness of it underfoot, to convince myself I'm not going to slip.

"I feel like I'm walking a plank." My voice sounds breathy in my ears. "Like Wendy in *Peter Pan*."

"Just imagine whatever weird dessert you're going to make based on this experience," he says. "High Dive Cream Pie."

"Acrophobia Apple Crisp."

Jack lets out a sharp laugh. It echoes across the pool deck, reminds me how far down he is and how far *up* I am. "There you go."

I teeter to the edge and glance down. The pool is empty. It's just cold enough now that the usual gym regulars who take over the pool after Stone Hall clears out of the lanes have taken to more winter-appropriate exercises, and the stillness of the pool gives it an eerie quality, like the water isn't really there.

"Hey," says Jack.

I want to turn to look down at him, but I don't trust myself to do it without losing my balance and teetering right off.

"You don't actually have to do this."

The only thing more stubborn than my fear might be my pride. But I feel something in my chest loosen, a little bit of the terror ease out of my bones.

"We made a bet," I protest, still staring down at the water.

His voice is so quiet that if there were anyone else around, I wouldn't be able to hear it. "Yeah, well. I won't think any less of you if you break it."

It's so still, I can't hear anything but my own breathing and the *thud thud thud* of my heart between my ears. The fear crackles through me like a second skin, like it's tightening my bones. I blink once, and then again, and start to turn to come back down.

"Pepper?"

Then, all at once, it isn't fear. At least, not the kind of fear I know, that I can put a name to. It's not just the high dive—it's watching the sun rise as I polish off the sixth draft of an essay. It's lying to the face of an admissions officer about what I want to do with my life because I have *no idea*. It's the beat of silence on the phone when I'm talking to Paige, and Mom comes up, and neither of us knows what to say without making the other one mad. It's the thousands of miles and winding roads that stand in the way of Pepper *now* and Pepper *then,* and I'm not even sure who either of them is anymore.

Suddenly this seems so silly. So conquerable. One stupid, ridiculous, fleeting thing that is nothing compared to the rest of it, to the questions I've been avoiding for years.

I let out a yelp and *jump.*

My stomach drops before I do. I crush my eyes shut, and then it's just air, air and infinity, like I'm falling forever. My breath swoops up into my throat and hovers in my lungs until my body is just one breath, buoyed in midair, falling, falling, falling—

I hit the water all at once, feetfirst, the *thunk* of it shocking but not at all painful. I let myself float down for just a moment, my eyes flying open. It's the same pool I've shoved my head into a thousand times, but it's different to me now, like the light is brighter where it's refracting off the edges, like I've made my own current.

I pop up with a gasp, ripping off my goggles. Jack is crouching at the pool edge, staring down at me.

"Holy *shit.*"

Jack's face cracks into a grin, and I get it now. That look in Jack's eyes when he pops out of the water after a dive, the look he's giving me right now. The shine in them, the rush.

"Now try it with your eyes open."

Not on your life, I want to tell him, but then he's holding his arm out to help me out of the pool, seizing my hand in his and pulling me up, and there's this unfamiliar surge in me. Not like I've been hit by lightning, but I *am* the lightning.

"Yeah," I say. "Yeah. I'm gonna go again."

A smirk curls on his face. "Atta girl."

And I do. It's slow-moving, and I'm terrible at it, but I climb up again, and Jack climbs up right behind me, waiting at the edge of the board for me to jump again. It's every bit as thrilling the second time as it is the first, watching the world swoop around me, letting myself go, and knowing there's something down below to catch me.

Jack lets out a *whoop* when I surface again, then promptly launches himself into a backflip, pretzeling and then streamlining himself into the water at the very last second.

"Show off," I gasp when he surfaces.

"Takes one to know one." He pushes his hair back again, splashing me in the process. I pull my cap off, throw it on the pool deck, and whip my hair right back at him. It gets directly in his eyes, and he winces.

"Oh, sor—*pfft!*"

I'm not ready for him to push what feels like a straight-up wave of water at me until I'm practically inhaling it. I let out a squeal, the kind of giddy, ridiculous noise I didn't think I was capable of making beyond the days of Velcro shoes and ice cream–stained T-shirts, and splash him right back. When it becomes evident his splash game is far stronger and more practiced than mine, I reach forward like I did during water polo and put a hand on his head to dunk him—only this time he's anticipating it, and presses his hand down on top of mine, holding it to his head so I go down with him.

For a few moments, we're just a tangle of legs and arms underwater, grabbing at elbows and hands, pushing water at each other. We're both laughing and snorting like idiots when we break the surface, and I launch myself away from him, doing a full butterfly kick on my back like a mermaid so he gets the maximum splash. He pitches forward and chases me down the pool length, but in this, at least, he's no match for me—I can swim circles around him, and he knows it.

Still, I find myself slowing down just a hair, long enough for him to catch up—or at least that's the amount of time I think I'm giving him, until he swims under me and I yelp like I just spotted a great white shark.

He pops back up out of the water with a shameless grin.

"You *ass*." I push my palm to his shoulder.

He leans his shoulder into my hand, lowering himself so he's at the same height. "What, you thought you were the top-dog swimmer around here?"

"*Please*." I roll my eyes. "In a real race, you couldn't take me."

"Oh, yeah?"

"I would crush you."

"So crush me."

It's shallow enough we're both standing, and Jack's smirk is so close to mine, I'm breathing into his face, staring right into the flecks of brown in his eyes and the water streaming past them. The water feels like it's lapping up behind me, nudging me closer to him. My head tilts upward, the challenge in Jack's gaze softening and giving way to something else, and just like that, something is washed away—there is nothing between us but the charge I've been ignoring for weeks, bare and uninsulated, like something inevitable.

"*There* you are."

I'm so alarmed to hear another voice cutting through the air that I jump, backward and away from Jack. The pool water sloshes around us and makes it all too evident what was about to happen, more evident than it was in the moments before it almost did.

My head swivels to see Landon on the pool deck, who, despite all appearances, looks oblivious to what he just interrupted.

I look at Landon, and then back at Jack, not sure which one of us he's addressing. But Jack's looking down at the water. A flush of embarrassment itches at my collarbone, works its way up my neck—did I misread things? Why won't he look me in the eye?

"I was hanging back outside the locker rooms—I realized I don't have your number," Landon calls over the water.

I blink. "My number?"

"Yeah. So I can tell you where to meet up tomorrow?"

Senior Skip Day. It all comes rushing back to me in one fell swoop, one that feels almost like an inversion of jumping off the high dive, like something is crawling back into me instead of out of me. The pact Wolf and I made to meet up tomorrow. Hanging out with Landon. Two things I'm almost certain will be one and the same.

Two things I'm not sure if I *want* to be one and the same.

"Right. Uh . . ."

I doubt if there's ever been a moment in my life more awkward than shouting my number across the pool as Landon types it into his phone, but then, directly following it, there is—the moment I look over at Jack and he looks at me, and there's something so wobbly and uncertain in his gaze that I almost want to apologize and I'm not even sure why.

It's over as fast as it happens. Jack flicks the water and sends a tiny drop in my direction.

"So you and Landon, huh?"

"We're just—it's for Senior Skip Day. Well, afterward. You know how everyone always ends up at the park after school lets out for real."

Jack raises his eyebrows the way he does when he's about to challenge me. "Well, it always *starts* that way, at least."

I wrinkle my nose. "It's not a date." Is it?

"But you want it to be?"

"I . . ."

It's not an answer because I don't have one—but Jack seems to take it as one anyway. He shrugs, the gesture not quite matching his tone when he says, "I didn't realize you guys were even friends."

"Well, we text," I hedge.

"You text?"

I don't even know what makes me say it. Maybe it's because he looks so genuinely perplexed. And why wouldn't he? I suppose I'm not the kind of girl a guy like Landon would casually text—as far as social circles go, we're in entirely different galaxies.

So I'm flustered and embarrassed, and before I can think through the ramifications, my stupid brain finds some way to justify it to him: "On Weazel."

The surprise splits Jack's face, widening his eyes, freezing the rest of him in place. I'm expecting him to ask for details—how we started chatting one-on-one, or when it was the app outed our identities to each other—but instead, he says, "I thought you said you weren't on it."

"I'm—barely. I'm not—anyway. It's just a group thing. You'll be there too, right? I'm pretty sure everyone is—"

"I have a shift to work," says Jack, turning his back to me and taking a few quick strokes over to the edge of the pool.

"Jack."

He pauses, his hand on the deck. I'm ramrod still, trying to think of something to say to make him stay, to bring two minutes ago back. Two minutes ago seems a lot more precious to me now that it's gone.

But all I can think of to say is, "The bake sale. We need to figure out which time block we're using so we can book it with Rucker."

Jack's shoulders give way to a sigh. "Let's say Monday. Then everyone has the weekend to bake."

"Right. Smart." I bite my lip. *Think of something else.* But Jack is already pulling himself out of the water, turning and giving me a close-lipped smile and a tight wave before heading into the locker room and leaving me treading water alone in the pool with a disappointment I can't name.

Jack

My mom sets a large piece of day-old cherry strudel in front of me.

"What's got you in a funk?"

I know she actually means it because she's offering me food at the register, which is a huge no-no in my dad's book. My mom's all about breaking tiny rules, though. I consider the strudel for a moment, and how I can't remember a single time I've actually had a dessert at this place the day it was made. Maybe Pepper's not even that good of a baker. Maybe it's just that her stuff is actually fresh.

Ugh. The taste of her Midterm Moon Pies from before the baking ban are still so fresh in my mind, I can't even lie to myself about it.

"I'm not in a funk."

"You are. Did uptown funk you up?"

"*Mom.*"

She nudges my shoulder with hers, which is no easy feat, seeing that Ethan and I dwarf her now.

"C'mon. Is it school?"

"No."

"Dive team?"

"No."

"Those big, scary college admissions interviews?"

I roll my eyes. "Definitely not."

She hums in agreement. "You're already locked and loaded after college, anyway. Who needs those stupid brand-name schools?" she asks, as if she didn't go to Stanford.

I can tell she's trying to be a *Cool Mom*, trying to take the pressure off me, but if anything, it makes it worse. It's enough of a shift that, for the first time since I left Pepper on the pool deck, she and stupid Landon are not the most aggressive things on my mind.

"Do you ever regret that?" I ask.

I've caught her off guard. "Regret what?"

"Going to school. The big brand-name kind. And then ending up here."

"I didn't end up here, kiddo. I chose to be here."

"But if you hadn't met Dad . . ."

I'm expecting her to be defensive. In all the times I imagined asking her about this, it never ended well. But instead, she smiles and tilts her head at me.

"I'd probably be working at some law firm here or in DC or some other big city, married to some other guy, with completely different kids."

I blink at her. "Oh."

She leans forward into the register, musing so casually, I might have asked her if she thinks it's going to rain tomorrow. "I knew that then, and I know it now. That's the thing, though—I love your father. I love this deli. And you two punks, even if your antics have probably taken a dozen years off my life." She puts a hand on my back. "I knew I'd never regret it. And you know what?"

I raise my eyebrows at her. "What?"

"I was right."

I should choose my next words carefully, but I've never been very good at that. "Even though it made Gran and Gramps mad?"

She clearly already knew this question was coming because she doesn't flinch. "They came around. It was my life, not theirs. I knew what I wanted. And that's lucky enough by itself—not a lot of people do."

I open my mouth and almost say it right then: *I don't want this.* But the problem is I do, and I don't, and my feelings are still way too tangled for me to be able to say I don't want to spend my whole future in this place when I also can't imagine a future without it. It's dumb, but I wish for a stupid, childish second I could just stay like this forever, with Mom and Dad running things so I can still love this place without feeling responsible for it. So I can still let it define me without letting it own me.

But then another swell of customers comes in five minutes to close, and we're all back in a flurry, the conversation over and the strudel long forgotten.

Jack

Later that night, I'm sitting on the couch with Ethan, both of us on our laptops. The fight we were in about the Twitter picture kind of ended by default, the way they always just seem to have expiration dates more than resolutions—when you're packed in quarters as close as ours and working together in a deli, staying mad at each other is just plain impractical.

A ping comes in from Weazel.

Bluebird

So. We still on for tomorrow?

I can't decide if whatever is churning in my stomach is relief or dread. Ever since this afternoon I've avoided getting on Weazel, even thinking about it. Usually I make a few sweeps during the day to make sure everything is kosher and to deal with any suspicious behavior the safeties in the app have flagged, but after that whole Pepper and Landon thing, I just want to wash my hands of it.

It's just—I don't know. It seemed like maybe we were having a moment. Like maybe we'd had a bunch of them, and they all kind of snuck up on me until they were right in front of my face, until she was popping out of the water with that full-wattage, ridiculous smile that made it feel like my blood changed its composition in my veins.

And weirdly, throughout this whole thing, Pepper and I have been . . . well, friends seems like a stupid word now. Like that doesn't quite cover it. I've told her things I've never said to Paul, not even to Ethan—heck, not even to Bluebird, who until now was the only person I could come close to saying anything honest to. Close enough I can still practically see her texts to me about Ethan the other night like my brain has screenshotted them—close enough that she managed to call me out for things I haven't fully understood myself.

She accused me of hiding. One straw short of accusing me of self-sabotaging. Well, then, this is the icing on the cake—I made this stupid app, and now this stupid app is the reason Landon and Pepper are going to ride off into the sunset.

I turn back to Weazel, to this weird beast of mine. I've never once regretted making it. With the exception of people occasionally being dicks the way dicks are prone to be, it's helped set up study groups, and given people a place to vent, and accidentally started friendships—relationships, even. Gina and Mel. Pepper and Landon.

Maybe even me and Bluebird.

Wolf

Yeah. But first—

Wolf

Emergency Cupcake Locator

It takes her a full minute to answer. I spend the first bit wondering if I've freaked her out, if the gesture wasn't funny or it was too personal or if this is going to put a weird pressure on something that, in some ways, hasn't even started yet.

But then, somehow, my thoughts slide right back to Pepper. I bet Landon doesn't even end up at the group thing. He'll say he is, maybe, and then oh-so-conveniently text her the wrong place for the meetup. Or maybe he'll wait until afterward—"Hey, want to grab some ice cream?"—and maybe Pepper will even take him to a Big League Burger, just to be funny about it, and pull out whatever ridiculous emergency dessert condiment she happens to have in her bag, and Landon will laugh and tell her it's cute, and her cheeks will get all red under her freckles and—

Bluebird
Oh my god. YOU DIDN'T.

Bluebird
YOU MADE A CUPCAKE VERSION?!?!

I finally let myself smile, easing into the couch cushions and tilting my phone away from Ethan, who is raising his eyebrows at me. It took the better part of all my free time this week, but I used the same map formatting I based the mac-and-cheese locator app on for a new one, one that lit up 450 different places selling cupcakes in Manhattan.

Wolf
Well, mac and cheese and cupcakes ARE the two
most essential food groups

Bluebird

I might actually be crying?????

Wolf

Your dentist will be, that's for sure

Wolf

Anyway, glad to know you weren't kidding about that cupcake obsession

Bluebird

Not at all. You don't even know how on brand this is for me

Bluebird

Okay, so you showed me your big secret project. But I held out on you

Wolf

Well now you're obligated to unhold out. What's yours?

Bluebird

It's super dorky so you have to brace yourself

Wolf

Consider me braced

Bluebird

ppbake.com

Bluebird

It's a blog. For baking

Bluebird

It's live and all, my sister and I run it together, but it's anonymous

Bluebird

And the stuff we make has ridiculous names because we basically bake like we're five, so

I tap the link, and it opens up a bright, cheery, robin's-egg blue web page. *P&P Bake*, it's called. It's clearly one of those WordPress blogs converted into a website, but that doesn't make it any less captivating—the pictures on the posts are so vivid, I can practically taste them through the screen.

I scroll down, glancing at the dessert names, lingering on the pictures. The most recent is Tailgate Trash Twinkies, which are apparently a homemade cake roll infused with PBR; I scroll down and see A-Plus Angel Cake, and Butter Luck Next Time Butter Cookies, and then—

And then, on Halloween, there's an entry for Monster Cake.

My breath stops before it can leave my chest, my entire body stiffening on the couch like a corpse. There's no mistaking it. I may have a bad habit of eating Pepper's baked goods so fast, it threatens the time-space continuum, but the bright colors and gooey mess of that cake are so distinct in my mind and in my taste buds, I could see it in another *life* and immediately identify it.

Yet my brain still refuses to process it, and I'm still scrolling as if I'll blink and it will disappear, a vivid, sleep-deprived teenage hallucination.

But the further I scroll the worse it gets. The So Sorry Blondies. The Pop Quiz Cake Pops she and Pooja were eating the other day. A few things I've never heard of before, with irreverent, silly names, some of which must be Paige's, but others that are so distinctly *Pepper* it stings to read.

I drop my phone.

"What?" asks Ethan, barely looking up from his screen.

Pepper is Bluebird. Bluebird is Pepper.

I can't decide what to think, what to feel, but my body seems to decide it for me, my heart beating all over my body and my chest suddenly so full of air, I'm not sure whether to use it to breathe or yell "PEPPER IS BLUEBIRD!" at the top of my apparently very melodramatic lungs.

"Is it Pepper again?"

If there was any blood left in my body, I'm sure it would drain from my face. "What?"

"Did she tweet something?"

Right. Twitter. My head must make some kind of involuntary nod.

"So much for her being done," says Ethan, rolling his eyes.

My mom walks in from Grandma Belly's room, holding a mug full of tea. "Pepper? Isn't that the name of the girl you were hanging out with the other day?"

The other day feels like a year ago. I try to think back on the last few weeks, the last few *months*, of talking to Bluebird and talking to Pepper, scrambling to untangle them in my head. What have I told Bluebird? What have I told Pepper?

"Yeah, that one," Ethan confirms.

And more important, what is Pepper going to think? How many things did she say to me on the app that she wouldn't want Jack Campbell, Twitter adversary and senior class disappointment, to know?

My mom beams. "And she saw that write-up of you on Hub Seed and asked you out, hmm?"

By some short-lived miracle, I finally find my voice. "Not exactly—"

"Pepper's the one tweeting from the Big League Burger account," says Ethan.

"Wait, what?"

I didn't even realize my dad was in the kitchen, just out of earshot, until suddenly he's standing in the doorway with a pan and a dishrag in his hands. He looks at me and then at Ethan, like he's not sure where to aim the question.

"Pepper Evans," says Ethan dismissively. "Goes to school with us. Her family owns the whole Big League Burger operation."

My mom frowns. "I thought it was some girl named Patricia?"

"Her real name's Pepper," I say. "No, her real name is Patricia, but her name is Pepper." Or Bluebird. Or Girl Who Is About To Be Pissed Off At Jack All Over Again. Take your pick.

"That woman."

If I hadn't watched my dad's mouth moving, I might have convinced myself I imagined him saying it. A shadow of an expression crosses his face; he lowers his head to look down at the pan so I won't see, but it's too late. I glance over at my mom, expecting her to look as dumbfounded as I do, but she's heaving in the kind of breath that can only give way to a sigh.

"What woman?" Ethan asks. Whatever is on his laptop screen has been thoroughly forgotten. When neither of them answers, he adds, "Are we . . . missing something here?"

My dad looks back up, his lips in a tight line. "No. Just . . . we put the Twitter thing to rest, right?"

"Right," I say dumbly.

He nods. "Let's keep it that way."

And then, in that eerie, psychic parent way, my parents wordlessly shift from what they're doing and head toward their bedroom. They don't shut the door—they never do when they're just talking—but it's only slightly ajar, their voices too low for us to hear anything.

My phone lights up in my hand.

Bluebird

So, what about tomorrow, bakery maestro?

Tomorrow. Senior Skip Day.

Whatever small, naive, truly embarrassing sliver of excitement pushed its way through the panic is immediately crushed.

Landon.

Maybe she does, and maybe she doesn't—but I don't think I imagined the look on her face in the pool earlier today, or the stammer in her words. She thinks Wolf is Landon.

No. She *wants* Wolf to be Landon.

"What the hell?" Ethan murmurs.

I look over at him, into the sometimes frustrating sameness of his eyes. Usually in moments like this, they are more alike than ever, the same furrow, the same confused squint. My ally. My brother. The other half of a rebellious split egg. But right now I'm so far past the weirdness of our parents, they could come back out speaking German and I'd still be rooted to this spot, sinking into what is about to prove to be a very self-indulgent, pitiful hole.

"Yo," says Ethan. He doesn't ask what's wrong, but the tone of the *yo* does, and so does the way his eyes blink out of his confusion and focus on mine.

And just like that, there's this ache in my chest, this almost irresistible urge to tell him everything. About Weazel, about

Pepper, about the future and all the parts of it I equally dread and doubt. No matter how I try to outrun Ethan's shadow, it is the shadow that understands mine best. No matter how I try to resent Ethan for the problems I've brought on myself, he is still and will always be my first and best friend.

It's not because I don't trust Ethan that I don't tell him. It's because I don't even want to accept it myself. Putting it out into the open would cement the humiliation of it, give it a permanence I'm just not ready to face.

I gather up my laptop and my phone. "I gotta catch up on sleep," I mumble.

"Yeah?"

Another opening. Ethan holds my gaze, and for a moment, it's just us. No school, no friends, no customers or straphangers or strangers in the way. The way it was when we were little, before the rest of the world wedged its way between us. Before Ethan became every bit as much a measuring stick as he is my brother.

I swallow hard. "Yeah."

I get to my room and kick off my shoes and fall into my bed face-first, shoving my head into my pillow. I need to sleep on this. For a night or for a lifetime, maybe. But my eyes are closed and my body is sagging into the mattress, and I am still equal parts aching and wildly self-pitying and indignant, like taking a shot of coffee from the espresso machine downstairs and then promptly getting smacked upside the head.

My phone buzzes again. I ignore it. It'll be Bluebird—no, *Pepper*—and still I don't know what to say, don't know what to *do*. I want time to stop passing. I don't want to have to make a decision about this. But that's the thing—whether I respond or I don't, a decision is made. A domino is knocked over that in turn knocks down a bunch of other dominoes in its path.

I'm just going to be a bystander in their cross fire.

But then the phone buzzes again, and again. I blearily pull my face out of my pillow and glare at the screen, but it's only Paul. Honestly, I should have recognized it from the rapid-fire nature of the texts; he's never been able to condense any thoughts into just one.

Today 9:32 PM

dude. DUDE. dude dude dude dude

you have to tell me who goldfish is
on weazel

i think? she is my soulmate????

or just like trigger the app to tell us
both. you can do that right

I rub my palms over my eyes, scowling into the screen.

Today 9:34 PM

No. I'm not doing that

but you CAN

right???

I put down the phone again, hooking it up to the charger and setting my alarm for the morning, determined to cope with this influx of information the only way my body knows how: going the hell to sleep. Just as I turn off the light, the phone buzzes again.

Jaaaaaaaaaaaaaacckkkk

And then, finally, whatever it is I'm feeling finds a point of focus, finds a place to funnel itself.

NO. Stop asking. It's not fair to the other people on the app and I'm not gonna be a dick just so you can cheat it

I set the phone back down with unnecessary force and flick off the light. The phone doesn't buzz for the rest of the night.

Pepper

By seven o'clock on Friday night, I am drafting a blog post for the next Pepper/Paige creation in my head: Pepper's Crappy Crap Day Crinkle Cookies.

Ingredients: First, add unresolved tension with one Jack Campbell, who is either out sick or out participating in the Senior Skip Day shenanigans taking place during the school day. Mix in nearly twenty-four hours without contact from Wolf, two seconds after essentially baring my soul to him by showing him the thing I am most proud of in this world. Add what is proving to be the most awkward hangout with Landon and a large group of *incredibly* drunk teenagers on the face of the earth. Add chocolate chips, butter, flour, salt, cocoa powder, eggs, and more embarrassment than the body of a teenage girl can possibly contain, set the oven to a bajillion degrees, and set the whole damn thing on fire.

"You look kind of . . . green."

I glance over at Pooja, who has been my literal only solace in this crinkle-cookie crapfest of a day. I spent most of it staring at my phone screen, waiting for either a response from Wolf confirming we were still on for tonight, or a response from Jack after I texted him that morning asking why he wasn't in class. Nothing, nada, the phone screen so blank, I could practically feel myself shrinking into my seat.

I considered not even going out to hang with Landon and the other seniors, filled with an inexplicable kind of dread as the day went on. But I couldn't miss it. Either Landon was Wolf or he wasn't, and I was too invested in knowing to back out now.

Well. It's safe to say now that Landon is very much not Wolf. In fact, there are a whole host of things Landon is and is not that have become extremely apparent in the last few hours I have spent in his company.

I got a text from him around five to meet up with the group just outside of the Met steps. I'd been ready for at least two hours, having carefully picked out an outfit for one of the rare few moments my classmates would see me out of uniform, applying and reapplying such an absurd amount of a lipstick Paige left behind that I was on the verge of accidentally tattooing my lips. I'd picked out a sweater dress with tights and a pair of smart boots, with a pretty pea coat my mom handed down to me and a scarf my dad got me for my birthday.

It was perfect for a crisp day in November, but all wrong for what I stumbled into—which was not my classmates, but the drunk, rowdy, raided-my-rich-parents'-liquor-cabinet version of them. Landon was the first to spot me, his hair all askew, wearing a pair of jeans and a Lacoste T-shirt, and red in the cheeks despite the fact it was forty degrees outside.

"If it isn't the Big League Burger heiress herself!" he yelled, prompting some hoots from our classmates that made the tips of my ears burn. "Better watch out, Campbell!"

Ethan glanced up from his perch on the steps, also red-cheeked and glossy-eyed but far more composed than Landon and some of the other stumbling boys were. "Hey," he said with a friendly enough wave, before returning to the far more important business of making out with Stephen.

I had an uneven, topsy-turvy sense that they had been talking about me before I arrived, which maybe I should have expected, given my new Hub Seed notoriety. Landon wrapped a drunken arm around me, a half hug of a greeting, and messed up my hair. My cheeks burned and my whole body went stiff—why couldn't I just be normal? Be casual and fun and lean into a hug, rib him the way he was clearly about to rib me, do something to flirt back?

The moment was over too late for me to do anything but be annoyed at myself for it—for the way I still felt like I had to make myself fit into this world, even after all this time. For the realization that for some reason, I'd hinged that feeling on this person who seemed entirely unaware of the way I'd thought of him, both at the beginning of Stone Hall to the near end.

I glanced around the group, hoping to make eye contact with literally *anyone* on the same level of sobriety as me, which is when, mercifully, Pooja showed up, looking every bit as thrown as I was. She got a similarly raucous greeting from the group, dodging a boy who tried to hug her with what seemed to be an open container of some sort of alcoholic concoction in his hands and ducking her way over to me.

"Uhhhh," she said, her eyes wide on mine.

I smiled in relief. "Yeah."

And maybe we both would have ditched right then—her eyes seemed to be asking me without asking if I was game—but then Shane announced he was drunkenly posting in the

Hallway Chat on Weazel, and then everyone was grabbing for their phones to either look at what he'd posted or do the same.

Pooja shoved her hands into her pockets, taking a step back from the madness as if to wash her hands of responsibility for it. "I guess we're not going to an actual place to eat," she said wryly.

I tried to match her tone, tried to keep the swell of disappointment out of my voice. "Yeah. Yikes."

A second later I flinched in surprise as Landon shoved his phone screen under our noses.

"Spell check from the brainiest chicks at Stone Hall?"

I froze like a deer in headlights. Pooja took the phone from him, which had a drafted text he was about to put in the Hallway Chat. I never even read what he was about to post; the username displayed on the screen was *Cheetah.* My eyes were stuck on it, reading it over and over and over until Pooja finally let out a breath of a forced laugh and handed it back to him.

"Good to post?" Landon asked, leaning in so close to the two of us, I could smell the sharpness of whatever he'd been drinking on his breath.

Pooja offered a tight smile. "There are no spelling errors, that's for sure."

"Awesome."

He hit send on his post—*Met steps, bring booze*—and walked away abruptly, leaving me on the edge of the steps with my mouth wide open and my chest tight with something I didn't quite know the shape of yet. Relief, maybe. Or disappointment. Or some mingling of the two.

Landon wasn't Wolf. That, surprisingly, didn't seem to move me in one direction or another; it was just a fact, and I accepted it with ease, like someone telling me what was on the menu in the school cafeteria that day.

But the rest of it hit me sideways—because if Landon wasn't Wolf, somebody else was. And whoever that somebody else was, they apparently wanted nothing to do with me.

Maybe it was the blog. There's nothing blatant on it that would connect it to me and Paige, but maybe he figured it out anyway. And maybe when he learned the truth, Pepper Evans became a hell of a lot less appealing than Bluebird ever did.

And maybe that's only fair. On Weazel I'm not the Pepper I am at school. I'm relaxed, and goofy, and free to say whatever I want—and the longer the app didn't reveal us to each other, the easier it got. But I can't expect whoever it was to reconcile that with the person I am at Stone Hall. Jack used to call me a robot, and I've always known there was a grain of truth to it. I've spent all four years at Stone Hall gritting my teeth, keeping my head down, and trying to crush everything in my path. Not exactly conducive to lasting friendships.

Of which I apparently had none at the moment. Jack was AWOL, Wolf was in the void, and I was . . .

"Thank god enough people have started coming to the study groups that we don't have to use Weazel anymore," said Pooja, closing out of the app with a roll of her eyes. "These doofuses are going to clog up the Hallway Chat with their shitposting for the rest of the night."

I bit my lip, forcing myself to rally. I wasn't alone.

"That's for sure," I agreed.

She took a seat on the edge of the steps, and I followed suit. For a few moments we just watched as the cluster of our classmates weaved in and out of each other like drunk pinballs. A few weeks ago I didn't know much more about them than their names and what their parents did, but thanks to Pooja's study groups, I've actually gotten to know some of them better—like Bobby and Shane, who launched a podcast where they read all the Twilight books, and Jeannine, who is so obsessed with Lady Gaga, she's seen her in concert nine times.

I glanced over and saw Pooja was pulling up one of the chain emails about the study group and responding to something.

"It isn't, like, too much on you?" I asked. "Taking all the time to set this up?"

Pooja shrugged. "It's worth it." She hit send on her email and turned to me, shoving her hands back into her pockets and bracing herself against the cold. "Besides, I kind of stopped caring about my grades so much. I think our education system is effed up. The way we're always teaching to tests. Defining each other by numbers instead of what we can actually contribute."

A gust of wind picked up, and I stiffened—both against the wind and the truth of her words. My whole body wanted to reject them. I'd defined myself by those numbers for so long, it felt like without them, I didn't have anything to anchor me in Stone Hall's world.

"That's pretty ballsy for this crowd," I said. "But that's—it's great. That you know what you want to do."

"You were kind of a part of it," she admitted.

It took me a moment to respond, so surprised that all I could say was, "Me?"

"Yeah." Pooja shifted her weight on the step, leaning a bit farther from me. "It's so dumb and you probably don't remember—like, so dumb—we were doing some quiz bowl thing, freshman year?"

For a moment I went so still that I couldn't even shiver.

Pooja's eyes flitted to the side at the memory, looking rueful. "And the teacher called on you, and you hesitated for a moment—and you just looked like, so miserable. Like you were on death row. So I gave you the answer. Or I thought I did. Turns out it was the wrong one."

"That was an accident?" I blurted, before I could stop myself.

Pooja's eyes snapped to meet mine. "You *do* remember."

Of course I did. It was the catalyst to four years of me trying to keep up with her, four years of trying to one-up her so I could be in a place where she could never one-up me again.

"I was so humiliated, and Mr. Clearburn was glaring at us, so I just blurted out my second guess and it was right. I tried to say something to you, and you wouldn't even look at me, and after class you just bolted. And that night I was so upset I told the whole thing to my parents, and they were so mad about it that they wanted to pull me out of Stone Hall right then. They're both professors," she said, by way of explanation, "and they're big into education being about learning, not—well. Whatever it is some of the teachers at Stone Hall are trying to accomplish."

"Another *Hunger Games*," I supplied.

Pooja let out a breathy laugh. "Exactly." She seemed almost shy, when she looked back over at me. "Anyway—I meant to say something to you, but I was in damage-control mode, trying to talk my parents out of pulling me out and *homeschooling* me." She shudders. "That's how it kind of started. I didn't want to leave. All my friends are here. So I've just tried to fix things, where I can. And having Weazel weirdly helped make that happen."

My throat was tight. All this time I had painted us both in these certain lights—me an underdog, and her some kind of bully—and using it to fuel this fire in me. Not just to justify my need to be the best, but to justify everything else—the chip on my shoulder. The way I didn't make many friends here. In one stupid moment that I completely misread, I decided it was me against the world.

"You're right," I managed after a few moments. "The system really is effed up."

I wondered if I should apologize. If the thing between us was as concrete for her as it was for me. But before I could decide, she hoisted herself back up and offered me her hand, pulling me to my feet.

"Looks like they've descended on the food carts," said Pooja. "Wanna grab a bite and see how long we can endure them?"

I realized then that she didn't want an apology. That the rivalry went unspoken, and the apology would too. We were on the other side of something that took way too long to cross, but at least now we were here.

"Yeah, let's."

We made a plan to grab smoothies, but while the alcohol in Landon's system made him forget things like appropriate conversation volumes and how to walk in a straight line, it apparently was not strong enough for him to forget his gallantry. He kept to his word and bought me dinner—a hot dog from the stand next to it, covered in ketchup and mustard and a mountain of relish.

He bowed a little as he handed it to me. "A hot dog for the burger princess."

I winced. I'd managed to go four years without anyone making a connection between me and the Big League empire, but apparently my luck didn't just run out, but went full into the red.

"Thanks."

I didn't really even mean to eat it. As snobby as it sounded, it was no Big League Burger Messy Dog, the toppings for which my dad and I once dreamed up on a ride back from a Nashville Sounds game. But I took a bite, and another, and polished off the whole thing, mostly so I had something to occupy my mouth so I didn't have to attempt to talk to Landon and his crew.

An hour later I am deeply, deeply regretting it.

"Seriously, you don't look so hot," says Pooja. "You wanna find a place to sit?"

Truth be told, I don't *feel* so hot. My stomach is doing that unsettling thing where it feels like it is trying to take up residence in my throat. We've been wandering around Central Park, loosely following the cluster of our classmates, which only seems to get bigger as more of them find us and join in on the hijinks. But thanks to me, we've been falling behind.

"No, no, I'm good," I lie.

"You sure?"

I stop for a second, do a quick self-assessment. It's probably just nerves—about Wolf, or Landon, or this whole mess of a Senior Skip Day.

"Yeah, I'm sure."

Before Pooja can say anything else, we're both cut off by the sound of Landon letting out a whoop and attempting to cartwheel on a patch of grass. He lands gracelessly on his back and laughs up at the sky like it's the funniest thing in the world.

"You know what's ridiculous?" Pooja asks. At some point in the last few minutes, we've stopped walking and started observing, ceased being part of the group and started to fully lean into being on the outside looking in. "I came out here because I had a stupid crush on Landon."

Landon gets up and lets out a belch so loud, I swear it stirs birds from their nests.

"Safe to say *that's* over," she deadpans.

I start laughing, even though it's making my gut churn.

"What?" asks Pooja, a self-conscious smile curling on her lips.

I'm half speaking for her and half for myself when I say, "You can do *much* better than Landon."

Pooja blushes. "Yeah, well. At this point I'm probably gonna wait until college to find out."

My stomach twists again as if in direct protest of this idea. The closer we get to college, the more distant it seems to me. I've been so focused on the finish line aspect of the whole thing, of just getting the admissions letters and knowing I didn't fail, that I still haven't given much thought to what happens *after*.

"Same," I say anyway.

"Aw, come on. Are you telling me you and Jack really aren't a thing?" asks Pooja, kicking at a stray rock in our path.

"No," I say, too quickly. "No, no, we're just friends."

"The people of the internet have spoken, Pep, and they ship Jactricia."

I pull a face, shuddering. "Please tell me nobody actually typed that ship name with their bare hands."

"I would, but that would make me a liar." She tilts her head back up to stare at the boys, who are now engaged in what seems like a drunken game of Red Rover that will inevitably end with at least one broken bone and two very angry coaches. "Anyway, he's clearly not as big of a dope as this lot, so he has *that* going for him."

I laugh, turning my head away from them because it is honestly starting to make me nervous. But just as soon as I turn away, I blink myself there again, standing in the shallow end of the pool, staring into Jack's face in that breathless, hesitant moment from yesterday. In some ways I've been there all day, the thought of it latching and tugging to every other thought, refusing to leave me alone. For a moment I just let it happen to me, let it take me to wherever it wants to go, and then—

"Oh, god."

"What?"

My stomach lets out one of those ominous, inevitable kind of roils, and I manage to blurt, "I'm definitely gonna hurl."

Pooja doesn't miss a beat. "Okay. Uh—sit tight."

She runs over to a trash can and comes back with a paper bag, just in time for me to shove my face into it and let out half the contents of my stomach.

"*Pepper*?"

It sounds like Jack, but that's ridiculous. And in any case, round two follows up round one so quickly, it's a miracle I'm still upright, with the amount of hot dog I'm presently upchucking. It's volcanic, and so disgusting the mere act of throwing up makes me want to throw up, like some kind of vomit-ception. Pooja had the foresight at least to grab my hair before the worst of it, and I turn to give her some messy combination of a thank-you and an apology when I realize the hand holding my aforementioned hair back belongs to Jack.

What are you doing here? I almost ask, but then I clamp my mouth shut—I'm sure my breath smells like a hot dog funeral.

"Hey, put your phone down, you asshole," Pooja yells.

I glance in the direction she's shouting and see I have accumulated quite the audience. Landon, Ethan, Stephen, Shane—the whole drunken crew has stopped what they're doing to stare, as have random people in the park.

The Pepper I was five minutes ago was so naive to think this day couldn't get any worse.

I straighten up and manage to put the vomit-filled bag back in the garbage. Jack's hand is on my elbow, following me like a shadow, and Pooja is charging forward and yelling at someone who must have taken a picture.

"Whoa," says Landon lowly, coming up to me with a broad grin on his face. "Props, Pepper. Never would have guessed you'd be the first party foul, considering the size of the stick up your—"

Jack moves forward with his fist cocked, looking like a cartoon character. I yank him back by his elbow, and he's surprisingly easy to pull, all momentum and lanky limbs.

"She's not drunk, you *dick*."

"Jack, it's fine," I mutter, pulling him back a little farther so he's next to me. He gives in to the tug like a very angry noodle, but doesn't look at me.

Landon's expression can't quite settle on irritated or amused. "Hey, man, chill out."

"Seriously, Jack," says Ethan, who has walked over to the commotion.

Jack scowls. "Really, Ethan?"

Ethan gestures vaguely, like he wants to apologize but his body doesn't know how to commit to it.

"Nice," Jack mutters.

Ethan sighs. "Shouldn't someone get her home?"

"On it," says Pooja. She hooks her arm into mine, and I feel a rush of gratitude so intense that for once, it doesn't make me ache for my own sister—for once it feels like I have someone as unquestionably on my team as a person can get. She steers us away, flanking one side of me with Jack on the other, who is hovering like he walked into the wrong reality and needs directions to get back.

"Are you okay?" Jack asks.

"Yeah. I weirdly feel better now."

"It was *definitely* that shady hot dog," Pooja concurs.

"In that case, I hope Landon starts chucking some up soon too."

"Why?"

Jack is in full Jack mode, his body like a live wire as he follows us.

"Jack, you don't have to—I mean, I live like six blocks away." I nod my head back at the edge of the park. "You can go hang out with the others."

Jack hesitates. Out of the corner of my eye I can see his arm lift, can see him scratch the back of his neck the way he always does when he's put on the spot. "Actually, I came to see you."

Pooja ducks her head in an ineffective attempt to hide her smirk.

"Oh." Something lifts in my chest. Thankfully this time it isn't dinner. "Sorry to be a buzzkill."

"Eh, I've seen worse," says Jack.

I look over at him and he's got this doofy kind of smile on his face, the kind that tricks me into thinking I look okay right now instead of the sweaty-browed, post-throw-up mess of a human I absolutely am. It's stupid how relieved I am to see him, how glad I am he's *here*. That he's talking to me. That he crossed the whole length of this overcrowded island to do it.

Pooja and Jack drop me off at the lobby of the building, Pooja hugging me and rattling off instructions to stay hydrated. Jack leans in unexpectedly and hugs me too, like it's the most natural thing in the world, and just like that it is. I hug him back, squeezing him for an extra beat, accidentally scrunching some of his jacket in my fist.

"Feel better," he says, his cheeks bright red.

I do. So much better, I forget to respond, until the doorman of the building clears his throat and Pooja's eyebrows go up as if to say, *Girl*.

"Yeah—you too." Shit. "I mean—well—"

Jack laughs, backing up and nearly stumbling into someone on the sidewalk. "Later, Pepperoni."

Pepper

For someone who has had the kind of day that ended in literal vomit, I have no right to be full-on grinning in the elevator. But I am, and it's wild, like there's something bubbling in me, pooling at the base of me and making me feel so light I feel as if I should tether myself to the railing. I let myself imagine things I never let myself imagine: what it would feel like to grab Jack by the sleeve of his coat and pull him close. What it would feel like to run my hand through his wet, messy, post-dive hair. What it would feel like to cross the distance to him in the pool yesterday, close my eyes, and kiss him.

I'm still dizzy in my own imagination when I open the door, completely miss my mom's suitcases lined up by the doorway, and walk straight into her poised on the couch with an expression that slams into my daydreams like an oncoming truck.

"Uh."

My mom raises her eyebrows at me. "Sit."

I consider my other options, which are limited to running away and seeing how far the five dollars in my purse will take me. Pooja told me the other day the Q train goes straight to Coney Island.

Too bad it doesn't go to Mars.

So I sit. Mom turns to me, her expression unreadable—I can't tell if she's mad or concerned, but she's definitely some kind of upset. "We have several things we need to discuss."

I wonder if it's too late to pull the *I just vomited in a public park* card, but it feels too risky.

"Okay?"

She pulls out her phone, and I can feel the anger inflating in me like a balloon. If she pulls up the Twitter page, I will explode. I will go full Paige Evans with a metaphorical baseball bat and yell until the neighbors think she's back from college. I may even lean fully into the teenage cliché of slamming and locking the bedroom door.

She passes it to me. It's not the Twitter page. It's my . . . midterm grades.

And they're not stellar.

"Oh."

I mean, it's not like they're *terrible*. But by Pepper standards, they are pretty bad. I feel an unfamiliar kind of swoop in my stomach, something I'm so unused to, I don't even recognize it for a moment: failure.

If this were Nashville, I could shrug and say, *Okay, so I have a couple of B's. So what?* But this isn't Nashville. And here, a B in the final stretch of college admissions is the equivalent of rolling over and playing dead.

"I didn't realize . . ."

My mom leans in, pulling the phone away. "What's going on, Pepper? This isn't like you."

Of course it isn't. I've run on a steady diet of five hours of sleep on weekdays for four years now. How could anything be *like* me? How am I supposed to know exactly what I'm *like* anymore?

And the past few weeks have dialed it up to eleven. There's no time, and this whole "war" with Girl Cheesing has stolen what little of it I have, carved it up, and chopped it into stupid tweets. I know it's not going to fly as an excuse, but it's the truth.

"The Twitter thing. It's taking up my study time."

"You send like two tweets a day. It's not exactly a full-time job."

I feel a twinge of sympathy for Taffy that is far from the first and certainly won't be the last. "It is exactly like a full-time job, Mom. It takes time to come up with those tweets, to figure out how to respond, to gauge the audience reaction to them—"

"I worry what's taking up most of your *time* is flirting with this boy."

And there it is. I sit very still, like an animal with the viewfinder of a gun targeted on its back, waiting to see where exactly she's planning to take aim.

"I finally read that article on Hub Seed," says my mom. "I didn't realize you were going toe-to-toe with your classmate. Or that you wanted this attached to your name on the internet forever."

My face is burning. "I had nothing to do with that. I didn't ask or want Taffy to put my name on anything."

I worry she's not going to believe me, but she's moved on too fast for it to matter. "And this Jack?'

It feels important to protect him. I didn't realize how intentionally I'd kept his existence from her until now. "He goes to my school."

The deflection is about as effective as hiding behind the couch cushions. In fact, my mom doesn't even seem surprised. "And he has nothing to do with these grades, or you ignoring Taffy's texts?"

"I stopped answering because we're done with this. The retweet war on the Hub settled it."

Her jaw tightens. "I can only assume that boy pulled one over on you with that picture."

"It wasn't his fault, it was—"

"A lesson learned. You shouldn't trust the competition."

It stings unexpectedly, hearing this right on the heels of my talk with Pooja. I bite the inside of my cheek. I'm not gonna say it, I'm not gonna say it, I'm not—

"Yeah, well, you shouldn't put your teenage daughter in charge of a massive corporate Twitter account."

My mom purses her lips. "You are *plenty* qualified," she says. "I wouldn't put you in charge of it if you weren't. But I'm less concerned about that than I am about the grades. Colleges still check first semester of senior year."

If that's true, she has a funny way of showing it. But instead of saying that, I say something that stuns us both.

"Who says I even want to go to college?"

My mom's elbow is propped on the couch, like she anticipated she'd be using her hand to hold up her forehead sooner or later in this conversation. Sure enough, she leans into it with a weary sigh.

"Pepper . . ."

"No, seriously." My heart is hammering in my chest like it's suddenly twice as thick as it usually is. I stare my mom down, not even sure where I'm going with this until it's coming out of me, pushed from some depth I haven't even acknowledged myself: "Maybe I—maybe I want to take a gap year. Or go back home for a little while. Or—or open my own business, like a bakery or something."

That last one takes me by surprise, enough that I clamp my

mouth shut as soon as I finish saying it, but my mom is oddly unfazed.

"Pepper, you're a smart girl. A driven one. If you know what you want, then take it."

I open my mouth. I don't know what I want.

"I thought . . ."

She actually looks amused, her face softening.

"What?" She waits for me to finish, and then I remember the thing New York sometimes makes it so easy to forget—she's on my side. We're on the same team, even if the team is considerably smaller than it used to be. "Pepper, I didn't finish college. Your dad and I made our own way in the world. You and Paige are both too stubborn and too smart not to be able to do the same."

I sit there for a moment, the anger so stunned out of me, I don't know what to do with myself. I unclench my fists and spread my fingers out on my legs, staring down at them, feeling more lost than ever—all this time I thought I was doing this to make her happy, or to beat Pooja, or to fit in. All the unhappiness or loneliness I ever felt, I was so prepared to pin on someone else. Only in this moment is it clear that it was nobody's fault but my own.

And more than that realization is the bottomless kind of panic that comes with it. I've just assumed there were certain directions my life was going to take. The safe kind. The kind everyone else was taking, and I plowed through with a vengeance. It hasn't been easy, but it hasn't been brave either. The idea of actually straying from it is either thrilling or terrifying, the two feelings swallowing each other and spitting each other back out before I can settle on one.

Then, suddenly, I can picture it: the thing Paige and I dreamed about as kids and joked about as teenagers and let fade into the periphery. A bakery tucked into the corner of some street, with a blue-and-white striped awning, with Monster Cake and Rainy Day Pudding in the window, with mismatched mugs and sticky-fingered kids and a little spot in the back kitchen that's all my own to make whatever it is I want to make.

I can see it so clearly, I feel like I just breathed it into existence.

"As long as you don't let some teenage boy stand in the way of it."

I should be more indignant on Jack's behalf, but I'm still reeling. "He would never."

"Well, those grades speak for themselves," says my mom. "You don't have to go to college, but you're in the endgame now. Finish strong and keep your options open."

I nod.

"And stay away from that Jack."

My mouth unhinges, and then I laugh. My mom doesn't. She stares me down like we're in a bad made-for-TV movie of a modern *Romeo and Juliet*, like she can actually forbid me from associating with a boy who goes to my school.

"Stay away from *Jack*?"

"He's clearly not a good influence." She stands, a clear bookend to this conversation. "And I don't see what the problem is anyway. It's not as if you actually like him."

She's testing me. *He's my friend*, I want to say, but even that's a trap—if I admit that, it's as good as admitting he's the reason why I've quit tweeting. But if I'm defensive, either swearing I don't like him—or worse, admitting I *do*—the whole thing blows up even further into my face.

In the end, I settle for none of the above, letting the verdict roll over me like some kind of wave I am willingly letting my-self drown in.

"And Taffy and I will take over the Twitter until you get your grades back up."

She slips out of the living room, then, and the dust settles on the not-quite-fight before I can tell which one of us has won.

Jack

How to Suck at Confessing to the Girl You Like that You've Secretly Been Messaging Her on a Platform You Created, Then Convince Her It's Not as Shady as It Sounds: a terrible novel, written by me.

The first attempt to tell Pepper the truth was noble enough—I begged off the end of my shift on Friday and took the 6 train uptown to where the Senior Skip Day shenanigans were going down, all inflated with this confidence and bravado, ready to lay everything out on the line. I was even going to be cheeky about it—sneak up and take a picture of her from behind, then message it to her on the app so when she turned around, she'd see me there, with a cupcake I'd brought from the deli.

I imagined Pepper would be surprised, and maybe angry, and then eventually hear me out. I imagined every possible scenario after that, from ones as ridiculous as her shoving me into the lake, as hopeful as her maybe even being into our whole accidental secret pals thing, and as realistic as her just plain being disappointed I wasn't Landon.

Of all these imagined scenarios, though, the one that did not come up was the one that ended with Pepper vomiting up some impressive chunks of a partially digested hot dog.

The second attempt goes about as well as the first. It's never hard to spot Pepper during a swim meet, especially now that she's the team captain—she runs warm-ups, harasses the freshmen boys who are dicking around when their heats are coming up, confiscates the chocolate espresso beans one of the junior girls started passing around to give everyone an "extra edge" on their relay race (only at Stone Hall). No, spotting her isn't the issue—it's getting her alone that proves to be impossible.

Especially because she seems very, *very* intent on avoiding me. Like, book-it-across-the-pool-deck-like-her-butt's-on-fire level of intent.

I finally manage to corner her after she pulls herself out of the pool from the 50-yard butterfly, headed for her towel in a cluster of other senior girls.

"Yo, Pepperoni, I was wondering—"

"Check your texts."

She says it out of the corner of her mouth, and so fast that it takes me a few seconds after she's passed me to rewind it in my head enough times to make sense of it. I hustle up to the bleachers and zip my phone out of my bag, where sure enough, there's a text from Pepper.

This is super dumb, but my mom is here and she doesn't want me talking to you. She's touchy about the Hub Seed article.

I glance up in alarm, like someone just told me a panther was let loose in the building. I don't look up with the intention of finding Pepper's mom, but in an instant I lock eyes with a woman sitting with the parents on the other end of the pool who can only be her—she has the same blonde hair, the same keenness in her eyes, and the *exact* same pinched look on her face Pepper used to get whenever I said something she didn't like.

Except the full force of that expression on Pepper's face isn't half as terrifying as it is coming from a woman dressed in a power suit in the middle of a pool deck. If it were possible for her to shank me with her eyes, I think she just might.

I look away, shoving my phone back into my bag, paranoid she somehow read Pepper's warning to me from across the pool. I don't bother trying to talk to her again for the rest of the night. I barely talk to *anyone* for the rest of the night. It's awkward enough that Pepper's mom clearly hates me—it skips past awkward and goes straight to eerie when, throughout the next few hours, I feel her mom's eyes watching me every now and then, as critical as they were the first time. It's jarring enough I even screw up one of my dives, landing with enough of a *plunk* in the water it's all Paul will talk about for the rest of the meet.

I wait until I'm home to text her back.

Today 9:14 PM

So . . . your mom is terrifying?

Which is to say, I kind of get your whole "my mom made me do it" thing with Twitter now.

Hoooly shit did she TALK to you?

Tell me she didn't talk to you

No, no, she just pierced me with the kind of stare that makes human souls shrivel

Oh man

She doesn't usually come to meets
but we were hanging out all day and
she's been out of town for a while so

YIKES

No it's fine I'm a new yorker. i'm used
to people giving me the stink eye for
no reason

Well, I guess technically she has
reason

Speaking of my mom I have noooo
idea where she stands re: using the
oven tomorrow for the bake sale

The ban is still in place?

If it is joke's on her I'll just go hide in
the big league burger kitchen down
the street

I mean we have like five ovens. Come
use one of ours

She doesn't answer right away. She's all the way uptown, but I can still feel her overthinking like she's sitting right next to me.

Today 9:27 PM

The 6 train isn't that scary. Call me and I'll talk you through it

Ha ha

For real. Worst that can happen is you end up in brooklyn, get kidnapped by hipsters, and your mom strangles me in broad daylight. What've you got to lose

Well when you put it THAT way

Does tomorrow afternoon work for you?

See ya then pepperoni

As it turns out, Pepper was not kidding about her lack of subway experience. The next day she calls me around three in the afternoon outside of the Eighty-Sixth Street subway station, where I talk her through using the spare change in her purse to get a one-way MetroCard, swipe, and find the platform for the 6 train that goes to Brooklyn Bridge. I get a few nervous texts from her—If I'm at 23rd, I haven't passed you yet, right?—but she makes it to Astor Place without getting kidnapped or stuck on a train going express and emerges blinking out at the new skyline like she just teleported to another world.

She pulls out her phone to text me, and I let out a loud whistle, raising my hand to get her attention. Her head snaps up, and her face bursts into this wide, blinding kind of grin, the same one that nearly knocked the air out of me when she jumped off the high dive for the first time.

"Hi," she says, running up to me. And then we're hugging, because I guess that's just a thing we do now, and it's great and it's awkward, but it's terrible because as soon as it happens, I don't want to let her go.

"You did it!" I say, at the same time she says, "You're here."

I shrug, glad it's cold enough now that my cheeks are already red from the wind. "I figured I'd give you a quick walking tour of the 'hood."

It's strange, seeing her in her everyday clothes instead of her uniform or her swimsuit. I mean, I guess I did on Friday, but the upchucking distracted from it pretty fast. We're both in jeans and coats, her hair tucked up into a bun with loose ends all sticking out of it, and the whole thing is just so relaxed and *normal*, it's like the usual thirty seconds or so it takes for us to fall into a groove together just falls away.

She sticks close to me on the short walk to the deli, close enough our hands brush a few times, and I have to fight the impulse to take it. It's weird—unlike Ethan, I've never actually dated anyone beyond the occasional awkward kiss with girls in our class at school dances. I always thought the motions of it would be so strange, like something that had to be learned and practiced. But it's the opposite of that—it would be too easy to grab her hand, to reach up and tuck her bangs behind her ear, to stop and stare at her and see if that moment from the pool was just a moment or something that led to a much bigger one.

I show her the ice cream shop, the little bookstore, the food cart where I sometimes get coffee even though it drives my dad nuts.

"You're so popular," Pepper notes, when the third person waves at me from behind a window or a cash register.

"Hah. No. They're all just scarred for life from me and Ethan running buck wild around this block as kids."

"I bet you guys were cute."

"Yeah, it's a shame what's happened since."

She ribs me, just as Annie, the bookshop owner, pokes her head out and says so loudly half the street can hear, "Jack Campbell, are you on a *date*?"

I freeze in my tracks, hoping lightning will miraculously strike me down where I stand.

"Let me guess," says Pepper, without missing a beat. "You bring *all* the girls to the deli."

Annie's grin is merciless. "He woos them with ham slices."

"Hey!" I protest, finally finding my voice. "I'm so clearly a cheese guy! I'm offended."

"And I'm intrigued. Come into the store on date two, and I'll tell you all the embarrassing stories about baby Jack you want to know."

Pepper laughs, and I'm expecting it to be one of those self-conscious laughs she muffles with her wrist, the kind that ends with, *Oh, this isn't a date.* Because it's not, really. It's just some pseudo-flirty, post–Twitter war, pre-baking *thing* I'm not sure how to—

"I'll swap you for the embarrassing dive team ones," Pepper promises.

Annie's eyebrows shoot up. "Ooh, I like her."

"C'mon, c'mon," I mutter through a smile, hooking my elbow with Pepper's and dragging her away as she waves goodbye to Annie.

The deli's in full Sunday afternoon swing when we arrive, the line not quite out the door but only because people have packed themselves inside to avoid the November cold. The woman who always comes in with her five grandkids waves at me, one of the line cooks who's on her break tweaks my shoulder when she walks by, an NYU professor who comes in from time to time nods from his coffee cup and turns his attention back to some book about seafaring.

Pepper stops just out of the doorway, staring with an inscrutable look on her face. It didn't occur to me until this moment to be self-conscious about showing her this place. I've never had to give the grand tour of it to someone whose opinion actually matters, because the people who are close to me have known this place as long as or longer than I have.

"What?"

"Nothing." Then she shakes her head to retract it. "It just reminds me of . . . well, the first Big League Burger."

"Oh my god. Are you *Patricia*?"

A moony-eyed middle schooler has approached, a group of her friends lagging about a foot behind her. They're all so pint-sized that Pepper and I tower over them, and I have an unfamiliar shift of feeling like—well, like an adult.

"Um, yeah?" says Pepper.

The girl's face lights up like a Christmas tree. "From the Big League Burger Twitter!"

"No *way*!" one of her friends crows. They're looking at me now. "You guys *are* dating?"

"Would you sign my backpack?"

"Let's get a picture!"

Pepper and I exchange mutual looks of red-faced bafflement, but end up submitting to the overexcited whims of our apparent fan club. We pose for a picture with them, and sign one of their cell phone cases, and by the time they're done, my mom is staring at us from her perch behind the counter with an eyebrow cocked like she's just waiting to make fun of us.

Ethan cuts in before she can.

"If you give her even a bite of our grilled cheese, we're all disowning you," he announces from the register, with a salute at Pepper to let her know he's mostly kidding.

Pepper salutes right back. "I'll stick to the baked goods."

"So *this* is the famous Pepper," says my mom, leaning in as if to inspect her.

There's a beat when Pepper freezes—our coloring and the messy hair is so similar on us there's no mistaking my mom is, well, my mom. She cuts a glance at me and then back at my mom, and only then does it occur to me she's worried we might also be holding a Pepper's mom–sized grudge.

My mom softens her eyebrow, makes her voice low and conspiratorial. "So you're the one I should send the bills to when I have to send my kid to Twitter therapy?"

Pepper eases up, letting out a breath. "He can just push them through the slits of my locker."

"Hah!" My mom gives Pepper that look she gets when she's decided she's sized someone up and is satisfied with what she sees. I don't realize I've been holding my breath too until I'm slouching in relief. "Can do."

Then she reaches out and nudges me on the shoulder. "Ovens two and four are cleared for teenage shenanigans. Try not to burn the place down, hmm?"

"Are these the Kitchen Sink Macaroons?" Pepper asks, her eyes wide on the display case.

"They sure are," says my mom, her hands on her hips. "A Campbell classic, according to your father. I whipped up a batch this morning myself."

I grab tissue paper and pluck one from the display, handing it to Pepper.

"What—are you sure—"

"He owns the place, he's sure," says my mom wryly.

I stiffen at the words, but then Pepper takes a hearty bite of it and closes her eyes. "Oh my god. Are there *pretzel* bits in this?"

"And you and that no-good brother of yours told me I was pushing my luck, adding those in last week," says my mom, pointing a finger at me.

"Okay, okay, but to be fair, that was right on the heels of the licorice experimentation, and I didn't want to scar any more customers for life."

Pepper takes another bite. "This version might actually be better than Monster Cake."

"Whoa. Don't get too carried away," I say, wondering when the tables turned so drastically on us that I'm defending her own food to her.

"Monster Cake?" asks my mom, intrigued.

"We'll have some ready in an hour," says Pepper. "It's an atrocity."

"A delicious one," I add.

Pepper beams like I've just handed her on Oscar. Then she hikes her backpack off her shoulder, revealing enough junk food and various dessert sauces that it could put Cookie Monster into a coma just by looking at it.

"Well," I say, "it looks like we've got our work cut out for us."

"Let the ridiculous dessert mash-up games begin."

Jack

An hour and a half later, we are the proud parents of two massive sheets of Monster Cake, some impressive concoction called Unicorn Ice Cream Bread, three dozen Kitchen Sink Macaroons, peanut-butter-and-jelly cupcakes, a three-layer Paige creation dubbed Sex-Positive Brownies ("Slutty Brownies," Pepper explained, "but Paige took a course on feminism and sex work, so."), an ungodly amount of banana pudding, and a bunch of misshapen cake balls we rolled around in melted chocolate and stuck in the fridge.

My mom comes in at some point, lured by the smell. She tries a sliver of the Monster Cake, groans, and says, "Don't look me in the eye," as she immediately cuts off a second slice.

"We actually need that for school," I remind her, as Pepper blushes furiously next to me, looking pleased with herself.

My mom holds up a finger. "Hush. I'm having a moment over here." Pepper snorts as my mom finishes having said moment, and then turns to Pepper, her fingers still sticky with cake, and says, "You are welcome to this kitchen any day of the week for the rest of your damn life." Before Pepper can respond, she turns to me and says, "But if you don't clean up this disaster, yours, my dear, is over."

By the time we finish scrubbing all the pots and pans, Pepper's cheek is dusted with flour, and a strand of her hair has come loose and somehow ended up streaked with melted chocolate. I reach up without thinking and run my fingers through it, trying to get it out. Her eyes dart over to mine, but not in alarm—in this hopeful, surprised kind of way that suddenly gives meaning to something I thought in the moment was meaningless, that makes me second-guess myself.

"Chocolate," I say dumbly, pulling my hand away to show her.

She rolls her eyes at herself. "Typical."

I shift my weight onto the foot that's farther from her. "We could, uh—chill at our place, while we're waiting for everything to cool down?" I point upward. "We live right upstairs, if you want to stay for dinner."

"Are you sure?"

I sweep my hand over to the other side of the kitchen, which is stacked to the gills with meats, cheeses, breads, and every weird sandwich accoutrement known to humankind. "If you can dream it, you can make it."

We both avoid grilled cheese, since the whole debacle is still a little too fresh. I make myself a pastrami on rye, and Pepper uses the bread ends of a baguette to fashion a swiss cheese, ham, and butter sandwich. I pull out the cranberry relish, and she mutters the word "genius" at me before adding it to hers, and I can still feel it inflating my chest five minutes later when we take our spoils back up to the apartment.

I'm expecting to see Grandma Belly in her chair when we walk in, but she must be napping. Instead, it's just me and

Pepper and suddenly a little more of myself than I counted on Pepper seeing, from the cheesy photos of me and Ethan hung up on the fridge, to the door to my room that is very much wide open, leaving an old Super Smash Bros. poster I forgot was even on the wall in plain view.

Suddenly I am so at a loss for what to do, I actually find myself *wishing* a parent would come in and interrupt.

"We could, uh, watch a movie?" I suggest.

"Yeah, sure."

I glance at the shelf, weighing our options, and turn to Pepper with a smirk. "*Mean Girls*?"

Pepper meets my eye like she suspects I'm kidding. "Don't laugh, but I'm obsessed."

I'm already walking over to pluck it from the collection. "Yeah, I know. You reference *Mean Girls* on the Big League Burger account more than you actually talk about burgers."

"I'm not a regular social media manager. I'm a *cool* social media manager," says Pepper, plopping on the couch with her sandwich as I queue up the DVD.

"You think that's what you wanna do? When we're finally freed from the prisonscape of Stone Hall?"

Pepper has already taken an absurdly large bite of her sandwich, but she wrinkles her nose in response. "No. God. What a nightmare."

"Eh, we had some good times."

I sit next to her, a little closer than I meant to, but she doesn't scoot away and neither do I.

"Are we going to wax poetic someday about the good old days on Twitter?" Pepper asks. "Has this been our heyday the whole time?"

We both lean back into the couch, and she turns her head

toward me, waiting for an answer that for some reason it takes me a moment to give.

I make a decision, right then—close a door I've been tiptoeing around now for months. I decide not to tell Pepper about any of it. About Weazel, about Bluebird and Wolf, about the tangled web of our friendship that is secretly more complicated than she could ever have guessed.

Because this, right here—whatever this is—has a strange kind of magic I feel as if I could accidentally breathe right out of the air if I say the wrong thing and puncture it. Pepper's eyes are on mine, and it's kind of scary, but it's also just so *simple*. Usually at least half my brain is preoccupied with self-doubt and second-guessing and my Olympic-sized twin complex, but right now everything is quiet. Just Pepper and sticky sandwich fingers and little smirks, and the feeling that whatever we're sharing between us right now adds up to something bigger than the sum of what we were by ourselves.

It's the talk about the future, maybe. Pepper using the word *someday*. Suddenly there is a someday, and that one spoken word seems to imply so many other unspoken ones—that we mean more to each other now than the people we were a month ago, who might have briefly nodded to each other at the all-night grad party in the spring and never seen each other again.

Not telling Pepper is easier than telling her, sure—but it's more than that now. I want to hold on to what's taking shape here. I don't want to compromise that *someday* by telling her something that doesn't even matter anymore.

"Nah," I say after a moment. "This was just the beginning. We'll go to war on Snapchat next."

She ribs me with her elbow and doesn't move her arm back,

so it's just tucked into my side. I watch the movie without really watching it, the two of us eating our sandwiches, Pepper saying her favorite lines with the characters often enough that it's clear in the first five minutes she has the entire film memorized down to the exact degree of exasperation in Tina Fey's face before she speaks. Still, she laughs like she hasn't seen it more times than she can count, hard enough I can feel the vibration of it through her arm and into my ribs like she's sharing it with me.

Just as Cady is about to throw up on Aaron Samuels's shoes, the DVD starts to skip, and then pauses.

"Oh, man. It does this sometimes," I mutter. "It'll start itself back up in a sec."

"I haven't had to deal with this in a while. DVD players—so retro."

I turn to her, somehow surprised by how close her face is to mine even though I've been fully and excruciatingly aware of all of her for over an hour. "Well, the East Village has to keep its hipster cred somehow."

"I guess that rep is more important ever now that we're famous, huh?"

I laugh, accidentally leaning in closer—or maybe she's the one leaning. "Those kids today—how freaking weird have our lives gotten?"

"I feel like I hallucinated that. Like I hallucinated the entire comments section of that Hub Seed article too."

"Jactricia," I snicker, before I even realize what I'm saying—and then we're both red in the face, because it's the first time we've mutually acknowledged the extreme awkwardness that is strangers actually, legitimately *shipping* us online.

Pepper clears her throat. "Well, obviously we need to petition for a better ship name."

Some of the awkwardness diffuses, but the tension is still there, tight like a coil between us.

"Jepper? Pack?"

"Pass," she says, nudging me with her elbow again—and then something shifts. The apartment is eerily still, with the same kind of quiet there was in the pool the other day, where you're not sure if it's actually quiet or if the rest of the world's sounds just don't apply to you anymore.

"Maybe just Jack and Pepper, then," I concede.

There's a ghost of a smirk on Pepper's face, but she's so close, I can hear it more than I can see it. "Pepper and Jack," she corrects me. Then her eyes light up. "Pepperjack."

It's ridiculous, but the word is like a key turning into a lock. And then impossibly, even though some part of me knew it would happen the moment I saw Pepper walk out of the subway, we lean in and our lips touch and we're kissing on my couch.

It is awkward, and messy, and perfect. We're so bad at it, but even in the first few seconds I can feel us getting better, her hand hesitant and then sure as she sets it on my shoulder, our lips giving way to each other's, this self-conscious, giddy little laugh escaping Pepper and humming in my teeth.

"Wait."

The laugh is already dissolving out of her face when I pull away, and *crap*, I don't know what I'm doing or why I'm doing it *now*, but I was wrong. I can't lie to her. I can't start something that feels this big built on what still feels like a lie. I just didn't understand how big it was until it was already happening.

"You're right," Pepper blurts, a mile ahead of me. "I mean, we're just—I don't know. My mom, and the whole thing, and I . . ."

"No, not—I don't care about that."

She looks equal parts panicked and exasperated. "You were the one who said wait."

"It's just that there's something I need to tell you."

"Oh."

Her eyes are already starting to dim, and my brain is scrambling for the words I need to recover when, without warning, the front door cracks open and a woman says, "Pepper Marie Evans, what on *earth* do you think you're doing?"

Pepper snaps herself away from me so fast, I might have burned her. My back is turned to the front door, but judging from the sheer horror in Pepper's eyes, I don't need to fully turn around to know it can only be her mother.

What I'm not expecting to see when I finally turn is my dad walking in right behind her, looking both exasperated and furious. It isn't until his eyes meet mine that I realize the fury is reserved for none other than me.

"*Mom?*" Pepper bleats. "How did you—what did you—"

"What, you didn't think I'd see *this* plastered all over the internet?" says Pepper's mom, walking into our apartment without even a beat of hesitation, as if her name is on the lease. She shoves a phone in Pepper's face, pointedly ignoring me. Pepper tilts the screen so I can see it too—the picture of the two of us with the middle schoolers has already accumulated four hundred retweets, with both the Big League Burger and Girl Cheesing accounts tagged.

I gulp. Literally gulp, like I'm in some bad sitcom, or maybe just a really off-the-wall dream that I'm going to wake up from any moment now. But it only gets weirder from there.

"Ronnie," says my dad under his breath, "there's no reason to—"

"I rarely, if *ever*, have set rules for you, Pepper." By now she is towering over the both of us, and we're sitting on the couch utterly paralyzed. "But I told you very specifically to stay away from that boy."

She says "that boy" as if I'm not even here, but I can't even let that demoralizing fact wrap around my brain—Pepper and I are both staring at each other, my dad's "Ronnie" still an open question dangling in the air between us.

"I—I needed to use the oven." Pepper is redder than I've ever seen her, and I can tell it's every bit on my behalf as it is for hers. "There's a bake sale tomorrow, and I know you didn't want me to bake, so—"

"Get your things. We are leaving, and having a *very* long discussion about the appropriate punishment on the taxi ride home."

Pepper reaches for her backpack, shoving her phone into it and zipping it up with shaking hands. She looks back at me, her eyes searing with a desperate kind of apology in them. I'm too stunned to react, my mouth hanging open, still buzzing from a kiss that feels like it happened in some other lifetime.

In her panic, Pepper reaches for the half of a Kitchen Sink Macaroon she hadn't finished yet. Her mom reaches her hand forward and picks it up first, holding it up and scrutinizing it. Out of context, I would have laughed—I've never seen a grown woman look so inexplicably furious at a dessert before.

"Figures," she mutters to herself. Then, for some reason, she turns to my dad. She opens her mouth to say something, and he tilts his head sharply—not quite shaking his head, but making enough of a movement there's no mistaking its intention.

She lets out whatever breath she was going to use to say something to him, sets a hand on Pepper's shoulder, and guides her out of the room. Then they're gone, the apartment door slamming behind them, leaving me and my dad in total silence.

I'm not sure what to say or if I should even speak. The air in the room is so thick, it feels like it's slowing down time. I glance over at my dad, cautious at first, but he's not even looking at me. He's leaning on the kitchen counter and scowling at his knuckles.

"Dad?"

He blinks, looking over at me. I'm expecting some kind of punishment of my own. A Time-Out Booth–level lecture, maybe. Something on par with whatever the hell just happened here.

But he seems so distracted that even when he does get around to the whole disciplining thing, it seems like more of an afterthought than anything else.

"You shouldn't be bringing a date into this apartment without supervision."

"It wasn't . . ."

Well. It kind of was. But it's not like Mom didn't know we were up here. And Grandma Belly is technically home.

But my dad's already pacing out of the kitchen, heading for his bedroom. He's not even waiting for me to apologize. And he's certainly not waiting for me to ask the dozens of questions on the tip of my tongue, chasing Pepper and her mom out the door.

"Sorry," I say—partially because I am, for Pepper's sake, and because I want him to stop for a second, so I can figure out what to ask and how to ask it.

My dad just nods.

So that's it. I've gotten away with . . . whatever it is I got away with, I guess. I'm still puzzling out what exactly that is, but my dad's *Ronnie* and Pepper's mom's *Figures* and the absurdly weighted look between the two of them just before they booked it out of here is still rattling around in my head like a pinball in a machine.

And then there's a *thud* from the other room, and both my dad and I stop in our tracks, everything else forgotten faster than it takes for us to get to Grandma Belly's door.

Pepper

Approximately eighteen hours after my kiss with Jack Campbell—my *kiss* with *Jack Campbell*—I am sitting at a card table with Pooja in the front entrance of the school behind our veritable army of baked goods, overanalyzing the situation to such an absurd degree, it is now less of a kiss and more of an FBI investigation.

Pooja, however, isn't having it.

"He likes you. You like him," says Pooja. "Honestly, it's old news. Even preteens in Iowa on the Hub realized it before you."

"But last night . . ."

"Talk to him."

"I've *tried*." It's a humiliating thing to confess, but Pooja needs context if I'm going to get any advice: "He hasn't texted back."

In fact, Jack has all but turned into a ghost. He mysteriously did not show up for homeroom. I only know he's here today because I saw him in the cafeteria at lunch, but he was way across the room and had slipped into his calc class before

I could catch up to him. And now he's conspicuously absent from the bake sale too—the only reason we even have the baked goods is because Ethan, in a rare moment of actually participating in his dive captain duties, dropped them off at the front office for us.

Granted, he is most likely making out with Stephen under the stairwell by the gym while we hawk all these goods, but at least he kind of tried.

"Well, he can't hide forever. So I guess you'll get your answers soon enough." Pooja leans back and props her foot on the chair that was supposed to be occupied with Jack. "Maybe he's just embarrassed, after the whole thing with your mom."

"Yeah, maybe." I shake my head. "His dad called Mom *Ronnie*. My dad doesn't even call her that. Vee, maybe, but never *Ronnie*."

"That, I have to admit, is intriguing. And I will be the first one to reblog the conspiracy theories when they hit Tumblr, because I personally suspect your parents are part of some weird underground fast casual food cult," says Pooja, popping another bit of a peanut-butter-and-jelly cupcake in her mouth. In her defense, she did pay for it. "But your mom can't ban you from seeing Jack. He's ridiculous, sure, but he's not, like, a delinquent."

"Maybe he wasn't yesterday," I mutter, thinking of his unexplained absence.

"And the kiss was good, right?"

"I mean, it wasn't *not* good." I shrug, trying to seem casual about it even as my heart starts beating a little faster and my palms are sweating where they're propped on the cash box. It was my first kiss, and one of those milestones I only realized I hadn't given enough thought to executing until it was actually happening—and boy, did it happen.

And then swiftly un-happen so fast my ears are still ringing from Jack's *Wait* and my mom's lecturing on the Uber ride back.

Still, even with all that lecturing, and the fact I am grounded until kingdom come, and my mom is quite possibly part of a food services mafia with Jack's dad, it was kind of absurdly, stupidly great.

Or at least it was until the second Jack brought it to an abrupt halt.

It's not just the kiss, though. I know I should feel bad about lying to my mom, about breaking her trust, and I do. Enough that I almost blurted out the whole thing to Paige on the phone last night, just so I could feel better when she inevitably took my side. But the guilt is completely separate from the rest of it, from the terror and the thrill of something as simple as getting on the 6 train and taking a twenty-minute ride downtown.

It was like emerging into an entirely different city. Not that there's any surprise in that—sometimes it feels like individual blocks here are their own islands, separate from the massive one they're all built on. It's just I've never seen a new part of the city or experienced it through my own eyes because of a choice *I* made.

And I guess, in a way, I still haven't. I saw it through Jack's eyes. The mingling of the newer, kitschier shops with storied buildings with storefronts so much older than we are that you feel like a blip in time. The bustle of NYU students and New York natives and street vendors and people wearing ridiculous outfits nobody bats an eye at. The people who waved at Jack like a parade all the way from the 6 train to the deli, as if he was every bit as much a fixture down there as the little shops and restaurants.

Girl Cheesing itself has its own magic, the way every shop

around it seemed to give way to it like it was the pulse of the block. And yesterday, I got to be a part of it. I got to see a whole new part of this city and still be myself in it without it spitting me back out, and I'm restless at the idea of it now, at how much more there is to see—the five or so blocks I walked with Jack function like their own separate planet, and there are hundreds, *thousands* of others squeezed into this city all around it.

I've spent so long resisting the rest of this place that I feel like I've had my hands over my ears and my eyes clamped shut ever since I got here, waiting to ride it out until the day I could leave. Now suddenly, graduation seems less like a jailbreak and a little more like an expiration date. The day I might run out of time here, to see the rest of everything I've been so determined to ignore.

I'm about to talk to Pooja about it, but we're interrupted by the sharp squeak of shoes on linoleum, a squeak so familiar that I know it belongs to Paul before I even look down the hall. Sure enough, he's hightailing it with his usual speed and talking a mile a minute—talking to Jack, who is walking a beat behind him, his face hovering in the beginnings of a scowl.

"Look who decided to show up," says Pooja—but Jack and Paul don't head in our direction, and instead divert sharply down into the music hallway. I catch just the side of Jack's face as he turns the corner, and whatever the scowl is about, it's way beyond the usual Paul levels of exasperation. He looks straight-up wrecked, like he didn't sleep at all last night.

Pooja is already looking at me when I find her eyes, like I need some kind of cue.

"Maybe he forgot," she says.

I raise my eyebrows at her, but only because it's that or give in to the alternative—that Jack regrets that kiss. That I was just imagining the moments leading up to it, building something up in my head. That somehow, over the course of one weekend, I've been rejected both by the anonymous friend I've been pouring my heart out to for months, and the very real friend I accidentally spilled it out to faster than I ever thought possible.

"I'll go talk to—"

"Listen, Pepper, I swear I didn't have anything to do with it."

I blink up at Landon, who is towering over the bake-sale table with an expression on his face I've only ever seen on people called into Rucker's office on the PA. Some mingling of guilt and sheer terror.

"Uh . . . I mean, yeah, I hope not. Unless you paid off a hot dog vendor to give her food poisoning," says Pooja.

Landon doesn't even look at her, his eyes still focused on mine. "I told anyone who had pictures to delete them. They were being dicks."

"The pictures of Pepper blowing chunks?" Pooja asks, her tone already heated.

Landon starts to nod, and I roll my eyes.

"Let me guess," I mutter. "Someone posted one into the Hallway Chat."

Landon's mouth opens and then stays open for just a beat long enough for me to feel a trickle of dread.

"You haven't seen?"

I narrow my eyes at him. "Seen what?"

"I didn't have anything to do with it," he says again. "It's, uh—you might want to check Twitter."

Landon takes off and is down the hall and out of sight before Pooja can pull the app up on her phone. Her scowl hardens, and then she passes it over to me.

It's a picture of me in the park from Friday night. My face is pinched and pale, just a half second away from retching into the bag Pooja grabbed for me out of the trash can—a bag that very visibly has the iconic Big League Burger logo on it, something I failed to notice as I was using it as a receptacle for my stomach contents. I look awful, like some drunk, stumbling teenage cliché, but more to the point, I look like *myself.* The picture was taken within close enough range that there's no mistaking it for anyone but me.

Especially because the picture was tweeted from the Girl Cheesing account, under the caption: Evergreen mood.

My stomach plummets all over again, this time in one heavy, lurching swoop. I thumb the picture and scroll down over a thousand retweets so far, and it was only posted an hour ago. oh ew un-stanning immediately, someone has tweeted. turns out patty's a party animal, writes another, along with a GIF of Kristen Wiig dressed like a drunk Cinderella on an old episode of *Saturday Night Live.* Another one, that hits a little closer to the vest than I thought it would, reads, No wonder her tweets sucked so much this week.

I've been so far removed from it since Jack and I settled the score that I haven't even been on the app all week—Taffy fully took the reins, and I disabled the notifications I used to get every time Jack tweeted. Maybe this shouldn't feel like such a slap in the face, but it still stings like one.

"He wouldn't do this," I say instantly.

"Then why hasn't he deleted it?" says Pooja. "Anyway, it looks like it's responding to something the Big League account said."

I pull it up and see a tweet from a few hours ago. It's so cringeworthy that I know Taffy couldn't have been the one who drafted it. It's a picture of our two versions of Grandma's Special Grilled Cheese along with the number of them we've sold versus theirs.

retweet all you want, but this grandma is wiping the floor with yours, it reads.

"Oh, for god's sake," I mutter.

"Go get him to delete that shit," says Pooja. "Someone already memed it."

I close my eyes. My mom just *had* to keep this stupid Twitter fight up, didn't she? And now I'm not only the laughingstock of the school, but probably poised to be the laughingstock of the country. No matter what I accomplish in this life, whenever someone Googles my first name for the next hundred years, a picture of me heaving my guts into a Big League Burger bag will probably be the first hit.

"I'll be right back," I mutter, getting up so fast from the bake-sale table that the chair legs screech across the floor out from under me.

I follow the little hallway they disappeared down. I can hear Jack's voice faintly before I reach the little offshoot of the hallway—and then he raises it, and it's not faint at all. I stop in my tracks, stunned by the level of irritation in it.

". . . cannot *even* begin to tell you how little this matters to me right now," I hear Jack saying from around the corner. He and Paul are standing in front of a row of lockers, where Paul must be grabbing his clarinet.

"Dude, I'm your best friend."

"Yeah? Then don't ask me to do dumb shit."

"It's not *dumb.* I just want to know who Goldfish is. We've been talking for a few weeks now, and I really think it could, y'know, be a thing. But I just gotta know who she is or I'm gonna embarrass myself."

Jack lets out a sigh like he's recalibrating himself. "You won't."

"Have you *met* me?"

It's about then that my brain makes sense of the use of *Goldfish,* and I realize Paul must be talking about someone he's met on Weazel. My face burns; the lingering embarrassment over the debacle with Wolf is still weirdly fresh, underneath everything that's happened since.

"Trust me, Paul, it's just—you don't want to mess around with this app. In fact, I think I'm just gonna—disable it, maybe. Make another version where people can't be anonymous, so we can still have all the study group setups and stuff."

I'm listening so intently, I'm not even breathing anymore. I don't fully remember why I came down this hall in the first place. *Disable it?* The words ricochet somewhere in my head and refuse to settle. *Make another version?*

There's only one scenario where it would make sense for Jack to say something like that.

"But *dude*, there are so many people who have become friends on it—"

"Yeah, but Rucker's right. Sometimes people are assholes on it. I monitor it whenever I can, but I just plain don't have time anymore, and I . . ."

"At least just tell me who Goldfish is."

"I told you I'm not going to do that. And besides, it's—you think you want to know, but maybe you don't, you know?"

Every muscle in my body tenses, like it already knows something I don't.

"No?" says Paul, his voice starting to lean into a whine. "I really, really do."

"Like—the other day I found out who someone I'd been talking to on it was before the app triggered it, and it just made everything weirdly complicated, me knowing and her not knowing."

The hallway suddenly seems smaller, like the ceiling is closer to the floor, like it's the only part of the school that's left, and it's going to compress and shove me into them at any moment.

"So you *did* cheat and find out who someone was on it," says Paul, both excited and accusatory. "I knew it. You don't just make an app like that and—"

"No, jeez, Paul. No, I didn't. She just—said something in the chat, sent me this link, and then I knew it was her and it just—it made everything weird. I hated it. I wished I hadn't known."

My heart is slamming in my ribcage. Paul says something else, but I turn and sweep up the hall before I can hear it, blinking back tears.

Jack is Wolf.

And I'm a goddamn *idiot*.

I don't even know how I make it back to the bake-sale table, because no conscious part of me is committed to getting there. *Jack is Wolf* is like a balloon swelling in my brain, knocking all the other thoughts aside. Because if Jack is Wolf, that means I've been talking to him for months. If Jack is Wolf, that means he not only knows who *I* am, but that he didn't want it to be me. Because if Jack is Wolf, he let me go to that stupid hangout in the park to meet him knowing *full well* I'd embarrass the hell out of myself thinking it was Landon on the other end of those texts.

Figures it would all come full circle. He let me humiliate myself there, and now his picture from that night will humiliate me for eternity.

It's not even that, though. I can live with the stupid picture, can live with Landon avoiding me for the rest of senior year, can even live with whatever fallout will inevitably come when my mom catches wind of all of this.

What I can't live with is the fact the nightmare has come true: Wolf knows who I am and is obviously disappointed. And the hurt is twice as big knowing Jack is disappointed too.

It casts a shadow of doubt on everything. I was the one who kissed him. I was the one who pushed for us to meet.

It made everything weird. I hated it. I wished I just hadn't known.

"What the hell happened to you?"

Pooja is looking at me like a ghost has approached her. I open my mouth—*Jack is Wolf!*—but that doesn't make any sense, not to anyone, because I kept it so close to my heart that I never breathed a word of it. So instead, what comes out is an ill-timed, too-loud blurt: "Jack is the one who made the Weazel app."

Pooja's jaw drops, and the blood seems to leave her face. While I expect a reaction, I'm not expecting a reaction that drastic—but Pooja isn't looking at me. She's looking behind me.

"Miss Evans, can I see you in my office?"

Shit.

Pepper

In the end, Rucker can't really do anything to us—the only proof he has that anyone did anything was me blurting it in a hallway with only Pooja as a witness, and Pooja was smart enough to grab another swimmer to put in charge of the booth and book it out of there the moment after Rucker called me in and sent one of the teacher's assistants to go find Jack.

It's fruitless. But I insist over and over, until all three of our ears are bleeding, that I was only kidding about Jack making Weazel.

"That doesn't seem like a joke, young lady," says Rucker, narrowing his eyes at me.

"It's, uh . . . it's part of the Twitter thing. I'm sure you've seen the article on the Hub about us?" I'm desperate. Grasping at straws. "We started, uh, pranking each other in real life too."

"Spreading allegations like this doesn't really seem like a *prank*."

Jack isn't even bothering to jump in. He was indignant when

they first brought him in, insisting he had nothing to do with it, but then his eyes swept up and met mine, and the fight drained out of them. Rucker told him what I said in the hallway, and he hasn't so much as looked at me since.

I don't know what else to do to save him, if he's not willing to save himself. So I play the only card that has a prayer of working. "I mean, it's Jack. He's not the brightest bulb. You really think he's capable of making an app like that?"

Jack winces. I don't move a muscle, determined not to break eye contact with Rucker.

They've already searched our phones. They didn't find Weazel on either of them—someone posted an app in the Hallway Chat to hide app icons weeks ago. The only way they'll find it is if another student rats us out and shows them how, and nobody can do that without incriminating themselves.

"I'm calling both of your parents—"

"Wait—could you . . ." Jack blows out a breath. "It's not a great time."

Rucker tilts his chin down in a way that would probably seem more effectively condescending if he weren't wearing pants with palm trees embroidered on them. "My apologies, Mr. Campbell," he says, his voice dripping with sarcasm. "When would be a more convenient time for you?"

He dismisses us, then, and we both walk out without looking at each other. I hover outside the office door, straddling an awkward line between guilt and rage.

"I didn't mean to rat you out," I finally say, so someone will break the silence. It's not an apology, but I can't find it in me to give him one.

Jack's lips thin. "How long have you known, then?"

"I didn't. At least not until a few minutes ago." The anger makes me bolder than it should. For the first time in months, I finally say the name out loud, the same name that takes up so much space in my brain it seems ridiculous I've never actually uttered it: "*Wolf*."

For once, Jack is utterly still, standing like a scarecrow.

"So," he says.

I'll say it if he won't. "You lied to me."

"I didn't—I didn't mean to," says Jack. "I mean, I rigged the whole thing so I *wouldn't* know who you were. I didn't want to know—"

"You've made that pretty clear."

"I get that you're mad, but—"

"And then you let me go to the park that day and make an ass of myself in front of Landon. And to top it all off, apparently you took a picture of me looking like a drunk hurling into a Big League Burger bag and *posted it on the internet*?"

I'm waiting for his face to shift into confusion, waiting for him to ask what I'm talking about. Waiting for that familiar tic where he scratches the back of his neck or moves like he doesn't know whether to step forward or back.

Instead, Jack closes his eyes. "I can explain that."

My voice is shaking. "Then explain it."

"First of all, Ethan posted it."

"I'm not an idiot. The angle that photo was taken from—it could only have been you. So how did Ethan get it?"

"The same way he always does," says Jack. "He opened my phone with Face ID. He must have found the picture and tweeted it himself."

"Then why didn't you delete it?"

"Because—because I thought we were *done* with Twitter. I thought we agreed. And then you came after my grandma." I'm about to interrupt him and defend myself, but his eyes are red-rimmed and his face contorts into the kind of hurt that goes way beyond jabs on Twitter. "And she's in the hospital right now, and I . . ."

Whatever I was going to say next is blown right out of me.

"So yeah, I didn't delete Ethan's little tweet, because I was *mad*, okay? And—and busy."

The hallway has never felt more empty. Jack is somehow looking at me and not looking at me at the same time, alternating between apology and defiance and what I now understand must be complete and total exhaustion.

"Is she okay?"

Jack nods. "Yeah, she—they're releasing her tonight."

I wait to see if he'll elaborate, but he doesn't. And after everything that's happened, I don't think it's my place to pry.

"I need you to know I didn't post that tweet. My mom did."

Jack swipes at his eyes and lets out a breathy noise that might have started its life as a laugh. "Well, shit."

It's not an apology, but the regret that so immediately sears across his face is more than enough of one.

"Yeah," is the only thing I can think of to say. Because all my other questions—about Jack, about Weazel, about what on earth almost did or didn't happen last night—dissolve all at once, drowned in a sea of something much bigger and more important than them.

Jack's phone buzzes and lights up in his hand. "I gotta . . . that'll be my mom. I gotta get back home."

I nod. "Let me know if there's anything I can do."

Jack nods back, and there's something kind of tentative in it, but also kind of final. Like we walked out to the middle of a bridge together thinking we'd cross to some other side, even lingered in that middle spot over the depths below for a while, but ultimately turned right back around and headed to familiar ground.

My eyes are burning when I turn and head back to the bake sale. I'm not even sure what those familiar grounds used to look like, back when Jack and I were just classmates. When I didn't know Jack's half grin had infinite degrees that all held different feelings, when I didn't know exactly what part of him was going to fidget before he even moved, when he called me Pepperoni and it didn't unfurl something quiet in my chest.

It's weird, how you have no idea how far you've come until suddenly you can't find the way back.

Pepper

I don't hear from Jack all night, but I do hear from plenty of other people. Pooja, checking in. Friends from my old junior high in Nashville. The Hub Seed reporter who wrote the article on me and Jack, asking for comment. My dad.

And then Paige.

"This has gone too far," says Paige, before I even finish telling her what happened. "She's out of her mind."

"Okay," I say, in a measured tone that I'm all too practiced in, "yes, it sucks, but it's not like she could have seen this coming."

"Bullshit. She should have known something was going to happen."

The thing is that I agree with her. This part is squarely on Mom. But telling Paige about this even though I knew it would only make things worse is decidedly on me. Now, yet again, I'm backtracking, trying to undo the damage.

Too late.

"Why are you always defending her?" Paige snaps. For once, it seems like some of the anger is directed not just at her, but at me. "This is all her, you know. Twitter. Those stupid Stone Hall kids. If she hadn't just uprooted you—"

"Paige, I came here by choice."

Paige huffs. "You were fourteen. You were a little kid who didn't know any better."

My eyes squeeze shut, the words slicing in an unexpected way. Maybe because they're true, but maybe because they're not—maybe because even at fourteen, there was something in me that knew, deep under the frizzy hair and the acne and awkwardness, that I was supposed to be here. That New York was something I might never grow into, but would grow around me, making space where there wasn't any before. That the future was going to be a big unknown either way, but I wanted to be with Mom when I faced it.

But in this moment, it doesn't matter what I thought, not at fourteen and not right now—because the anger is suddenly so white-hot that I can't stop myself from saying what I say next.

"But you did." My voice is shaking. I don't want to say it, but it feels like I've been pushed and pushed to an edge that I can't lean over anymore, and it's all just falling out. "You did know better, and you came out here anyway, and wrecked things with Mom when you could have just stayed and let it be."

Paige doesn't hesitate. She says it with a conviction so quiet and firm that I know there's no way it isn't true. "I came to New York because of *you*."

The indignant breath I was sucking in stops in my throat, almost painful. It hovers there in the awful silence, as I scramble to make sense of something that makes too much sense all at once.

Some of that firmness is gone when Paige continues, like her voice is farther away than it was moments ago, farther even than the miles separating us. "I came because I thought you'd get eaten alive. And I thought—I thought maybe Mom would see how miserable we were and change her mind."

I close my eyes, already anticipating the wave of regret before it crashes into me—only it isn't a wave. It's searing, like my blood is suddenly on fire with it.

"But you weren't miserable. It only took you a few weeks to fit in. And I . . ."

She stayed miserable. I remember. The slammed doors, the long walks—the way she went from being one of the most popular girls in her old school to being this angry, pale version of herself, stalking in and out of the apartment like a ghost.

"I didn't know." My eyes are stinging, my face burning. I don't know what to say, except to say it again: "I didn't know."

There's a beat. "Yeah, well." The words are wet, like she's crying too. Before I can say anything else, she says, "I'm sorry, I've got to go."

Then she hangs up. I don't try to call her back; I know better than that. And I know better than to think that whatever just fractured between us won't eventually heal. But it still hurts just the same, in some core of me that I thought was too deep to be shaken.

All this time, I have blamed Paige and Mom for the fights that tore us apart. I never once thought the root of it all just might be me.

Pepper

I wake up the next morning feeling like I've been smacked by an MTA bus. In the five hours or so I manage to sleep, the internet sure hasn't. Before I even fully peel my eyes open, I see there are no texts or calls from Paige—but that worry is almost entirely forgotten when I realize there's a Twitter Moment, a Hub Seed article, a Jasmine Yang video, and a few other viral sites with roundups of the memed versions of me. People have been photoshopping the Big League Burger bag, first with other logos, like one from a recent superhero movie that flopped in theaters. Then people started labeling it with things like "your hot takes on Twitter." It's come so full circle, someone wrote "seeing this meme 15 times on my dash in one minute" on it.

There's even an article on Know Your Meme talking about the origins of the meme, which has officially dubbed it "Vomiting Girl."

Points for originality, I guess.

I don't even dare Google my name to see what comes up

now. I pull the covers up over my head the way Paige and I did when we were little kids and shut my eyes, willing myself to disappear between the sheets, or wake up to find the whole thing is some bake-sale-sugar-high-induced dream.

Eventually my mom knocks on my door, looking more spent than I've ever seen her. She's in her work clothes and her hair and makeup are done, but her posture is all wrong for it, like someone else dressed her. She doesn't look angry, which is why I'm not expecting her to say, "Your vice principal just called. You're suspended for two days."

"I'm what?"

She stays there in the doorway. "That boy confessed to making whatever app it is the school's been emailing about. Rucker said you intentionally withheld information about it to protect him."

I grit my teeth. Level her gaze as if I'm not pajama-clad and lying in bed, but on equal ground. "Well, then, I guess I'm not going to school today."

My mom blinks, but recovers. "That's all you have to say for yourself?"

I can't believe we are having this conversation as if she didn't just burn a Pepper-shaped corner of the internet to the ground. "What about *you*, Mom?"

"What about me?" She still hasn't moved from my doorway, like she's some kind of vampire who needs my permission to cross the threshold. "I saw this coming from a mile away, and I tried to stop you. And now you might have just compromised your entire future over this stupid boy."

I consider standing, the anger so electric under my skin it feels like I have to, but even that seems like too much of a concession. "For someone so concerned about my *future*, you sure don't seem to care that I'm the literal laughingstock on the internet because of you."

She's already shaking her head. "What on earth are you—"

"Jack and I ended the Twitter war. It was ridiculous from the start, and then it got way too personal, and it was *over.* But you just had to get another stupid, cheap shot in, didn't you?"

"There was no reason for it to get personal, which is exactly why I've been saying you shouldn't—"

"But it is personal, Mom. For me and obviously for you, because this whole thing with Girl Cheesing wasn't a coincidence, was it?"

Her arms are crossed so tightly against her chest that her whole body looks like it's on the verge of snapping. Her lips are drawn, her eyes skimming the floor, and when it's clear she isn't going to immediately answer, I go ahead and plow on without giving her the chance.

"Anyway, it doesn't get any more personal than this. Jack's brother responded to your tweet with a picture of me that's all over the internet now. It's bad enough that I'm actually *glad* I'm suspended."

That sure gets her attention. "What are you talking about?"

I pull my laptop from where I abandoned it on the other side of my bed, and open it to nearly two dozen open tabs of meme roundups and Tumblr posts and some website's super creepy deep dive into my life, including old Facebook photos from *Paige*'s account. My mom sits on the edge of my bed, and I watch her flit through them, feeling a grim satisfaction in watching the way the shock loosens the scowl on her face.

She closes the laptop and holds her hand there for a moment. "I have to ask. Are you drunk in that picture?"

"No, Jesus, Mom. I had food poisoning."

She nods and puts a hand up in defense of herself, brushing the matter aside so quickly that at the very least I know she believes me. Then she goes very still, seeming to absorb it all. I watch the familiar shape of her face, the frown that says there is a problem but she's going to find a way to solve it, but it doesn't last nearly long enough. We both know there's nothing we can do.

"I'm sure this will all blow over in a—"

"I have voicemails on my personal cell phone from *national publications* requesting comments, Mom. This isn't blowing anywhere."

There's a beat, the wobbly kind where it seems anything could happen. We are still so unused to fighting that there's no script to follow, no obvious move to anticipate next. But the last thing I'm expecting is for her to stand abruptly to leave the room.

"Where are you *going*?"

She pauses in the doorway, her back to me and her head turned just enough for me to see some of her chin. "To talk to your principal and straighten this suspension out before it goes on your permanent record."

"But, Mom—"

"And when I get back, and I've sorted through what on *earth* is going on here . . . we need to have a talk."

She turns fully then, stiff in that distinct way she always is when she's dealing with Paige. It stings more than anything she could say to me.

"Yeah. Let's talk, *Ronnie*."

It is somehow the worst but most effective hit I could aim in that moment. My mom is unflappable enough that I've seen her nearly get clipped by taxis and not so much as flinch, but the nickname seems to hit her in the one place she didn't think to protect.

She sweeps out the door before I can see just how lasting the blow is, leaving me there with my bedhead and my laptop and an infinite void of pictures of me throwing up into various pop culture phenomena.

For a good ten minutes or so, I'm too stunned to move. There's no distraction from the itch, the hurt, the *anger*—I can't call Paige. I can't even go to school. There's no place to shake it off, nowhere to go.

And suddenly I *need* somewhere to go.

I kick off the covers, my eyes stinging, my face overheating. I grab an old pair of jeans, a T-shirt covered in cartoon doughnuts that I stole from Paige, a ratty old pair of sneakers, and yank my hair into a ponytail. I slip myself back into the *me* I once was, and for a few moments, in my old clothes and my old shoes and my old state of mind, I can let it go: the endless homework, the college applications, the Twitter notifications, the stupid meme.

What I can't let go of is the way I tried just now to tell my mom my world was falling apart, and she *left*.

Well, if she's allowed to leave, then so am I. I grab my wallet, my keys, the MetroCard Jack talked me through buying the other day. There's only one place I want to go, and it's the last place I should be.

Jack

I'm really raking in the superlatives. It kicked off with Worst Pseudo Pen Pal on the Planet, veered sharply into Worst Best Friend in the Galaxy, and now, to top it all off, Worst Son/ Grandson in the Known Universe and Every Infinite Reality Hereafter.

There are so many people to apologize to, I don't even know where to start. It feels like there's a fire in every corner of my brain, and instead of putting any of them out, I'm just frozen and watching it spread across the room.

The mess with Pepper is terrible enough on its own. There are so many things I could have, would have, should have done—like take down that stupid picture when I saw Ethan tweet it—but the moment we heard Grandma Belly fall over in the other room, anything beyond it was out of my mind so quickly and so thoroughly, there wasn't space for anything other than *panic* and this gray look on my dad's face I don't think I'll ever forget.

She slipped getting out of a chair and ended up hitting her

head, and in the end had a concussion and a few stitches. They released her last night, and she's back at home and going to be fine. But that first minute when we walked in and saw her on the floor with blood on the carpet, before my dad started shouting for me to get the phone and the commotion stirred her awake, was probably the worst minute of my life.

And while that was by far the worst of it, it turns out it was just the beginning of the long, lingering shitstorm that has since taken over my life.

"I don't even know what to do with you," says my dad. It's bright and early in the morning, a time when he's usually overseeing things in the kitchen or going over our stock to put in orders to our meat and cheese suppliers, but instead we're sitting in the Time-Out Booth so the whole world is witness to my humiliation.

Not that my dad can really do anything to me now. I can't see how he can possibly make me feel any worse than I already do.

In the last twenty-four hours, not only have I let Pepper get turned into the meme of the week, but I've basically wrecked Paul's life too. After I left to help my mom get Grandma Belly out of the hospital, Paul apparently decided to ignore everything I said to him and agreed to meet this *Goldfish* person on the roof of the school. After about a half hour of waiting last night it started to get dark, and Paul realized not only was he locked up there, but Goldfish had posted a picture of him stuck up there and written, can u believe this guy actually self-described as "hot"? weazel app i want my money back.

Paul didn't even call me to tell me, and I was too busy at the hospital to be monitoring the Hallway Chat the way I usually do on and off during the afternoons. By the time I saw it, it had a comment thread a mile wide, and multiple unflattering photoshops of Paul with bad captions alluding to him being on the dive team like, dumpster diving? and looks like someone dove in with two (hobbit) feet.

The first thing I did was break my one rule and trace Goldfish back to some girl named Helen, a known bully in the senior class. The second thing I did was email Rucker to turn her in—and myself right with her.

I should have known it would only make things worse. As far as I know, Helen's off scot-free, Paul's still embarrassed out of his mind and not talking to me, and not only am I suspended for a week, but—plot twist—Pepper's suspended for two days for not ratting me out when she had the chance.

The TL;DR: Paul hates me. Pepper hates me. And it's only a matter of time before it gets around that I made Weazel, and then the whole *school* will hate me too. There isn't one corner of my life I haven't actively sabotaged, and I'm so far past rock bottom, I'm basically in the earth's molten core.

Hence, the most pointless father-son guilt trip in the whole of human history. My dad could literally start spitting flames right now, and I'd probably just tilt myself over and lean into the blast.

"I'm sorry, Dad."

And I am. I really am. Just not particularly at him, because it seems like he and Mom are the people *least* affected by this entire thing. And the people who are *most* affected, I could be spending this time getting in touch with, instead of being on the receiving end of a lecture within earshot of half of the morning egg-and-cheese-bagel rush.

"What were you thinking?"

I open my mouth to tell him just that, about what Weazel actually is—or was, I guess, since I disabled the whole thing last night. But he doesn't even let me get a word in edgewise. Instead, he leans farther into the table, propping his elbow above the spot where Ethan carved a Superman logo when we were kids, and lets out a Dad-sized sigh.

"You're on shift immediately after dive practice and every weekend for the next *month*," he says, without even looking at me.

I laugh. On the list of appropriate reactions I could have had, this is so far down that for a moment my dad doesn't even seem to process it, looking over at me, temporarily stunned out of his anger.

"Jack."

The laugh has now dissolved into an undignified snort, and before I know it, I'm saying, "Honestly, Dad, if that's 'punishment,' looks like I'm grounded for life, huh?"

My dad raises his eyebrows at me, warning and curious. He doesn't say anything, giving me the space to keep going, which judging by the sudden heat of what seems to be about a decade's worth of repressed insecurity bubbling to the surface right now, he probably shouldn't.

I jam my finger down into the Time-Out Booth. "I'm already here *every day*. After school. On the weekends. My whole *life* is here, and you've made damn well sure of it."

My dad closes his eyes for a brief moment, so wearily I'm not even sure if he's hearing half of what I'm saying. It's the wrong time and the wrong way and most *definitely* the wrong place, but it feels like if I don't say it now, I might never get another chance.

"Jack—"

"You know, I've always wondered why you pushed me instead of Ethan to be the one who takes over this place. Because it's *always* been that way. And at first, I didn't get it."

My dad is too stunned to say anything back, so I just keep going like a derailed subway car.

"But I caught on. Ethan's the golden twin, the *better* one, the one who gets to go off and take over the world, or whatever. Because lucky for you, you made a spare, stupider twin to keep this place running."

"What on earth makes you think working in this place makes you any less? Jesus, if that school is putting ideas in your head that working here is some kind of—"

"You just called it a punishment yourself! Which is *stupid*, by the way, because if that's what this is, you've been *punishing* me for years!"

My voice is loud enough the egg-and-cheese crowd is staring at us like we're some kind of side show. If we've stopped New Yorkers long enough for them to pull out their earbuds, we must really be a sight.

When I finally look over at him, my dad's eyes are hot with the kind of fury I have never seen in them before. "Go upstairs."

And just like that the anger that did such an annoyingly good job of grounding me a moment before is gone, crumbling out from under me so fast, I can't latch onto anything else to replace it. It's like I'm six years old again, senseless and stupid and running in and out of this conversation with no strategy at all, aside from saying things at him until I've finally run out of things I need to say.

"You don't even *care* that I—that I did something cool. That I *made* something, something that actually *helped* people before it . . ." I'm floundering, my face burning, my voice starting to shift dangerously toward something close to a whine. "Dad, I'm *good* at this. The app thing. Good enough that it might be something I want to do with my life."

He's not even looking at me anymore. "Go. Upstairs."

Now that I've dug myself so far into this hole, I'm so unsure of what to do with myself, I'm almost grateful for an instruction.

I pull myself out of the booth, avoiding the curious stares of people waiting for their food, and duck back out into the cold air to let myself in the apartment.

My mom's in Grandma Belly's room, the two of them watching something in there with the volume down low enough they definitely hear me come in, but nobody says anything. I beeline straight for my room before they can, and the click of the door shutting behind me is the permission I didn't realize I was waiting for to immediately start crying, the stupid, angry, little-kid kind of tears I haven't cried in so long that for a few moments I'm too overwhelmed to even let it properly happen.

I remember myself just enough to lock the door. I don't even make it to the bed, sitting on the floor for no real reason, really, except the bed seems too comfortable, and I don't deserve to ride this misery out in any kind of comfort. I end up grabbing the first thing I can find on the floor to muffle my face into, and only after I've snotted it up and ridden out the worst of the crying do I realize it's my apron from the deli, the one my dad got me a few years ago with the Girl Cheesing logo and my name sewn into it.

I crumple it into a ball and toss it across the room.

He probably hates me now. My whole life I've been working nonstop at the deli so he *wouldn't* hate me, and now I've gone and blown the whole thing up so fast and so effectively, I honestly should win some kind of Olympic medal for wrecking things. I want more than anything to be able to blink and undo the last twenty-four hours, or maybe the last month, or the last *year*—stop myself from making Weazel, from posting from the deli's Twitter account, from doing all the things that led to the veritable disasters and me spewing at my dad like an angsty teenage volcano in full view of half the East Village.

But I guess if none of that happened, I wouldn't have Pepper in my life.

Well, wouldn't have *had* Pepper. Who even knows what our deal is now.

I blink, and for a moment the tears stop entirely. It's the thought of Pepper that snaps me out of myself just enough it reminds me that, of all the times in the world, this is probably the least convenient for me to be emoting above the deli. I may resent the hell out of being down there right now, but the fact of the matter is, someone has to run that show and someone has to be up here with Grandma Belly, meaning we're down a pair of hands.

I swipe at my eyes and take a quick glance at myself in the mirror. My eyes are so red, I look like Ethan that time he snuck home after getting high. I splash water on my face and run my fingers through my hair, attempting something close to decent, and once I look somewhat like a person who hasn't been crying on the floor for an hour, I head back down the stairs.

I pause at the door to the deli, making sure there aren't any customers still lingering who witnessed my one-man shitshow, and bracing myself to face my dad. But it's not my dad at the register, or even my mom—it's *Pepper.*

At first I am so certain I am dreaming that I stand there like a goon for a solid five seconds, blocking the door so nobody can get in or out. Someone has outfitted Pepper with a purple Girl Cheesing hat and apron, and she's squinting down at someone's order and the price cheat sheet taped under the register and talking to one of our regulars. Her hair is tucked into a low bun, and she's smiling this bright, practiced customer service kind of smile, looking so in her element but also so unlike any Pepper I ever imagined that even after those five seconds pass and someone on the street nudges my shoulder to get past me, the image refuses to make sense in my head.

It takes Pepper a few moments to spot me when I walk in. Her cheeks immediately flush, but she finishes the transaction without missing a beat. I walk up to the register, so unused to being on the other side of it that it adds yet another layer of disconnect.

"What're you . . ."

It's all I can manage.

"I figured I could, uh, lend a hand today," says Pepper. "If that's okay."

It feels like my face is going to crack right down the middle. Just like that, my throat is swollen again, like I didn't spend a good hour crying already. "Yeah."

Pepper's eyes flit away for a moment, and then I realize whatever has happened to my throat must also be playing out on my face. Before I can panic and say or do something awkward, my mom swoops in from the back, takes one look at me, and says, "Hey, kiddo. We've got everything handled down here. Why don't you go sit with your grandma for a little while?"

I stare at her dumbly. She must have ducked down here at some point while I was in my room, but I didn't even hear the door.

"Yeah. Yeah, I'll go do that." I turn to Pepper. There are probably half a dozen things I need to say to her, but all that comes out is a thick, "Thanks."

I turn back around before she can answer, mostly because I don't trust my face to keep what little amount of composure it has left in it. I climb back up the stairs and let myself into the apartment, my blood rushing in my ears, my eyes still blinking like they made Pepper up. I'm so distracted, it doesn't occur to me until I'm opening the front door that if my mom is downstairs, it can only mean my dad is up here.

I full-body flinch at the sight of my dad sitting on the couch in the living room, which somehow feels more jarring than what's happening downstairs. And maybe it is—I'm so used to my parents being down in the deli during daylight hours, it seems strange to see him up here right now, in the middle of a day when he would usually be in the corner office in the back and I'd be sitting behind a desk. It feels like we're looking at each other through a different lens, on unfamiliar ground, even though this is the place we call home.

My dad's eyes lift to meet mine, and I brace myself all over again. I almost want him to yell at me, just to have the relief of it being over, but he doesn't seem angry. He seems like something I don't know how to navigate, something soft in the eyes and hard in the mouth that makes me waffle at the door like I came in here by mistake.

"How's Grandma Belly?" I finally ask.

My dad nods toward her room. "Taking a nap."

I nod back. An excruciating quiet settles between us, and I'm already counting the seconds it will take for me to get to my room and close the door on him when my dad says, "Why don't you sit down?"

He motions to the space next to him on the couch. I walk over and take it, even though the middle cushion is Ethan's spot, not mine. I look at my lap for a beat, resenting that even in a moment like this, I can't think for myself without making space for him too.

"When you were little, you hated this apartment. You told me you wanted to live under the table in the Time-Out Booth."

"I did?"

My dad's lip quirks.

"We might have let you too, if we didn't catch you trying to peel used gum off the bottom of it."

It cuts through just enough of the tension that I stop waiting for some other shoe to drop. "Well, that explains a lot."

He lets out a breath, leaning in a little closer. "What I'm trying to say is—you loved the deli. Right from the start. Loved being down there, and getting to hit buttons on the register, and nipping at the heels of everyone in the kitchen."

He doesn't speak for a moment, like he's giving me space to cut in. But I am suddenly too desperate to know what's on the other side of those words to say anything myself.

"I don't want you to think I pushed you into it because I thought any less of you," says my dad, lowering his voice. "If anything, it's the opposite. I guess I pushed it because—well, your brother and your mom, they're so alike in a lot of ways. And I've always—maybe it's selfish, but I've always seen a lot of myself in you."

The words feel like they burn on the way down. "Well, not so much anymore, I guess, huh?"

"No. The way you step up for this family—not just with this silly Twitter thing," he says off my look, "but every day. You're here. You show up. Without being asked." He runs a hand through his hair, staring at Grandma Belly's door. "Even I wasn't half as dedicated to this place growing up, and your grandma can speak to that. You've always been above and beyond. More than we could have ever asked for from a kid. And I'm sorry if I ever made you feel less than for it."

The words settle in between us, my dad gruff but earnest, me near paralyzed. I have this sudden feeling of wanting to grab the words from the air, put them somewhere permanent in me, like they can anchor me in a way nothing else has. I want to remember this feeling—the strange, happy crush of it in my lungs, the pride, the relief, even the mingling guilt.

"And for what it's worth—your mom had an *eerily* similar talk with Ethan earlier today."

I find this hard to believe. So much so that I almost snort. "She did?"

"He was all bent out of shape. Seemed to think *you* were the—how'd you put it?—golden twin. That we trusted you over him, with everything to do with the shop and Twitter and everything else." My dad's voice is wry, but also a little bittersweet. "If that helps you . . . put things into perspective at all. I think maybe you both need to understand that you're good at different things, and stop beating yourselves up about what you think you're not good at."

I cringe, unsure if it's for my sake or for Ethan's. It's always been like this—even at my most embarrassed, I'm never quite sure what part of it ends in me and begins in him. Even knowing that, I didn't think it extended this far.

But maybe it makes sense, even if I don't want it to. The way Ethan was so touchy about the Twitter page. That weird, unresolved fight we had outside of the community center after Pepper hacked the account. I was so wrapped up in how I thought of Ethan that it never once occurred to me what he thinks of himself.

We'll talk about it, someday, maybe. For now I know what will happen: my dad will tell my mom about this conversation the way they tell each other everything, and she'll tell Ethan, and the two of us will quietly know what we know and feel how we feel until it either goes away or doesn't. But right now, having this long overdue conversation with my dad, is the first time I've ever been confident that someday it will.

"He's sorry about that tweet he sent. And he called Pepper

this morning to say so. He was just upset about the timing of it with what happened to your grandma, and . . . I think he was trying to be helpful. More like you."

This time I really do snort. My dad nudges my shoulder with his.

"Truth is, you're both pieces of work." He pauses, a wince starting to take shape on his face. "But since we're on the topic of that . . . Twitter thing."

Oh, man.

"I don't know what is or isn't going on between you and Pepper, but since it is or isn't happening, I feel like I owe you a bit of an explanation. And from the looks of things, Pepper's mom might owe her one too."

I nod. "You guys know each other."

"Yeah, well. That, and . . . we dated, briefly."

My eyes widen to the approximate diameter of those useless dollar coins the MTA card machines are always spitting out. "Oh."

My dad raises his hands up in defense of himself. "A long, *long* time ago. Like, long."

I try to picture my dad and Pepper's mom in this "long, *long*" time ago, but my imagination refuses to de-age them. My dad is just my dad, the way he is right now, and Pepper's mom is—well, terrifying. But also such an unknown quantity to me, it's hard to imagine anything about her at all.

"How long is long?"

He has to think for a moment. We both raise our hands to scratch the backs of our necks, and I hide a smile at my shoes and stop myself just in time.

"It was—well, it was just before I met your mother."

I raise my eyebrows. "Did you dump Pepper's mom for *our* mom?"

My dad stares at the coffee table.

"It didn't—happen—*exactly* like that."

Which is to say, from the rueful look he is not doing a very good job of suppressing, that's exactly how it happened.

"*Dad.*"

"She was just here for the summer before heading back to Nashville. It was never meant to be anything serious. Not that—okay, that's enough, that's all you're getting from me on it," says my dad, pointing a finger at me. "No smirking."

It's so rare I ever get to hear about my parents' pre–Jack and Ethan days that I can't help myself. "You *scoundrel.*"

My dad shakes his head. "I fell in love with your mom within a minute of meeting her. Nothing in the world was gonna stop it."

Then all at once he gets misty-eyed the way he does sometimes when he talks about Mom. This time, I don't feel the usual rush of secondhand embarrassment. This, maybe, is the real anchor, the one that's always been there—knowing I have parents who love each other so much it was never a matter of *if*, but always a matter of *when*.

"But you pissed off—Ronnie, was it?"

My dad presses his lips into an exasperated line. "Yeah. I got a few angry phone calls. She, uh—she was working at the deli that summer. Trying to learn the ropes because she wanted to open her own place. That's how we met. We hadn't quite called it off when she went back to school in Nashville, so things were a little . . . tangled in that regard."

My dad's eyes aren't fully with me when he says it, so I know there must be more to the story than that—but whatever it is, he doesn't offer it up.

"So rather than working it out, you just waited until your kids were old enough to duke it out on Twitter instead?" I ask.

"Hardly," says my dad. "That's why I didn't want you on it at all. That whole Grandma's Special stunt at Big League Burger had Ronnie written all over it, and if I'd had my way, we would have just ignored it altogether."

I feel a pang of remorse. "Well."

My dad nudges his shoulder into mine. "But then it got half the city buying our sandwiches. I'm not going to lie—we were in a tight spot a few months ago. All this Twitter insanity . . . it's made a huge difference to our bottom line."

For a moment I almost pretend this is a surprise to me, but we both know I'm way too invested in the deli and its goings-on not to know we were in the red. I nod quietly, and my dad cuts his gaze to his lap, obviously not expecting it. I can feel the slight puncture to his pride so immediately that it feels like my own.

"So all this was thanks to your spurned college ex, huh?" I ask, to take some weight off of the silence.

"No. All this was thanks to my very clever *son*, who is nothing if not loyal to this family. And would probably make an excellent social media manager one day, if he wanted to be."

I open my mouth, but it's suddenly drier than it was after trying to eat the stale rye loaves my mom used to make our lunch sandwiches from when we were kids. But I can't chicken out now. It's my opening. I know it's not now or never, but it's now or some other less appropriate moment when I don't have my dad's full attention.

"I know this whole Weazel thing kind of blew up in my face, but—I think that's what I want to do. Develop apps, I mean."

My dad considers this. "I really didn't have any idea you were even into that," he says, leaning forward and propping his elbows on his knees.

I pick at a loose seam on my jeans. Years and years of work—of teaching myself to code, of stumbling through online tutorials, of watching the weird things I've envisioned come to life on screens—and now that the moment has come to justify all of it, to explain how much it means to me, I'm at a complete and utter loss for how to do it.

"I'm—it's something I think . . . I could be good at," I say.

The words aren't right, maybe, but the understanding must be. My dad breathes out a sigh that is just as much in resignation as it is pride.

"I believe you, if those screenshots your vice principal sent me are any indication." There's a subtle edge in his voice to let me know I'm nowhere near off the hook for that, but it doesn't do anything to dampen my relief. "I just wish you'd told us."

It's somehow easier and harder to say than anything I have in my whole life, coming out of me too quickly for me to overthink it: "I didn't want to let you down."

He puts a hand on my knee. "Of course I'm disappointed you don't want to stick around here. But only because I don't think I'll ever find anyone half as good as you to run this place," he says. "I'd be much more disappointed if you didn't go out in the world and do something you loved because you wanted to make *me* happy."

I clench and unclench my fingers. "I don't want to—get away, or anything. I want to be here." I don't understand just how much I mean it until I'm saying it. There are all kinds of lives I've envisioned for myself beyond the corner office of the deli, but none of them have ever been too far from home—from this city that raised me, from the block that knows me better than I know myself. "I just . . . want it to be on my terms."

My dad nods, and it's an unfamiliar kind of nod. There's a respect in it beyond the respect of father-and-son; it feels for the first time like he's looking at me as more than that. As someone who is less of a kid and more of a peer.

"Does this mean the Twitter war is over?"

My dad and I both snap our heads up to Grandma Belly, who is leaning against the very much open door of her bedroom and peering at us critically through the thick lenses of her glasses. We both open our mouths at the same time—me to ask how the heck she knows about the Twitter war I thought I'd gone to great lengths to hide from her, and my dad clearly to ask why she's up when she should be resting—but she raises her hand to silence us both.

"I'm fine," she says to my dad. Then she turns to me. "And as for you—I'm old, not dead. I've been following this saga since the beginning. Have you and that Patricia girl made out yet or what?"

I somehow manage to choke on oxygen. I lean over to my dad mid-cough, expecting him to say *something* to stop her, but he's gone redder than I am and already leapt to his feet.

"Let's, uh, get you back into bed, Mom."

"That girl is a hoot and a half. You two got me through an entire two months of waiting for new episodes on my favorite soaps," says Grandma Belly, with a wink. "You tell her she's welcome to let that sassy mom of hers copy my recipes any day of the week."

I wait until she's safely in her room with her back turned to bury my smirk into the palms of my hands.

Jack

"So."

"So," I echo.

We're walking down the street, just me and Pepper, both of us armed with aluminum foil–wrapped grilled cheeses, plastic cups full of lemonade, and a giant Kitchen Sink Macaroon to split. It was easy enough to be around her for the two or so minutes when my mom was setting us up with the food, insisting on Pepper taking a lunch break, but now that we're alone, every single one of the wits I used to have has left me.

"I'm sorry," we both blurt at the same time. We pause, momentarily stricken, and then laugh—hers breathy, and mine an accidental cackle, loud enough people move an extra step out of our way when they pass.

"What are you sorry about?" I demand. "You didn't do anything."

"I—I don't even know, really. I feel like I kind of did. I'm—sorry for thinking you were Landon, first of all." She takes a long sip of her lemonade, her face scrunching like she's trying to wash the taste of that thought out of her mouth. "And sorry for—well—thinking the worst of you, a few times, when I didn't have the full story."

I wish my hands weren't occupied with holding my food, so I could shove them into my jacket pockets.

"Well, I'm sorry for real stuff. For lying to you about the Weazel thing, mostly." I gnaw on my lower lip. "The thing is—I was actually going to tell you that night. I took that picture because I was going to be a smart aleck about it. Send you the picture over the app as Wolf, so then you'd put two and two together and realize it was me."

The implication, of course, is unspoken—that she'd have the space to put two and two together and pretend she *didn't* realize it was me, if she didn't want it to be. I see I haven't done anything to fool her because her eyes immediately soften.

"Anyway," I say, before she can address it, "that obviously backfired when you, uh, threw up instead."

Pepper snorts. "Yeah. Safe to say, I'm off hot dogs for the foreseeable next hundred years."

"And then—I was going to tell you when you were here. When we were kissing. And instead, I just kind of shoved my foot in my mouth and wrecked the whole thing."

Pepper spots a place for us to sit in Washington Square Park, on a bench with a view of the little gated area that makes up the dog park. She sits, watching me studiously as I take the place next to her, with the kind of care I'm still not used to even after all these weeks of being on the other end of it.

"I wouldn't say wrecked," she says.

"Yeah. But you're a meme now. And suspended."

I don't know why I'm pointing all of this out to her, except I have to—suddenly it all has to be on the table, every stupid thing we've said and done, every mistake we've made. She's still here, and she's still staring back at me, but I can't trust it yet.

"Truc." Pepper thins her lips, her eyes not meeting mine for a second. Before I can start spiraling into the panic I've been keeping at bay, she turns back to me and says, "But weirdly, this is one of the best days I've had in a long time."

I laugh self-consciously, but only because I can tell she means it. There is something more personal in that, maybe, than any kind of insecurity we've told each other, than even the kiss we botched. Even if it was just for a few hours, Pepper knows the landscape of the inside of my world.

It's not enough to erase everything that's happened, but maybe it's a step.

"And your mom . . ."

Pepper blows out a breath. "I don't know. But I'll deal with it when I get home."

"My dad—he said he and your mom used to know each other."

Pepper doesn't seem nearly as fazed by this as I was. "Yeah . . . I thought as much." Off my look, she shrugs and says, "I may have made some less-than-polite remarks on my way out the door this morning."

I wince. "Hard same."

"Whatever it is though—it's their problem, not ours."

I'm relieved to hear her say this, mostly because I don't want to have to tell her what went on between them myself. I feel like it's the kind of thing she should actually hear about from her mom, and not through a game of telephone from me.

Still, it doesn't make this any less complicated. It feels like this whole thing has been a giant heap of Monster Cake from start to finish—good, but messier than either of us could have ever anticipated.

"Could we just—start over?" I ask. "No Twitter, or Weazel, or parents, or . . . screens in the way."

Pepper smiles this easy, patient smile. The kind that a few months ago I never would have been able to picture on her. There's something so grounded and assured in it that I know it's not just her—it's rooted in something between us. Something steady and quiet, a kind of understanding that maybe has been there all along, buried deep under the tweets and the jabs and the occasional staredown in the hallway.

"I'm all for leaving that behind. But I don't want to start over," says Pepper quietly.

She leans in, then, and pauses just in front of me. I'm so wrapped up in what's about to happen, I don't realize for a moment that she's waiting for me, for permission to do this thing that seems so natural, so inevitable, that even in the beats before it happens I can't imagine it not happening.

I bridge the distance between us, and then we're kissing again—and this time it's slow, and small, and simple, but fills me with the kind of full-body warmth nothing else ever has.

We pull apart, smiling like idiots, and just stare at each other for a few seconds. Then some hipster on the bench next to ours who doesn't know how to mind his own beeswax pointedly clears his throat.

"We should probably, uh. Eat these before they get cold," I say, just barely managing not to stammer.

"Right." Pepper unwraps hers, face still red, her fingers fumbling. She pauses just before she lifts it to her mouth. "So is this the Grandma's Special?"

The grin that bursts on my face almost cracks from the cold air. "Wow. My mom really does like you."

Pepper is poised with it in front of her mouth and raises an eyebrow at me. "Do you trust me?"

"Not a bit. Take a bite."

She does, and I prop my head on my palm and lean in close enough she has to muffle a laugh as she chews.

"Well?" I demand. "Finally willing to concede that our grilled cheese is vastly superior?"

She looks like she's about to give a begrudging nod, but then her eyes go wide. "The secret ingredient." She peels apart the grilled cheese, staring at it and then up at me, her face so incredulous. "It's sweet bell *peppers*?"

It isn't the first time I've wondered how Pepper would react if she knew. But somewhere along the line that imagining shifted from a nightmare to this moment now, with a full Pepper grin so infectious, I can't help but match it with one of my own.

"Shhh," I say, grabbing a half of her grilled cheese and taking a bite. "It's a secret."

"Yeah, well." She leans forward and kisses me on the cheek, shy and quick. "I think we've had our fair share of those."

Pepper

In the text I sent my mom this morning, I told her I'd be home by 3 p.m. so I make sure I'm in the elevator on my way back up by 2:55. I use the ride up to collect myself, dusting some of the flour off my shirt, trying to dim the smile that keeps creeping its way back on my face.

I'm expecting a fight, or at the very least some kind of passive-aggressive exchange. My mom didn't tell me not to leave the apartment, but I can't play dumb—even in my lacking experience with actually getting in trouble, I know skipping downtown is pretty high on the list of *things I don't want my teenage daughter doing when she's suspended*. Never mind that it's pretty high on the list regardless.

But when I open the door, my mom isn't angry. She isn't even irritated. She's sitting on the couch, clutching a mug of something and wearing a ratty old robe I haven't seen since our Nashville days. She stares over at me with puffy, makeup-less eyes, looking so much younger in this state that for a moment I have to blink the image of Paige out of my eyes. She tries to look stern, gearing herself up for the scolding we both know I deserve, but then the tears start leaking out of her eyes, and whatever she's going to say dissolves right out of her.

"What happened?"

She shakes her head, but the stream of tears thickens and the panic only coils tighter in my chest.

"I just—you *left*, and I . . ."

"I texted you." I sit next to her, at a loss for what I should do. I've never really seen my mom cry before, at least not like this—not when I'm the only one around to do anything about it. "I came right back—"

"I know, I know," says my mom, her voice tight and wet. She swipes at her eyes. "I just—it started like this, with Paige, and then she left. And then she *left*."

I feel myself teetering on that same edge, the divide of my loyalty to her and my loyalty to Paige. Paige, who still hasn't called or texted since our fight, a short time that still might be the longest silence between us we've ever had.

"She went to college," I say carefully.

My mom lowers her chin and looks at me with red-rimmed eyes. I don't know what to say.

"So, where were you?"

There's no point in lying to her. "I was at Girl Cheesing. Jack's grandma was in the hospital, and I just wanted to—to help out, is all."

My mom is quiet for a moment. "Is she all right?"

"Yeah, she's gonna be." I prop my feet up on the coffee table, mirroring hers—mine socked, hers slippered. I can smell now that it's hot chocolate in her mug, the kind we used to make with cinnamon and maple syrup.

She offers me a sip, and it's like raising a white flag. I take it, and the taste of it is so comforting and familiar, it somehow makes me ache for my mom even though she's sitting right here.

"I've been talking with your dad all day. And—and you're right. I've been . . ." She smiles this grim smile. "I shouldn't have pushed you into this. It was my business, not yours, and—I hate that you've been dragged into it like this, Pep. I really didn't mean for it to escalate the way it did."

"Yeah. About that." I'm testing my luck here, maybe, but I have to know. "What exactly did Jack's dad do to piss you off so much?"

To my surprise, my mom lets out a sharp laugh. "I should have known he'd tell you. Him or one of those kids of his."

I shake my head. "They didn't. I mean—I just figured, after that scene at Jack's place."

My mom eases into the couch, mulling it over for a moment like she might not tell me. "Well—aside from dumping me over the *phone*," she says, "he's not exactly innocent in this whole copycat thing."

"So you did copy their grilled cheese."

My mom doesn't even seem one inch sorry about it. In fact, there's a ghost of a smirk on her face. "How did you like those Kitchen Sink Macaroons?"

I furrow my brows at her.

"Those were all my doing," she says. "As was 'The Ron,' which was one of their bestselling sandwiches. And a few of their other desserts that were mysteriously pulled off the menu when Sam figured out I was back in the city."

"You didn't know?"

"Oh, I knew." Her gaze cuts to the side for a moment, like she's half here and half somewhere else. "You know I never finished college, but what you don't know is I had a good reason. I was going to open my own place. A café."

She's right. This is the first I'm ever hearing of it. It always sort of seemed like my parents didn't have lives before Paige and I were born, so it never even occurred to me to ask.

"I'd always worked in cafés and restaurants growing up. But I spent the summer after my sophomore year in New York for a class and fell in love with the city, and decided that was where I wanted to start a place of my own."

She smiles to herself, and I can see some reflection of the girl she must have been at twenty—stubborn and hopeful, a more concentrated version of the woman she is now.

"So I took a summer job at Girl Cheesing, to get in the swing of big-city small business. And even before I went back to Nashville, I started branding my own vision—the menu, the logo, the color schemes. I stayed in touch with people when the semester started back up again. Once I had some investors, I quit school and headed back to New York to find a space to rent."

Something in my stomach drops, like I know where this is going before I can even form a picture of it in my mind. I can feel the ache of it before anything else.

"By then, Sam had already broken up with me. I decided to be civil, swing by and say hello. Well, imagine my surprise—Sam had taken over the deli from his mother and was hawking my Kitchen Sink Macaroons. Added my sandwiches to the menu. Even switched the Girl Cheesing branding to the same color purple I wanted for my own place."

"He didn't."

She laughs. "Oh, he sure did." The laugh tapers, her voice lowering. "The macaroons were such a hit that the entire city was talking about them, back then. And it sounds—ridiculous. But my stuff put Girl Cheesing back on the map so quickly that the biggest investor I had caught wind that a place was already doing what I wanted to do, and he backed out. Then so did the other two."

I know the story ultimately has a happy end, because I am that story—but it doesn't make me feel any less indignant, or any less upset about what must have happened next. "And you didn't try again? Or even try to open a place in Nashville?"

She shakes her head. "I banked everything on the idea of New York. I didn't have any money left. I started waiting tables again, thinking I'd go back to school, or try again . . . life happened a little faster than I thought it would."

It's strange, how quickly the path that led us here rearranges itself, now that I can see it through her eyes. All this time I thought we were in New York because my mom was looking for a fresh start. Only now am I starting to understand that she didn't come here to find something—she came here to take it back. The dream she had before I even existed.

A dream that's starting to take some form in me now, that I never knew we shared.

"It's stupid. But being back here . . . seeing those stupid macaroons again, and seeing Sam . . ."

An immediate horror grips my chest. "You don't—you and Jack's dad aren't—"

"No." She looks genuinely repulsed at the idea. "Not on his life or mine."

Good, I almost say. But I'm still not entirely sure where my mom stands on the Jack front right now.

She takes a sip of her hot chocolate then stares into her mug.

"I know your sister thinks this whole divorce was my fault, but you should know—it was a long time coming. That's why your dad and I have had it a little easier than most with the transition. We were always better friends than we were ever going to be husband and wife."

I can tell she's telling me this because she doesn't want me to think she ran off to New York for an old flame, but that part doesn't matter to me. It's just nice to hear for its own sake. It hurts—it probably always will, to some degree—but it helps too. Even if they weren't in love, I never made up that we were a team.

"And that whole café thing—I didn't know it at twenty, but I was better off for it in the end. What I was imagining would never have taken off the way Big League did. We built that together. You, me, your dad, Paige. Made something better than I could have ever made on my own." She lets out a contented sigh and says the thing I didn't realize I needed to hear most: "Even if it never got any bigger than that first little restaurant in Nashville, it was perfect, just the way it was."

I steal her hot chocolate and take another sip, thinking of that old home away from home—the milkshakes we invented that are still on the menu. The drawings Paige and I made that are still framed on the walls. The beating heart that still pulses in all the Big League Burgers that have opened since. It may be bigger than we ever thought it would be, but I hope, at least, people walk in and feel the way they do at that first restaurant. Like they're walking into something made with love.

"But after we got here, walking past the deli and seeing he was still selling some of my old stuff, pawning it off as his own—I don't know." She takes a moment to choose her words, like she is still not quite certain of the feeling behind them. "That feeling just came back. That anger."

I stare at our knees, leaning my shoulder into hers. She sighs. "Do you ever feel like someone just took something from you?"

Yes, I want to say. Sometimes it feels like it's been four years of this place taking and taking, and I'm all out of pieces to give—like I don't even know the shape of myself anymore.

But I think I'm finding her. Some outline of what she is, or what she could be. Somewhere beyond this little block I've been hiding on, in a city where there are more outlines of me than I could ever fathom, a city I'm opening my eyes to now a little bit more every day.

I take my mom's hand, and she squeezes it in hers.

"So—revenge via grilled cheese?"

"Not revenge, really. I just—he knocked me down to rock bottom once. I guess I wanted to knock him down a peg too. Make him see we were better off despite what he did. And when corporate started talking about adding grilled cheeses . . . well, I knew that would get at him the fastest."

"And Grandma Belly," I remind her.

To my surprise, my mom isn't defensive or even rueful about that at all. Instead, she smiles. "You know, I was close with Grandma Belly once too. Only she was just Bella, then." For a moment I can picture it—my mom every bit a part of Girl Cheesing as I was just hours ago, standing in the same spot at the register, feeling like a part of the same magic. "And truth be told, she used to buy that sourdough bread for the Grandma's Special from a supplier downtown. I was the one who convinced her the deli should start making their own."

Another bakery-related plot twist, and this one even weirder, considering I'm still digesting it.

Off my curious look, she says, "Bella figured out what Sam did a few months after he took over and called to apologize. Told me she gave him hell for it, and I was more than welcome to too."

"That's some kind of raincheck you took."

"Give or take a decade," she says wryly. "She said she told him to stop selling my stuff, but I'm guessing he just slipped some of it back in over the years, not counting on me coming back." She shakes her head. "Anyway, it's Sam I meant to piss off, and clearly I did. Just didn't count on his kids going to bat too."

"Or yours?" I ask, not without a healthy amount of sarcasm.

My sharpness only seems to soften her. "I never imagined it would play out like this. I really am sorry about that."

Despite everything, I almost smile into the hot chocolate mug. "Yeah, well. It wasn't all bad."

"And if you really do want to open a place of your own, like you were saying—I hope nobody ever stands in your way."

I think of Jack, and that unabashed way he's always bragging about my desserts. Of that cupcake app he built. Of all the little ways he is a person at our age that his father clearly wasn't. There will be plenty of things to worry about further down the road, but that, at least, isn't one of them.

"I know things have been stressful, and you've been handling all of it like a champ."

I press my lips together, already feeling the wobble in my voice before it comes out of me. "Not always."

She wraps an arm around me and pulls me in, and we sit like that, curled into each other. She runs a hand through my hair, and I close my eyes, tempted to pretend we're *home* home, in Nashville home, but for the first time, I am rooted here in a way I don't remember being. As if I'm already where I'm supposed to be.

"Are you going to go run off to college and not answer my calls too?"

"No." I burrow a little further into her warmth. "But, Mom?"

"Hmmm?"

"I think we need to take a bus and go to Philly."

Mom looks at me quietly for a moment. I hold my breath, waiting for her answer like the whole world hinges on it.

"You don't think an Uber will go that far?"

The relief is so immediate, it feels like it might liquefy my bones. She smiles at me, her eyes still wet, and nods. There is some kind of unspoken promise in it—we can fix this. We are bent, the four of us, but we're not quite broken yet.

We spend the rest of the night baking, using the ingredients I have left over to make another batch of So Sorry Blondies—this one modified with extra peanut butter, Paige's favorite. We turn on an old Taylor Swift album and eat the dough raw and catch up on each other's lives. We talk about how she and my dad came up with Big League Burger in the first place, and weird dessert hybrids we want to try in the city, and fall asleep watching *Waitress* with fingers still sticky from chocolate and toffee.

And then, in the morning, we get on the bus to Philadelphia, a tin of So Sorry Blondies perched in my mom's lap.

Epilogue

ONE YEAR LATER

Paige swats at Pooja's hand before she can grab a waffle off of the massive tower she's made. Pooja moans.

"Instagram first, eat later," says Paige—words I'm hearing more and more often now that Paige actually comes home for breaks, and even some weekends too. Sure enough, she angles her lens at the stack, documenting the Where Are They Now? Waffles for our now-public baking blog.

"Sheesh," says Pooja, "you're even bossier than your sister."

"I resent that," I call from the couch, where a good portion of my limbs are tangled with Jack's. He's in full Thanksgiving break form today, in a pair of worn jeans and a faded flannel so soft that even if I weren't so partial to his face and everything that comes with it, it'd be scientifically impossible *not* to glom onto him.

"Surprised you can hear anything at all, sucking face over there!" Pooja singsongs.

I raise my eyebrows at her. "What's that saying about the pot and the kettle . . ."

"*This* pot only makes out with her boyfriend at parties and Instagrammable locations," says Pooja—which is an out-and-out lie. I may not be anywhere near Stanford or the swim team captain who swept her off her mermaid fin, but if her Snapchats are any indication, her face is attached to his more often than not. At least they're both putting their impressive lung capacities to good use. "You two, on the other hand, are in exhibitionist territory."

Jack pulls maybe an inch away from me, just enough I can see the hint of a sheepish smile. "Lay off me, I haven't seen her in like seven hours."

I can't see Paige's eyes rolling so much as I can feel them. "You two are the grossest thing to ever happen to the internet."

"Speaking of, can we hurry this up?" says Ethan from the other couch, where he's perched next to Stephen. They've been off-again, on-again ever since Ethan headed to Stanford with Pooja, and Stephen stayed in the city with Landon to get their startup off the ground—but now, it seems, they are decidedly on, if their aggressive proximity is any indication. "The Hub Seed article's been live for like half an hour."

Pooja heads to the waffle maker and eats the little cooked pieces that dribbled off on the counter. "We're waiting on Paul."

Right on cue, there's a frantic series of knocks on the front door to the apartment, which can only belong to him.

"Sorry I'm late," says Paul, out of breath as usual. "Forgot to pick up our Thanksgiving pies for tomorrow."

"Dude," says Ethan. "Pepper could have just brought them to you. She was on shift at the deli, like, all day."

Paul stops dead in the doorway. "I'm an idiot."

"An idiot with a spot saved over here," says Paige, gesturing to the couch. "Peanut butter or lemon curd on your waffle?"

Paul goes the tomato shade of red he always does whenever Paige addresses him. They ended up at UPenn together, and she generously took him under her wing, telling him all the campus hot spots and which teachers to avoid and how to make some cocktail called the Pennsylvanian. Paul only recently graduated to speaking full sentences in front of her without stammering. We're all very proud.

"Um—you decide. You're the dessert whiz."

"Pepper's the dessert whiz." Paige points a knife covered in Nutella at me. "What the heck did you put in that apple pie again?"

It's more than a little conceited of me that I'm drooling at the thought of my own creation. "Mascarpone and almonds."

Jack nods, beaming like a traffic light. "They're completely sold out for the holiday. Mom and Pepper have been baking them round the clock."

"Well, that explains why she comes home smelling like the inside of a Bath & Body Works candle every night," says Paige.

She sets down a massive platter of waffles on the coffee table in front of us, and everyone reaches forward and grabs the paper plate with their waffle on it, all customized for them by me and by Paige. Over the summer, before we all dispersed for college, the group of us started convening in our apartment so often, we have everyone's preferences memorized like we've got GPS on their taste buds. After all these months, it's a relief to have us all here together again—to have something as familiar as Pooja's obsession with adding syrup to everything, and Stephen's love for any kind of jam, and Paul's numerous food allergies. Like we're settling back into a rhythm again.

"Are we all accounted for?" says Ethan.

"Aye-aye, captain," says Pooja, plopping herself down next to him and shimmying her butt to volley for more space on the couch. She turns to Jack. "Load up the post, maestro."

Jack obliges, pulling up the computer screen he synced to my mom's giant television. My dad's in town for Thanksgiving, so he and my mom are grabbing dinner to catch up—and also, I suspect, to give us some rein over the apartment so we can read the new Hub Seed article about us in peace.

I take a bite of my Where Are They Now? Waffle just as the post—appropriately subtitled "~*~Where Are They Now?~*~"—loads up on the screen. Headline: *Um, We Have The CUTEST Update About That Big League Burger Twitter War From Last Year.*

"Oh em gee, the CUTEST update," Pooja deadpans.

Jack flings a peanut at her, which she unexpectedly and deftly catches in her open mouth.

"*Sick*," says Paul.

"Scroll down!" Paige demands.

I'm delighted to see the first image on the post is of a bunch of my new dessert creations, all on display in the case at Girl Cheesing. I'm enrolled at Columbia, and hoping for a spot in the Business Management concentration next year, but all the time I'm not in class or studying, I've been working at Girl Cheesing to learn the ropes of owning a small business. As a result, Jack's mom has given me free rein to add any desserts I want to the menu.

And, uh, I might have gotten *slightly* carried away.

Hey, kids! Remember last year when we all semi-creepily (but with the BEST OF INTENTIONS!!) started shipping the two teens behind the Big League Burger and Girl Cheesing Twitter accounts that were warring on this here internet?

Well, I am delighted to be the bearer of slightly-less-creepy news—the teens are dating IRL! And also super successful in their budding professional ambitions! But more importantly, THEY ARE DATING IRL!!!

"Oh my god," says Jack. "I'm blinded by the caps lock."

"Not the majesty of my desserts?"

He and his half smirk lean in and kiss me on the cheek. Paige gags theatrically, and Pooja leans from her perch to grab the laptop from Jack so she can keep scrolling.

Yes, the teens are very much in love, and—in the ultimate plot twist—have Parent Trap'd themselves. You see, young Jack is reportedly taking classes in mobile app development at NYU, while interning with an app team . . . at Big League Burger HQ in New York.

(Hub Seed reached out to BLB for comment on what this new app is about and when we can expect a launch, and received a response of three winking emojis, so. Y'know. Interpret that however you will.)

Meanwhile, Patricia, who started at Columbia this semester, is working for—drumroll please, y'all—none other than Girl Cheesing. And ICYMI, homegirl is nothing short of a dessert genius.

The newly revamped Girl Cheesing Instagram account is such goals I want the pics of her desserts tattooed

on the inside of my eyelids. (Word to the wise: If you haven't had Monster Cake yet, you have not fully experienced what this mortal realm has to offer.)

"Yesss, more Monster Cake stans!" Paige cheers.

Stephen grimaces. "Three *winking* emojis? Dude."

I shrug. The biggest relief of my life is that I no longer have any hand in any of Big League Burger's internet presence—not the Twitter, the email account, or even Taffy's newly launched Instagram, where she and her dog have been touring the recently expanded Big League International locations in Europe and Asia while taking lots of adorable, curated pics (a job she is *much* better suited for than BLB's Twitter, which is now being run by an extremely snarky outside hire who lives and breathes memes, thank god).

Jack shrugs. "I mean, it's not *that* top secret. It's just for like, mobile ordering and delivery. And some interactive chats and games."

I hike my knees up and nudge him with my foot. "Chats and games they're letting Jack develop on his own. He was the one who pitched them in the first place."

Jack smiles down at his lap. "Should be fun," he says, chronically underselling himself as usual.

"Congrats, man," says Stephen. "Hey, you should take a look at this client we're trying to pitch a chat platform to right now that's kind of like Weazel—do you freelance? Because if you had any ideas, we c—"

"*Please* embargo this nerd-palooza for another five minutes," says Pooja, knowing that, left to their own devices, Jack and Stephen will start talking about the respective apps they're working on until they're blue in the face. She scrolls down.

Jactricia—or PepperJack, as they've come to be known, once Patricia's nickname came to light (seriously, HOW STINKING CUTE are these two?)—has stayed pretty chill since the war died down. They still don't have Twitter accounts of their own, and their Instas, if they exist, are private.

But they were kind enough to provide the Hub with a recent pic, posing with the latest permanent offering on Girl Cheesing's menu: the PepperJack Grilled Cheese. Cue the collective "d'awwww."

Paul and Pooja let out an actual "d'awww" at the same time, hers mocking and his unabashedly earnest. The picture is one Ethan took of me and Jack the day we all had a picnic in Washington Square Park just before the first semester of college started—sandwiches from Girl Cheesing with massive shakes and fries from Big League Burger. Naturally, Jack and I were hamming it up for the camera, both trying to shove our grilled cheeses into the other's face. Even I have to admit we look insufferably cute.

There you have it, folks. A fitting end to the cheesiest romance ever told, and a love we can all brie-lieve in.

Paige raises a paper cup full of hot cider, prompting us all to do the same.

"To my little sister and her weird dessert brain."

Ethan chimes in. "To my little brother—"

"By *eleven minutes*—"

"—and his secret dorky hobbies."

We all cheer, and Pooja looks up from her now-empty waffle plate and says, "Okay, okay, that's enough cuteness for one night. Turn on *Mean Girls* before we all get diabetes."

Paige does the honors of pulling it up on the TV, and I look around the room at the happy, mismatched lot of us—Pooja in her Stanford Swimming sweats, Paul in a bowtie, Stephen with his face full of waffle, Ethan making fun of him, Paige watching it all with an amused kind of exasperation—and Jack, already staring at me when I look for his eyes, the same way he always seems to be. He smiles one of those half smiles, the kind I return without thinking. Of all the unexpected recipes this "weird dessert brain" of mine has ever come up with, I doubt I'll ever create anything as perfect as the one right in this room.

This may have started with a war, but whatever it is now, there isn't an end in sight—not as long as we're both still winning.

Acknowledgments

First, holy guacamole, thank you to my agent, Janna Bonikowski. I can only describe the last few years as "everything happens so much," but you were never once fazed by any of it, with the kind of counsel and support that goes way beyond the agent call of duty. This book may have been inspired by a tweet, but it happened because of you—I never would have written it without your encouragement and insight. Basically, my dreams came true, and it is all your fault.

Thank you to my editor, Alex Sehulster, who gave me the best advice of my life before we were even working together, and told me I was supposed to be writing YA. I am a much happier writer for it, and now I am also a writer who knows the ridiculous joy of getting to work with you and learn from your ideas, both plotwise and dessertwise. Thank you also to Mara Delgado-Sanchez and the Wednesday Books team. I could not be more excited to be making my debut with you guys.

Thank you to Gaby Moss—may every overexcitable green bean who moves to New York immediately meet someone who so fiercely takes them under their wing and teaches them how to savor the good things and laugh at the scary ones. To my writers-in-crime: Suzie Sainwood, who has held my hand through every step of this journey; Kadeen Griffiths, who is too pure for this human world; and Erin Mayer, the spooky teenage witch of my heart. Thank you to Yumee Cho, who taught me that your organs don't spontaneously fail if you read each other's work. May we all be swapping ideas and mopping one another off the floor until pen do us part.

Thank you to the women of *Bustle*—my coworkers, my friends, my guides. I hope we are all still fighting about the best kind of potato until the Earth flies into the sun. (It's tater tots, and I just got this published, so I'm right.)

A massive, dweeby thank-you to the fanfiction community that raised me and made me the writer I am today. From the day I posted my first fanfic at eleven years old, y'all have taught me, supported me, and watched me tank at more dreams than I can count, but never, ever, ever let me give up on this one.

(Thank you also to the girls in the back row of my college stats class for not tattling on me for updating my Spider-Man fan fiction during lectures. Lol, math.)

Thank you to my teachers, Lori Wagoner Reiner and Eleanor Henderson—you both gave me a place to write, but more important, a place to belong.

Thank you to the stone-cold pack of nerds who share my DNA and have pulled me out of more plot holes than I can count. Thank you to Evan, the big brother who tried to teach me to read with way too many books about wolves, and has been teaching me ever since. To Maddie, the little sister who helped me post my first fanfic, and always has the answers to life's hardest questions and the patience to give them. To Lily, the littler sister who has read every manuscript my brain has ever churned out, untangles the plots in my books and my life, and thought of me as an author long before I did. I love you guys. Being your sister is the best thing that ever happened to me. (Aside from cake.)

Finally, and most important, thank you to my mom and dad. You raised us to believe we could turn every *if* into a *when*. Watching you made me brave, but knowing you support me in everything I do makes me braver. I am a girl built on Minnie Mouse cheese and made-up swing-set songs and handmade superhero costumes, on sparkles and show tunes and more ideas than I'll ever have the time to write, because you always gave my imagination room to grow. I've had a big, exciting life both inside my head and outside of it, but so far the best part has been getting to call you to tell you about this book. I hope one day I can be half the parent to my own kids that you are to us.

Read on for a sneak peek of *You Have a Match!*

It starts with a bet.

"Abby, I'm one hundred percent more Irish than you are," begins said bet, when Connie—who, admittedly, is about as ginger as they come—challenges me at the lunch table.

"Having red hair is not the be-all end-all of Irish-ness," I point out through a mouthful of Flamin' Hot Cheetos. "And my grandparents on my dad's side were like, so Irish they bled potatoes."

"Yet between you and all three of the gremlins you call little brothers, not one ginger," Connie points out, narrowly avoiding slopping her chili on the mountain of study guides she has propped on the lunch table.

"Dodged a bullet there, huh?" I tease her.

Connie lightly kicks my foot. I'd feel worse about it if she weren't so staggeringly beautiful that she has been mistaken for the actress who plays Sansa Stark more times than I can count on one hand, an especially impressive feat considering we live in a suburb of Seattle some bajillion miles away from any famous person who isn't Bill Gates.

"Not that I support this Anglo-Saxon nonsense—"

I flinch, and then Connie's chili *is* on Connie's pile of study guides. It is a testament to how committed she is to pretending things aren't awkward between me and Leo that she wipes the beans off the one loudly titled "AP FUCKING GOV! IS! YOUR! BITCH!!" without one threat to murder me.

"—but I'm doing one of those send-away DNA test things," Leo finishes in a mumble, planting himself and his lunchbox down next to Connie.

"Oh yeah?" I ask, leaning across the table and making deliberate eye contact with him.

Leo, the anchor of our trio, has known us both since we were little—me because we live in the same neighborhood, Connie through youth soccer. So we've both known him long enough to understand that this is kind of a big deal. Leo and his sister were both adopted from the Philippines and know next to nothing about their birth parents or their backgrounds, and up until now, he didn't seem to have any interest in looking into it.

But we're all taking Honors Anthropology and are right in the thick of a project where we're learning the proper way to track and denote lineage in our family trees. Hence, the Irish-off that Connie and I are currently engaged in, and probably Leo's new curiosity about tracing his roots.

Leo shrugs. "Yeah. I mean, I guess I'm more curious about the health stuff it'll tell you than anything else."

We both know that's only a half truth, but Connie pokes at it so I don't have to. "Health stuff?"

"It can also connect you to other biological family members if they've taken the test," Leo says quickly, more to his massive Tupperware of jambalaya than to us. Before we can ask any follow-up questions, he adds quickly, "Anyway, there's a discount if you buy more than one. If you're in, I can buy yours with mine and you guys can pay me back."

Connie moves Mount Study Guides off the table to make room for the rest of Leo's lunch, a bunch of delicious mismatched leftovers from his weekend culinary adventures. "You know what, I've got some money saved up from the ice-cream shop."

I wrinkle my nose. We all know I have money saved from babysitting aforementioned "gremlin" brothers during my parents' Friday date nights, but I also have my eye on a new lens for Kitty, my camera, that I'm obsessively tracking the price of online.

Except Leo's eyes find mine and linger in this way they haven't really in the last few months. At least, not since the Big Embarrassing Incident—more colloquially known as the BEI—I am still actively trying to scrub from my brain. Whatever it is in his gaze cuts right past it, and I understand at once that it isn't about the discount.

"Yeah. Yeah, let's do it."

Connie grins. "Loser has to make the other one soda bread."

Leo, the only one of us who can actually cook, perks up at this. "I'll help the loser."

Connie and I shake on it, and Leo starts talking about some soda bread fusion with cherries and chocolate and cinnamon, and the bet is finalized by the time the bell rings to end lunch.

To be honest, hours after we all spit into tubes and send off our kits, I forget about the whole thing. There are perilously low grades to juggle, endless tutoring sessions to endure, and worried but well-meaning parents to dodge. Plus with Leo focused on graduation and Connie focused on more extracurriculars than I have fingers and toes to count on, all three of us are basically spun out into different planets.

But there it is, a month later: an email in my inbox, directing me to a website that apparently knows more about me than my sixteen years of knowing myself.

I scroll down, morbidly fascinated by the details. It tells me I'm most likely brunette (check), have curly hair (aggressive check), and am prone to getting a unibrow (rude, but also check). It tells me I'm probably not lactose intolerant and probably don't have issues with sleep, and that I am more likely than others to flush when drinking alcohol (noted, for future college endeavors). It also tells me I'm 35.6 percent Irish, a fact I immediately tuck away to rub in Connie's face when the time comes.

But whatever else it knows about me is abruptly cut off by the hum of my phone. It's from Leo, texting the group chat: DNA results came in. Big fat nothing.

It's the kind of text that I don't even have to wait for anyone to respond to in order to know we're all going to head over to Leo's. Still, I wait a few minutes, putting Kitty in her case and popping some gum in my mouth, giving Connie a chance to catch up to me so we'll get there at the same time.

"Where are you headed, kiddo?"

Allow me to clarify, because in the last few months of him shifting into working from home more often, I've become semi-fluent in Dad. In this case, *Where are you headed, kiddo?* loosely translates to *I'm pretty sure you haven't finished rewriting that English essay you tanked, and I'm 100 percent using this as a loving, yet still deeply passive-aggressive way to bring it up.*

I tighten my grip on my helmet, keeping my eyeballs as still as I possibly can even though resisting an eye roll right now might actually be pressurizing something in my brain.

"Leo's."

My dad pulls one of those affable, apologetic smiles of his, and I brace for the usual segue into the routine he and my mom have been perfecting since the start of junior year, when my GPA first took a swan dive.

"How's the old Abby Agenda?"

Ah, yes. The infamous "Abby Agenda." This chipper turn of phrase includes, and is not limited to, all the exhaustive tutoring sessions my parents signed me up for, the student-run test prep meetup for the SATs they keep making me attend, and a giant running list of all my homework assignments put on a whiteboard in the kitchen (or as I like to call it, the Board of Shame). I will give them points for creativity, if not subtlety.

"Dad. There are like, five days before summer vacation. I'm good to go."

He raises his eyebrows, and just as he intended, there's a fresh wave of guilt—not because I care all that much about anything on Abby's Annoyingly Alliterative Agenda, but because he looks straight-up exhausted.

"I'll *be* good to go," I correct myself. "But it's Saturday. And it's illegal to talk about homework on Saturdays."

"Says the kid with two lawyer parents." His smile is wry, but not enough to let me know I'm off the hook.

I blow a stray strand of hair out of my face. "I've got another draft ready, okay? I spent half the day on it. Now can I please go look at the sun before it swallows up the earth?"

He nods appreciatively. "We'll take a look at it when you get home."

I'm so relieved by my successful jailbreak that I basically tear holes into the street with my skateboard on my way to Leo's. It's only after I roll to a stop and shake the helmet head out of my mass of curls that I see the text from Connie, who is yet again held up at a Student Government Association meetup, and has essentially left me for dead.

"Well, shit."

If this were a few months ago, hanging out with Leo one-on-one would have been just another Saturday afternoon. But this isn't a few months ago. This is right the heck now, and I am standing like an idiot in his driveway, the shadow of the BEI creeping over me like an extremely humiliating, pheromone-ridden ghost.

Before I can decide what to do, Leo spots me and opens the front door.

"That'll be the Day," he says.

In lieu of nicknames, Leo's greetings of choice include any and all idioms about the word *Day*, which happens to be my last name. I start to roll my eyes like I usually do but pause at the sight of him in the doorway—the sun is starting to set, casting warm colors on his face, honeying the brown in his eyes and gleaming in his dark hair. I'm itching to know what it might look like through my camera lens, an itch I'm not so familiar with. I almost never photograph people.

Actually, these days my parents keep me so busy I barely photograph anything at all.

Leo's expression starts to shift, probably because I've been staring too long. I look away sharply and pop a wheelie on the way up to his front porch.

"Show-off," he says.

I prop my skateboard by the door and stick my tongue out at him. It's a relief to be on teasing terms again, but it's immediately punctured by what he says next.

"Where's Connie?"

He winces as soon as he asks, but I do what I do best and walk it off.

"Busy with last-minute details for tomorrow's Keyboard Wash for the junior class fundraiser."

"Keyboard Wash?" Leo's a senior, along with his non-Connie-and-Abby friends, so he's out of the loop on half of our goings-on. "Like a car wash for keyboards?"

"I've watched you use yours as a dinner plate, so I'll pencil you in."

I follow him into his house, inhaling warm butter and burnt cheese and, as always, the faint waft of cinnamon. Leo flicks on the front hall light, which exposes the precarious tower of pans, pots, and miscellaneous ingredients crammed into the small bit of counter real estate he has in his kitchen. His laptop is propped up on the table, open and exposed enough that I figure his parents his sister, Carla, must be out.

I'm about to ask about the DNA test results displayed, but he puts a plate in front of my face first.

"Lasagna ball?"

I pull a wrapper out of my pocket and spit my gum in it. "Hell yeah."

"Careful, they're—hot," Leo says with a sigh, seeing I've already blatantly ignored his warning by popping it into my mouth.

The roof of my mouth instantly burns, but not enough that I don't appreciate how absurdly delicious it is—the legendary lasagna balls, one of Leo's many workarounds to actually cook in his house. He's become something of an oven snob and doesn't trust his to stay at a steady temperature, so he got himself a high-end toaster oven—hence, a lot of bite-size, dollhouse recipes, so I always feel like I'm in some fancy culinary pop-up when I'm just as stuck as I always am in the depths of Seattle suburbia.

"Are you okay?" he asks, with his usual mingling of exasperation and concern.

"You could've come over," I say, the ricotta legitimately steaming out of my mouth.

This is part of the reason Leo has been essentially absorbed by the Day family—our kitchen is humungous. And while we appreciate all that extra counter space for laying out several boxes of Domino's pizza during a feeding frenzy, nobody in our family actually cooks. Leo, on the other hand, is basically the Ina Garten of our high school and needs the space to fully manifest his Food Network dreams (plus, if we're being real, the ego boost of the Day brothers hollering about his six-cheese pizza at the top of their tiny lungs).

Not that Leo comes over much these days. We're not so great at being alone like this anymore. And as supportive as I want to be, I can't help the way my eyes keep skirting to the door, the way I keep waiting in the beat of silence that Connie usually fills.

"Is that Kitty?" Leo asks, looking at my camera case.

There it is again—that squeezing cycle of panic and relief. The teetering line between *are we okay?* and *we're okay enough.*

"And all nine of her lives."

"She's probably down to about six by now," says Leo. He would know—he's the one who gave the camera her name, after she survived more than a few harrowing drops, near plunges into bodies of water, and that time I thought it'd be cool to hang upside down from a jungle gym to get the sunset through the metal bars and ended up with a mouthful of playground rubber.

"You mind?" he asks.

I tuck my chin to my chest, hiding my smile as I pull Kitty out of her carrier. Leo reaches over my head into the cabinet to grab his mom's nice white plates, and I start arranging the lasagna balls on them. For a bit we're so locked into the easy quiet of this old pattern that I almost forget to wish Connie were here: I take a few shots of Leo's creations with Kitty, he uploads and posts them on his Instagram, and I promptly eat all the spoils.

He has a habit of uploading all my other photos, too. I'm not expecting him to today, though, until he surprises me by holding a hand out for Kitty. I try not to watch him as he clicks through views from the top of my mom's office building in Seattle, a sweeping, pre-dusk skyline punctured by the Space Needle, the clouds stark and heavy in the air.

I stand on my tiptoes, peering into the screen. My head barely clears his shoulder, forcing me close enough to him that the heady smell of cinnamon is thick in the air, warm in my lungs. That's Leo's calling card—sneaking cinnamon into everything. Muffins, burritos, pudding, grilled cheese. Even when it's not supposed to work, he'll find a way to make it. Ever since we were kids he's always smelled like he was rolling around in the display case of a Cinnabon.

He stops on an image, tilting the camera so I get a better view. Leo claims not to know jack about photography, but of the dozen or so pictures I took, he still chose my favorite—the one where the shadows are a little harsher, right as the sun was gearing up to poke out from behind a cloud.

I glance up to nod my approval, but he's already watching me. Our eyes meet and there's something soft in his that holds me there—and without warning, the warmth of his knuckles skims under my jaw. My breath hovers somewhere unhelpfully in my chest, suspending me in the moment, into something brewing in Leo's eyes.

"You, uh—there was some cheese," he says. "On your . . ."

I touch the spot where his hand met my face. It feels like it has its own pulse.

"Oh."

"So, um, post it?"

I try to meet his eyes again, and when I do all I see is that familiar honey brown. You'd think I would have enough experience with my camera to know when something is only a trick of the light, but I can't ignore the tug of disappointment I know better than to feel.

"Yeah, if you wanna," I say, shrugging myself away from him and his autumnal smell and over to the table.

Leo clears his throat. "Sweet."

For a while he's been uploading these photos on a separate Instagram he made for me, even though the idea makes me feel a little topsy-turvy. He keeps saying it will be good to get a following, to have some kind of portfolio and a way to connect with other photographers, like he and some friend of his from summer camp have been doing with their own Instagram accounts. But the truth is, I viscerally dread the idea of sharing my photos with anyone. The thought of people out there seeing my work makes me feel so weirdly naked that I don't even look at the account.

Plus, if anyone's actually following it, I'm sure they're bored out of their skull—most of my pictures from the last year are the same places over and over, since the academic leash I'm kept on gets tighter by the day. And even if it weren't, I haven't been out as much lately. Photography was my *thing* with Poppy. It's been harder to go anywhere outside my element without my partner in crime.

A zillion hashtags and one masterfully shot blob of cheese and noodle later, Leo's lasagna ball Instagram is posted, and a large percentage of them are in my stomach. Leo sits on the couch, watching the likes trickle in, and I sit on the arm, hesitating before letting myself slide down with a *plunk* into the worn cushions beside him.

"So are we going to keep putting cheese in our faces, or talk about this DNA test thing?"

I'm not so good with the whole art of segueing. None of us are, really. I'm too blunt, Leo's too honest, and Connie—well, Connie just plain doesn't have the time. So Leo's fully expecting the question, the anticipation easing out of him with a sigh.

There's a silence, and this wobbly, uncertain moment when I think he might try to blow the whole thing off, and I won't know how to not take it personally. But then he turns to me with more frankness than he has in months.

"It's—I don't know. Like, how you know that statistically speaking, the odds that there isn't some other form of life in the universe are like, zilch." He picks at a seam in his jeans that hasn't quite come loose yet but is on its way. "But why the quiet? Do they not want to know us? Or can they just not reach us yet?"

I nudge Leo's shoulder with mine, tentative at first, but then he sags some of his weight into me. The relief is almost embarrassing. I hate that it takes one of us being upset for things to feel okay between us.

"My family tree is the Fermi paradox."

I wait in case he wants to elaborate. That's the thing with Leo, though. I always understand more about him in the beats after he says something than when he says it.

"Well, whatever that means—I'm sure it's that they can't reach you," I tell him. "I can't imagine anyone not wanting to know you."

Leo bristles. I take some of the edge off, because we both need it: "Even if you are kind of a dork."

This earns me a sharp laugh. "*Hey.*"

"Facts are facts."

He bops me on the knee with the palm of his hand, his skin touching mine where my jeans are ripped. His eyes linger on an old scar, just above my kneecap. I have no memory of what it's from, but Leo does. He always keeps score of that kind of thing, like it's some personal failing of his—ever since we were little, I've been the daredevil, and he's been the safety net. Me climbing and jumping and shimmying into places I shouldn't, and Leo a few feet behind, warning and worrying and probably developing Abby-shaped ulcers in every one of his organs along the way.

Before he can comment on it I rest my head on his shoulder, like when we were kids and napped on each other on the bus—one of the few times I was ever still for more than a few moments. Only it doesn't feel quite like it did. There's a new firmness to him, and he's so tall now that my head doesn't fall in the same place. It presses us closer, me trying to find some purchase on him, him scooting to let me fit.

I really shouldn't do this. I know better. But it feels like I am playing a game of chicken with the universe—like I can make this whole thing feel normal, even when it actively is not.

Because normal isn't my heart beating in my fingertips and in the skin of my cheek on his T-shirt sleeve. Normal isn't noticing the way that cinnamon smell of his has gone from grounding to dizzying, taking on something sweeter and too innate in me to name. Normal isn't having a big, stupid, ridiculous crush on one of my best friends, especially when he most certainly doesn't have one on me.

And there it is: the BEI bubbling its way back to the surface and popping all over again. My brain is so into reliving it that sometimes I'm almost glad my parents keep me busy—the more time I sink into trying to keep up at school, the less time I have to think about how I colossally messed things up with Leo and almost took down our whole little trio with it.

I take my head off his shoulder, turning to face him. "And you know, the database on this thing updates all the time," I press on. "You could check in a few months and maybe someone related to you *will* have taken the test. This isn't game over."

Leo lets this sink in. "I don't know if I want to be like, waiting on that, you know?"

"So give me your password and I'll check on it for you."

He huffs out a laugh that's equal parts appreciative and dismissive. "I'd still be waiting on it."

I hop off his couch, reaching for his laptop. "Then I'll change your password. Write it down on a teensy piece of paper and eat it."

"You're ridiculous," he says.

"I'm serious," I tell him, poised to type. "Minus the eating part."

"What would the eating part even have accomplished?"

We're veering off course, but I can tell he hasn't fully gotten this off his chest yet. And even though he's not going to tonight, and it will likely manifest into another one of his cooking and/or baking frenzies that will keep me and Connie fed at lunch for the next week, we can at least try.

I glance back at him, waiting.

"I don't even really think about it that much. I mean, I didn't, until recently. But I always kind of figured if I wanted to know, I could."

"You can't ask your parents?"

Leo glances at the driveway, as if one of them is going to jump out from under the porch window. "Well—the adoption was closed, so . . ."

"You don't think they'd be chill with you looking?"

"No, no, they—of course they would," he says, his eyes lingering on the front of the house.

The most Leo thing about Leo is this: he's always putting other people's feelings before his, always trying to keep the peace. Someone nearly ran him over in Pike Place Market running a red, and when the driver immediately burst into hysterics, Leo apologized to *her*. It's like he's a barometer for human emotion, and anytime someone is out of whack he feels obligated to tip the scale back in their favor.

This is somewhat mitigated, at least, by the fact that Leo's parents are both psychology-majors-turned-teachers and knew this about him before he even started forming full sentences. They're both pretty busy with work, but they make up for it with enough family game nights, weekend outings, and infinite parental empathy to make the parents from *The Brady Bunch* look like chumps. If anyone is prepared to handle their kid asking questions like the ones Leo has, it's them.

But that doesn't mean Leo won't talk himself out of it anyway, for everyone's sake but his own.

"It's just, there's really no wikiHow page on how to tell your white parents you're looking for the family that actually, y'know, looks like you." He pauses before adding, "That, and Carla doesn't want to know."

Ah. Carla and Leo were adopted together and are full-blooded siblings so close in age they're mistaken for twins more often than not. But that's all either of them has ever known about the adoption—that they came as a pair, when Leo was a year old and Carla was brand-spanking new.

"I guess that's fair," I say cautiously.

"Yeah. But it's—I don't know. I've never been good at . . . not knowing things."

Leo and I may be different in a lot of ways, but here we are too alike: the "latch" factor.

Leo's *knowing* thing goes as far back as I remember him. He's always trying to understand how stuff works, whether it's whatever paradox Fermi's dealing with or the precise amount of time it takes to use a mixer on egg whites for the perfect cloud eggs. As early as preschool he was driving every teacher he had up the wall, ending every explanation anyone gave him for anything with "But why?" To this day, his mom still mimics his piping little voice—"But why? But why? But why?"—a teasing glint in her eye.

For me, though, it's a *doing* thing. While Leo's been busy asking questions, I've been busy not asking enough of them. An idea pops into my brain and I can't talk myself out of it: Cut my hair to see if it would grow back overnight. Hop past the NO TRESPASSING sign on a trail to get a better view. Commit to whatever the hell was going through my head during the infamous BEI.

Maybe it's why we've always kind of gravitated to each other. I pull Leo off the ledges of his thought spirals. He pulls me off literal ledges. We've got each other's backs.

"Here," I say, pulling up my results. "Show me how to get to the ancestry part so I can hack into your account later."

Leo goes rigid. A van decked out with soaped-up words in our school colors loudly idles in front of Leo's place and comes to a stop, and Carla hops out and waves to the other cheerleaders in her carpool. Leo stands up from the couch so fast someone might have electrocuted him.

Then his shoulders slump, like something he's held together too long is starting to fold up inside him.

"It's, uh—it's pretty straightforward," he mumbles. "Just tap the 'Relations' thing under 'Ancestry.'"

Carla spots me through the window and picks up the pace, her backpack bouncing on her shoulders and her ponytail bobbing. I wave at her, waiting for the page to load, and Leo lets out a sigh.

"It's probably better to drop the whole thing," says Leo. "It might just be a waste of time, and I should be focusing on my future, you know?"

He says something else that gets drowned out by the words on my phone screen, which are somehow impossibly loud.

"Abby?"

I'm on my feet so fast that I trip on the carpet. Leo grabs me before I pitch forward, and there's this momentary shock of his warm hands on my skin. Before I'm totally paralyzed by it, we're interrupted by the clatter of my phone bouncing off the carpet and onto the faded hardwood.

"Uh—am I interrupting something?" asks Carla, looking between me and Leo with a faint smirk.

Leo releases me so abruptly that I feel like a balloon someone accidentally lost hold of—I'm untethered. Aimless. Unsure of where to go, except that I need to get out of here *fast*, away from walls and words on a screen and the way Leo is looking at me, like he's already ten minutes ahead anticipating whatever stupid thing I'm about to do next.

"I have to—I just realized—I have tutoring," I blurt.

Leo reaches down to pick up my phone, but I dive for it, grabbing it before he can. He tries to make eye contact with me, but I can't, or it's all going to spill out of me before I even know what it means.

"Abby, what's . . ."

"On a Saturday?" Carla asks, scowling.

"For, uh—" They're both staring at me. I try to think of a single school subject I'm taking or even one passable word in the English language I can use to excuse myself, but there's only room for one thought in my brain right now, and it's swelling like a balloon. "I just have to—I gotta—I'll text you later."

Leo follows me to the door, but I'm too fast for him. Within seconds I've yanked my helmet onto my head, grabbed Kitty, shoved my phone into my back pocket, and torn onto the sidewalk faster than my rickety old skateboard has ever gone. Halfway home, the stupid thing Leo no doubt predicted happens: I roll right into a crack in the pavement, end up flying like a crash test dummy, and find myself a few mortifying seconds later on my very bruised butt with my skateboard lying in the grass of someone's front yard.

I sit there, my heart beating in my ears, my mouth tasting like pennies from biting down on my tongue. I do a quick body-check and discover that, while the embarrassment may be lethal, the rest of me remains relatively unscathed.

Only after I pull myself up does my phone slip out of my back pocket, revealing one majorly cracked screen. I cringe, but that doesn't stop the phone from unlocking, or opening to the page that's been burned into my eyes ever since I saw it—a message request from a girl named Savannah Tully that reads, Hey. I know this is super weird. But do you want to meet up?

A message request from a girl named Savannah Tully, who the DNA site identifies as my full-blooded sister.

About the Author

© The Lock & Co.

Emma Lord is the author of *Tweet Cute* and *You Have a Match*. She is also a digital media editor living in New York City, where she spends whatever time she isn't writing either running or belting show tunes in community theater. She graduated from the University of Virginia with a major in psychology and a minor in how to tilt your computer screen so nobody will notice you updating your fanfiction from the back row. She was raised on glitter, grilled cheese, and a whole lot of love. Her sun sign is Hufflepuff, but she is a Gryffindor rising.